To the town of North Brookfield, Massachusetts where magic ignited the imaginations of two young girls that has lasted a lifetime.

CHAPTER 1

1977

THAT NIGHT

"As Tears Go By" – The Rolling Stones

EVA

"N OT NOW, GOD DAMN IT!" Automatically, I looked heavenward and touched my forehead, then my navel, then each shoulder.

It was 12:30 AM on a cool, star-speckled, July night; I was alone and five miles from home on one of the town's most infamous back roads. I coaxed my sputtering blue sports car onto the gravel shoulder of the deserted road and rolled to a stop. As always, I tried to think through the problem logically and troubleshoot, point A to point Z. Does the car have gas? Yes, I'd filled the tank two days ago. Oil? Yup, Dad showed me how to check all the fluid levels and I had done that too, only last week. Battery? I turned the key in the ignition. Click… click. Not even a feeble attempt to turn over. Headlights? The faintest glow. Radio? Nothing.

I peered through the darkness, quickly calculating my options. Every one of my eighteen years had been spent walking, biking, driving, and riding my horse, Smokey, while exploring the back roads of North Brookfield, Massachusetts. I already knew there wasn't a single house nearby.

I cracked the window and strained to hear. Only the disinterested chirping of the night peepers filled the crisp air. I opened the door and stepped out, my eyes automatically searching for any sign of Rag Doll Man, the elusive local legend who'd been shadowing my life for as long as I could remember. Shivering, I pulled the crocheted poncho my mother made for my birthday tighter.

As I walked, my mind wandered. It was turning out to be the best summer of my life. Warm days at Brooks Pond beach, sleeping late, being in love for the first time, and, best of all, lazy days at the pasture with my beloved Smokey. My job at the nursing home was going well and my bank account was growing—luckily, since come September a new life awaited me at Worcester State College. I would need new clothes. And books. And gas for the car. And... *new clothes!* I pictured the fashions I would wear. Starting all over in a new school—college, no less—where no one knows me: the girl with the baggy hand-me-down jeans and army boots, the girl with the over-bite and mouth full of metal from eighth grade to the end of junior year. I was ready for a new start, the opportunity to make myself over. Going from a high school of twenty-six in my graduating class, with the same kids I'd been with since kindergarten, to a state college. College! I had actually purchased the latest issue of Cosmopolitan, the one with the bold headline proclaiming "Sneak Peak! The latest fall fashions 1977!" and had practically memorized the pages. I loved the lace-up knee-high leather boots, plaid A-line skirts, and high-collared prairie blouses. And, I would wear make-up and have my auburn hair cut into a Farrah Fawcett style. My mind raced. Working full-time at the nursing home, I was making $120 a week. That would give me at least $60 to spend at the mall, $40 for gas and books, and $20 just to spend. I felt rich.

The sound of an approaching car snapped me back to reality. My heart beat wildly until the car drew close enough for me to recognize it. I released my breath and smiled.

"Well, well, Eva Thompson," he said, touching his fingertips to the brim of his hat in greeting. "Is there a problem?"

"I was coming home from work and my car broke down. I'm not sure what's wrong."

"Well, lucky for you, I came along. It's not safe for a young girl to be out here alone at this hour," he said.

Apprehension tingled through my chest, but I pushed it away and forced myself to continue smiling.

He leaned across the passenger seat and opened the door, smiling back.

My mother always told me not to get into a stranger's car. She'd drilled that into me from the time I was little.

But, he's not a stranger, I chided myself. *I've known him my whole life.*

I took a step toward the open car door.

An hour later, I stood bruised and bloody at the front door of my house. My bewildered mind tried to kick start a sensible analysis of what had happened. Was it a dream? Or a hallucination? I wasn't sure, but I did know I couldn't say a word to my parents about this. He told me how disappointed they'd be in me. How they would never look at me the same again. That they may not even love me anymore.

4

What about Tim? What would he say? I was *his* girl. But, he wouldn't want me anymore. Not after what I'd done.

Justine. My confidante. My best friend since the day she burst into my life. I could tell her but I wasn't sure how she'd react. She might kill him. Or, maybe she'd remind me of all the crap I'd given her over the years about how provocatively she dressed. She'd feel awful for me, I knew, but somehow no matter what predicament she got us into, she still managed to skate through life unruffled. I was the modest one. The careful one. The good girl.

Now look at me.

I slipped through the unlocked front door just as the grandfather clock in the front hallway slowly began its chime, never sounding so loud as it did during that deathly still night.

One... Two... Three... 3 AM!

I took off my shoes and crept up the stairs toward my room. On the landing midway up the stairs, I caught a glimpse of myself in the mirror: even in the darkness with only the faint glow from the porch light outside, I could see my left eye was swollen and dark colored. I climbed the remaining flight of stairs, taking a giant step to avoid the top stair—the one that creaked just outside my parents' room. I reached my bedroom door and opened it slowly to prevent its usual groan of protest. Holding my breath, I listened in fear for the sound of my parents stirring. Slipping into the room, I closed the door gently and took a relieved yet quiet breath.

I crawled into my bed and pulled the covers up. Silence, except the rhythmic ticking from the clock on my bedside table filling the room. My eyes adjusted to the darkness as I looked around. Clippings from travel magazines on a US map pinned on one wall marked the places I'd been and planned to go. An album collection sat upright across two shelves in my book case. The crucifix, a treasured gift from my parents for my First Communion, hung next to my bureau mirror. Staring at it, I trembled as tears burned down my face. Blinking rapidly, my eyes shifted toward the horseshoe nailed above my door. It had been there since 1973, the summer I first met Justine out by Smokey's pasture. She'd given it to me the day we found it in the old barn at her great-aunt and great-uncle's house.

"For good luck," she'd said.

I wish I were a kid again, like I was then. Life was so much simpler.

CHAPTER 2

1973

THE TWERP IN THE WINDOW

"You've Got a Friend" – Carole King

EVA

I CRASHED. A KLUTZY, WILE E Coyote-esque pratfall, head-first off my bike and into the picker bushes by the edge of Smokey's pasture. And, it figures, all while Peggy and John Miller's grand-niece from New Jersey spied on me through the front window of the Miller's house.

I'd been attempting a high-speed escape from her probing eyes. The pasture on Miller Ave was the one place where I could be myself, far from the scrutiny of classmates or, even worse, the butt of cruel jokes. I loved my solitary time with Smokey—brushing him, hopping on his bare back for a ride, or simply watching him. Mid-June meant the promise of a fantastic summer was finally before me. Long, warm days; a pasture on a nearly deserted road; tall grass, a pond, and the apple orchard with miles of dirt roads for leisurely trail rides. At the end of the summer was the Spencer Fair, the largest annual festival in central Massachusetts, and I would enter Smokey in the horse show. He would be glossy and fit, with rippling muscles and a silken mane, and we would surely win a ribbon in every class.

Yes, this summer would be perfect. It was going to be heaven. Except for one fact. This mile-long, dead-end road was not deserted. Other than the farm at the end, out of sight past the heavy screen of trees and slopes and bends in the pavement, there was one other house, and it was directly across the street from my pasture. I knew the girl was spending the entire summer with them and, although I'd smiled shyly at Peggy and said, "yes, I would love to meet her," nothing could have been further from reality.

My time here was mine, and I treasured it. I played back the recording of what I wished I could have said to Peggy. *"No, I don't want to meet her. No, I don't want someone to talk to. No, I don't want to play with a seventh grader." A seventh grader! "What would she possibly want to talk about: 'Who's your favorite, Donny or Marie?' I don't want to spend my summer babysitting!"*

I'd felt prying eyes from the front window of the Miller's ancient house as I fed Smokey his nightly ration of grain. While talking to him in the sing-song voice he loved, I tried to look at the house from the corner of my eye.

There! The curtain moved! That little twerp is watching me. I don't want to talk to her. I'm leaving, dreams of my perfect summer bashed.

I jerked the bike from the fence where it rested about ten feet from the road, and decided to show—whoever—exactly how fast I could ride. I usually walked the bike back to the edge of the road, but I wanted out, badly and fast.

Hey, little twerp in the window, I don't want to talk to you!

I hopped on the bike and cranked the pedals as fast as I could. In my haste, I hadn't even made it past the brambles by the side of the pasture when a stick, no doubt stirred up from my bat-out-of-hell retreat, jammed firmly into the front spokes, sending my bike and me catapulting head over heels.

Smokey eyed me, chomping on a mouthful of straw, as I wrestled with the brier. Oh dear God, just what I'd tried to avoid. The girl who'd managed to wreck my one safety zone came running. And, she was puny! No way was she even as old as Peggy said. She had to be about eight. On top of everything, there I was, about to be rescued by a puny baby.

"Are you okay?" she asked.

"Do I look okay?" I said, struggling futilely.

"Here, lemme help you." She gingerly pulled at a prickly tendril attached to my forearm.

"Ow! You're hurting me!"

"Gee, I'm sorry." She looked stricken, pushing her glasses firmly onto the bridge of her nose, then raising her eyes barely enough for me to see a flicker of blue. "I didn't mean to make it worse."

My wounds screamed as I dragged myself to my feet. Touching my face, I fingered several abrasions and the goose egg growing on my forehead. After yanking up my sleeves, I gasped at the crisscrossed scratches all over both arms. Brushing myself off and summoning my remaining pride, I climbed back on my bike, tossed my hair over my shoulder, and said, "Well, then. Thanks for your help. Bye."

My dramatic exit was thwarted by the mangled front wheel of my bike.

And, to make matters worse, that... that... kid... was taking advantage of my plight.

"Uh, I'm Justine Andrews," she said, taking a quick step toward me. "You sure you're okay?"

Propping my worthless bike against the gate post of Smokey's pasture, I crossed my arms in front of me and examined her. She was a skinny thing with long blonde hair, dressed in a tie-dyed shirt and frayed shorty shorts. Most annoying was how she'd placed the ball of her sneakered foot on top of one of the crabapples on the ground and was rolling it around.

"Yeah, I'll live," I scowled at the twirling apple. "Uh, I'm Eva Thompson."

Justine didn't say a word. Her foot just kept rolling that apple.

"Right. Well, I've gotta go." I reached for the bike I was resigned to walking home.

"Wait!"

Now what? I was supposed to meet Lynn. I already knew she'd quiz me about my injuries, laughing at yet another incident to be added to my Dork List. I certainly wasn't going to mention this child to her. This child who probably spent her days with coloring books and a Crissy doll.

"That your horse? What's his name? Is it a boy?" That crabapple still twirled lazily under her foot.

I had no patience for this line of questioning. "His name is Smokey. He's not a boy. He's a gelding."

"What's a gelding?"

I concentrated on not rolling my eyes. "A boy who's been fixed."

"Oh. How old is he?"

"About twenty-six," I said, climbing through the split rails of the gate and caressing Smokey's neck.

"Oh." She stared at him. "Is that old?"

"Yup."

"How old do they live to be?"

I blew out a loud sigh. "About twenty-five."

"How long have you had him?"

"A few years. I used to keep him at a different place, but that property was sold so I had to find a new pasture to rent. That's how we ended up here this year."

"Doesn't he get cold in the winter?" she asked.

"He lives in the barn behind my house during the winter, but it's only got a small corral. For the winter it's fine, but when the weather's nicer, he needs more room."

"Why'd you name him Smokey?"

This time I couldn't help myself. My eyes rotated a full 360 degrees. "Because of his coloring. Grayish white. Like smoke. See?"

I was waiting for the response I'd heard from the boys at school who taunted me. Or, from the snotty girl at the 4-H camp: "He looks like a plow horse. Where's the plow?"

Instead, Justine continued to gaze at him with wide blue eyes. Placing one finger on the bridge of her glasses, she pushed them back up her sweaty little nose. Finally, she said, "He's pretty. Can I pet him?"

"Uh-yuh... sure. If you want. Horses like to be petted on the nose, or on the neck, or shoulder. But don't reach up suddenly towards his ears and don't walk behind him." I repeated the warnings I'd been told even though Smokey had never given any indication of being startled by those things. "You can give him an apple." I kicked her foot away from the crabapple and picked it up. "Like this." I demonstrated, keeping my hand flat and extending it towards him.

Justine picked up another crabapple, laid it on her flat hand, and held it over the fence as I had done. When Smokey nibbled at the apple, it rolled around on her palm and her fingers closed around it automatically.

"No, no, no," I warned her. "Don't do that. He could accidentally bite you. Like this." I held my hand flat against the softness of Smokey's lips as he nuzzled the apple.

"Gosh, he's groovy," Justine said in an awestruck voice. "You're so lucky. I wish I had a horse."

Streaks of Sunlight Across the Lawn

"Stand By Me" – Ben E. King

Justine

STRETCHING MY BODY TO ITS full length, sleep began to fade and it occurred to me that even though this was my first summer without my brothers to entertain me, it might not be so boring. Punching my pillows, I snuggled back into my favorite part of the morning and enjoyed the sounds and scents of a rural summer at dawn. The birds chirped in the big maple tree right outside my room. Uncle John's footsteps crunched on the gravel as he went to dump the rubbish in the incinerator barrel. The early chill in the air carried the smell of cut grass through the window.

I huddled beneath my covers until the start of the morning ritual. Finally, the hands of my old Big Ben clock eased to 7:30 and the floorboards on the landing began to creak. Aunt Peggy was making her way down the long, curving staircase, her shaky knees threatening to give out with each step. My stomach tightened with each groan of the wood. Although I had seen her descend the stairs at least a hundred times, I'd begun to realize every passing year had left its mark on her. Each step was slower, more careful, and more agonizing. I shut my eyes tight and pulled my knees up to my chest as I pictured every move. With her left hand clutching the worn banister and her right gripping her cane, she went down backwards, leading with her left leg to plant her foot on the step below, then bringing her right foot to join it on the same step. Then the thump of her cane, and another step. Left foot down, right foot to join it. At last I heard the final creak from the bottom stair and allowed myself to breathe.

I waited until the smell of sizzling bacon reached me, then leapt from bed and threw on my clothes. Checking the time, I knew Eva would be coming to take care of Smokey shortly. When I'd arrived a few days ago, Aunt Peggy said, "There's a girl from town who's keeping her horse in the pasture across the street. I think she's about your age." I could have ignored the information and settled into Uncle John's bulky rocker, committing myself to another reading of the Bobbsey Twins series or playing Operation against myself. But, as I'd watched her fly off her bike the other day, I had to admit I desperately wanted a friend. So I'd rushed out to make sure she was okay and to introduce myself.

Skipping down the stairs Aunt Peggy had traveled painfully, my fingers lightly trailed along the rail that used to double as a slide when I was younger. I couldn't imagine how many young bottoms before mine had whizzed down the four-inch wide, makeshift sliding board, zipping down backwards in seconds. I was three the first time Mom followed next to me as I rode, her outstretched hands steadying me when I wobbled. She told me how her father had done the same when she was a child, and his father had taught him. Generations of banister-sliders, from the time my third great-grandfather built this house, had left their memories beneath my fingertips.

"Good morning," I said, kissing Aunt Peggy's cheek as she set out breakfast. Passing Uncle John seated at the kitchen table, I brushed my hand across the top of his head, delighting in how it felt. He had a buzz cut, left over from his time in the army, and the bristles standing up on top were softer than they looked.

"Mornin', Justin." He chuckled at his own humor.

"Jus-*tine*," Aunt Peggy reminded him. "It irritates me when you call her 'Justin.' It's *Justine!*"

"Aye-yuh." Uncle John made that vague New England sound which could mean anything from 'yes, ma'am' to 'what did you say?' He was already attacking his eggs and bacon.

Used to his running joke, I dove into my own breakfast of Aunt Peggy's special scrambled eggs, heavily salt-and-peppered, with hunks of melted Velveeta.

When Mom was pregnant with me, Uncle John discovered she had kept all the baby clothes from my two brothers 'just in case' her third baby was another boy, and dubbed me 'Justin Case.' I never did get a straight answer from my parents about whether Uncle John's silliness had any influence on them naming me Justine.

"So, Justin," he continued as if Aunt Peggy had never spoken, "have you read the book, *The Yellow River*?"

"No, Uncle John. Who wrote it?" I asked, my fork poised over my plate as I waited for the punchline.

"I P Freely," he said. "Aye-yuh. Here's another one. Who wrote *The Unknown Rodent*?"

"Never heard of it. Who?"

"A Nonny Mouse!"

We both burst into laughter.

"How 'bout that, Justin?"

"It's Jus-*tine*!" Aunt Peggy shook her head.

"Give me one more, Uncle John."

"Who wrote *The Fall of a Watermelon*?"

"I don't know. Who?"

"S Platt," he said, chuckling to himself.

Giggling, I accidentally dropped a piece of crispy bacon on the floor for Lucky.

"Quit feeding the dog! He's getting fat!" Aunt Peggy scolded, then quickly turned back to the stove to hide her smile. While she had a strict 'no feeding the dog at the table' rule, Uncle John and I constantly broke it. Besides, Aunt Peggy could never be strict with me no matter how hard she tried. She was love in its purest form.

"Are you seeing Eva today?"

"Yes, we're hanging out," I said with an air of maturity. "She'll be down any time now to feed Smokey."

After breakfast, Lucky and I wandered outside, into the last of the morning mist gently swirling and fading. The sunlight poked through the woods behind Smokey's pasture and cast streaks on the lawn. Crossing the yard, my canvas sneakers got soaked from the dew and coated with grass clippings from yesterday's mowing before I reached the road. Smokey bucked his head up and down, snorting in greeting, his tail swooshing at the flies. I grabbed a crabapple from the ground and held it out for him like Eva had shown me. Climbing to the top rail of the gate, I sat and waited, watching as Lucky wandered around the yard, dashing off now and then after some creature. If it was a good day, he'd be outrun. A not-so-good day was when he came back, proudly carrying his latest victim in his mouth. Sometimes it was a squirrel, sometimes a chipmunk, and sometimes—yuk!—still moving.

This pasture was my earliest memory of North Brookfield. Before Smokey lived here, a little donkey named Pedro spent his days munching on the fallen crabapples. Before Pedro, the field was overgrown with long grass and wildflowers—Queen Anne's Lace and Indian Paintbrush, Aunt Peggy taught me. I could remember sitting in the field with the bright sun in my eyes making my head hurt, tiny insects flying up my nose and into my mouth, while Mom called, "Smile, Justine. Smile!" Maybe it wasn't even a solid memory, but more a glimmer when I looked at the faded Polaroid she had taken that day. A tiny, pointy-chinned girl with pale blonde hair flowing to her waist and deeply tanned skin, surrounded by flowers, squinting into the camera.

Pulling my hair into a ponytail, I wiped the sweat from my neck. It was still early, but I could already smell the June heat and my clothes were beginning to stick to me. Eva came speeding down the hill toward me on a different bike than the one she destroyed yesterday. She was flying so fast her thick chestnut hair whipped behind her like a banner announcing her arrival. Just as she reached the gate, she slammed on her brakes and skidded to a stop, spraying a cloud of dust into the air.

"Wow! That was groovy! You're like Evel Knievel." I removed my glasses, mopped my slippery face with the bottom of my shirt, then replaced them.

"I'm working on it. Who's this?" she asked, bending over to rub Lucky's back while glancing up at me through her long, windblown bangs.

"Lucky."

"What a good dog. Is he a Dalmatian?"

"Actually," I said, proud to be able to teach her something, "he's a Bluetick Coonhound. He's a good dog, except when he chases cars."

"Yeah? So, how old are you, anyway, Justine?" she asked, scanning me from head to toe. "Nine? Ten?"

"I'm twelve and a half," I replied, stretching my spine taller. "I'll be thirteen in March."

"March what?" she asked.

"March 29th."

"Mine's March 5th. I'll be fifteen," Eva said, straightening. "So how long have you been coming here?"

"Every summer since I was born."

"Are your parents here too?"

"No, they're back in New Jersey."

Eva pushed unruly hair away from her eyes and swiped the back of her hand across her sweaty, freckle-smattered cheek. "You mean you're here for the whole summer by yourself? What do you do all day?"

16

I thought hard. What did I do? The 19-inch black and white television offered a whopping three stations. I'd outgrown dolls. There was only so much solitaire I could stomach. And, the Silly Putty looked a little tragic after many hours of lifting and stretching the Sunday comics. Even with a closet full of games like Monopoly and Parcheesi, I needed a second player.

"Well, I like to read," I said, tracing a big curve in the dirt with the end of my sneaker.

"You do?" She tucked her overgrown bangs behind her ear. "I like to read too."

Eva handed me a brush from the supply box and showed me how to use long, firm strokes as she worked on Smokey's other side. "Do you have any brothers or sisters?"

"Two brothers. Greg is sixteen and doesn't come up here much anymore. Randy is fourteen. He comes up when he can. He likes history, especially family history. His favorite thing's exploring in the attic."

Eva paused in her grooming. "Attic? What's in the attic?"

"Ghosts." I stifled a smile.

"Nuh-uh! Ghosts?"

"People say they hear sounds when no one's there."

"I don't think I believe in ghosts. What else is up there?"

"Lots of old family stuff. You know: letters, pictures, clothes. Things people have left behind over the years."

"Let's check it out sometime," said Eva. "Hey! Have you ever heard of Rag Doll Man?"

"Who?"

"Rag Doll Man. He's not some ghost story—he's real. They say he escaped from a local mental hospital about ten years ago. He lives in the woods right outside of town." Eva's eyes grew large as she looked over my head toward the thick growth of trees halfway up Miller Ave.

"In the woods?"

"Yes, and he goes after little girls."

"Little girls? What does he do to them?" I hoped she didn't hear the fear in my voice and decide I was too young to hang out with.

"I don't know, Justine. I don't think he's ever caught one. But he wears a trench coat and nothing else underneath!"

"I don't know...."

"Oh, Rag Doll Man's real. Trust me. People have seen him. He's wicked tall and skinny, and always carries his old, dirty doll with him."

My eyes did a quick scan of the woods on the far side of the pasture.

"Just don't go out alone and you'll be fine." The left corner of Eva's mouth twitched. "What else do you do while you're here?"

"Well…" I deliberately adjusted my glasses higher on the bridge of my nose while searching for something worth telling. "Do you know Meg from the farm at the end of the road? I've hung out with her sometimes." I began to feel a little bolder as Eva contemplated my statement, and not wanting to sound twelve, added, "She has a cute brother, Mark."

"She has a brother Mark? How old is he? I never heard of him."

"I think he's about fifteen," I said, hoping to impress the older girl with my worldliness.

"Fifteen? That's funny. Her brother, Mahhck, is fifteen."

"Yeah, that's what I said. Mark!"

Eva fired me a sideways look. "So, anyway… have you ever been to Shadow Hill Cemetery, down the road apiece?"

"Sure I have. All of my relatives are buried there. I've gone lots of times."

Eva pulled out a hoof pick. She positioned her back to Smokey and gripped one hoof at a time between her knees to dig out wedged particles. "I love going up there and reading all the old gravestones. I make up stories about the people… you know, what they were like when they were alive. What they did for fun. And, how 'bout the old frog pond? You never saw it? I used to count the frogs. Once, I counted twenty-three." She tossed the pick into the storage box. "Both of my grandparents are buried in Shadow Hill. Hey, I know! I'll show you my relatives if you show me yours!"

I tried not to look childishly eager. That wasn't cool. Instead, I gave Eva a casual glance while thinking maybe I'd found someone who dug the same kinds of things I did.

Her eyes traveled from my hair to my shoes, then she blurted out, "So, why do you talk funny?"

"I don't tawk funny! *You* tawk funny!" I said, my temper kicking up inside. I took a deep breath and did what Mom had taught me to do when I was mad. I pictured myself as an inflated balloon, then imagined sticking myself with a pin and letting my anger whoosh out through the hole as I slowly counted to ten.

Eva continued to study me like I was some kind of exotic insect. "Tell me how the people in the house are related to you, Justine."

"Peggy's my great-aunt and John is her brother, my great-uncle. On my mother's side."

"See! You said 'ant.' It's not 'ant.' An ant is a little bug. It's 'ahrnt.'"

Ha! It was my turn to feel triumphant. "'Aren't'? What the heck is an 'aren't'? It's like, 'aren't you going to the store with your 'aren't'? That's weird, Eva."

"You're weird, Justine!"

"So are you!"

We eyed each other. Her hands were planted on her hips. I felt the grin stretching across my face. She was quick with the comebacks, and cracked me up quicker than any of my friends back home. Judging by her lopsided smirk, she found me funny too.

Maybe I'd found the friend I was hoping for.

Good Times in the Cemetery
"Time in a Bottle" – Jim Croce

Eva

I've always had a fascination—almost an obsession—with events that came before me. I wanted to know all about the places I visited, and sometimes went on archeological digs in my backyard, under the porch, and behind the chicken coop. Discovering a piece of an old doll, a plastic cowboy or Indian, or a split baseball felt like discovering a bit of the lost Ark. When I was ten, I found an old set of wood pocket doors in the shaky loft over our garage and immediately ran to tell my mother of the discovery.

"Oh, those used to be in the house between the living room and the dining room, a long time ago," she'd told me.

"Why'd ya take them down, Mom?"

"We didn't. They were taken down before we lived here. Probably because they're not in good shape."

"Then how do you know where they were?"

"Because there used to be an opening in the door casing in that room, the same size, and there used to be a track on the top part of the frame. That's where they would have gone."

I was incredulous. "How come you never told me this before?"

"Because I didn't think it was important." She stopped weeding long enough to turn toward me with a look of exasperation and a hint of a smile. "What do you want me to do? Take you on a tour and say, 'Eva, here in this woodpile, we have a hinge that used to be on the front door?'"

I couldn't believe it! How could she not have told me about the doors? I wanted to tell her of my disbelief, but… "A hinge? What hinge?"

My interest in the past was something I never talked about with the kids at school. They couldn't care less about the 'olden days' when today's gossip was so much more exciting. I wondered if this new kid, Justine, truly liked the cemetery or was only telling me that so I'd talk to her. She seemed sincere, though, with her ancestors buried there and all.

At the top of Miller Ave, Lucky took off after a speeding car and Justine, arms flailing, screamed at him to come back. I prayed I wouldn't see anyone I knew. I couldn't help wondering which would be the bigger butt of the town jokes: 'Hey, Eva, whatcha doin'? Babysitting?' or 'Look! There goes Eva, hanging out with all her friends in the graveyard again!' The coast was clear as I hurried us through the open gate, past the limestone sign with Shadow Hill Cemetery boldly etched on it, and into my sanctuary.

Stretching before us were rich green, manicured slopes and rolling hills with crackled paved roads branching off from the circle around the central Memorial Garden. There were rows of white and gray headstones. Huge monuments marked the plots of families and tiny pillars memorialized children. A mausoleum was tucked away beneath a hill.

"See that one?" Justine pointed to a modest-sized stone as we passed. "That's where my great-great aunt Eliza is buried. She had schizophrenia, but back then they called it 'demerits.'"

"Dementia?"

"Yeah. And, that one?" She pointed to a gray stone. "My great-great uncle Fred and his wife are buried there. And, over there. That white one? That's their daughter Ruth. My geology in North Brookfield goes almost all the way back to the Revolutionary War when Captain Samuel Miller first came here and settled at the end of Miller Ave."

"Geology?" I asked, chuckling. "Don't you mean genealogy?"

Her bottom lip poked out a little as she tossed her hair over her shoulder. "That's what I said!" Tilting her chin up, she continued to enlighten me. "Aunt Peggy always talks about Uncle Fred's daughter Ruth; says Ruth was like a big sister to her growing up. She died in a car accident a couple of years ago. I don't really remember her."

"Do you think her spirit is here with us? Right now?" I grabbed her arm. "Ruth? Ruuuth!?"

"Don't *do* that! There's such a thing as ghosts, ya know!"

I watched Justine's cocky chin-jutting posture quickly change to wide-eyed terror, and felt the tiniest pang of guilt for freaking her out. She kept pushing her glasses up her nose and glancing over her shoulder. I wanted to continue toying with her, but her naked fear made me back off. "Oh... ghosts only come out when it's dark, anyway."

21

Justine held my eyes with hers and resumed her self-confident air. "Maybe we could come up some night and see?"

I chuckled as I steered us toward the shiny black stone marking where my grandparents were buried. My memories of coming here as a child were dim snapshots. My tiny hand tucked in my grandfather's; my grandmother's grave lovingly trimmed and planted; looking up in wonder at Pop Pop's bowed head; placing a single fresh flower at the base of the headstone. We rarely missed a day. When I was six, he was laid to rest in Shadow Hill too. My parents brought me every Sunday after church to pay our respects until I was old enough to ride my bike alone. They had no idea how often I went. Several times a week. Every day, still, I missed Pop Pop's laughter, the stories about when he was young, and the way he'd wink at me when he would sneak me a root beer barrel candy from his pocket.

Plenty of other kids I knew had lost grandparents—some had even lost parents—but it didn't seem to affect them the same way. When some of them found out I went to the graveyard by myself and spent hours with my dead grandfather, I was the talk of the school for nearly a week. Until Lisa Stanley, a junior, could no longer pretend she was simply getting fat. Her expanding baby bump took the heat off me.

"You were close? You and your grandfather?" Justine asked.

"Wicked close. He lived with us until he died. We loved to look at old pictures. His family... people I never met. I remember he told me once, 'See, Eva? Those people are frozen in time, at that exact moment. And, that's how we'll always know them.'"

"I don't get it."

"Well, in one picture he was a little boy posing with his parents and older brother. Two years later, his brother drowned. So, only three of the four people in the picture were left. Of course, both of his parents were also gone by the time he showed me the picture. He was the only one still alive. But, in the picture, they'd always be a young family. Same with his wedding picture. That moment was frozen in the picture, but the people in it were no longer the same."

She was quiet, absorbing my explanation, then looped her arm through mine. "Come on. Lemme show you my favorite relatives. I never knew them, personally, but I know a lot about them."

Continuing toward the back of the cemetery where the road ran next to the low stone wall boundary, Justine showed me several more headstones and explained how all those people were related to her. She stopped in front of a square, white stone with 'Miller' engraved on one side. On the other, it read: John C and his wife, Faith E. "They were my great-grandparents. Aunt Peggy and Uncle John's parents. And my grandpa's. Faith Ellen died a couple of days before I was born. March 26, 1961. Isn't that weird?"

Pointing to three small stones nearby, she continued, "They had three children who died when they were little. Mom says her grandmother could never talk about them, even all those years later, without crying."

The tiny stones were so weather-worn I could barely read the engravings. Tracing my finger along the names, I made out 'Baby' on one, 'Dorothy' on the second, and 'Sweet Alice' on the third. "What happened to them?"

She shrugged. "Different illnesses. Things they'd probably survive if they were alive now. I'm not sure about the baby, Harold. He died before my grandfather was born, but Dorothy died from a ruptured appendix and Alice died of impetigo."

"Impetigo? She died of a skin rash?"

"Nooooo! You know, the flu."

Influenza. I let it go. Scanning the gravesites, I imagined Justine's ancestor-types as flesh and blood people. Not two-dimensional, photographic black and white. I could almost see the lively children—the girls with hand-stitched pinafore dresses and buttoned-up ankle boots, chasing each other in a game of tag; their squeals and giggles echoing across the hills while their baby brother watched, chortling and clapping his chubby hands.

Movement at the opposite corner of the cemetery snapped me out of my daydream.

"Eva, who's that?" Justine asked.

My eyes tried to make out the shadowy figure that had stopped right behind an eight-foot obelisk.

"I can't tell," I said, pulling Justine after me as I jumped over the nearby fieldstone wall and crouched down.

"Is it a ghost?" Justine crouched low, clinging to my arm.

"I don't—"

"He's carrying a doll!" Justine peeked over the wall. "It's Rag Doll Man!"

"I don't think so. Too short to be Rag Doll Man."

"It's him! What if he gets us?" Justine asked, her widened eyes looking to me for answers.

"Rag Doll Man lives in the woods, remember?" My reassuring tone didn't hush the pounding in my chest. He was wearing something that flared past his knees. *A trench coat?*

23

"There's woods right behind the cemetery!"

"Shhh! He's coming!" I glanced for the quickest way to escape. *Could he outrun us?*

"Wait, wait! It's a girl… in a dress? It's a little dog she's carrying," Justine said, beginning to stand. "Let's go."

"No!" I yanked her back down. "It's my classmate, Jane Williams. Duck! I don't want her to see us!"

"Why?"

"Just trust me, Justine. She does wicked nasty things."

"Like what, Eva?"

"Like… she pulls wings off of flies. And *eats* them!"

Gasping, Justine said, "Ewww! Really?"

"No! But, I bet she would if she could catch them! Quiet! Here she comes."

Once Jane passed, I climbed back over the wall, Justine scrambling after me with her questions. "What does she do that's so mean? Is she in your class at school? Why didn't you want her to see us?"

"Nothing. It's nothing. Don't we need to get back?" I walked faster, checking in every direction.

Even as we exited the cemetery and were heading back down Miller Ave, Justine was still bugging me, her shorter legs working double-time to keep up with my longer stride.

"Who is this Jane? Why are you afraid of her, Eva? Why did we have to hide?"

"She's a bitch, okay? She wrote a note and passed it to the cutest boy in the class and said it was from me. Another time, she taped a sign on my back that said 'Slut' and I walked around all day with it before someone told me. She's rotten. If she sees me hanging out with a little girl, I'll never hear the end of it!" I snapped, the words escaping my mouth before I could stop them. I spun around in time to catch Justine's reaction.

Her mouth had dropped open and her cheeks were bright red. She regained control and regarded me with an astonishingly poised face. "I may be small, but I am *not* a little girl!"

A HORSESHOE FOR GOOD LUCK

"You and Me Against the World" – Helen Reddy

JUSTINE

MY BROTHERS AND I HAD spent our childhood summer days on Miller Ave, roaming through the woods and picking wildflowers. We explored all the trapdoors and hidden passageways of the old barn. Around the outside, there were low walls made of field stones like the ones at Shadow Hill—the kind that cropped up everywhere in New England. We could spend an hour just waiting, watching, to see if a toad or a chipmunk would come out from those walls. At the very least, we were usually rewarded with a few big, black crickets. A Bosc pear tree stood to the right of the barn, most of its fruit ending up rotted on the ground and sending up a sickeningly sweet scent. With some smashing and squishing, we had a homemade version of a Slip-n-Slide. Mom put a stop to that little pastime after my oldest brother ran and slid a bit too hard, pitching into the stone wall and ending up in the emergency room with a broken arm.

They were too busy back home to come much anymore, so it was only me keeping Aunt Peggy and Uncle John company. Each June, my heart danced as Mom turned the car onto Miller Ave. Cruising down the narrow road, heavily wooded on both sides with trees so tall they met overhead to create a darkened tunnel, we'd burst into the daylight with open fields and untold adventures as far as my eyes could see. Craning my neck to see through the windshield, I'd hold my breath until I got my first glimpse of the old family homestead in North Brookfield, Massachusetts, rising on a hill to the left with the gravel driveway circling around the back and the red barn behind.

My days were blissfully unplanned except for the chores, errands, or occasional family visitor until late August, when Mom returned to take me back to my real life in New Jersey. Every year, with my heart breaking and tears flowing, Aunt Peggy and Uncle John grew smaller through the rear window as we pulled out of the driveway, entered the tree tunnel, and disappeared from my view well before we reached Shadow Hill.

Since my brothers were no longer around to make up new games, I hadn't rummaged through the barn in ages. When Eva suggested it, I'd jumped at the chance.

"Hold on! Hold on! I can't find a place to get a grip. Wait… okay, I'm getting it. Shit, it weighs a ton! Here it goes." Eva groaned as she worked to slide the door open. The wheels in the track, nearly rusted in place, screeched in protest. "Whoooaaa!" Her eyes bulged as a trove of treasures opened before her. "Look at this!"

Every inch of the walls was crammed with a display of antique tools— scythes, hoes, rakes, and pitchforks. Shoved to one side and tilting awkwardly was a narrow, primitive table with a broken leg. It was piled with nail-filled jars. A couple had slid down the surface and crashed to the floor. There was a hint, maybe a memory, of the smell of livestock mixed with the mustiness of the long-sealed room. The floor was covered with remnants of hay and sawdust.

"Here, Eva." I handed her a discarded horseshoe.

"What's this for, Justine?"

"For good luck. If you hang it on the wall like this," I held it like the letter U, "then the luck stays in it. If you hang it upside down, then your luck falls out."

"Oh, hey, thanks. I'll put it in my bedroom when—"

"Oh, gross, look! See that old cow ramp?" I pointed at the rickety wooden slope descending to the bottom floor. "When my brothers and I were little, we used to play hide 'n' seek and, one time, I hid under there. It's all cobwebby with spiders and probably mice. I kept waiting for them, but they never came. When I finally went looking for them, they were sitting in the kitchen eating ice cream! They said they'd forgotten me. Jerks!"

Eva let out a snort. "You have two older brothers you think torture you? I've got six older brothers who treat me like their personal servant. It's 'Eva, go get my baseball glove', or 'Eva, go make lemonade for me and my friends.' And, my two sisters! Jeez! They were the popular girls. With all the boyfriends and president of this club or head of that club. Try living up to that! Believe me, you don't know torture!"

"Oh, boo hoo!" I fired back, momentarily forgetting I wasn't talking to one of my friends back home. I froze and watched her face. What if she wouldn't want to hang around with me anymore? What if she thought I was too immature?

"Yeah, I'll give you something to boo hoo about," Eva said, lifting her clenched fist in mock payback.

We crossed the room and I opened the door into the main part of the barn. The biting smell of gasoline from Uncle John's lawnmower greeted us. I scanned the room that once housed farm equipment. Boxes, piles of timber, discarded furniture, a warped 1920s-style bicycle, huge wooden barrels, and countless artifacts from eras past were jammed into the space. Overhead was a long-empty hayloft that used to be a fort for my brothers and me.

"Whoa!" Eva exclaimed, squeezing to see around me. "How long's it been since animals lived in here?"

"Not since my great-grandfather died in the fifties."

"Look at that!" She jabbed her finger in the direction of her discovery.

"What?"

"It's a spinning wheel. See, Justine? For spinning thread or yarn. They used to operate those pedal things with their feet to make the wheel go around." Eva grabbed an old rag and wiped shredded pieces of newspaper and old hay off the seat. "It reminds me of Rumpelstiltskin. Here, give me some straw and I'll spin it into gold." She sat down and began to demonstrate how it worked.

Who in my family would have used a spinning wheel? Obviously someone did. My great-grandmother? It must have required a lot of strength. "Aunt Peggy could never have done that."

I didn't even realize I had spoken out loud until Eva asked, "What's wrong with Peggy, anyway?"

"She has arthritis," I said, letting out a sigh. "You usually think it's something only old people get, but she has the kind you can get at any age. She was in college when she had her first symptoms. Her knees got swollen; she had a lot of pain and problems walking. The doctors didn't know what was wrong and said it was all in her head. By the time her parents found a doctor who figured it out, she could hardly get around."

"Jeez! I'm trying to picture Peggy all of those years ago as a student, with her hair long and dark—young—just starting to have problems. I wonder if it was wicked hard for her, going up and down stairs, carrying her books."

"I guess." I picked up a stray piece of hay and rolled it back and forth between my thumb and fingers. "I've only ever known her the way she is now."

Eva was silent. Suddenly, she grabbed my arm. "Hey! Let's pretend Rag Doll Man is after us and...."

"...we have to hide!" I scanned the room and spotted a large rusted ring sticking up from the floor. "This way!" We scurried toward it, hunched low, furtively watching for our imaginary pursuer.

"It's a trap door!" Eva lifted it up and we both peered through the opening. "There's a ladder attached to the wall!"

"Hurry!" I moved my foot toward the top rung, but she was quicker— down the hole like Alice in Wonderland's White Rabbit she went. I scampered after her and landed in the old feed room.

"Come on!" She looked back up the ladder. "He's after us!"

"There's no place to hide in here. We'll have to go that way!" I hurried toward another door, hanging by wheels on a track overhead. She passed me, racing through the mounds of sweet-smelling hay scattered across the floor.

"Justine! He's coming!" She slid the door open with ease.

I was four steps behind her when my foot landed on something pointy. Reflexively, I looked down just as the handle of a rake came whipping toward my face. I felt the crack in the center of my forehead, light exploded, and my tailbone smashed to the packed dirt floor.

"Are you okay? Are you hurt?" I heard a voice and when my vision finally cleared, I found Eva's face six inches from mine. I couldn't speak. I took several slow, deep breaths. Tears gathered in my throat, but I'd be damned if I'd cry in front of her.

"Let me help you, Justine." She grabbed me under the armpits and started to pull me up.

I brushed her hands away. "I got it, I got it." With my head spinning, I dragged myself to my feet. Luckily, my glasses weren't broken. I touched the lump growing between my eyebrows. I needed to get some ice on it. I swallowed hard and gave Eva what I hoped was a carefree smile. "I'm fine. Really. Let's get out of here before Rag Doll Man catches us."

SUMMER ENDS IN A PUFF OF SMOKE

"Seasons in the Sun" – Terry Jacks

EVA

A T SOME POINT, THE SUMMER of my fourteenth year became one of the best I would remember. I didn't care that I rarely spent time with kids my own age. My siblings had been my companions, and I'd tagged along with them and their friends. Games of Man Hunt, flashlight tag, teenage parties. Emergency room visits for stitches and broken bones. My family still laughs about the time when my brother Steve was nine years old and somehow locked himself in his room, climbed through a window, got stuck on a ledge, and had to be rescued by the fire department.

I loved the nights we'd hear the jingling music of the approaching ice cream truck and, when we dashed into the house, Dad would give us each a quarter to run back out and make our selections. The evenings we'd all walk up to the Common for a baseball game, usually several of my brothers joining in, then play hide 'n' seek in the shadows created by the streetlights. When we reached our front yard, the spicy-sweet scent of our mother's fresh-baked doughnuts lured us into the house.

They'd all gone off to start families and live their own lives by now, except for Craig. He was still at home, but so busy between work and college that I didn't see him much. I spent a lot of my time with Smokey. Or alone.

I wasn't sure how I'd feel about that Justine kid. Turned out, she was okay. Actually, I found her entertaining. She had her own ideas about how things should be and certainly wasn't shy about voicing them. Within the first few days of meeting her, she instructed me on the finer points of style.

"Aren't you suffocating in those jeans, Eva?" she said.

"They're fine. I like my dungarees. They used to be my brother Craig's."

Justine's unreadable blue eyes peered at me through her glasses. She deliberately pushed them up on her nose in that way she had of preparing to unleash her opinions on me. It was always unnerving when she did this.

At last she asked, "Did you make that shirt out of a horse blanket, Eva?"

"Don't you know that the 1960s are over, Justine?" I glanced down at her hip-hugger denim shorts and peasant blouse.

Her eyes widened as she comprehended the question. Then she grinned. "Touché!"

Neither of us spoke. We looked at each other, waiting.

Justine said, "You could cut those jeans into *wicked* cute shorts—I'll help you fray the bottoms."

"Maybe you can wrap a leather band around your head. Wouldn't that look *groovy*?"

With a burst of laughter, Justine countered, "You dress like a... like a... hick!" Still chuckling, she added, "I guess we both have our own ideas about fashion."

"I don't have any ideas about fashion!"

"Obviously! That's why you need me!"

That made me smile. I'd miss hanging out with her every day after she went back to New Jersey.

"THIS'D BETTER WORK. IT'S OUR last match." I struck the long match on the mostly worn sandpaper side of the box. Justine huddled close, cupping her hands to shield the delicate flame against the late summer breeze. We were crouching in the clearing behind the barn, backs to the wind. I carefully put the flame to a dry leaf. It smoldered, then caught. We collectively held our breath. Justine fed a single piece of dried grass into the growing flame, then another, then another. At last, we had a respectable blaze burning. Sitting on the log we had found nearby, we let out a sigh as if we were one.

"I think the key is not trying to burn too much at once. Not until the flame gets going a little," ventured Justine.

"Yeah, you're right. I never built a campfire before. I was in the Brownies, but didn't make it to Girl Scouts. How 'bout you?"

"Nah, me either. But, I do other things."

"Like what?"

"*Lots* of things." Justine giggled, embarrassed, and fed more twigs into the fire.

"Like *what*?" I pretended to be impatient with my new young friend.

What kind of adventures could this twelve-year-old have had, I wondered. *Crossing the street alone?*

"Like baton camp."

"Baton camp?! Baton *camp,* Justine? They have a camp for that?"

"Yep. I've been twirling since I was six."

"Really? Twirling? Like a majorette?" I didn't know whether to be skeptical or impressed. "I've never met anyone who can do that."

"Look, I'll show you." Justine jumped up, quickly found a thin branch, then snapped off a section about two feet long and fairly straight. Extending her right arm and holding the middle of the branch between her fingers, she expertly twirled it, making it roll over each of her fingers in turn. Then, giving the branch a quick fling into the air, she turned and gracefully caught it behind her back.

I was dumbstruck. "Wow, that's good! Can you teach me to do that?"

"Well, it's not a real baton and I could have done it better if I had one. But, yeah, sometime I'll teach you."

The fire was crackling with glowing embers beneath the flames, the burning grasses giving off a delicious, woodsy scent. We sat quietly on the log.

I warily eyed Justine with admiration. "What else can you do?"

"Ummmmmm, I don't know. I play the piano. For about four years, now."

As my eyes grew even larger, Justine reached into her jacket and said, "And, this."

She pulled a cigarette from her pocket and, grabbing a dry leaf from the ground, reached into the flame and deftly held the burning leaf to its tip, inhaled deeply, then exhaled.

This time, I was speechless.

Propping her elbow on her knee and extending the cigarette between outstretched fingers, Justine put it to her lips, bending only her wrist, and inhaled again while leveling a mock-serious stare at me in an exaggerated 'I'm-so-bored-I-could-die' Bette Davis impression.

"D*ah*ling, we've got to do this more often."

I leapt to my feet, unable to contain myself any longer. "*Shazaam!* You smoke?!"

"I took it from my mom's purse when she got here yesterday." Justine tried to sound casual. "I've been sneaking them for a while. If I take one at a time, she doesn't notice. You want a drag?"

"Sure!"

Justine passed the cigarette and I inhaled deeply, trying to imitate her. On the exhale, I was overcome by a fit of coughing.

"Oh puke! That was terrible! I would give my entire album collection to look as cool as you."

"Take a drag, hold it, then let it stream out," Justine said eagerly. "It's easy. I've taught all my friends back home how to do it."

I stared. Who *was* Justine? She was unlike anyone I'd ever known. Watching her, I wondered what other surprises this twelve-year-old kid had in store for me. Twelve, going on sixteen.

I could only imagine.

CHAPTER 3

1974

THE CHURCH BELLS CHIMED

"Smokin' in the Boys Room" – Brownsville Station

JUSTINE

R UNNING OUT TO MEET EVA at the pasture gate on the day I returned for summer vacation, I prayed she could see how much older I looked now that I'd turned thirteen.

She scanned my full height up and down, then said, "So, you finally grew a little, huh? How was your school year, anyway?"

"Well, if you wrote to me like you're supposed to, you'd know!"

"So who's the new boyfriend this year? Or, should I say boyfriend*s*?"

"Well, there's Jimmy. Lemme tell you what happened—"

"Hold on!" Eva paused from her horse grooming with the hard bristle brush in midair. Her eyes were glued to some far off point, her brows all scrunched up. Her lips moved soundlessly, counting the distant tolling of a bell. It rang three times and stopped.

"Wha—?"

"Sh! Sh!" She shook her head and put a finger to her mouth to silence me. The chiming started again. Slowly and deliberately, the vibrations from each chime faded completely before the next one sounded. One... two... three... I watched her counting them on her fingers. After thirteen, the ringing stopped.

Eva gave me a quick glance before going back to her work on Smokey's coat. She didn't comment so I continued with my exciting news. But after her fourth "uh-huh" during the fascinating story about my first kiss, courtesy of a neighborhood boy back home, I realized she wasn't paying any attention to me.

"Hey, Eva," I poked her in the arm. "You aren't listening. My friends back home wanted to know every single detail. I'm the first of all of them to even *kiss* a boy!"

35

She tossed the brush into the wooden box. "It's the bells. Do you know what they mean?"

"No," I said. "Is it something to do with the church? A service or something?"

"Well, sort of. It's a tradition. When someone in North Brookfield dies, they ring the bell at the Town Hall on the day of the funeral."

"Why do they do that?"

"Because it helps people remember. Even for a minute, people look up from what they're doing to remember the person who died. It reminds me of an old saying: 'People die twice. The first time, when they stop breathing. The second, when no one remembers them anymore.'"

"Far out. So, Jimmy and I sneaked up to the school and were making out when he goes to put his hand up my shirt and—"

"Justine! Did you even hear me?"

"Yeah, but...."

"There's a code. If it rings three times, it was a woman. Two times for a man. Then, they ring the bell once for each year the person was alive."

"Wait," I said as a chill tingled up my spine. "It only rang twelve times."

"It was thirteen."

"Thirteen? She was my age? Who was she? How'd she die? Did you know her?"

"She was found dead over at Five Mile River. No one knows much yet. The police are investigating."

"That's weird. Was it an accident? Do you—" The sound of an approaching engine cut me off. A car of any sort on Miller Ave was rare, but this was a police cruiser. "What's a cop car doing out here?"

Eva shrugged. "Ever since the girl died, the cruiser's been seen all over town."

I'd had countless arguments with my friends in New Jersey. Our feelings about cops were completely opposite. Most kids my age had an automatic respect for authority. They'd bought into the whole Officer Friendly campaign. But, I remembered my mother's cousin, Jen, the first real hippie I'd ever met. She lived with us for about a year when I was eight and I remembered the impression she made on me. She wore floor-length, colorful, flowing dresses and let her hair tumble down her back, unlike her peers with their bouffant flips and mini-skirts. Dinner conversation usually ended up with Jen yelling about why authority figures, especially police, weren't to be trusted. She'd pointed to the recent Kent State shootings as yet another example of how those in power abused it.

As the car slowed to a stop, I was caught between a 'screw-you' attitude and 'uh, oh, am I in trouble?' I stood a little taller as the officers stared at us.

"Mornin', girls," said the light-haired cop, his fingertips briefly gripping the brim of his police cap as if he were about to tip it.

"Mornin'," Eva said, nodding her head in return.

The cop with dark hair and cocoa-colored eyes in the passenger seat smiled at us and, for a moment, I forgot to feel contrary. The corners of my mouth pulled into an answering smile until I looked back at the blond. While his face was soft with the corners of his mouth turned up, his hard, icy blue eyes creeped me out. I took a slight step backwards.

"You girls aren't out here alone, are you?" asked the blond. I noticed a splattering of freckles across his cheeks and barely visible beneath the thick blond hair on his arms. I couldn't remember ever seeing a grown up with freckles before.

"No, the Millers are home."

"Okay, good," he said. "Tell Peggy and John 'hello.' Oh, and be careful."

"Why do...?" I began, but stopped when Eva jabbed me in the ribs with her elbow.

"We will," she said. "See ya."

As they drove off, those cold blue eyes held mine as I stared back.

"Justine, stop! They're just the town cops, O'Reilly and Costa. They're okay. Really."

"Yeah, well, they're not gonna intimate me."

"You mean intimidate!"

I gave the police one last glance before tossing my hair over my shoulder. "Come on. Let's blow this popsicle stand!"

Behind the barn, we lit up cigarettes and looked into the distance across the lush green, half-mile pasture, splashed with hues of orange, purple, red wildflowers, and grazing Holstein cows, to the only other house on Miller Ave. The run-down farmhouse was built a century and a half ago by my fourth great-grandfather, Captain Samuel Miller, the first of my ancestors to settle in North Brookfield. With the gigantic gray barn to its right and the scattered collection of tractors and plows, I could imagine artists camped here to paint the picturesque landscape. Except the police car was parked up there, ruining the otherwise unblemished country scene.

I took a long drag off my cigarette and blew out a smoke ring.

"Does your mom know you smoke yet?" Eva asked.

I could easily imagine Mom's reaction. Her perfect daughter, with perfect grades, and perfect manners. The carefully crafted image she could hold up to society as the example of skillful parenting. I pictured her horror and disappointment if she caught me with a cigarette.

"Ha! God, no! She'd kill me. I just won't get caught," I said. "Oh crap! Speaking of not getting caught, I can't believe I forgot to tell you. Guess what my friend Laura and I did a couple of weeks ago. We went," I crushed the butt of my cigarette against the ground, "*streaking*!"

"You mean like the guy who streaked at the Academy Awards?" Eva said.

"Yup! I told my parents we were camping in the backyard. When it got late, we stripped off all our clothes and snuck out. We went running down the sidewalk, scared that all the neighbors would see us and tell my mom."

"Then why'd you do it, Justine?"

"Duh, Eva! That's the fun of it. We went about halfway around the block when these headlights came toward us. We hid behind a parked car, watching the lights get closer, then it pulled right next to us on the other side of the car. We thought we were busted, but it kept going. We ran around the rest of the block and were almost back to my house when this other car came up behind us. We didn't even know until it was right there, shining its lights on our naked asses. Talk about scared! We about killed each other racing the rest of the way to get back into the tent." When I finished, I sat back to savor Eva's reaction.

She stared at me with a look I'd never seen before.

"Are you gonna shut your mouth or are you gonna sit there like a guppy out of water?"

Eva closed her mouth.

"For the first time since I've known you, you're speechless. What is that? Newfound respect?" I proudly thought about the same response I'd gotten from my New Jersey friends when they heard about the streaking. It was quite different from just a year earlier when my shyness made me feel invisible in the neighborhood social circles. All that had changed one night during a sleepover at Maggie Jenson's house when I'd worked up the guts to dare the other girls into sneaking out after midnight. I'd bravely led them all around our neighborhood, hiding in shadows in our nightgowns and bare feet, shivering with nervous excitement. Since then, my adventurous reputation had put me on the invitation list for every gathering with the kids from school.

Eva hit my thigh with the back of her hand and jerked her head toward the farm. The police car had pulled away from the house and, while crouching low behind the tall-growing grasses, we listened as it came down the road toward Aunt Peggy and Uncle John's house. The sound of the motor rose as it neared, then faded as it passed. We remained still, pulling out blades of grass, one by one. My thoughts drifted to a nameless thirteen-year-old girl who was gone. No longer someone I might see walking through town or who would smell the heat of the summer sun on newly cut hay. Had she explored the woods with her friends and stolen cigarettes from her mother? Was she blonde like me or dark-haired like Eva?

Eva nudged me and smiled. "Streaking. That's wicked cool. I can't picture anyone from here doing something like that."

I gave her a playful push and the ghostly image of the dead girl floated away. "Life's short, Eva. We need to make our own fun. Did you ever think about that?"

EVERYTHING CHANGES

"American Pie" – Don McLean

EVA

WHEN YOU'RE A KID, YOU think of life as a constant. That thought makes us feel protected and secure. For all of us, the illusion is shattered at some point. I was six when it happened to me. As I watched my grandfather take his last breath, I was struck with the realization that life doesn't stay the same. Like those pictures he showed me with people frozen in time.

Since I was eleven, I'd had this unshakeable feeling of time starting to move backwards. First, it was only my parents, then they had one child after another, after another. Then, time seemed to hold in a balance for a while before ever so slightly tipping, as if a great ship was starting to sink. Kids graduated, enlisted, married. Left home, one by one. Craig and I remained, but soon it would be only my parents once again. Then, like a scene fading to black, one by one, they'd be gone too.

Yes, everything changed. And, the news in today's *Worcester Telegram* was a harsh reminder of that.

"You're not going to believe what's going on! See, Justine? You disappear all day with Peggy and John and come back to the Town Crier over here!" I was excited to be the one with a story to tell. Justine always had a big saga—about making out with some boy, or some lip-gloss-stealing stunt she'd pulled to impress her friends, or sneaking out at night. Sometimes I wondered if half of what she said was true.

Ha! Look at her. She's dying to know and hell bent on not letting it show. She'd glanced at the newspaper tucked under my arm, but made no mention of it. I think she's going for 'aloof.' Well, two can play that game!

We were perched on the edge of one of the defunct train rails, sheltered by the bordering woods stretching as far as we could see. Tufts of grass grew between the ties, creating emerald squares that blurred into distant green lines. I sneaked a sideways look at Justine through my lowered eyelids, the flaming sunset creating a pinkish glow on her blonde hair. I took a long, unhurried drag on my cigarette, keeping her in suspense. She played it cool, blowing out strings of smoke rings.

We each held out, waiting for the other to give.

We waited.

And waited.

Oh... *damn!* "Do you want to know what happened?"

Justine smiled victoriously as she ground her cigarette against a rail. "Sure, Eva. Go for it."

"Well, remember the bell tolling when you first got here this summer? For the—"

"—thirteen-year-old girl?"

"Right. It turns out she'd been camping with her family and disappeared. When they found her near the river, they knew it wasn't an accident." Then, whipping out the newspaper with a dramatic flourish, I added the clincher. "She was murdered!"

Justine's mouth dropped open. "Murdered? Someone *murdered* a thirteen-year-old girl?"

Murdered a thirteen-year old girl?! Her horrified reaction burst my thrill of one-upping her in storytelling. Dear God, this wasn't some made-up tale! That girl was real, of flesh and blood. With heartbroken parents, maybe brothers and sisters. Softening my tone, I said, "Lynn's uncle's a cop in Ware so she gave me the inside scoop. He said her head had been bashed in. They found the bloody rock next to her body. Look. Here's the story."

We smoothed out the newspaper on the ground in front of us. The headline reinforced what I'd said. "13-Year-Old's Death Ruled a Murder." A photo of the victim covered the entire top half of the front page.

Justine studied the picture. "She was blonde. Her headband looks like something my mom used to buy me. With the big flower on it."

"I still can't believe it."

"She looked so happy, didn't she?"

"She did. Poor thing. She had no way of knowing what would happen to her."

"She looks a little like me, don't you think?"

"Yeah, I can see it." I glanced from the picture to my friend.

"You didn't know her?"

"No. The family had just moved here from Brookfield."

Justine's eyes didn't leave the paper. "Do they know who did it?"

"Not yet, but I ran into some kids in town this morning. They're saying it's Rag Doll Man."

"Rag Doll Man? Why do they think that?"

"People say he's been hanging around lately. One boy from my class said he saw a tall man in a trench coat, carrying a doll, over in that area the day before it happened."

"So why don't they arrest him?" she asked.

"I don't know if the cops believe it's Rag Doll Man. Lynn said she asked her uncle but he didn't really say much."

Justine fell silent.

"You know...." I began, uncertain if I should tell Justine about the newest gossip I'd heard regarding her Uncle John. The kids in this town had nothing better to do than talk about other people—make up stories, even—just to amuse themselves.

"What?"

"Oh, never mind."

"Come on!" she said. "What were you gonna say?"

"Uh, I forget." I decided to drop it. Maybe the rumors would die on their own.

She stared, analyzing me with her typical intensity, waiting for me to continue.

"Well," I said, reaching to refold the newspaper and stick it under my arm, "I need to be getting home. I've got a curfew now."

"Because of the girl?"

"That and Rag Doll Man. Thanks, Rag Doll Man!" I said loudly enough for anyone who might be listening.

By this time, the sky had turned a foreboding gray and heavy clouds blocked most of the glow from the stars and crescent moon. Tripping along the tracks, we found the path that would eventually bring us out behind Peggy and John's. With the high-growing grove to our left blocking any remaining light, we groped our way. A strong breeze rustled through the woods, stirring my hair and making me unseasonably chilly.

Crack!

"What was that?" Justine whirled around.

"A tree branch," I said, rubbing my hands up and down the goosebumps on my arms.

Justine hugged her own arms across her chest. The trail, bordered by sinisterly tall grasses and darkened by shadows, narrowed until we were forced to trek single file. Justine led tentatively. I kept my head forward, eyes darting side to side. Could that strange, black shape be a homicidal maniac with a rock? Was he creeping along behind us? Would he jump out at us? Add two more girls to his trophy case? Where is that damned light at Peggy and John's, anyway?

"Eva?" A quivering voice drifted back to me. "You don't think anyone's in those trees, do you?"

"N-no way. There's n-nobody around but us. You aren't s-scared, are you?"

A branch snapped right behind us.

Oh shit! My heart dropped as my head whipped around to scan the pitch-black grove. *Who's there?*

"Puh-leeze! Not me." Justine's voice cracked on the last word.

I was walking more quickly, still checking over my shoulder, when I crashed into her, sending us both stumbling.

"What're you doing!? Why'd you stop?" Reaching down, I rubbed my throbbing ankle.

"Why weren't you watching where you were going?"

"I was!" I tried to put weight on my foot, but yelped in pain. "Come on." I took a few tenuous steps before resorting to a lopsided hobble.

At last, the back porch light at the house reached toward us, guiding us to safety. Lucky gave a quiet "woof" as he trotted to greet and escort us the final distance. We plunked ourselves onto the Adirondack chairs and I propped up my aching leg.

"Do you want me to get you something? Ice?" The dim light cast by the porch lamp exaggerated the paleness of Justine's complexion and the hollows under her eyes, giving her an otherworldly look.

"No, no, I'm good. Let me rest it for a minute." I massaged my foot and ankle, then settled back. "Do your contact lenses bother you at all? I've heard they hurt." With the thick glasses gone, her restless blue eyes seemed to glow even more intensely.

Justine relaxed back into her own chair, the shadows across her face shifting so her features were darkened beyond distinction. "They took some getting used to, but now they're fine. And, Mom says she'll let me start wearing make-up to school this year. Far out, huh? All of my friends already do. Do you ever wear it?"

"Nah! I'd just smear it."

"You should, Eva. It'd look good."

I shook my head. "The clothes are enough." I glanced down at the shorts and t-shirt she'd insisted were a step up from the jeans and flannels I used to wear. I still wasn't sure, but I had to agree they were certainly more comfortable during the heat of the day.

She was still scrutinizing me. "It'll give you confidence. Make you feel good about yourself. That's what people see, you know. Not the clothes or the make-up. They'll see your hard-ass attitude."

I chuckled at my young friend. The girl with all of the answers. "We'll see."

Justine leaned toward me. "So, remember how we never got around to looking through the attic last summer?" Her animation and the change in her position had recast the lighting on her and, with her skin's yellow hue and her wildly glittering eyes, she looked downright wicked. The hair on the back of my neck tingled. "It's gonna rain tomorrow. What do you think?"

"Uh, okay. Sure!" A smile stretched across my face. She'd tried to convince me there were ghosts in the Miller house. Generations of her ancestors' spirits who were trapped there, confused, rattling chains, and moaning. Who did she think she was kidding?

Standing, I found my ankle had settled down and I could put my full weight on it. "Well, I need to get home before my parents send out the search party. Oh shit," I said, feeling under my arm, then searching around the ground by my chair. "What'd I do with that paper?"

"I haven't seen it since we got back."

"I must have dropped it back by the grove. Remember? When you tripped me?"

"What?! I didn't...!"

"My dad's going to kill me. I'd better go before I'm late for curfew too, or I'll end up getting grounded." At Smokey's gate, I grabbed my bike and climbed on. "Catch you on the rebound."

Justine and Lucky stepped back as I pushed off. "Okay, bye." Then she added, "Watch out for Rag Doll Man!"

"Gee, thanks. See ya!"

"Bye," said Justine.

I coasted toward the tunnel of trees. "Bye."

"Bye." I heard through darkness.

"Bye!" I yelled, spotting the first glimmer of the street light at the intersection with Elm Street. Could she still hear me?

"Byyyee!" Yep, fainter but still audible.

Taking a deep breath, I screamed as loudly as I could. "Byyyeee!"

"Bye," came a whisper.

"Byyyyyyeee!" Could she *still* hear me?

"Bye," floated on air.

Wow! I veered onto Elm Street, Shadow Hill was on my left. At the top of my lungs, I hollered, "Byyyyyeeeee!"

I'm not sure, but thought I heard the faintest of faint "byyyeee's" come back.

With a laugh, then a deep breath, I belted out my loudest one yet. "Byyyyyyeeeee!" and waited for a response.

I soared, pedaling faster, and strained my ears to listen. And listen. As silence greeted me, a twinge of apprehension began to nag. I kept my eyes focused on the road in front of me and pushed away thoughts of Rag Doll Man. Of cracking branches in the woods. Of spirits waiting for me in the Miller's attic. Of comments from my classmates, suggesting that John Miller was in fact, Rag Doll Man. I raced the rest of the way home, slammed on the brakes, dropped my bike, and leapt to the porch. I yanked open the door, then turned and did what I do every evening before going in for the night. I scanned the yards up and down the street to see if any of the neighbors were turning in too. Sometimes I'd see Mr. Herdman, or maybe Terri Smith, and we'd amicably wave to each other. Tonight, I only saw shadows. The screen door slammed as I dashed into the house.

A Haunted Attic

"Superstition" – Stevie Wonder

Justine

A NARROW DOOR, CREAKING IN PROTEST, opened from the second floor hallway. The attic stairs loomed ahead. Unlike the grand, sweeping staircase leading from the main floor to the upstairs, these steps were steep, straight, and narrow. Although they were enclosed on both sides, the handrail abruptly stopped halfway up, and the only light was from a bare bulb dangling from an ancient ceiling fixture at the top of the stairs. I'd traveled these steps a thousand times and ran my hand along the wall for guidance. This was Eva's first time and I couldn't help but laugh when I looked over my shoulder and saw her scurrying up, bent forward at the waist, using both her hands and feet.

"Come on, we don't have all day!" I taunted when I reached the landing. "Jeez, you go up the stairs like my three-year-old cousin."

"Well… well, *you* can break your neck, but I'm not going to." Eva tried to make up for that weak comeback when she straightened at the top of the stairs and wiped her hands on the back of my blouse. I yanked my shirt away, too excited about my next bit of news to give her the satisfaction of pretending to be mad.

"Hey! I just remembered something. A long time ago, my great-great-uncle Harry fell down these stairs… and *died*." In the dimness, I could see Eva's eyes grow large with interest.

"Really? Was he old?"

"He was in his eighties. He didn't die right then and there, but he never recovered from his injuries. He was Faith Ellen's older brother, and back in those days, when people came to visit, they'd sleep up here in the attic. I didn't know him because he died before I was born, but my mom told me he used to whistle all the time, morning and night. And…" I dropped

46

my voice to a whisper, leaning close to Eva to extract every ounce of drama from my story, "and people still hear whistling up here... and they say it's *Uncle Harry!*"

Eva let out her suppressed breath in a slow, steady stream. "Wowww!"

"Ready?" I smiled, happy I'd rattled Eva, as I turned the knob on the door opening into the room to the right.

Despite the daylight, the room was dim. A window a few inches above the floor faced the farm at the end of the road, its wavy glass panes clouded by decades' worth of grime and intricate cobwebs. It was still gloomy outside, and at the top of the house, there was no mistaking the light patter of rain on the roof. I hurried to the center of the room and pulled the chain of another bare fixture, and the room brightened.

The room had once been wallpapered, and scraps of faded green with enormous pink and white flowers still clung to the walls. The roof had leaked, and streaks of brown trailed down the walls in several places. Plaster dust from the cracked ceiling coated my family history, bundled, stored, and forgotten for a generation. A piece of worn linoleum, curling at the edges, covered the floor; at least, what could be seen of it. At the room's edge, where the ceiling sloped, was a simple iron bed with a stained mattress; a round-lidded, forlorn-looking trunk; and a few pieces of worn or broken furniture. On the other wall was a small, schoolhouse desk with an inkwell and attached chair. Beside the desk, in front of an elf-sized door, were several pairs of shoes.

"It's like the room is waiting for visitors to return." I scanned the collection of cast-offs.

"Yeah, I get that feeling too." Eva's eyes settled on the boxes stacked as tall as Eva herself. More than a dozen. Some were water-stained and mouse-chewed, but they were intact.

"What's in all those boxes?" By her breathless tone, it was clear Eva was fascinated.

"I have no idea."

"No *idea*?"

"Hey, I don't live here, remember? I haven't been up here for a long time. I doubt Aunt Peggy and Uncle John have either. Aunt Peggy's too disabled to make it and, well, Uncle John...." My words drifted away as I thought about my gentle great-uncle.

Eva's brows raised. "I know about Peggy, but what's the story with John?"

I paused, instinctively bristling in defense. But I knew Eva. She wasn't judgmental or cruel. She wouldn't laugh or make snide comments about someone I loved. Drawing a deep breath, I said, "He's schizophrenic."

Eva waited.

"He was in Pearl Harbor during the war. He was a switchboard operator when they were attacked and the military doctors thought the stress and all of the flashing lights on the board, caused him to break with reality. That's what schizophrenia is. People don't know the difference between reality and fantasy. Most of the time he's pretty good, but he's on a lot of medication. Aunt Peggy keeps track of it all."

"I never knew that." Eva's voice was soft. "To me, he's always been this sweet, sorta different guy. Sort of in his own world."

"Yeah, well...." I tried to think of something to change the subject. "The rain seems to—"

"How did he get schizophrenia? I mean, do they know what caused it?"

"I don't know a whole lot about it, except it can run in families. Remember I told you about my ancestor up at Shadow Hill who had it too?"

"Oh right. Um, I know it's nothing, but some kids were talking...."

"About Uncle John?"

"Yeah, uh—"

"What kids?"

"You know, just kids."

"And...?"

Eva shifted back and forth, unable to meet my eyes. "Well, they were saying, maybe, uh, it might be, uh, possible that he and Rag Doll Man...."

"He and Rag Doll Man what?" I asked, my face getting warm.

"That, maybe, they're the same...?"

"The same? You mean, the same person?" I heard my heart pounding. "Uncle John *is* Rag Doll Man!?"

"It's only a stupid rumor."

Eva's eyes were on me, anticipating my reaction. The rage building inside made me want to scream, to throw and break something into a million pieces. I pictured myself flying at them, tearing into them. I closed my eyes as I blew out my fury in a long, ten-count stream, then turned to the uppermost box on the pile nearest to where we were standing. I pulled at the heavily taped edges of the box. "Got your pocket knife?"

"Yup." Eva slipped it from her hip pocket and passed it to me. I slit the brittle, yellowed tape while Eva pulled a child's rocking chair close and squeezed into it. When I lowered the box to the floor and knelt, examining its contents, I forgot all about Rag Doll Man.

We'd hit the jackpot! There must have been a thousand pictures. Some faded gray and white, some in sepia tones, some with curlicue-embossed oval cardboard frames, and most with the photographer's name in gold on the lower corner. Women with high-collared blouses, hair pinned up, wearing elaborate hats and wistful expressions. Men who stared into the camera intently, some with arms crossed, in suit jackets and bow ties. Many of the pictures showed families—children standing stiffly at their parents' sides, little boys in knickers, young girls dressed like miniature versions of their mothers. Other pictures were less formal; kids standing proudly next to a Shetland pony; a group of people in front of a brick building; two smiling little girls standing together, arms linked.

"I wonder who they are." I examined each picture before handing it to Eva. "And if any of them are still alive. It's like your grandfather said. These people are all frozen in the moment the photo was taken. Weird to think most of them are probably gone."

"Anyone you recognize?" Eva studied each in turn.

"Hmmm. Hey, look! This one was taken right here!"

Eva leaned over my shoulder. The photograph was faded; a young couple standing together. The woman wore a straight, loose-fitting, ankle-length dress and smiled shyly. The man wore a bowler hat and a suit and held his head high, with a hint of cockiness. They stood in the gravel driveway, next to a car that was clearly ancient, with the Miller house in the background.

"Far out! Look how small that maple tree is in the front yard. When do you think this was taken?"

Eva studied the picture. "I think that's a Model T. Either that or a Model A. I'm not sure, but I would say definitely it's from the early 1900s. 1910, maybe? And that woman looks like you!"

"Like me?!" Was she *serious*? The woman in the picture was old, at least twice my age. And I could never show my face in the high-necked formal dress that looked like something out of the Middle Ages.

"She has the same chin as you. See that little dimple? And the same eyes."

"I don't see it. The resemblance. Nope, don't see it." I shook my head adamantly.

"Well, then you're blind."

"How could I look like her? Huh?!" My voice climbed. "She's got short, curly hair and she looks like a... a flapper!"

"Forget the dress, Miss Hoity-Toity. If you were alive sixty years ago, you would probably wear something like that instead of your little shorty-shorts. And, you would probably have worn your hair short too, and curled it instead of straightening it. And you probably wouldn't have been blonde, either!"

I had to admit, I did love the zingers Eva slung at me. "Yup, that's me. Thank goodness for Sun-In."

Eva added in her most serious television golf-tournament-announcer mock whisper: "Ladies and Gentlemen, does she or doesn't she? Only her hairdresser knows for sure. And most of the boys in her eighth grade homeroom!"

I barely heard her as my eyes were glued to the next photo. Wordlessly, I handed it to her.

The picture was no doubt taken on the same day and showed the same couple. Only this picture was taken from a different perspective: closer. Neither the house, nor the car, was visible. Instead, something else was in the picture. In front of the pretty woman with the bashful look and the cocky young man was a pram. A small bundle peeked out from under the hood of the old-fashioned baby carriage. This time, I could plainly see my resemblance to the woman. There was writing on the bottom of the photo.

Eva squinted to read it. "September, 1911. John Carl, Faith Ellen, and," Eva stifled an involuntary gasp, "Dorothy Justine!"

"You know who they are? Those are my great-grandparents! Remember? I showed you their graves up in Shadow Hill." I stared at the picture more closely. "I've never seen them when they were younger. Only pictures of when they were really old."

"And Dorothy Justine?"

"You know the children's headstones? She's one of them. She died when she was really little." I looked again at the date. "She must have died soon after this picture was taken."

"Did you know her middle name was Justine?"

"No."

We explored the contents of the attic room for the rest of the afternoon. Box after box held undiscovered treasures. Mostly old pictures. One box contained letters and autograph books. Another was filled with old high school diplomas, handwritten recipes, land sale deeds, and various legal documents. An ancient baby-doll with eerie blue eyes and painted-on blonde hair wore a stained Christening gown. While we sorted through the contents of each box, we were distracted by the worn leather shoes lined up near the bed.

"Years ago," Eva said, "people didn't throw shoes away when they became worn; they were so expensive. Every village had a cobbler, and the cobbler would make new soles or repair the shoes. In fact, the cobbler is the town symbol for North Brookfield."

"I can't imagine." I lifted up one leg to display my latest footwear—my backless 3-inch heel with the wide, tan leather strap that showed off my glittery polished toenails. "New soles for my Candies?"

Eva ignored me. "Hey! Look at these boxes!"

"They say 'Justine's dishes'! Mom told me Aunt Peggy has been collecting dishes forever, to give to me when I get married! Even though she has other nieces, she and I have always had a special relationship."

We slit one box open, by now expert with the old switchblade.

"Oh, look!" I said, holding up a white dinner plate with a blue floral pattern. I couldn't believe they would be mine someday.

Eva examined it. "Staffordshire. Hamilton. Yes, very nice."

"She's been sending to England for it for years."

Eva stood up and stretched. "We still haven't seen the other room. Do you want to check it out?"

"You know I do!"

We straightened out the boxes. I slipped the picture of my youthful great-grandparents and baby Dorothy Justine into my back pocket.

The second attic room was in worse condition than the first. It was smaller, more cramped, and the hot, stale air held a heavy mustiness barely stirred by the square floor fan I lugged from the other room. Mice had taken up residence: shredded cardboard, clothing, and mattresses littered the floor.

Eva peered into the room from the doorway with thinly masked disgust. "Ummm. Yuck. I would say it has an old-fashioned homey quality, but I don't think I'd want to sleep here."

"That's quite a statement, coming from you!"

"What do you mean?"

"I've seen *your* room!"

Eva turned, poised to respond, but I held up my hand to silence her. "Wait. Did you hear that?"

"Hear what?"

"Ssshhh! It's Aunt Peggy. She's calling me. She must need something. I better go see."

"Hey, wait a min—" Eva began, but I was gone.

Giggling to myself, I set the stage for my biggest 'gotcha' yet. I'd grabbed a shoe before leaving the first room and hidden it behind my back. I quickly tossed it to the bottom of the stairs with a thud. Peeking around the corner of the door, I watched as Eva pawed at the air through the dimness, fumbling for the pull-chain of the light fixture. Her head whipped from side to side as she walked toward the window.

I put my lips together and did my best Uncle Harry impression—I whistled. Eva stopped abruptly.

I continued, softly. "Yankee Doodle."

She turned in slow motion toward the door. I kept whistling, backing silently across the landing and into the darkness of the other room.

Her racing footsteps came toward me, then stomped down the stairs. I rushed out and followed her, my laughter finally escaping my throat.

"Oh my God, that was a hoot! I should have had a camera!"

Eva was panting so hard she couldn't talk.

"That look on your face! I saw you when you came out of the room and ran down the stairs! It was priceless!" I was practically rolling on the floor.

Eva scowled, still unable to speak and gasping, bent over with hands on knees.

"You should have seen yourself!"

Eva continued to glare, wordlessly.

"Aunt Peggy never really called me. I just faked it. I threw a shoe down the stairs and hit the door so it opened a little and squeaked. Then I went and hid in the room across the hall. It was perfect!"

Eva pretended to be mad, but couldn't help conceding. She even looked a little pleased her apprentice had outshined her.

"I better put this shoe back before someone trips over it. You've got to admit, it was a good one, wasn't it?"

Eva found her voice, at last, and cackled in her witchy imitation, "I'll get you, my pretty! And your little dog too!"

As we mounted the stairs, I noticed how the darkness threatened to end our day. Our endless days in June, so full of promise, had faded to early August. While we were grasping onto every second of summer as it raced toward September, we knew it soon would be over. I'd return to New Jersey. We'd both be back in school. Smokey would go home to his small barn behind Eva's house. Winter would force us indoors.

"Hey!" Eva broke into my thoughts, snapping me back to the moment. We were standing on the landing. "I thought we turned that light off." She pointed toward the first attic room.

"Me too. It was dark a minute ago, when I was in there."

"I *know* we turned it off."

I dropped the shoe next to its mate and crossed the room, Eva following. Then, we noticed. From the rounded trunk by the iron bed, something was protruding from beneath the lid. A piece of lace. A skirt.

I pointed to it. "Hey! I didn't see this when we were in here before."

"Me either."

We stared at the trunk.

I walked over, lifted the lid, and grabbed the garment. I stood up straight as I hauled it from the trunk, backing up to allow it to extend to its full length. It was a long, faded, ivory-colored lace dress with a high collar; puffed sleeves; a full, hand-sewn skirt; and at least a hundred buttons from neck to waist.

"Look at this. It's wicked pretty." Eva circled it to examine every angle.

"And it's tiny. A tiny wedding dress. I don't think it would even fit me!"

"Wow, I guess not."

I looked at Eva and her eyes locked on me.

"It's funny how the light was on."

"I know, and this dress was spilling over the lid of the trunk."

"It's almost like it was waiting to be found."

Softly, we both heard a faint sound. *Whistling!*

Together, we listened. I recognized the tune from one of Eva's many history lessons: "Over there, over there/Send the word, send the word over there..." The old World War One song by George M Cohan.

There was no one else here.

The whistling continued, on and on.

Eyes wide, staring at each other, we were frozen.

JUSTINE'S ROSE-COLORED GLASSES

"Summer Breeze" – Seals and Crofts

EVA

MY EYES KEPT STRAYING BACK to her boobs. She probably thought I was a perv for staring but I couldn't help myself. I mean, what was going on there? It was like she turned into Raquel Welch. Overnight!

"Evaaaa? Whatcha lookin' at?" Justine asked in a sing-song drawl, gently tugging at a low-hanging branch on the mature, fifty-foot tall maple tree in the front yard of Peggy and John's house.

"Uh, nothing."

Justine squinted her eyes at me.

"What the hell's going on with you?" My eyes were still focused on her bulging chest.

"What? What do you mean?" The branch bounced back into place when she released it to cross her arms in front of her, blocking my view.

"Those." I pointed. "When did you get... *those?*"

The blush rose from the location in question, up her neck, and spread to her cheeks. "I don't know what you're talking about."

"Get real! You didn't have those yesterday!" I extended my finger to poke one. Would it pop like a balloon or would my finger bounce off of it like a trampoline?

She swatted my hand away before I touched her. "It's a padded bra. I'm trying it out to see how it looks." She glanced down, then grinned. "Too much?"

"Uh, yeah! Like, three cup sizes too much. You're thirteen. Give it time. You'll grow." Laughter erupted from me as I blatantly ogled my friend's jugs.

"Stop!"

I pointed at them, tauntingly, one last time. "*You* stop! Stop doing... *that!*"

Something else was different since yesterday. Other than those breasts, she looked the same. Almost. Straight, blonde hair. Her skin was browned from all of our outdoor romping. She was certainly more confident this summer. But, something was different. She didn't have her usual swagger as she went into her house to change clothes and get her beach bag. I studied her as she returned, walking toward me with her head held high, but... what *was* it?

Her eyes. Her big, blue eyes. All summer, they'd glimmered with mischief, sparkled with excitement yet to be discovered. That's it! That impish glint was gone.

"So, are you looking forward to going home?" I asked offhandedly as we hopped on our bikes, Justine on my old banana seat bike and me on Craig's discarded ten-speed. I'd learned by her clipped responses that she hated being asked what was wrong directly.

"I guess," she said, pumping her bike pedals as we headed toward town.

"Anything you want to talk about?"

"Well, I hate leaving. I don't want to go back to my real life—pressure from my parents and all...."

"I'll be better about writing this year. Promise."

"You suck at writing back! Don't make promises you can't keep." A small, genuine smile finally crept onto her face. "It feels like forever, but I'll be back before we know it."

"I don't get you. I'd give anything to go to some of the places you've been. California, Florida, *England!*" I wagged my head. "But you always want to come to this boring old place instead."

Justine had a romanticized view of North Brookfield through her rose-colored glasses, with visions of her long line of ancestors walking these familiar streets. She hadn't seen, or allowed herself to see, that living in this small town was exactly like any other place. With its share of sketchy people... and monotony.

"Well, I don't get *you!* Why do you want to leave so badly?"

"Oh, don't get me wrong. It's not that I don't like North Brookfield. I do. It'll always be home for me. But, *you* see it as a destination. From wherever you are, this is where you want to end up. It's kind of the opposite of how I see it. I see it as a starting place—my center—then I go a little bit farther, then a little bit farther. Sort of like concentric circles, right? I start at this town, then travel throughout Massachusetts, then the Northeast, eventually the whole country. See?"

"What does 'concentric circles' mean?"

"It's something I learned this year in Geometry. It means—" I was interrupted by jeers coming from the baseball field.

"Hey, farm girl! Where's your old nag?" Two boys, Jane Williams's fiendish sidekicks, were perched on the bleachers at the Common, their faces lit with the prospect of torturing me. At school, I'd walk past and pretend I didn't hear their comments. If I spotted them in time, I'd duck into a classroom or take the long way around to avoid them. Today, there was no hiding from them.

"Yeah, don't you think it's about time for the glue factory?"

I took a deep breath and kept my eyes down. Suddenly, I realized Justine wasn't beside me. She had dropped her bike to the ground and was storming toward the bullies.

Oh shit! I quickly did a U-turn and raced back to intercept her. She stopped when I approached, her eyes wild with fury. *How is it that this girl, this scrawny twerp who's two years younger than me, looks so fearless and about to kick both boys' butts?*

"Please, *please*, don't do anything!" I begged. "It'll only make it worse. Just count to ten the way your mother always says."

"I don't *wanna* count to ten!" Justine's cheeks had angry red splotches bursting across them. "You're gonna let those putzes talk to you that way? Are you *kidding* me!"

I found myself balancing between the anxiety of a confrontation making my life at school more miserable and the fascination of seeing how Justine would handle them. I decided it wasn't worth the risk.

"Come on. Let's ignore them and go. They'll tell Jane and then she'll never leave me alone."

"They're friends of *Jane's*?" She resumed her march toward them.

"Justine, *please!*"

She stopped and looked at me. Then she turned and glowered at the boys, pulling her slight, 5'1" frame into an intimidating stance until they stopped laughing. She picked up her bike and, casting a fierce, prolonged gaze at them, we continued.

She was still seething as we rode the remainder of the way in silence. I was heavy with embarrassment and, truthfully, a little unnerved by Justine's reaction. When we veered onto Brooks Pond Road and I saw a smirk pulling at one side of her mouth, my mood lifted.

"Those dorks almost croaked, didn't they?" she said, her eyes glowing in their old, familiar way.

"Did you see their faces? I can't believe you were going after them! What would you have said?"

"No clue!"

"And you wonder why I want to get out of this town?"

"Eva, they're assholes, but you need to stand up to them. Then they'll leave you alone." The shimmering pond came into view in front of us. "Ooooo, far out! Look at that war-der!"

"War-der," I repeated, chuckling at her pronunciation.

"How've I never seen this place before? Hey, cool rope! Do you use it as a swing?"

In no time, we'd dropped our bags and unfurled our towels. The sun was scorching hot and Justine ripped off her clothes, revealing an aqua blue two-piece bathing suit beneath; she wasn't the same scrawny girl I'd met last year. Even without her ridiculously padded bra.

She raced toward the rope and grabbed it, swinging far out over the pond, and yelled, "Geronimooooo!" She splashed into the water.

As the rope swung back, I caught it and joined her seconds later.

We spent the next two hours swimming, splashing, and talking. After our lunch of Fluffernutter sandwiches washed down with cans of Tab, we slathered ourselves with the baby oil and iodine mixture needed to top off our rich summer tans. As we were stretching out on our towels, I continued to school Justine on the virtues of "good" music. None of that bubblegum, teeny-bopper crap. I discussed several rock bands, but because of my personal preferences, the majority of my instruction centered around the Beatles and Rolling Stones.

"My brother, Randy, likes all of the same music," Justine said. "We hang out in his room, listening to his albums. I think I like the Beatles better, but now that Paul McCartney's with Wings, I like them too. What do you think?"

"Well, anything Paul does is good. I'm not sure how I feel about the Beatles versus the Rolling Stones, though. I think I'm leaning toward the Stones." I turned onto my stomach to let the sun color my back. "When you come back next year, we'll go to my place. I have most of their records. You can listen to both bands and decide for yourself."

Justine sat up. "Okay. Then I can choose which one is transcendentalist."

"Wait, what? You mean like Emerson and Thoreau?"

She tilted her head to the side with one eyebrow raised. "Those were writers, weren't they? I was talking about the bands."

"You said 'transcendentalist.' That's someone who studies the philosophy they wrote about."

"No!" she insisted. "I was saying I could pick which band I thought was better. You know. *Transcendentalist!* One *transcends* the other."

"Transcendent? Transcendental? Is that what you meant?"

"That's what I said." She gathered her towel and shoved it into her bag.

"I'm not sure if that's exactly the word you want. But, I know what you mean. You can decide which one you think is the best."

"Ready? We need to get back."

Despite myself, I laughed as I got to my feet. I bent down and picked up a small stone. "Wait," I said, tossing it into the pond for good luck. The rock broke the smooth surface of the water, then created a series of rippling rings. I pointed to the pattern. "See? Concentric circles."

"Justine," her mother called from downstairs. "You need to practice the piano."

"I know! I'm just getting Eva the book I promised. I'll be right there."

"Jeez! You're leaving tomorrow and you still have to practice?" I asked.

Rolling her eyes, she collapsed onto the edge of the bed. "Every day. I have to practice piano for an hour, *every single day*! During baton competition season, I have to practice that for an hour too."

"She's wicked strict, huh?"

"My friends are allowed to go out during the week. Not me. I'm only allowed to do stuff on the weekends." She hesitated, then added, "As long as I keep my grades up."

"Why's she so hard on you?"

"Well, she's always saying I need to 'make something of my life... do something meaningful... change the world.' I get good grades so she expects a lot of me. She works with me at home too. Like reading, grammar, vocabulary."

"Vocabulary?" I teased her. "You mean like 'transcendentalist'?"

"Shut up!" She whacked me, stifling a smile. "She expects me to have some high-powered career, probably to make up for what she gave up to get married and have kids. I think she's trying to live vi—" She stopped, confusion wrinkling her forehead.

"—cariously. I thought she was a social worker."

"She is, but she always dreamed of being an attorney. Like my dad. Anyway, lemme get you that book I told you about."

Resting on the edge of Justine's bed, I avoided looking in the direction of the attic stairs. They lay right on the other side of the closed door. Neither of us had talked about the day we were up there—the dress and the whistling—but I hadn't stopped thinking about it.

Stacked on one side of the room, Justine's suitcases were ready for her to leave in the morning. The windows were dressed with yellow flowered curtains over white roller shades and there was a rocking chair in the corner. In the fading light, I could almost imagine a middle-aged woman in a long skirt and high-necked lace blouse sitting there with knitting needles in her hands and a ball of yarn on her lap, rocking back and forth. My eyes found the mirror above the dresser: on the picture stuck into the frame of the mirror. It was the one we had found in the attic. The one with John Carl and Faith Ellen. And little Dorothy Justine in the carriage. I was riveted by the image of the pretty, young mother and, when Justine turned toward me, her latest favorite book, *The Reincarnation of Peter Proud*, in hand, my eyes darted back and forth from her to the picture. The undeniable likeness between the two faces was unnerving.

"Maybe we'll find out we were sisters in a previous life," Justine said, chuckling as she dropped the book into my lap.

I barely heard her. Glancing from the cover of the book to the grainy photo of Faith Ellen and back to my friend, my heart stood still. While I stared at the girl who was nearly a carbon copy of her late great-grandmother, I was positive I saw the rocking chair across the room move ever so slightly.

CHAPTER 4

1975

Bullies Beware

"You're My Best Friend" – Queen

Justine

"**I**t's called a mood ring. It tells you what your mood is by whatever color it turns." I extended my hand, displaying the round, blue stone. "See? I'm chill and relaxed."

Eva paused from brushing Smokey and glanced at the ring. "Here, let me try it." Slipping it onto her pinky, the blue deepened instantly to a rich black. She looked at me with raised eyebrows.

"Hmmm. That means you're stressed out or upset." I replaced the ring on my finger.

Eva had arrived an hour ago. Usually, I dashed out to greet her. Today, I'd hesitated when I spotted her through the front window. Instead of her usual bustling about while caring for the horse, she was still. Her normally squared shoulders were slumped as she leaned into Smokey, her forehead against his, arms around his neck. Averting my eyes from the intimate scene, I sank into Uncle John's chair and concentrated on the ticking of the grandfather clock. I picked up *Sports Illustrated* and pretended to read it. Each time the count of tick-tocks reached twenty, I checked out the window. Finally, Eva had patted Smokey's back and reached for the curry brush.

Now, as I absently twirled Smokey's forelock around my index finger, my friend pretended everything was normal. She babbled about her family—Craig was thinking about becoming a lawyer... her sister Jan was having a baby... her parents were taking a cruise next winter. Streams of consciousness—she was so glad to see me... we were going to have *such* a great summer... she loved getting my letters... some town kids had called her "lezzy" when she'd gone up town this morning. My ears perked at that last buried comment and, when I added it up with her puffy reddened eyes and the reaction of the mood ring, I knew everything was *not* normal.

63

"I'll get my bike. We're going up to the railroad tracks to drink the blackberry brandy I brought. Okay?"

She stopped with Smokey's brush in midair. "What?!"

"Oh, come on. You didn't think just because Mom stuck me in that snooty private school, I'd given up my wild ways, did ya?" I grinned at her.

"Yeah, what happened there? You never said."

"Well, she didn't know I was cutting classes at my old school to go drinking with my friends. She only knew I got a C in Home Ec because I couldn't learn to section a grapefruit. And, we both know, Justine's only allowed to get As. So she transferred me in October."

Eva leaned toward me with interest. "A private school, huh? What's that like? Do you have to wear uniforms?"

"No," I said, taking the brush from her and working on Smokey's side. "But there's a dress code. Boys have to wear dress pants, jacket, and tie. Girls can wear skirts or dresses, or nice pants. No jeans, no t-shirts, that kind of thing."

"Do you have to live there?"

"I live close by, so no. About a third of the students are boarders, though."

"Really?" She ducked under Smokey's neck to stare wide-eyed at me. "What kind of kids live there?"

"They're from all different states and around the world. Really rich. Oh, and one of the princes from Saudi Arabia is in my class."

"You're kidding! A *prince*? Do you hang out with him?"

"No, he kinda keeps to himself."

"What does the school look like?"

"It's actually pretty cool. It looks like a college campus. We have a huge gym with sports fields, academic buildings, dorms, a student activity center...."

Eva smirked. "Where do they keep the polo ponies?"

"At another facility, about five miles away."

"Really?" she asked, her eyes wide in disbelief.

"No!" I laughed, shaking my head. "Gotcha!"

"But do you like it? Better than your other school?"

"Well, the classes are a lot more interesting, I have to admit. I'd rather be learning French," I wiggled my eyebrows suggestively, "than learning how to sew a whip stitch." Tossing Smokey's brush to her, I said, "And that's all she wrote. Ready to boogie?"

We pedaled our bikes through the downtown section of North Brookfield, which looked like something in a Norman Rockwell painting. The classic Main Street had a variety of retail shops, restaurants,

Cumberland Farms (affectionately known as Cumby's), and a package store that sold liquor. The Lunchroom was a favorite with the locals where they could pick up the weekly newspaper and a cheap meal. The grand Town Hall, with its high-arching windows and decorative finials, was topped with an enormous, intricately carved gazebo-shaped bell tower. Passing the classic Greek Revival-style Congregational Church, the centerpiece of this village, we caught up on each other's lives. She wanted to tell me what her brothers and sisters were up to. I wanted to talk about the cute boys in my new school. Suddenly, Eva veered onto School Street, her head lowered, pumping her pedals furiously. I followed, ready to question her, when I heard the taunting jeers trailing after us.

"Oh, Eeevvaa. Where ya going? You with your *girl*friend?"

"Are those the kids who were bothering you earlier?" I whispered to Eva. She nodded once, eyes fixed on the ground beneath her bicycle.

I slammed on the brakes and my bike tires screeched to a halt. Although a film of red had dropped before my eyes, I took a deep breath, held it, then let it out slowly as I counted. One, two, three... all the way to ten. With exaggerated care, I laid my bike gently on the ground. Calmly combing my hair with my fingers and straightening my clothes, I turned toward Eva's tormentors. Two scuzzy, pimple-faced creeps. And *they* had the nerve to make fun of *Eva*?

I heard an urgent, "*Justine! Don't!*" but ignored it. High time someone put these cretins in their place.

"Hi!" I smiled my most charming smile and extended my hand toward them. "I'm Justine Andrews. You must be Eva's friends." Their dopey-looking faces gaped as they limply shook my hand. "I'm Eva's friend from New Jersey. Well, actually, I'm Eva's *boy*friend's sister. She and Randy are going out, but I guess you already know about him, right?"

By the time a flaming-faced Eva sidled up to me, probably figuring I'd completely ruined her life, Benny, Ronny, and I were jolly good friends.

"I was introducing myself to your buddies, Eva. I can't believe you never told them you and Randy have been dating for two years. That's not cool!" I pushed her playfully as I winked at her. "He'd be so *hurt*, keeping him a secret!"

"Uh, yeah. Mmm hmm. Two years. Er, her brother. Yup!"

Five minutes later, after cheery "good-byes" and "see ya laters," we continued on our way down School Street and bumped along off-road to the railroad tracks.

Eva's eyes were still bulging in astonishment as I cracked open the pint of blackberry brandy, took a long swig, and handed it to her. "And that, my dearest friend, is how to deal with your enemies!"

"Wow! Wicked impressive! Be careful, though, Justine. Sometimes when you're pissed, you don't stop to think about the consequences. I know you mean well, but if it's the wrong person, you might make it worse."

"I was being good. I didn't yell or anything," I said, pouting. "I thought you'd be proud of me!"

"I am! You did great! I'm just saying, please make sure you think before you react." She nudged me with her shoulder. "And thanks. I bet those two don't bother me anymore."

"I guess you'll need to meet my brother since you guys have been going out for so long, huh?" I nudged her back.

The sky had grown dark as we drank our brandy. I lay sprawled in the grass next to the tracks, hand on one rail to stop me from spinning. "Evaaaa! Light me a shigarette?"

The stars above glimmered brilliantly. Raising one wavering arm, I connected the dots in the constellations with my finger. "There's Orion. That's Cath... Cash-i-o-pe-ia!" I giggled uncontrollably until Eva laughed with me.

We were in our own world, surrounded by woods and quiet. Away from the safety of our familiar turf, yet oddly sheltered in the nothingness.

"What are you thinking about?" Eva asked.

"Rag Doll Man."

"What about him?"

"I'm thinking that if he were real, this would be the kind of place he'd be. With the woods, and being so dark...."

"What do you mean, 'if he were real'?" she asked. "He *is* real."

"I don't know. I've been thinking about it since last year. What proof do you have? Not what the kids in town say, not what the rumors are, but you—Eva Thompson."

"Just because I haven't seen him personally, doesn't mean it's not true. Have you seen gravity? Or God? We know they exist!"

"Well, gravity obviously exists because we're lying here instead of floating off into space. As for God, I can't say I'm very convinced of that, either."

"Don't be so cynical, Justine! Obviously God exists. How else do you explain the creation of everything? The whole universe?"

"The Big Bang theory?"

Eva was exasperated. "Oh, Justine!"

"Anyway, I bet Rag Doll Man is some old folk tale."

"I remember the story of how he escaped from the hospital. I was little, but my brothers and sisters told me all about it. They said he attacked the guard, hit him over the head with the metal leg he'd broken off of his bed, then beat up one of the nurses who tried to stop him. They said Rag Doll Man tore the nurse's face off with his bare fingers!"

"Eww!" I said, sitting up. "That's gross! And you believe it?"

"Well, people who've seen him all describe him the same way—tall, skinny, carrying the doll, sometimes wearing a trench coat. Sometimes, even wearing a fedora style hat."

"The way you describe him, always lurking around, reminds me of that scary guy from *To Kill A Mockingbird*. That Bo Diddley character."

Eva burst into laughter. "Boo Radley!"

"That's what I sai—"

The approaching sound of raucous voices sent me stumbling to my feet and squinting through the darkness. I made out three silhouettes pitching and weaving down the tracks toward us. Eva yanked me into the cover of nearby shrubs. Her eyes glowed in the moonlight as she held her finger to her lips, silencing me.

"Who're they?" I asked, the ground swaying beneath me.

She shook her head and mouthed, "I don't know."

In a gravelly whisper, she wailed, "Hel-loooooo," starting low then growing in force.

I snorted with amusement, then slapped my hands over my mouth. The three on the tracks froze. When Eva called out again, a cloud of dust rose as the shadowy figures tripped over each other in their race back toward town.

Beaming, Eva grabbed the empty brandy bottle and flung it into my purse. "Come on. We have to get back. Peggy wants you home early. Remember?"

It took me a couple of rotations of my bike pedals to gain my balance, but then, with blood pumping in my ears, we hurtled along the railroad tracks until we veered onto the well-worn path hugged by tall grass and undergrowth. Eva cycled fiercely, with me charging close behind. The trees around us grew taller, eclipsing the crescent moon, pitching us into near total darkness.

"Faster!" I screamed.

Careening blindly along the narrow trail, we squealed, "Wheeee!" at the same time when we were catapulted from the top of the hill. Landing upright with a strangled *"Oh shit!"* from Eva, we continued at a breakneck pace on the downward slope. Finally, the trees opened into the field behind the barn. Slowing as we climbed the rise and pushed into the driveway, the porch light welcomed us home. Dropping our bikes, we collapsed into chairs out back of the house.

"Man, that was a*maz*ing!" I said, gasping for breath. "This whole *night* was amazing!"

"I never rode my bike so fast in my life! I thought we were going to crash! Remember how last summer you didn't even like walking down that path at night?"

"You didn't either!" I shot back. "You were all freaked out about Rag Doll Man."

"So were you! Seriously, though. We'll have to do this again. Maybe tomorrow."

"Nope! We've already done it. It's on to our next challenge."

"Hey! Let me see that mood ring." Eva slipped it onto her pinky and held it up to the light. "Huh. What does that mean? It's like an orangey-red color."

"That means daring or exciting," I told her. "Glad to know you're feeling better! Because—get ready—I know what our next challenge is going to be."

Haunting Jane Goes Wrong

"Midnight Rambler" – The Rolling Stones

Eva

"YOU WANT TO DO *WHAT*?" My voice was high, incredulous. Justine appeared calm, relaxed, her voice low and quiet. She took a long drag on her Newport and exhaled slowly, staring into space as if thinking, milking the moment for maximum dramatic effect. At last, she turned and faced me.

"Scare Jane. Let's spook her out of her mind, man."

We were in our new favorite spot, sitting on the arms attached to an ancient bulldozer blade, on a wooded ridge high above the cemetery. We had stumbled upon the blade by accident while exploring the woods, and were immediately drawn to the decaying metal structure. It was enormous, as wide as a dump truck and undoubtedly as heavy, and at least a foot thick and four feet tall. Most fascinating of all, it was landlocked. Trees grew around it and through it, leaving no doubt it had been left in this spot long, long ago and forgotten. The monstrosity had the name "Wausau" etched on one arm. We were certain we were the only people who knew of Wausau's existence. Peeking over the top of the immense blade, we could see the road to the north and the cemetery to the west without being seen. The rusted, hulking structure blended into the trees, brush, and earth around it. If anyone tried to peer into the woods at the sound of our distant giggles, we could slip undetected behind the massive plate.

"You want to scare Jane. Jane Williams. Crazy Jane. Crazy, homicidal Jane." My voice was calm and flat. It was Justine's turn to be excited.

"Yesss! We can… we can *haunt* the cemetery, tomorrow… *tomorrow night* around midnight." Justine's words came rapidly as her ideas germinated, grew, and culminated.

I had to smile inwardly. Justine's ideas always began that way. She was transformed, as if her thoughts seemed to tumble forward too quickly to process before erupting from deep within her, until she was unable to contain them. She leapt to her feet.

"I'll sneak out. Can you? We can... we can throw pebbles at her windows to wake her up and keep whispering her name. *Jane, Jaanne, Jaaaannne,*" Justine stage whispered her creepiest Vincent Price impersonation.

In spite of myself—the logical thinker—I was sold. But I know Justine, know how she can throw caution to the wind, and her reckless attitude can be dangerous. After all, Justine was a *juvenile*, and if worse came to worst, nothing would happen to her. With her dad being a civil rights attorney, punishment was all the less likely. And, most of all, she didn't *live* here. I decided to play devil's advocate. Digging into my pocket, I fished out my last Marlboro, lit it, and took a long, deep drag.

"And if we get caught? Trespassing. Curfew. Criminal mischief...." I flicked the hair away from my face with my fingers.

It was Justine's turn to speak quietly. She stubbed her cigarette into the dirt and studied it, relaxing against Wausau's blade, legs straight out with ankles crossed. At last, she looked up, her piercing eyes on mine.

"That's easy," she said. "We don't get caught."

Jane Marie Williams was the perfect target. In spite of being a tough girl who never backed away from a fight, she was not above befriending anyone she saw as beneficial to advancing her social position in the complex hierarchy of North Brookfield High's sophomore class. She schmoozed with the cheerleaders while bashing them behind their backs: "Did you see Carol's eye shadow? It's blue. *Blue!* And the way she's wearing her hair. She's trying to look like Marcia Brady. And, did you know she's *doing it* with Willy Pehlam? I heard it for a fact. She's acting all innocent and"— eye rolling—"yeah, right?" In Jane's book, the cheerleaders and popular girls were phonies and sluts, the outcasts were losers or pot heads, and the athletic girls were lezzies. Jane elbowed her way into lines, mugged underclassmen for lunch money, told lies about her own friends, and was insufferable to enemies. Despite her vile personality, Jane remained on the guest list of every class party; equally revered, despised, and feared by every clique, group, and sub-group. But what made her the one ideal and absolute perfect target was where she lived.

"I can see the lights on in her bedroom window," I said, calm again.

Justine's mouth hinted at a smile. Dusk was creeping in; the street lights were slowly coming on one by one, up and down lonely and deserted Elm Street.

"I was thinking… you know that old organ we have? I can play some low notes that sound wicked creepy. I can tape them and, since it runs on batteries, I can bring it."

"That's cool, man." Justine's smile broadened.

We leaned back against the cool metal of the plow, staring at the little house standing alone and isolated behind the stone wall at the far corner of the cemetery.

I could feel my enthusiasm growing. "And, we have this old lantern in our cellar. It runs on batteries too, and it flickers."

"Perfect." No matter how outrageous the plot, how silly, or how preposterous, Justine knew somehow I always ended up thinking exactly like she did. She'd never say that to me, though. Instead, she grinned and lit her last cigarette.

"Perfect. Just perfect."

I DIDN'T HAVE TO WORRY about sneaking out of my house the next night. By 11:30, my parents were turning in.

"Lock the door when you go upstairs," Mother called over her shoulder as she disappeared around the landing.

"Okay, will do." I sat in front of the TV pretending to be absorbed in Johnny Carson. I listened to the bathroom door upstairs open and close, and then my parents' bedroom door shut, then slipped through the screen door onto the front porch. My tape player held a fresh recording of low, groaning notes from the organ where I had experimented with unearthly sounds while Mother did the supper dishes earlier. The wooden front steps creaked, but I was certain my parents hadn't heard. I left the TV on like I was staying up late any other summer night, often until 1 or 2 AM. In a minute, my parents would be sound asleep.

My bike was parked on the back sidewalk and I easily slipped a leg over the seat, tucked the recorder under one arm, and began pedaling the half mile down the street to Shadow Hill Cemetery. Although I'd ridden down this road at least a thousand times, I guessed, it suddenly looked unfamiliar. The early July night was chilly and the houses I passed were dark, except for an occasional lone porch lamp. The streetlights made pools of light on the deserted road. Somewhere way off in the distance, a dog barked. I knew every inch of this road and was confident I could see and not be seen almost anywhere. At last, I came to the crest of the hill—the stretch of road where the houses become more distant—and then disappeared altogether. A long, neatly trimmed hedge to my right signaled the boundary of the cemetery. I dismounted and walked, peering through the darkness for Justine.

"Pssst. Hey." A small figure stepped out of the shadows right in front of me.

"Jeez! You scared me to death!"

She was wearing black pants and a black shirt. Her hair caught the moonlight and, if it weren't for that, she would have been invisible.

"Scared to death?" Justine giggled. "Well, this is the perfect place. Did you bring them?"

"Yeah, right here. I couldn't find the lantern." I slid the cassette player from under my arm. "No Lucky tonight? I thought you'd bring him for protection."

"I thought about it. I was afraid he'd bark or something… give us away."

We walked our bikes past the hedge, through the gate, and turned down the road leading into the cemetery. I'd never been afraid of a cemetery before. Although I had read hundreds of stories depicting graveyards as terrifying and haunted by the restless dead, I was never bothered. Growing up down the street from Shadow Hill, I saw it as comforting, not foreboding. In fact, I considered the ancient stone walls, gently rolling topography, green lawns, and crumbling gravestones as somehow soothing.

With the half-moon hanging in the sky, the burial ground in near blackness, the chill in the air, and the brittle silence, I felt an involuntary shiver go up my spine. Goosebumps broke out on my bare arms. As we pushed our bikes down the curving road into the heart of the cemetery, Justine was unusually quiet.

I stopped short and grabbed my friend's arm. "Sssssshhhhh! Did you hear that?" I hissed, my voice piercing the stillness.

"What, hear what?"

"That! Look! Over there! Do you see that? It's a freshly opened grave. Someone must have died today and is being buried. It wasn't there yesterday!"

"Where?" Justine strained her eyes to see through the darkness.

"Right there in front of you." I goosed my friend from behind while sticking out my leg in front to trip her. We both went down. I was hysterical while Justine fumed.

"You moron! That's not cool. I oughta kill you." Justine pretended to be mad while I pretended to be sorry, all the while dabbing my eyes and sniffling, trying to collect myself. We'd almost risen to our feet when Justine kicked my legs out from under me and we both fell to the ground again, laughing.

"That was a good one," I said as I rose to my feet.

"Jerk off!" Justine grumbled, brushing grass off her skin-tight bell-bottoms.

A clanking sound, as if from a metal gate, echoed behind us. We fell silent.

"You did it," Justine said. "I'm not falling for that again."

"No, no, I didn't. I swear."

We stood facing each other, hushed. We waited. We listened.

"Wish I had a cigarette," she said.

The metal gate clanked again, this time unmistakably. We peered towards the street and saw it at once: headlights! How could this be? In one light-hearted moment, we'd missed the sound of an approaching car. It had turned into the cemetery and was headed down the winding road, straight at us! Without anywhere to run, we dove behind a headstone. The closest one was too small for two of us so we crouched as low as we could, burying our chins into our chests. Praying we were hidden, I instinctively drew my bare arms up underneath my t-shirt. As the car pulled alongside, I could make out Neil Sedaka singing over the static on the radio, smell the tobacco of the driver's cigarette, and hear the gentle crunching sound of gravel. And, I could feel the trembling from Justine, curled up and huddled against me. Or, was it my own?

Oh no! I had a sickening thought. *The bikes!* They were in plain sight! We'd left them laying in the spot where we'd stopped to horse around only ten feet away! I held my breath.

"Who is it?" Justine asked, pressing closer to me so I could hear her.

"Dunno."

"Ooh, I hear laughter in the rain/Walking hand in hand with the one I love...." crooned Sedaka as the car stopped.

Justine and I were silent, barely breathing. The music switched off. The click of the car door handle sounded, followed by the creak of the door opening. One foot crunched on the gravel, then the other. I lifted my eyes and shifted slightly, just enough to glimpse around the side of the headstone. I saw the entire back half of the car and, with the modest light from the moon above, recognized the town cruiser.

"It's the cops!" I said as softly as possible. "Keep still."

"Will we be in trouble if—?"

"Ladies." A deep voice spoke above our heads. Simultaneously, we turned our faces toward the sound. I couldn't make out the details of his shadowed face, but recognized the police cap and husky figure hovering over us.

"Uh, good evening, Officer O'Reilly," I said, scrambling to my feet. As Justine rose beside me, he reached up and grabbed the brim of his hat with his fingers. "We're just...."

"You know the cemetery is closed at sunset, Eva. It's after midnight." He gave us a reassuring smile. "Come on. Let's put your bikes in the car and I'll take you home."

As he leaned past me to grab my bike, the stink of beer, as if applied like after-shave, rose from him. He popped the trunk of the car and hoisted my bike in, then stopped to consider.

"The other won't fit. We'll stick it in the back seat and you can both ride up front with me," he said, reaching for the banana seat bike. This whole time Justine had remained silent, hands clasped behind her back without so much as a single trademark fidget of her foot.

"This is very nice of you," I said. "But it really isn't necess—"

"I can't very well leave the two of you out here, can I?" He let out a big hearty laugh, the sound echoing throughout the cemetery and bouncing from stone to stone as it traveled away from us. I automatically smiled. In relief, I turned toward Justine. Her face was unreadable. But her eyes never left him.

"Er, this is my friend, Justine. She's staying at the Miller's for the summer."

Again, he tipped his hat in greeting. She barely nodded in return while continuing to stare mutely at him.

As I climbed into the car, Officer O'Reilly placed his hand on my mid-back. Justine went next and, when he tried to help her, she recoiled and said, "I've got it," then slammed the door behind her. O'Reilly steered the car around the circle at the Memorial Garden and, when we approached the front gate, I could see that he had closed it when he'd first entered. After opening it, driving through, then locking it again, he turned the cruiser onto Elm Street. When he put on his directional signal to make a right onto Miller Ave, Justine spoke up.

"You can take me to Eva's," she said. "I'm spending the night there."

74

"Wha—?" She jabbed me in the side. "Uh, yes. You can drop us both at my house."

The officer didn't say a word as we coasted to a stop in front of my house, the hum of the car engine barely perceptible above the song of the night peepers. He set our bikes at the curb, winked, and then touched the brim of his cap before returning to the driver's seat and gliding away. After he made a left toward town and vanished from our sight, I finally questioned her.

"I don't know," she said. "I felt weird leaving you alone with him."

"*Whaaat*? He's a cop, for Chrissakes! Plus, I've known him my whole life. He and his family go to the same church as mine."

"I don't know. There's something…."

"You're imagining things," I said, giving her the hairy eyeball. "You don't like cops so you're suspicious of all of them."

"Maybe," she said. "Anyway, ride me halfway home. In case he comes back."

Elm Street was dark and quiet and, somewhere off in the distance, a dog howled. I considered what Justine said about Officer O'Reilly. *Nah! He's a nice guy. A good Catholic. A family man.* The air was cool and I shuddered as we headed toward Miller Ave.

Bells and Brookfield Orchards

"Listen to the Music" – The Doobie Brothers

Justine

A THICK MORNING FOG WAS HOVERING over Miller Ave and Eva was nowhere in sight. Keeping watch by the window in Uncle John's chair, my head resting against the slatted back, I listened to the rattling of the dishes as Aunt Peggy finished cleaning up from breakfast. Lucky was curled up on the far end of the couch and, somehow, had pulled the knitted afghan off the back and partially covered himself with it. His nose twitched in his sleep and I wondered if he was still savoring the smoky scent of bacon too, wishing Aunt Peggy had cooked up another half-pound. Outside, Smokey's ghostly image waited as hopefully by the gate as I did by the window.

"Do you want to help me, sweetheart?" Aunt Peggy shuffled into the living room. Leaning her cane against her chair, she placed a hand on each of its sturdy arms and slowly lowered her body onto the thickly padded seat with a muffled "umph!"

I quickly turned my eyes away. When I was little, before I'd started questioning His existence, I'd bargained with God to stop Aunt Peggy's pain. *I'll be good… I won't fight with my brothers… I won't talk back to Mom… I won't have any more temper tantrums.* Was anyone even listening? Was anyone even up there?

As she caught her breath, she said, "Uncle John won't be back from The Lunchroom until later, so I thought this might be a good time to get some other chores done. My bells need to be dusted. Would you do that for me?"

I sprang up to find an old rag and opened the fronts of the barrister bookcase. While Aunt Peggy made it sound like I was doing her a favor, we both knew sharing the stories surrounding her huge bell collection was something we looked forward to every year. I'd never counted how many bells there were, but it must have been hundreds. They were of all shapes and sizes—some fancily decorated, some heavy and plain. Each had its own sound, from the highest tinkle to the deepest, hollow clang. Some had names and pictures representing a city or a popular tourist spot. Some had holiday themes. Some had sweet little animals while others had intricately sculpted flowers. There was a miniature Chinese gong and a porcelain dancing lady. I loved every single one of them.

I took each out, carefully dusted it, and listened closely as Aunt Peggy told me the history behind it. She'd collected these bells her entire life. It had started with a couple of discarded cowbells she placed on the shelf in her bedroom when she was a girl. As she grew, she began to pick up bells for different occasions—Christmas, Easter, when the barn cat had kittens (I loved the bell with the mama cat licking the baby), when she went to Princeton, NJ the first time to visit her older brother, my grandfather. When Aunt Peggy's disability cut short her traveling, her friends and family continued the hobby on her behalf, bringing her bells from places visited, events celebrated, or achievements earned. Throughout Aunt Peggy's life, her bell collection grew to represent the lives of those she loved. It was still growing.

"They're all beautiful, but if I had to pick my favorites, I think it would be these." I held out a bell in each hand. One was a heavy pewter bell with a turtle on the top. The turtle's shell was made of rich blue and green glass. I liked it because… well, obviously, the turtle was adorable, but also because I loved how the glass reminded me of my favorite part about church—the stained glass windows. I always thought they were so pretty and colorful, and entertained myself with the stories in each of them during the never-ending sermons. In the other hand was a ceramic bell with a big gray elephant, cartoonishly sitting up on his back legs, holding a wreath and sporting a Santa hat. Written in cursive on the bell was "Merry Christmas." *Look how friendly he is, with his long trunk happily curved upward in front of his face!*

An hour and a half later, I'd finished wiping each bell, cleaned the shelves, and replaced them. Aunt Peggy didn't care in what order they were arranged; she just preferred the taller ones in the back and the shorter ones in front. She said she could sit across the room and still see each of them while her imagination traveled to far-off lands like Nepal and Tahiti. As I lowered the last of the glass fronts, I glanced out the window and saw the morning fog had lifted without leaving a trace. Eva was across the street, putting away Smokey's grooming tools. With a quick kiss on top of Aunt Peggy's head, I dashed outside so we could start our day.

RIGHT PAST SHADOW HILL CEMETERY, the untamed forest gave way to endless, ordered rows of apple trees on both sides of the road. In the early August heat, the fruit ripened to a deep red, dotted against the lush green leaves on gnarled branches. Some of the apples had dropped to the ground and begun to rot, releasing a sickeningly sweet scent and drawing a steady *bzzzz* from a swirling cloud of frenzied yellow jackets. The main building at Brookfield Orchards was a converted barn, a combination of a country store and antique market. In the front room, wrapped in the cinnamon-apple aroma of baked goods, were bushels of apples, breads, cakes, pies, caramel dipped apples, and jugs of cider. Every inch of shelf space was crammed with memorabilia and bric-a-brac, from antique cameras and toys to Depression glass and collectible pitchers. Framed newspaper front pages and vintage ads covered the walls, with hundreds of ancient farm tools like those back in our barn scattered among them.

"Come *on*!" I was impatient to get to my favorite room. Eva, as usual, was lingering over some boring headline, this time an old story from the *New York Times*. "Quit prevaricating!"

"Hold on. Check this out. It's from April 16, 1912. 'Titanic Sinks Four Hours After Hitting Iceberg.' This is unbelievable! It's the real thing—it's *history*!" Eva's mouth moved as she silently read the article printed over sixty years earlier. Abruptly, she tilted her head toward me and smirked. "Besides, I'm not lying. I'm *procrastinating*."

"Yeah, yeah, yeah. I'll meet you by the candy." I skipped off to prepare for my sugar fix. I entered Paradise—a room filled with shelves and island displays of every sweet imaginable. Bottles of maple syrup in different shapes and sizes; maple sugar candy, the kind that started off solid in your mouth and melted into syrupy goodness in seconds; homemade jams, jellies, and apple butters. Endless oversized jars displayed a colorful assortment of penny candy, from caramels to sourballs. Rows of gum, a seemingly infinite assortment of chocolate bars, wax lips, and candy bracelets and necklaces. Grabbing a small paper bag, I chose blue raspberry and watermelon flavored stick candies, a cherry Blow Pop, and a handful of assorted hard candies. Eva finally joined me and filled her own bag with a Marathon bar and a mix of other chocolates. That's all she ever wanted. Chocolate.

In the corner of the room was the used book section. Heaven on Earth to us. We could spend hours lost to the world outside, leafing through piles of magazines and reading the back-cover synopses on the stacks of books. When one book's description pulled us in, we were tempted to sit cross-legged on the floor and be drawn into the lives of the characters, forgetting about anything else we'd planned to do that day. This time, Eva chose a Daphne DuMaurier collection of short stories and I settled on *Go Ask Alice*. We paid for our books and candy at the register and headed home.

"Crap! I forgot to get apples for Aunt Peggy. She wanted to make a pie. We'll have to go back."

Eva continued walking.

"Eva?"

"I have an idea!" Her eyes glowed in her animated face. "Why don't we just, oh, I don't know, happen to pick up a few apples that, oops!, might have already fallen onto the ground? There's nobody around, anyway, so no one will see us."

"Are you kidding?" I stopped dead in the middle of the road, mouth gaping. "In broad daylight? What if we get caught, Miss I'm-Always-So-Cautious-And-Sensible?" Visions of being thrown into handcuffs and hauled down to the police station danced before my eyes.

Eva's voice was bold as she turned to me. "Well, to quote an old friend of mine: 'That's easy, we don't get caught!'" Chuckling, she gave me a shoulder push, hard enough to send me tripping off the pavement onto the grassy edge of the orchard.

By the time I caught my balance, I was convinced. Playing along, I said in a breathy little girl voice, "I'm so sorry, Officer O'Reilly. I don't know how those apples ended up in my bag!"

"So, here's the way it'll go. When the coast is clear, we'll run to the closest trees and grab apples on the ground that look like they're in good shape. Don't get any with holes—they might have worms. And don't get any that are too green. *And*, remember to stay low so no one sees us."

Not a car was in sight. We raced the forty feet to the nearest trees, searched around on the ground, and discovered most of the fallen apples were in terrible shape. Partially rotted, many gnawed by animals, several with holes. As my heart sank, thinking about how let down Aunt Peggy would be, it was impossible not to notice the perfectly symmetrical, plump, scarlet fruit hanging right above my head. Begging to be picked.

My fingers reached up and wrapped themselves around one of the lovely, ripe McIntoshes, instantly freeing it from its branch. "Uh, uh, ooooo, lookie what happened here!" Within seconds, eight more luscious apples had found their way into my Brookfield Orchards bag.

The horrified look on Eva's face sent a bolt of apprehension through me. "I *told* you… just the ones on the ground!"

"It's cool! They'll never miss them!" I gulped, then said, "Eh, it's time to get back, anyway."

Eva yelled, "Hurry! Let's get out of here!"

We crouched low, stealthily racing toward the road. We were thirty feet from safety when we heard the high-speed roar of a car engine. And, there we were, right out in plain view! Spotting a shallow ditch in front of us, nearly concealed by tall grass, I pointed. "Hide!"

We dove into the ditch and buried ourselves as best we could in the high grass. Holding our breath, we listened. It was getting closer. Were we covered? What if they saw us? We remained frozen until we heard the car zip past without slowing. When it was gone, we peeked up, looked around, then darted the remaining distance to the road.

"We were right there, *right there*!" I thrust my finger at the ditch. "On the edge of the field and they didn't even see us! It's like something out of a movie. Hey!" I said, grabbing Eva's arm. "You know what it's like? It's like that time my friend Laura and I hid when we went streaking. Remember?"

I was all jumpy inside like a junkie needing my next high. My addiction was excitement, and I knew exactly how I wanted to get it. I'd been thinking about our failed mission at the cemetery the other night. I don't like to fail. Eva had avoided the topic, but I forced her to listen: we were *going* to haunt Jane Williams.

Eva's thoughts were often veiled. When she was happy, she chuckled and looked away. When she was mad, she chuckled and looked away. Even when she was nervous, she chuckled and looked away. This was frustrating; I was used to gauging my responses based on the other person's reaction. How could I know what she was actually thinking? But, I'd discovered, she had a 'tell': her hands. When caring for Smokey, they were strong and in charge. Same with when she was on top of him, controlling him with the reins. If it was one of those rare occasions when she was serious, they were motionless in her lap. Or, when she was giving me a piece of her mind, they were planted firmly on her hips, sometimes with one scolding finger wagging at me. I also noticed she crossed herself a lot, asking forgiveness for her sins. *Does she do that more often when she's with me? I'll have to ask her, sometime,* I'd thought at the time. But, my favorite was when her hands flitted like butterflies, trying to poke holes in my stunt du jour. They only did that when I'd finally swayed her cautious spirit with whatever exploit I'd thought up for our amusement. I think they were trying to defend against my ideas. I preferred to interpret them as the final gasp before giving in to what we were about to do.

The way they were now.

Because that's when I knew we were in business.

HAUNT OR BE HAUNTED

"One of These Nights" – Eagles

EVA

JUSTINE'S ANCESTRY IN NORTH BROOKFIELD dated back as far as mine. Maybe even further. She lucked out, though, coming from a branch on her family tree that moved away and settled in a more exciting part of the country. My branch stayed put, leaving me stuck. At least for the time being.

Even though Justine didn't live here, plenty of people knew who she was because of her heritage and relationship to Peggy and John Miller. Everybody knew them. Growing up, I heard people speak of them in high regard, as pillars of the community. Except for the occasional hushed, behind-the-hand comments about John, nothing overt. Little snippets I'd hear in passing—*"tsk, tsk. Such a shame for the family…"* or *"not quite right"* or *"sweet, but…"*—accompanied by a sorrowful head shake. I never understood what the problem was until Justine told me. And there were still occasional whispers from the kids at school, suggesting he might be Rag Doll Man. I generally ignored them or told them they were full of shit.

I'd formed a close friendship with the Millers since keeping Smokey across from their house. Peggy was maybe the dearest woman I'd ever met. John fascinated me. It bugged me when people talked to him as if he were stupid. He was quite smart, although a little tough to engage in conversation. Except when it came to sports. Then, he became quite chatty.

The other day, I ran into him and was excited to share my recent find. "So, John. I just finished reading a book you'd like. *Seeing It Through*. Have you heard of it? It's the biography about—"

"Aye-yuh. Tony Conigliaro. Tony C. I read it when it first came to the library."

Of course he did. John Miller was a baseball encyclopedia, probably having read every book and publication ever written on the subject. I never knew anyone who could rattle off facts about the game, including players' stats and histories, the way he could. I came to enjoy our early morning talks when we happened to meet by Smokey's pasture. Our exchanges tended to take place in a rapid-fire, call and response style:

Me: "What year did he retire?"

John: "Officially, 1975. From the Red Sox."

Me: "Who'd he play for before the Red Sox?"

John: "Well, in 1971, he played for the California Angels for a bit. But the rest of his career was with the Red Sox."

Me: "What was the pitcher's name who hit him in the eye with the ball?"

John: "Jack Hamilton. Ironically, from the California Angels."

Me: "How many games did he play for the Red Sox?"

John: "Eight hundred and two."

Me: "Home runs?"

John: "One hundred sixty-two. And, four with the Angels."

Me: "Batting average?"

John: ".267 with the Sox, .222 with the Angels."

Me: "RBIs?"

John: "501, Sox. 15, Angels."

I paused, trying to remember any other information I learned from the book. During the years we'd been having this contest, I never managed to stump him. Not once. I only needed one obscure detail he might possibly have overlooked....

"I've got one. What award did he win in 1969?"

Again, without hesitation, he responded. "Comeback Player of the Year." With a chuckle, he added for extra credit, "Aye-yuh. After his eye injury, he returned and had twenty homers and eighty-two RBIs in one hundred forty-one games."

"Okay, I give up. You win, as usual."

Abruptly, he turned and ambled up the driveway toward the house, whistling for Lucky to follow.

"I FIND HIM ENDEARING," I concluded, relating my conversation from earlier in the day to Justine as we lounged at Wausau, finishing our pre-haunting bottle of blackberry brandy. "You just have to understand him."

"Exactly. Can you see why I love coming up here so much? Between him and—"

"—Peggy. Yeah, yeah. I guess so," I grudgingly agreed. "But more because of them, not because of this Podunk town. What kinds of problems has John had because of his schizophrenia? I don't want to pry, but I'm curious."

"It's hard to describe. Most of the time, because of the medication, he's fine. Maybe a little… awkward?… when he talks to people. But, if the medication isn't working, or if he forgets to take it, he gets confused. I know a couple of years ago, he started reliving what happened in Pearl Harbor. With the bombings and people being killed. The thing with him, though, is he wasn't just having nightmares or memories. He actually believed he was there. He had to stay in the hospital until he was better."

"Has he ever been violent?"

"Never. Why would you ask?"

"It's, well…."

"That shit about him being Rag Doll Man again?" Justine's voice was so tight she sounded as if she were being strangled. "Besides the fact that Uncle John would never—*never*—hurt anyone, he doesn't even look the way people say Rag Doll Man looks. Rag Doll Man is supposed to be tall and skinny, right? Uncle John is built like Santa Claus!" She paused to catch her breath and, almost imperceptibly, I heard her counting deliberately. "… four, five, six…"

"I know! I know! It's absolutely ludicrous."

"Besides, Eva, you know him," she said more calmly. "Why aren't you putting an end to that crap? Nip it in the butt when you hear it."

I stifled a smile. "Nip it in the *bud*. And, I do! I always tell her—them—that it's nonsense. He's wicked sweet and wouldn't hurt a fly."

"Who?" Justine asked, astutely catching my verbal slip. "Exactly who is it that's saying this about him?"

"Uh, well, it's a lot, well…." I stumbled over my inability to lie while her piercing eyes were fixed on me. "Jane Williams."

She hesitated for only the briefest second, then shoved the empty brandy bottle into her purse. "It's dark enough. Let's do this!"

"Justine…."

"You're not getting cold feet, are you?"

I considered Jane Williams. The endless years of torture under her direction. More recently, her malicious gossip about John Miller. What if tonight's scheme back-fired? What if she found out it was us? Maybe this wasn't such a great idea.

Justine continued to stare at me with an expressionless face.

My thoughts swung in the other direction. I envisioned bringing justice to my long-time oppressor. Could this finally put an end to the ridicule and humiliation? I was torn as I counted the pros and cons with my fingers. Make Jane feel like the victim for a change... let her feel scared, maybe embarrassed... knock her off her pedestal so she'd treat people better. Or, she'd find out it was me and my life would be over... my parents would ground me... the cops would arrest me. Should we or shouldn't we? I looked up at Justine.

She smiled.

Here's the thing about Justine. She's determined to keep her deepest feelings to herself. It was often difficult to know what was going on behind those blue eyes. But, she couldn't control what that smile betrayed. Sometimes, it was tinged with hurt or sadness and, while her words said, "I'm fine," I learned she actually meant "leave me alone." Most of the time, it was what I called her "mischievous grin." Even if I wasn't absolutely certain of what she was thinking, that irrepressible grin with the one eyebrow raised and the glint in her eyes was a dead give-away that she was about to ignore convention, maybe even the law. I was beginning to understand it revealed a rebellious rush that seemed to fuel her.

That smile—the one that simultaneously ignited my excitement and made me queasy with anxiety—was the smile that always convinced me. "Hell, yeah! Let's do this. You grab the tape player and, here, I'll bring the lantern. I finally found it in the basement."

Justine tipsily stood up. Impulsively, I reached out and pushed her. She lost her balance and went crashing down the hill, somehow blindly dodging the trees in the near-darkness. Racing after her, I gasped through my hysterics and we both landed in the cemetery.

"Shh!" Justine hissed at me sternly, finger to her lips.

"*You* shhh!" I whispered even louder.

"I swear! One of these times, I'm gonna get you!" She glared at me.

Hiding a smirk, I edged forward and beckoned for Justine to follow. "Listen, we need an exit strategy."

"A what?"

"A plan. How are we going to get out of the cemetery without getting caught?"

We stopped, hunched low, and weighed our options. Since Jane's house was behind the cemetery, going out the back wouldn't work. To our left, the chain link barricade ran the length of the cemetery and behind that was the heavily wooded stretch leading to the apple orchard. Navigating unfamiliar land in the dark seemed foolish. To our right, after crossing through the huge expanse of cemetery plots, we would reach another fence with more woods. Scratch that. Our only remaining option was the front of the cemetery. Again, it was a long way to run if being chased, especially without any cover. But once there, we could escape through the open main gate onto Elm Street.

"Hey! I've got it! We run in the shadows by the fence." Justine pointed to the left. "When we get to the hill where Wausau is, we split up. You go to the right, I'll go to the left. We go up through the woods from behind until we get to Wausau, and we hide there. She'll be looking for us out on Elm Street, but voila! We vanished into thin air. What do you think?"

"I think it's wicked brilliant!"

We crawled as close as we dared and squatted behind a large, rectangular headstone. Justine set the tape player on top and looked over at me. "Now what?"

"Let's wait until her bedroom light goes off," I decided.

"Which one's hers?"

I pointed to the only lit window on the second story, where I'd attended numerous slumber parties as a little girl. "That one. Up there."

The stillness of the night amplified the closing song from The Carol Burnett Show coming from the television somewhere in the house. Peeking around the stone, we watched as the first floor went dark and, finally, Jane's bedroom. Only the back door of her house remained visible in the dull mustard-yellow glow from the porch light.

Setting the lantern on top of a stone, I flicked it on. Justine switched on the tape recorder and the mournful organ strains pierced the silence. We called Jane's name over and over, moaning and groaning for effect. Glancing across the graveyard, not another living soul in sight, I could feel the flesh tingling on my arms.

A light came on inside the house. Then another. The door flew open. Jane and her mountainous father appeared in the lit doorway. My heart exploded in my chest and the next '*Jaaanne*' got stuck in my throat.

"Who's there!" Her dad roared as the porch shuddered under his feet.

"I'm calling the police!" Together, Jane and her father stomped down the stairs toward the cemetery.

I grabbed the tape recorder and we sprinted to the camouflage created by the dense trees along the fence. "They're coming. Hurry!"

As planned, I stayed to the right of the wooded hill and Justine swerved off to the left. She started up the back incline while I, with a quick look around, found a baseball-sized rock. Grabbing it, I waved her off, urging, "Go! Go!" I turned and lobbed the rock with all of my force and sent it crashing into the trees on the other side of the street. Then, sprinting noiselessly, I joined Justine who was already nestled in the safety of Wausau's arms. I crouched next to her, trying to draw a deep breath into my heaving lungs.

We listened, but didn't hear a sound. Not a twig breaking, not a footstep approaching. I heard Justine's rapid breathing, but that was all. Peering through the trees, we saw Jane and her father retreating across the cemetery. We did it! We successfully haunted Jane Williams! The terror. The school bully. The malicious gossiper.

I was elated as I recounted our success. "I can just see her creeping in shame around the school hallways! She'll be humble, maybe even nice! She'll know there's somebody—*somebody*—who is now the reigning tormentor. She'll...."

"Shit!" Justine grabbed my arm. "The lantern! We forgot the lantern! It's still on!"

We watched Jane and her father march in a direct line toward the light. "Oh no! We're busted!"

"Can they trace it back to you?" Justine asked.

"Can they....?"

"Think! Is your name on it!"

"Is my....?"

"Eva! You *have* to know!"

"I don't. I don't remember." I pulled myself to my feet and wrapped my arms across my chest. "I knew this was a bad idea! Why do I listen to you?"

"Don't always blame me! We both forgot it!" Justine scrambled to her feet.

"You, with your innocent face and big, blue eyes. Yeah, no one ever suspects you! Not sweet little Justine. Shit! They've got it!"

Jane and her father were almost to the back door of their house, the captured lantern swinging back and forth in Jane's hand.

"Eva."

"I swear, if she finds out it was me, she's going to…"

"Eva!"

"…make my life a living…"

"*Eva!*" Justine poked me in the ribs. She was standing on her toes, peeping over the top of Wausau's blade toward Elm Street.

"What?"

"Who's that?" Her whisper sent a shiver through me.

On the edge of the woods across the street—the very same woods where I'd just thrown the rock—was a figure. Tall, skinny, and unmoving.

"Ho-*ly shit*." I pulled her arm so we both ducked behind the blade.

"Did he see us?"

"I don't know."

"Is he coming up here?"

"I don't know!"

"Eva! Is it Rag Doll Man?"

"I don't *know*!"

"Come on. Run!"

"Hold it!" I needed a second to rationalize. *Would he chase us? Was he faster? Was it even really Rag Doll Man? If it was, would he try to hurt us?* "He can't get us both at the same time. We'll have to be faster."

We rose quietly. Took a tentative step. Then Justine stretched to take another peek over Wausau's blade. "He's gone!"

"What? Where?!"

"I don't see him. Maybe…."

We heard the muffled sound of leaves rustling under foot, then a stick snap. Without a word, I grabbed Justine's wrist and, as quickly as caution allowed, we made our way down the back of the hill. My mind raced as I tried to plot our next move. I pulled Justine behind a headstone and we huddled together.

"Is he still c-c-coming?" Justine asked.

"I d-d-don't think so," I said.

We listened for any hint of movement. At last, I worked up the nerve to look over the top of the stone. I scanned the cemetery and both sides of Wausau's hill. Nothing.

"*Shhh!* We're going out on the back road. Let's haul ass!" Clutching the tape recorder against my chest, I skirted along the fence with Justine one step behind me. By the time we made it to the road, we were certain no one was after us.

"I think I'm done haunting the cemetery," said Justine, attempting to bring levity to our predicament. "First, that cop. Then, Rag Doll Man."

"So, do you believe in Rag Doll Man now?" I couldn't resist teasing her.

"Maybe. I wish Jane had seen that guy, though. There's no way—*no way*—it could have been my stubby, round Uncle John. And, another thing. How am I going to get home? I'm not walking down that road by myself!"

"We'll go to my house. Craig will drive you home."

Adolescent Boys of Summer

"You Ain't Seen Nothing Yet" – Bachman-Turner Overdrive

Justine

"OH, I DON'T KNOW," I sighed, dramatically. "So many boys, so little time. There's Dean, and Chip, and Pete. All so cute. What's a girl to do?" Giving my hair a devil-may-care flip with my hand, accompanied by an exaggerated shrug, I turned my eyes back to watch the pick-up baseball game we'd happened upon in the empty lot across the street from Eva's house.

Having grown up with two older brothers, I was used to being around their male friends. Recently, though, my interest in them had changed. I stopped plotting how to outsmart them and began dreaming about how it'd feel to kiss them. Mom realized it was time to dredge up the old story of the birds and the bees when I replaced my 'Hang in There' poster—the one with the kitten clinging to a tree branch—with pictures of my current crush, David Cassidy. Luckily, my precocious cousin, Lisa, had already told me everything I needed to know, so I secretly chuckled as Mom blushed and stammered through her big Mother/Daughter Talk.

"Are they all in your class?" Eva asked, her wide-eyed interest spurring me on.

"Yeah, but there's my brother's friend, Mark, too. He and I went out a few times. He's pretty cool." I shifted uncomfortably on the prickly grass and crossed my legs at the ankles.

"What about your mom? Does she know about all these boys?"

"Eva. My mom's been drilling it into me since I was little. You know, being a 'liberated woman,' not needing a man, not letting them treat me like a 'sex symbol,' blah, blah, blah. I can recite Gloria Steinem almost as well as I can Dr. Seuss! Mom's not exactly the first person I'd go running to when I like a guy."

90

"That's too bad. That you can't talk to her about dating and all."

Do other girls talk to their mothers about boys? I hadn't given it much thought before. "It's fine. That's why I've got you, right?"

She shook her head and leaned back, stretching her legs out while supporting herself on her elbows. Squinting, she gazed toward the boys on the baseball field. "Which one of your many guys do you want to go out with?"

"One? Why pick one? I want all of them!"

"You're too much, Justine!" She jerked her chin toward the ballgame. "How about any of these guys? Anyone here interest you?"

I scanned the group playing on the Elm Street lot, many who had been throwing curious looks my way since we'd arrived and plunked ourselves down on the grass behind left field. "Eh, I see some that might tickle my fancy, but, really, I'm leaving tomorrow. What's the point?"

They seemed like your typical ragtag group of adolescent boys. One tall, gangly kid did catch my eye. Curly, dark hair, pretty good-looking. I pointed him out to Eva.

"His name's Danny," she said. "I don't think he's your type."

"My type? My *type*?! He's male. He's cute. Seems like my type to me." Laughing, I considered my friend. Summer was over and I knew what that meant. "Gonna miss me terribly when I leave, Eva?".

"Nah. I need a rest after this summer!"

"Glad to be of service!" Then, more soberly, I got to the point. "What about school?"

"I don't know how I'll possibly manage it without you," she said with barely a hint of seriousness. "Speaking of school, I forgot to tell you I saw Jane Williams at church yesterday. If my name *is* on the lantern, she certainly didn't let on. I don't think she's smart enough to be able to pretend. Actually, she was pretty nice to me."

"Jeez, I almost forgot about her. After we were almost murdered by Rag Doll Man, you know."

"Exaggerate much, Justine?"

"Actually, I'd kinda hoped it was our imaginations working overtime or we were having an alcohol-induced hallucination," I said.

"No, there was definitely someone there. I can't believe it was Rag Doll Man, though. I've never heard of him being this close to town."

"Yeah, and I'm still not sure I believe he's real, Eva."

"Well, you won't have to worry about walking down Miller Ave at night anymore. By the time you come back next summer, I'll have my license and the Opel GT I'm buying from Craig's friend."

I was only listening with one ear. The cute baseball player was at bat. He swung and missed. The next pitch was high. On the third pitch, he connected and the grounder headed right toward us. The left-fielder missed it and the ball continued rolling until I leaned forward and stopped it with my hand. Picking it up, I held onto it for a second longer than necessary, allowing the batter to round second. Then, I gently tossed it to the outfielder, intentionally making it fall short. By the time he retrieved the ball and sent it sailing toward the plate, it was the game-winning home run. The at-bat team was cheering and congratulating their hero, who smiled at me. I smiled in return before he ducked his head.

"I can't wait for us to go cruising!" I said, returning to our conversation. "I know! We'll go hunting for Rag Doll Man. Figure out once and for all if he's real."

"I'm telling you, he's real!"

The ball players were gathering their equipment so we scrambled to our feet. I brushed the grass and dust off my bottom, glad I'd worn jean shorts instead of something that would show dirt, and glanced over at the dark-haired boy pretending not to notice me. Even from here, I admired his huge, blue eyes. Jeez, he really was cute. Too bad I was going home tomorrow. Oh, well. I peeked at him one last time before scurrying to catch up with Eva who was already walking down Elm Street toward my house.

"I can't believe I'll be a junior this year," she was saying. "Man, I'm getting wicked ancient!"

"Ha! Next year, you'll be rolling around in your wheelchair instead of your sporty car, you old bag." I was about to give her my customary shove when we were distracted by a loud squawking.

"What are they doing?" I asked, pointing to two boys about my age by the side of the road with slingshots in their hands. They were shooting rocks at a nest of birds in a nearby tree and the mother blue jay was swooping around their heads. Meanwhile, an injured baby flapped helplessly on the ground.

My heart ripped open as the fury erupted. Eva was quicker. She sprang toward the boys, grabbed the slingshots from their hands, smacked one on the head, and pushed the other with such force he fell on his butt in the street.

"What is *wrong* with you ass wipes?" Eva was a furious shade of red.

"You don't treat animals like that! Get the hell out of here before I break your necks! If I ever see you doing anything like this again, you'll have *me* to answer to!"

Maybe it was shock or maybe they truly felt threatened, but those young terrors began to run. Not before Eva took her foot and pushed the bigger one in the ass, sending him stumbling, arms flailing. Meanwhile, I tried to get a closer look at the broken bird, but its protective mother wouldn't let me near. The poor little thing! And, its poor desperate mother. Finally, the baby stopped struggling and lay still on the crackled pavement, barely breathing.

"It won't live," Eva said, wiping the back of her hand across her nose. "And see, its mother has left it. She knows."

"What should we do?" I asked.

"It needs to be put out of its misery."

I looked up to see the cute, lanky boy from the baseball lot.

"Why don't you two go on and I'll take care of it," he said.

Eva nodded her head and swallowed. "Thanks, Danny. I don't think I could do it."

By the time we reached Miller Ave, we'd worked up the nerve to look back. Danny was gone, and so was the little bird.

I turned and stared at Eva. "Who were those boys?"

"A couple of local jerk-offs. They're lucky I didn't beat the shit out of them!"

"I kinda wish you had," I said. "I've never seen you stand up to anyone like that before, Eva."

She chuckled and dropped her eyes. "I wasn't even thinking."

"You're a tough guy, aren't ya? A real bad ass. Maybe I need to be scared of *you*!"

"Yeah, maybe you do, Justine."

I couldn't get over it. This new Eva. With her shoulders a little squarer, her chin cocked a little higher. "Come on. I need to get home," I said, shoulder-checking her before returning her grin.

CHAPTER 5

1976

TRAIPSING THROUGH WEEDS

"Born to Be Wild" – Steppenwolf

EVA

"WHAT DOES IT FEEL LIKE?" Justine asked. She leaned toward me, her face growing larger and more distortedly detailed. Closer. Closer.

What would she do if I flicked her in the forehead? A tickle started in my stomach. *Don't smile. Doooon't smile!* I bit my lips together, but they refused to cooperate. I burst out laughing. Her curious stare struck me as funnier and funnier, and my private joke seemed to irk her.

"Come *on!*" She crossed her arms. "Tell me how it *feels.*"

"It's hard to describe," I said, pressing my foggy brain to concentrate on her question. "I feel sort of out of body. Like I'm here, but not really. I hear my words coming out, but it's like a stranger is talking from far away." The laughter bubbled up inside me and, despite my best efforts, boiled over again. "I'm *sooo* stoned!"

When I'd pulled out my stash, I wasn't sure how Justine would react. Lynn and I discovered a whole new world when we started smoking pot back in October. We'd become part of this cool, elite group that hung out to share a few joints and deep, enlightening conversations. I'd bought a dime bag at the start of the summer, excited to share it with Justine, then had second thoughts. Briefly. Sometimes I forgot she was younger.

With the joint stuck between my lips, I'd steered my sweet, royal blue coupe south from Main Street onto Route 67. After I'd lit it and drawn heavily, I held it out to Justine. She hesitated, looking from my hand to me and back to my hand. I knew exactly what she was doing. It was what she always did when weighing her options. In the course of twenty seconds, she ran the pros/cons list in her mind, debating between living up to the good-girl image designed by her parents and abandoning all of their expectations to feed her wild child nature. She first pictured her trusting mother's shocked and horrified face, then was seduced by the vision of carefree hippies. The allure of dabbling in the forbidden, countered by the thought of calling her father to bail her out of jail. As her expression shifted, I'd remained confident of her decision.

She sounded disappointed as she snuffed out the remainder of the roach in the ashtray. "I don't think I'm feeling anything. Maybe it doesn't work for me."

"Give it a chance, Justine. Most people don't feel anything their first time."

Using every ounce of mental focus I could muster, I eased off the accelerator to exactly 25 mph as we entered West Brookfield town limits. Justine leaned across me to check the speedometer.

"Careful, Eva," she said. "You wouldn't want to do anything crazy like speed through town doing 26!"

"Hey, you don't know what these local cops are like. Pulling over speeders is what they live for."

"Exciting lives they lead. Uh, oh… watch it! You're at 27… 27 and a half…."

A group of teenage boys on the street in front of Town Hall pointed to us as we cruised by. I was positive they were riveted by my new-to-me sporty car, but in true, egocentric, Justine-style, she hung her entire upper body out of the window to call out to them and blow kisses.

One boy yelled, "Hey, aren't you forgetting something?"

Justine yelled back, "What?"

"Me!"

She waved, blew him one last kiss, then plopped back into the passenger seat. "This summer is gonna be *decent*! Cruisin', boozin', and boys. What more could a girl want?"

"Careful there, Hussy. You 'bout lost your shirt!"

Justine glanced down at the red tube top emphasizing her natural voluptuousness—artificial padding no longer required—and raised one eyebrow. "And that would have been bad?" She gave her new Farrah Fawcett hairdo a toss.

"Oh Jeez! Is this what I have to deal with this summer? Trying to keep you in line?"

"Look who's talking, Sexpot. All hot in your tight shirt. Who'd have guessed? You've got boobs!" She nodded her head toward my chest. "My philosophy is, 'If you've got it, flaunt it.'"

"Obviously! You're *almost* wearing your clothes!"

We continued on the narrow, curving roads, Justine alternately leaned halfway out of the car to let the wind sweep over her and bounced up and down on the seat while singing at the top of her voice whenever *'oohh, my absolute favorite song of* all time!' came on the radio. I slowed and pulled to a stop at our destination in Ware. "Okay. Here we are. Here's my surprise."

"What is this? Shadow Hill? I don't get it."

"It's another cemetery with the same name. Just two towns over. Can you believe it? Lynn and I came over and checked it out a couple of months ago."

This cemetery wasn't meticulously maintained and tranquil like the other Shadow Hill. It looked like a scene straight out of the new horror flick, *The Omen.* There were no paved roads and the headstones were scattered haphazardly. The wrought iron gate, with its line of spiky finials across the top, screeched as we wrestled it open. Not another soul was in sight. The only sound was the distant hum of the occasional passing car. Wandering through the ankle-high grass, we read inscriptions on the ancient stones. Unlike the glossy marble or polished markers found in our cemetery, these were rough slabs, mostly chipped rectangles, some with rounded corners. No cheerfully planted geraniums or tidily trimmed plots. Weeds and tall, scraggly grasses partially obscured much of the writing on the awkwardly listing stones. The old style engravings, with decades-accumulated grime in the letters, had permanent rain marks streaking down the length of the plaques like a grieving widow's mascara.

A sudden cool gust sent a chill through me. Rubbing at the goose bumps on my bare arms, I silently cursed the day I let Justine talk me out of wearing my old flannel shirts. A mass of threatening clouds moved to block what remained of the fading daylight. The sight of the gravestones' crooked, eerie shadows stretching toward us made me rub my arms harder. Shivering and swaying back and forth in an unconscious warmth dance, I realized Justine was noting every move I made. And snickering. I hunted through the haze in my head for a witty remark to clobber her with when, right behind her, I glimpsed a fleeting silhouette.

"What was that?" My head snapped toward the apparition.

"What?" Justine followed the direction of my eyes.

"Where did it go? I saw something. Over there."

"Maybe it's Rag Doll Man."

"No, no. Can't be Rag Doll Man. He's in North Brookfield."

"Maybe my Uncle Harry's ghost?" she asked, eyes wide in mock fright.

The hair on the back of my neck bristled. "He's in the att—Justine! Quit trying to freak me out!"

"*Me?* Freak *you* out? Ha! Look who's talking!" She jerked her chin at some nearby headstones. "Speaking of freaky, check out these stones. Did you see them?" She dragged me behind her and began reading an inscription. "When I am dead and in my grave, and all my bones are rotten. While reading this you'll think of me, when I am long forgotten."

Black clouds brought a premature dusk. The breeze rustling the tree tops sent a fresh shiver through me. I peeked around, half-expecting to come face-to-face with a ghost.

"Hey! Here's another one!" she called, crouching before a crooked stone, densely covered with lichens, and peering through the gloominess. "The worms crawl in and the worms crawl out. The ones that go in are lean and thin. The ones that crawl out are fat and stout." Her eyes glimmered with sinister glee.

"Eww!" I cast my eyes around the shadowy periphery of the graveyard.

Justine was on a roll. "Oh, oh! Here's a decent one: The spirits of the dead, who stood in life before thee, are again in death around thee, and their will shall overshadow thee; be still. Hey! That's Poe! I love his creepy stuff! And, look. Here's another—"

"Hold on, Justine! Wait! Wait! Who's that?" I thrust my finger toward a shady-looking person all the way on the other side of the cemetery. At least I *thought* it was a real person. I was no longer sure of anything.

"Who?"

"Right there! Don't you *see* him? That old man over there! What's he doing? Is he coming after us?"

"Oh my God, Eva! That's the groundskeeper, you dope! See his tools?" Pulling a cigarette from her purse, she lit it and handed it to me. "Listen. You need to ease up on the ganja if you're going to be traipsing around in cemeteries, Miss Paranoia. You're starting to see things." She gave me a nudge.

I released my breath. "Oh okay then, Cheech." I took a long drag on the cigarette as the first drops of rain began to fall. "Ready to go, Justine?" I seized a topic I knew always distracted her. "I've got a wicked case of the munchies. McDonald's?"

LOW TO HIGH IN A DAY

"Roundabout" – Yes

JUSTINE

THIS EVENING WAS GOING TO suck. S-U-C-K! I could tell already. Eva sat cross-legged, moody and quiet, drawing pictures in the dirt with her finger. She'd been sulky since we met up nearly half an hour earlier at Smokey's gate and headed off to hang out at our favorite hiding spot atop the cemetery, and I couldn't figure out why.

I tried another angle. "So, when am I gonna meet this Lynn chick you always talk about? She sounds pretty decent…?"

She barely glanced at me. "Soon."

I collapsed against Wausau. I didn't have the mental energy to jolly her out of her funk. I'd been counting on Eva to make *me* feel better. Mom called that morning and balled me out.

"I can't imagine what happened, Justine," she'd said in her controlled voice that instantly caused my temper to simmer.

"What are you talking about?" I'd asked in the snottiest tone I dared. "I got three As and two Bs."

"You must have blown your final exams. You didn't study enough for them. You're spending too much time thinking about boys these days."

"My friends' parents would be thrilled with those grades!"

"Well, I'm not your friends' parents," she'd said as I'd mouthed the words in unison with her. "I expect more from you."

"I know you do! You expect me to be perfect!"

"Justine, you have so much potential. I just don't want to see you waste it."

"Stop pressuring me! All you ever do is pressure me!" I'd slammed the phone down.

Aunt Peggy tried to distract me by suggesting we organize the massive pantry with its rich smells of exotic spices and ripe fruit, and endless supply of goodies for my sweet tooth. While I was in no mood to do any work, I would never say no to Aunt Peggy. By the time we'd finished wiping each shelf and organizing every last can and jar, I was sweaty and cranky. After showering, I'd called Eva in the hope that she would improve my humor. She'd been fighting with her own mother, though, and was even grumpier than I was. Frankly, she was being a ginormous pain in my ass.

"Are you gonna tell me what's going on with you, Eva? Or should I just go home?"

"It's my parents. They're on my case about college, again. 'Eva, you have to do your applications! Eva, what are you going to do with your life? Eva, why can't you be more like your sisters?'" She sighed. "You're so lucky you don't have to worry about any of this shit, yet."

"You aren't the only one with problems, ya know!"

"Oh yeah? What do you have to deal with? You've still got time before your parents start forcing you to make all these decisions. How should I know what I want to do? What I want to *be* when I grow up?" She drew a question mark on the dusty ground with her index finger, then rested her back against the steel blade of Wausau, legs stretched out before her. "That's me. A great big question mark."

I momentarily forgot to feel sorry for myself as I stared at my friend. She was the steady one. The one I counted on to tether *me* when I was dashing off in five directions at once. I tried to think of something helpful to say. "Well, you don't have to make some big life decision now. Take it one step at a time. How about you start by sending in the applications?"

"Why bother? Who needs college, anyway?"

"I thought you were the one who wanted to get out of this town so badly? Isn't this supposed to be the next ring in those concentric circles you told me about? How you were going to travel farther and farther from North Brookfield?"

"Maybe." Eva fired up a joint she pulled from a plastic baggie, inhaled deeply, then passed it to me.

I took a long hit but still didn't get what the big deal was about smoking pot. I'd tried it, what, half a dozen times? It didn't seem to have any effect on me. "Have you ever heard of 'predestination' or 'freewill'? It's about whether we have real control over our own lives or if we're controlled by God or the Universe, or something. For me, it's my *mother* who rules my life!"

"So, let me get this straight. You're saying, in your house, your mother is God? I think we all feel that way!" Eva glanced across the cemetery and watched the lone remaining car wend its way toward the front gate. Someone would be by soon to lock up for the night.

"Seriously, though. If I don't get straight As, she's all over me. If she ever caught me doing half the shit I do, she'd kill me."

"She has high hopes for you, Justine. You've got a pretty good deal, really. Keep your grades up. Then she'll lay off."

"It's never good enough. I can never make her happy. Eh… whatever. It's fine."

Eva took one last hit of the joint. She carefully returned it to the baggie before she directed her gaze at me. "You know you don't have to do that."

"Do what?"

"Always trying to be who you think others want you to be. Creating this… *image*." Eva swept her hand in front of me, gesturing to my entire self. "You're trying to be the perfect daughter with the perfect grades to live up to your parents' dreams. Then you're this wild and crazy hellion with your friends. You always think you have to be… *something*. Why do you do that?"

I sat silently for a moment, considering her question. "I guess it's what's expected of me."

"Expected? By who, exactly? And, what about you? What do *you* want?"

What did I want? No one had ever asked me that before. About any of it. *My* goals, *my* dreams, *my* thoughts… *my* life. Who *was* I? I mulled over her words but was having trouble forming a reply. I turned toward her, but drifted away, immersed in a thick liquid. I was aware my mind was trying to grasp onto something, but it was like grabbing Jell-O.

My mouth formed the words, "I'm stoned. Oh shit!" Forcing the sound out of my throat took as much effort as when my cousin Lisa and I tried to talk to each other underwater in her swimming pool. With equal difficulty, my ears clumsily caught the unfamiliar sound. *Who said that?* Oh, right. It was *me*! I burst into laughter.

"That's wicked cool! What do you think?"

What *did* I think? I was suddenly wise and philosophical, the answers to all of life's questions readily within reach. Through the haze, I offered my profound response. "Am *I* thinking? Am *I* in control of my thoughts or is there some larger force controlling them for me? Do you know what I mean? Remember free will? Does it really exist at all?"

"Exactly! There are, like, billions of people on this one little planet, right? And, that's just on *our* planet. Look at all of those trillions and trillions of stars in the sky. Are we supposed to believe there isn't life on any of those? Imagine if a fraction of them had people on them. Multiply all of those planets by all of the millions of other beings and you have, I don't know, an infinity of people or creatures living all over the universe. And, other universes. See what I mean, Justine? Who's controlling all of these people all over the place?"

"Some mastermind? Some Great Force?"

Eva nodded. "That's right! You're absolutely *right*. Whoa! We're, like, real intellectuals."

"Yes, we are. But who do you think it is, doing all of the thinking for us?"

We sat quietly. Who *was* doing all of our thinking? All of the people on Earth and in the Universe. And what about animals? What about horses and dogs and cats and pigs? Who does their thinking?

"So, Justine?"

"So what, Eva?" I asked, picturing thought bubbles over Smokey's and Lucky's heads, wondering what words would be printed there.

"Justine! The one who is controlling the thinking!"

"What are you talking about?"

She laughed so hard she couldn't speak. I wasn't sure why she was laughing, but obviously something was funny. Funny enough to make me laugh too.

"Oh shit, Justine! We were talking about someone controlling all of the thinking. Who is controlling all of the thinking?"

"All of the thinking? Uhhhh… maybe it's God?" The last word echoed in my head—*God… God… God.* It expanded and filled in every millimeter of space inside my skull.

Darkness had crept in and the only sound was the melody of the night peepers. My thoughts drifted tranquilly on their peaceful music until, what felt like hours later, Eva's response roused me. "No, I don't know if I'd call it God. I think of God as a creator, not a controller. I'm leaning more toward something kinda evil."

More silent contemplation.

I glanced at Eva. *Check her out. All serious.*

I wasn't used to seeing her this intense. It was funny to see her like this. *Hysterically* funny. The flutter in my stomach spread upwards until my body was helpless with laughter.

"Come on, you waste case, let's go find some food. We can walk up to Cumby's." Eva dragged me by the arm down the wooded hill.

I was still chuckling as I floated after her. "I want something salty. Potato chips. Or Pringles. I *love* Pringles. Or wait, wait! I know. Those new Combos things. Have you tried them yet? Pretzels with cheese filling? Oh my God. I'm starving! Maybe sweet. Chocolate. I need chocolate. Snickers. No. Three Musketeers. *Ohhhh!* A Clark bar. No, no! Your mother's doughnuts. That's what I need. Come on!"

"No, you spaz! You're going in the wrong direction. Town is *that* way."

We'd barely gone thirty feet when we caught the glow of car lights coming toward us.

My heart pounded in my head. What if it was someone we knew? Eva's mother. Or, *my* mother. "Hide!"

I dashed to the side of the road and leapt over the low stone wall running the length of the woods. Eva was right behind me and we both dropped flat to the ground behind the rocks, my body quivering at the sound of the approaching engine.

"Shh! Quiet!" Eva commanded.

As the car grew closer, we held our breath and waited until the brightness passed and dwindled, then lay there for a moment longer to be sure.

"I've got it! This is our new game… our *quest*. When we're out walking at night, no matter what we're doing, we can't let cars see us." The details developed in my mind as I simultaneously spat them out. "As soon as we see the lights we have to hide behind a tree, in a ditch, or behind a fence. If they spot us, we lose."

"What do we lose?"

"We lose the game, duh!"

We walked along the dark, abandoned road, eager for the next car to come. Finally, when the first glimmer appeared ahead of us, we knew what to do. We split like two sides of a wishbone, Eva dashing to the left and swinging herself over the fence into the cemetery while I ran to the right and sprang over the stone wall. I huddled in the ditch, listening as the car grew closer, then faded.

"Okay, this is our best game, ever!" Eva said when we met again in the middle of the street.

"This has been one of my best nights… *ever!*"

"Mine too." Her dark eyes, earlier weighted and lackluster, sparkled in the moonlight. "Okay, I've decided I'm gonna go ahead and mail out those applications. I *do* need to see what else is out there. It's time for me to go."

Raising one eyebrow, I said, "You think I'm too boring for you?"

"Why yes, yes I do, now that you mention it." She forced a stern expression on her face. "You think some game of hiding from cars in this back water town is enough to keep me here?"

I crossed my arms and turned my head away. "I won't even indignify that with an answer."

"Indignify?" She gloated. "*Indignify?*"

"Ha! Gotcha! I did that on purpose. I conflated 'indignant' and 'dignify' to make a new word. You like it?"

"I do," she said. "Not dignifying it because you're indignant. Indignify. That's great. Oh, and 'conflated'? *Niiice!*"

Chasing Mortals and Phantoms

"Spill the Wine" – Eric Burdon & WAR

Eva

Her cartoonish eyes seemed to pop out of her head. Justine was always an irrepressible storyteller, but when stoned, her imagination ran on overdrive while her mouth struggled to keep up with her chaotic thoughts.

"The attic... Uncle Harry... I *knew* I heard it. Then Aunt Peggy was telling me... he's up at Shadow Hill too... footsteps!"

"You heard footsteps in the attic?"

"I just said that!"

"Peggy said she thinks it's Uncle Harry?"

"Yeeaaahh...?" she said sarcastically, as if talking to an idiot.

"And, he's buried up in Shadow Hill!"

"Eva! I told you all that. Pay attention!"

I smiled as I eased my Opel GT onto the grassy shoulder and killed the engine. "You up for a party?"

Justine peered through the dark across the shadowed field. "Party? Here?"

We'd turned past the Quabaug factory and arrived at the Common, one of the focal points of this small village. On a warm summer afternoon, it wasn't unusual to see kids tossing baseballs or playing pick-up basketball. Most nights, though, had a different vibe. The idyllic, wholesome picture from earlier in the day turned into a haven for bored and restless teenagers, couples hoping for some time alone, and groups getting wasted on cheap beer or pungent smelling pot they'd managed to score. At some point nearly every evening, someone yelled "Cruiser!" and black silhouettes scattered in all directions, jumping fences and running through nearby yards to dodge the glare of the spotlight circling the grounds. Complacent police officers seemed less interested in making a bust and more interested in the amusement of sending dozens of kids scurrying.

"I heard this is where they are tonight," I said.

"They?"

"The kids from the area. North Brookfield, mainly, but sometimes other towns too. The 'Portable Party'."

"'Portable Party'? What does that mean?"

"Well, a lot of times we meet at the Common. But if the cops start busting us, we move someplace else. See? Portable."

Justine adjusted her halter top and rolled some Maybelline Kissing Potion across her lips. "Decent," she said, checking herself in the rearview mirror. "Any cute guys?"

"Uh, control yourself, Floozy. I have to live in this town!"

I'd learned Justine and I had vastly different ideas of what 'cute' meant. I leaned more toward the long-haired, rock 'n' roll type while she liked clean-cut, pretty boys. At least we'd never fight over the same guy. It occurred to me I'd known the kids in this group for so long, I never even thought of them like that. I tried to picture them through Justine's hair-measuring, physical-attractiveness-judging, thrill-seeking eyes.

All conversation stopped as we approached the group.

One guy murmured, "Oh baby, where've you been all my life?"

Justine pretended she didn't hear the comments as she accepted a beer.

"Justine. This is Benny. And Ronny. You met them last year, remember?" These were the two bullies Justine had confronted so impressively. Now, we hung out all the time. I watched as she smiled coyly, giggled flirtatiously, and mentally put them into the 'Friend' category.

"And, this is Vicki."

Justine visibly perked up as she told my neighbor how excited she was to finally meet her.

"This is Joey."

Justine's thoughts were nearly transparent: *Too short, hair too long.* But, I knew him to be quick-witted. *Friend.*

"And, Kenny."

Shoulder-length hair—acceptable. Kinda cute. This was one of the townies I'd been thinking might interest her and, from the batting of her eyelashes, I guessed she put him on her 'Maybe' list.

"This is Rob."

Sweet — shy, but *Friend.*

"And, Carl."

"Well, hello there, Justine." Carl adopted what I assumed he thought was his sexiest voice. "What's your sign?"

"Aries. That's a fire sign. You know what they say about playing with fire," she said. *Friend.*

"This is Jimmy, Chuck, and Larry."

Friend, Friend, Friend.

"And, may I present... Lynn." I waved my hand in a flourish. "The infamous Lynn."

Justine's smile appeared genuine, but, knowing her as well as I did, I detected the stiffening posture. She extended a hand and said with a chilly undertone, "Hello, it's a—"

"Justine! I'm so glad to finally meet you. I was starting to think you were a figment of Eva's imagination. But, look! Here you are!" Lynn lunged toward Justine and threw her arms around her.

"Well, hi there!" Justine laughed, allowing herself to be embraced. Even though Justine was taking inventory of my other friend—glancing from the bare feet to the hip-hugger bell-bottom jeans, to the skimpy halter top, to the long blonde hair—Lynn's natural charm could sway anyone. In fact, I don't know why it had never occurred to me before. How alike these two were!

Justine finished her beer, then another, followed by a third. She was in her usual hair flipping, provocative arm-touching, sexpot form. Even a little more over-the-top than usual. I suspect it had something to do with Lynn, judging by the frequent sidelong looks she threw in the other blonde's direction.

Most of the kids I knew had never traveled outside central Massachusetts. Meeting Justine from as far away as New Jersey was almost like meeting someone from a foreign country. She adeptly fielded questions being tossed at her from every direction, playing up the Big City Girl act she'd honed.

"That's right, from New Jersey. Near Princeton University. No, no! I don't actually *know* any mobsters! New York? Of course! I can hop on the train and be in the city in an hour! Yeah, sometimes I see celebrities walking down the street. It's no big deal. They're just people too, ya know. Well, of *course* we have big parties. Do you think you're the only ones who know how to party?"

By her third beer, she'd begun shifting back and forth and responding "huh?" enough times to signal her attention was wandering. I gave a subtle jerk of my chin in the direction of the car and she began her goodbyes. "I *know*! It *has* been so much fun. We'll do this again real soon. It was so great to meet you all."

As she skipped toward the car, I glanced back and saw Lynn following us with her eyes.

Justine caught the direction of my gaze. "Hey, Lynn!" she called. "Come on!"

Lynn trotted to catch up, then we all broke into a race for the car. I came in first and whipped around to watch Justine and Lynn scramble for second place. Lynn pulled into the lead, but Justine grabbed her by the back of the shirt to slow her down. They reached the car at the same time, gasping for air through their laughter. Magnanimously, Lynn jumped into the back seat to allow Justine to sit shotgun.

"So, Lynn," Justine said once we'd settled in the car. "I've gotta know. What's with this Rag Doll Man? Is he real? Eva swears he is, but I don't believe it."

"Oh, he's real. I know at least three people who've seen him," she replied.

"But, have *you* seen him?" Justine asked.

"Well..."

"How can you still not believe it?" I asked. "After what happened last year at Shadow Hill? Remember? Up at Wausau? That guy coming after us?"

"It was dark; there were shadows," Justine said. "That whole night's a blur."

"Alright, Miss Skeptical. We're going over to the woods where he's been spotted," I said. "Maybe he's out tonight. Then we'll prove it to you once and for all."

Traveling past the high school and Brooks Pond, I drove until there were no houses along the road at all. The dense trees made it impossible to see past the first couple of feet into the woods.

"I bet he's in there somewhere," I said.

"Pull over," Justine said, pointing to a slight hollow. "Put your brights on."

We sat quietly, the song of the night peepers accompanied by the occasional *hoot-hoot* of a passing owl. The headlights from my car tunneled into the blackness, allowing us to see white pines, evergreens, and even a red maple or two. Nothing else.

"Keep driving," said Lynn.

I pulled back onto the road and continued along at a crawl. All three of us searched for the elusive Rag Doll Man who might, at any second, appear before us.

"Wait! What's that?" Lynn pointed to the left.

I stopped abruptly. We all strained our eyes, waiting for movement or a shadow. Still nothing. I continued on.

"I saw something!" Justine called, this time pointing to the right. "Something moved by the side of the road!"

I cranked the wheel to aim the lights in the direction she indicated. Nothing.

"I'm freaking myself out," Justine said. "I still say he doesn't exist."

"Yeah? Why don't you get out and take a closer look, then?" I challenged her. "If he's not real, then you'll be fine walking around in the woods, right? At night… in the dark… no one around."

"Okay, I will!" Justine pulled on the door handle.

"Justine, don't!" Lynn reached from the back seat to close the door. "Can we go? You might not be scared, but I am!"

I did a U-turn, the sweeping headlights providing one last glimpse into the woods which may or may not be hiding the mysterious Rag Doll Man. Cruising back toward North Brookfield center, I thought we were about to call it a night. Not Justine, though.

"Stop!"

"What? What is it?" I pulled onto the shoulder of the road. "Did you see him?"

"No! New game. Come on!" Justine jumped from the car before I'd come to a complete stop and sprinted across the front yard of a ranch-style home set back from the road.

"What's she doing?" Lynn asked. "What are you doing?" she called out of the open window.

Justine motioned for us to join her and, by the time we did, she'd yanked the wooden stake of a Ford/Dole '76 political sign out of the ground. We watched her race to the neighbor's yard and pull up their Carter/Mondale sign, then shove the Ford one in its place. Returning to the first yard, she planted the Carter sign where Ford had originally stood. The entire operation felt like it took a year to complete, but in reality, she did it in seconds.

"Justine!" I said when I'd recovered my voice. "You can't do that!"

"Shh! It's not hurting anyone!"

"Justine…" Lynn looked nauseated.

"Come on, it's funny!" Justine said, leaning into the car. "They'll wake up in the morning and find out they're voting for the other guy."

"But, trespassing, destruction of property, criminal mischief...." I said, the familiar Justine-induced anxiety rising in my stomach.

"Chill out with all that legal crap, Eva. It's just a joke." She pointed to the houses lining both sides of the street. "Look at all of those signs. We'd better haul ass. We have a lot of work to do!"

The quiver in my stomach turned into a full-scale quake. Somehow, I feared this wouldn't end well. Truthfully, I wasn't sure if we'd get into trouble. Was switching political signs *really* that big a deal? Maybe the cops wouldn't even care? I glanced at Lynn and, seeing the uncertainty on her face, turned to Justine, determined to put the kibosh to her latest hair-brained scheme. Then, I met her eyes.

She grinned.

Damn!

Crouching low and hugging the shadows, we proceeded to change signs around down the street, around the corner, and up the next street. We moved stealthily, systematically swapping every sign along the way. Nearly an hour later, Justine seemed satisfied.

"Do a quick drive-by to make sure none of the signs fell over," Justine said.

"How many do you think we did?" asked Lynn.

"At least forty or fifty," I said, steering us through the neighborhood to inspect our work.

"I was sort of surprised to see that many signs," Justine said wryly. "I didn't think so many people way out here in the sticks would even know who's running for President, much less care!"

"Shut up! We don't live in a cave, you jerk!" I said. "Can't you see the expressions on their faces when they wake up in the morning? I only hope—"

"It's fine," Justine said. "Honestly, it's fine."

Later, after we'd dropped Lynn to her house, Justine and I reviewed the events of the evening. She waved goodbye when I left her at the Miller's and I smiled as I headed toward home. As I traveled through the tunnel of trees on Miller Ave, I found my eyes sweeping through the woods for any sign of Rag Doll Man. When I turned onto Elm Street and spied a political sign on someone's front lawn, my stomach flipped. I heard Justine's voice in my head saying "it's fine... honestly," but it didn't settle me.

"It's fine," I said, pushing the prank from my mind as I pulled in front of my house. "It's fine."

CONSEQUENCES
"Baba O'Riley" – *The Who*

JUSTINE

"**M**MM! MMM!" I GRUNTED, FLAPPING my hand to get Eva's attention. I'd managed to get my Bubblicious into perfect bubble-blowing consistency, and this bubble was nearly the size of my head. It may be the biggest one I'd ever done! I tried to work it with my tongue to close off the air hole and seal it like a balloon, but it burst and splattered all over my face.

I gleefully waited for her "*ooooos*" and "*aaahhhs*" of appreciation while I picked the sticky remnants from my nose and chin, but her expression was as flustered as when she'd first thrust the newspaper in front of my face. Seeing panic widen her eyes, my shoulders drooped. *Dear God, she's a wreck! Why does everything make her so uptight lately?*

"Eva! Don't be such a drag! They have no idea who did it."

In a full-blown tizzy, she had driven over to Smokey's pasture earlier than usual to show me today's headline:

Political Flip-Flop
Prankster Pulls Sign Switcheroo

She was babbling nonsense about "electoral fraud" and "harassment," and said the article reported the police were "following several leads."

"How will they ever trace it back to us? No one saw us. Jeez! It's not like we committed first-degree murder or something. Get real! It's a bunch of old farts with their knickers in a twist. They'll get over it. So," I adeptly switched topics, "are we still going out cruising this afternoon?"

Eva stared at me. "Are you kidding me? Don't you take *anything* seriously? We could be in real trouble over this. Lynn says people in town are demanding that the police get to the bottom of it. I don't think they're just going to 'get over it'!"

Clearly, I wasn't as adept as I thought. Heaving a long, exaggerated breath, I conceded. "Alright. Here's the plan. Keep an ear out. I can always call my dad. He'll know what to do. But," I shook my head with certainty, "I'm telling you. It won't come to that."

"Okay, as long as your dad can help if we need it." She carefully refolded the newspaper, deliberately pressing the crease, then reached through the open window of her car to place it on the passenger seat. "So, what'd you think of Lynn? She's cool, huh?"

I'd often wondered why Eva hadn't introduced me to Lynn. She'd talked about her for years. "Lynn and I did this..." and "Lynn and I did that..." Honestly, I was a little sick of hearing about this always-ready-for-fun Lynn who got to hang out with Eva all the time because she lived in North Brookfield and I didn't. I was expecting to hate her when we finally did meet, especially once I laid eyes on the pretty hippie chick with flowing blonde hair and enviably flat stomach. But, who could resist the dainty free-spirit with the pixie dimples?

"Eh, I guess she's okay." Her head snapped up in surprise and I couldn't contain my laughter. "I'm kidding! She's decent! When will we see her again?"

"She's around. Too bad she doesn't want to hang out with you, though."

"What!?"

"Ha! Gotcha, punk. She liked you too. Oh, speaking of liking you," she continued, "one of the Portables called to ask about you. Kenny. Do you remember him? He was wondering if I thought you'd go out with him."

"Which one was Kenny? Did we even talk?"

"How should I know? All he said was he'd like to get to know you better. He's in my class at school. He's a really good guy and wicked cute."

"Yeah, sure," I said. "That might be fun."

"Listen," she said, an edge returning to her voice. "He's a *nice* guy. If you're only going to play head games with him, then never mind. He doesn't deserve that."

Wow! She *was* in a huge snit today. "Eva, what do you want from me? I don't really remember him, but I said I'd like to see him again."

"You know what? Forget it." She headed for her car. "I'll pick you up after lunch?"

"Yeah, great."

It was a temperate August day—low humidity and bright sunshine—and we were cruising aimlessly around North Brookfield and the surrounding towns. The tension between us from earlier had begun to ease with the help of cold beer and the Beatles. And, there was something about traveling through the familiar scenery that always put me in a good mood. Mostly visible along these routes were huge expanses of rolling farmland with herds of cows, sprawling farmhouses, barns, and silos. Or, miles of unbroken wooded vistas on both sides, with a small pond or two, barely visible through the trees. Occasionally, you might see a produce stand or antique store by the side of the road, or signs pointing toward the nearest apple orchard.

"My sister, Jan, got me a job where she works," Eva said, taking a swig from her beer. "At a nursing home, as a nurse's aide. I start in three weeks."

"How will that fit with school?" I tossed my empty beer can into the back and popped open my second.

"It's afternoons, when I'm done with classes. Four days a week and one weekend a month."

"Full-time?"

"Not quite, but it's a real job. It'll be my first steady paycheck."

When we reached Brookfield, Eva slowed the car as we approached Cumby's. She was distracted, scoping out a group of boys hanging in front, but *ick*. They all had long, stringy, nasty hair. She hesitated until their boisterous voices reached us. I urged her to keep going. They were stumbling and pushing each other, and it was obvious they were plastered. But, Eva's eyes were glued to one low-life in particular.

"That one's kinda cute," she said, but they all looked the same to me.

"Hey, babes!" called the obvious head delinquent. "How 'boutcha get your asshhes over here and suck on thishh?" He staggered, nearly falling while grabbing his crotch. His buddies hooted and egged him on.

I was stunned into silence as the car idled to a stop.

"Show us your tits!"

"Yeah! Let's make some putang pie!" More laughing and whooping.

I felt the heat surging up my face. Who said such repulsive things? Who the hell did they think they were talking to? My wits rebounding, I yelled, "I wouldn't touch you with a ten-foot pole, you filthy piece of shit!"

"*Justine!*"

The ring leader lurched toward us, slurring, "Lish-en, you li'l cock teazhh. I'll make you shut thefuckup!"

"Justine, no! *No!*" Eva yanked my hand away from the door handle. I was delirious with rage as I lunged to get out of the car and put that asshole in his place, but, with a vise grip on my arm, Eva slammed on the accelerator and we barreled tire-squealing, car fishtailing, down Route 9.

"*Really?* You're gonna let them get away with that?!"

She sped out of town, putting plenty of distance between us and the dirtbags before pulling into the parking lot at the Clam Box. How could she be so calm about this? I could barely breathe, but Eva looked completely unrattled!

"Use your head, Justine! They were jerks, but that could have been wicked dangerous!"

Seriously? Seriously?! *Was this somehow my fault?*

"Besides, Justine...." She pointedly eyed my shorty shorts and shirred crop-top.

"What the *hell?*" I could feel the burn spreading up my neck.

"I mean, they shouldn't talk like that, but they probably thought they were being funny."

"Why'd you look at my clothes like that?"

She stared at me, unspeaking.

"Get bent!" I reveled in the hurt look on her face.

Still, she kept her cool. "They were definitely out of line. That's not what I'm saying. But, sometimes when you dress and act a certain way, it gives the wrong impression."

I sat on my hands to keep from smacking her. I swallowed, took a deep breath, then released it slowly. I forced my voice to sound neutral as I tried again to get through her thick skull. "Eva. It doesn't matter how I dress. They were total assholes. I don't care if they *were* drunk. They were gross. Beyond gross. *Disgusting!*" I spat out. Despite my attempt at self-control, I could hear my tone rising. "Don't you *get* it?"

"I understand why you're upset. They're assholes. Of course you can dress however you want, but don't be surprised when it gets a rise out of the guys. More importantly, you've *got* to watch that temper! You don't *think* before you go off. You don't know what those guys could have done to you!"

I absorbed what she was telling me, but didn't want to listen anymore. Maybe she was right to some extent, but I would only admit it over my dead body. Maybe we didn't have to mention this again. Maybe I could try harder and it'd all blow over.

"Consequences, Justine. You need to think about the consequences of what you do and say. And, not only with guys. With your little schemes too. Like those election signs. Just think first. Okay?"

A moment passed without either of us speaking. I finished the remainder of my beer, tossed the empty can into the back seat, and turned toward Eva. Pushing the sides of my mouth into a smile, I answered, "How I dress is nobody's business but mine. But, I'll take the rest of what you said under advisement."

The Moon Over Spencer
"Wild Thing" – The Troggs

Eva

"**H**AVE YOU EVER HEARD ABOUT the woman from East Brookfield named Bathsheba Spooner?" I asked, steering the car toward the McDonald's in Spencer, a town over and east of home.

Justine and I were doing what we did best—cruising with a six-pack while looking for cute guys. Things were better between us, but it had taken us a few days to get past our fight. Not so much a fight—a difference of opinion.

I think she was trying, though. Yesterday, when we'd gone to Howard's Drive-In for fried clams, a couple of guys in a car whistled at us. One had yelled something about "wanting to get a piece of that." Justine liked being admired, never objectified—it was one of her pet peeves. In this case, her best choice would have been to ignore it. Instead, she smiled and said calmly, "yeah, keep dreaming" and continued walking. Not perfect, but a big improvement. She'd looked pleased when I told her I was proud of her.

She shook her head. "No. Who's this Bathsheba chick?"

"She's kind of a local legend. Supposedly, she lived back during Revolutionary War times. They say her husband was horrible to her—beat her up, or left her, or something. She wound up getting pregnant by a seventeen-year-old Continental soldier who stayed at her house on his way home. I guess she must have been scared because her husband would know he wasn't the father. So she convinced these two soldiers who'd deserted from the British army to kill her husband. I don't know all of the details about how she did it and how they got caught, but they were all sentenced to hang. The most interesting fact, though, was Bathsheba was five months

118

pregnant and they wouldn't wait to execute her until after the baby was born. They ended up killing her baby too. Isn't that wild?"

"Jeez! I can't imagine, can you? One little mistake and look what happens."

"One *little* mistake? She committed murder!"

"I meant the cheating part, Eva."

"Still, I don't think cheating on your husband is *little*."

"I thought you said he treated her badly."

"Yeah, but that doesn't make it okay, Justine!"

"I didn't say it was okay. I said it was a mistake. But, obviously, there were reasons she did what she did, Eva. I bet the law didn't protect women back then. That's probably when they were still considered property."

"I don't know. If you get married in the eyes of God, then that's it. You make it work."

"Ha! You think I'm bad? Sometimes, you're pretty judgmental, you know. Life isn't always so black and white."

I thought about my sister, Nancy, who'd been having so much trouble with her marriage. She'd left her husband and stayed at our house for a while until my parents convinced her she'd taken vows and needed to make it work. Now, she was pregnant. In the back of my mind, I was concerned about her safety; I'd seen the long bruises across her back when she bent over and her shirt rode up. No one in my family talked about it. I also knew if things got that bad for Nancy and it couldn't work out, my parents, or any one of our siblings, would take her and the baby in. What if Bathsheba didn't have anyone? Maybe her husband had brought her to this country and she'd left her whole family behind in England. Maybe she had a lapse in her morals because she was miserable with her life.

"Maybe." I relented. "But whatever her reasons, the whole plan went haywire. Hiring the soldiers to kill her husband, then the hangings. What a story, right?"

Justine chuckled. "I guess all my boys back home seem like nothing compared to hers!"

"Oh, I don't know. I think she was the Justine Andrews of the 1700s, all slutting around."

Gasping in feigned horror, she hit my arm and shot back, "Shut up, you big jerk!" With a grin, she added, "Okay, you can call me a slut. Just not a murderer."

After picking up our chocolate shakes and extra-large fries in the McDonald's drive-thru, we rounded the building toward the exit. Several cars were parked together and a horde of teenage boys was hanging out. I glanced over to read Justine's demeanor. She must have guessed my apprehension because she was already looking at me with a reassuring smile.

"I'll behave. Promise." Holding up a three fingers pledge.

"You were never a Girl Scout, so that doesn't count. Besides, I'm not sure you know what it *means* to behave."

"Say what?" she asked, already distracted by the guys.

I'd zeroed in on a tall boy about my age with thick, curly hair cascading halfway down his back. His eyes locked on mine as we crawled toward the exit.

Justine, meanwhile, was working double time to prove to me she could be charming. She was leaning out of the window, calling out, "Hey, Gorgeous! Hey, Handsome! Whatcha doin'?" and blowing kisses to the entire group.

"See?" she said, pleased with herself as I reached the end of the drive. "I was good. I was showing my appreciation to each and every one of them. Wasn't I nice?"

I turned left, then left again, back into the parking lot on the other side of the building. "That one guy was wicked cute. Did ya see him?"

"You're going back through?" Justine squealed with that wicked glint in her eye.

"Whoa there! I don't trust you. What are you scheming?"

"Nothing."

As we reached the back of the fast food joint, I hunted for the cute boy with the luxurious mane. There he was! He looked familiar. Had I seen him before? Well, it wouldn't be surprising. It's not like we lived in the middle of some metropolis where you might never in your entire life see someone a second time. He grinned at me and I swear I felt actual butterflies fluttering in my stomach. As I smiled in return, ready to stop my car near his, I saw a blur to my right. Time slowed like something in a movie as, frame by excruciating frame, I was helpless to stop Justine when she jumped up on the seat, unzipped her shorts, pulled them down in the back, and stuck her naked butt out of the window.

"Noooo Juusstinnne…" My voice elongated in a deep moan. My euphoria crashed as I slammed on the accelerator, the whistles and cheers following my speeding car back to the Stop sign. This time, I turned right and raced away. Justine had pulled up her pants and was back in her seat, happily chomping on a handful of fries.

120

"Shit, Justine!"

"What? They showed *proper* admiration of my ass. When *I* chose to have them admire it. What's wrong with that?"

"You know I'll never be able to go there again, right? They'll never forget the 'Moon Over Spencer'!"

"Oh, relax, Eva! My ass isn't that memorable."

She couldn't seem to help herself. And I couldn't resist a little smile at the thought of the boys' shocked faces. At the same time, I wanted to strangle her for wrecking my chances with Mr. Wavy Locks. Again, consequences.

DEEP AND ENLIGHTENING DISCUSSIONS
"Rock and Roll All Night" – Kiss

JUSTINE

THE PORTABLE PARTY KIDS PROVIDED a whole lot of entertainment for me this summer. I tried shortening the group's nickname to 'Porta-Party' and pronounced it the way people in New England do, with the flat 'a' so it sounded like 'Porta-Pahty,' which sent me into hysterics every time. For some strange reason, Eva didn't find me funny. It was an ever-rotating group—sometimes larger, sometimes smaller. The core group I'd met that first night at the Common remained pretty constant. They were a nice bunch, but mainly I got a kick out of listening to them discuss the great mysteries of the universe when they were stoned.

One of my new favorite games was to engage in their conversations, make some profound contribution, then listen to how they eagerly tossed my ideas around, somehow believing even my most ridiculous statements. Once, when we were talking about time travel—a subject about which I'd read extensively—they regarded me as the expert. After throwing out enough information to wow them about the theory of relativity, the book by H.G. Wells, and the grandfather paradox, I'd said with utmost conviction that Madeleine L'Engle in *A Wrinkle in Time* proved beyond a shadow of a doubt that by folding the fabric of space and time it was possible to time travel. They'd never heard of Madeleine L'Engle and praised her writings as if they'd been published in respected scientific journals.

When I was high, I found I had a small piece of my brain that was still semi-functional. That piece loved being outrageously absurd and watching the others react as if I knew what I was talking about. Did Eva play the same game? She appeared to be as intellectually engaged as I pretended to be, but I'd seen her smother a smirk after she'd made a particularly ridiculous remark. I kept meaning to ask her, but the rest of my brain, the part which had given in to the effects of the pot, kept forgetting.

Another recent discussion we had was: *Is there life on other planets?*

Me: "How could there not be? Could we possibly be the only planet in our entire galaxy that has life?" I pulled out my trusty secret weapon. "Madeleine L'Engle says there's life on the planet Camazotz."

Eva: "Of course it exists. Based on the odds. Of the billions of other planets and stars? And, in other galaxies? The odds support the facts. Life exists on other planets."

Carl (the blond, beefy guy with the ponytail that looked exactly like Smokey's tail, and whose incessant bragging couldn't hide the fact he wasn't terribly bright): "I don't think so. Maybe those other planets have some sort of life, but not with our advanced intelligence." He erupted into his loud, braying laugh that made me jump every time. "You don't think they're driving around in something like my Trans Am, up there in the Big Dipper somewhere, do ya?"

Me: "But imagine if those planets light years away are also light years ahead of us. Maybe their cars are actually able to fly. Like in the Jetsons."

Carl: "Nah! No way. We've evolved into the most advanced species in the universe. Besides," he brayed and I jumped, "that's a stupid cartoon."

Joey (who I found to be witty, and who grew his hair long—down to his waist—maybe to compensate for his 5'4" height): "Yes, and you're the perfect example of evolution."

Carl, oblivious as usual, nodded: "You got it, man!"

At some point during all of our exchanges, Benny and Ronny chimed in. I think they fancied themselves as a brilliant comedy team. They tried to model Abbott and Costello with their razor-sharp timing and snappy comebacks. Unfortunately for Benny and Ronny, neither was smart enough to pull off being the straight man, which left both as the dim-witted bumblers. Therefore, when they tried to pattern a bit after 'Who's On First,' they ended up deteriorating into the squabbling slapstick of Lenny and Squiggy. Which actually, in my own shit-faced condition, was even funnier.

Benny: "Well then, who's on Mars?"

Ronny: "Yes."

Benny: "I mean the alien's name."

Ronny: "Who."

Benny: "The Martian."

Ronny: "Who."

Benny: "The guy on Mars."

Ronny: "Who."

Benny: "The guy living...."

Ronny: "Who is on Mars!"

Benny: "What?"

Ronny: "No, What's on Venus."

Benny: "Wait. What?"

Ronny: "No, Who, you idiot."

Benny: "I thought Who was on Mars. I said What."

Ronny: "I said Venus!"

Benny: "Wait. Is it Who is on Venus?"

Ronny: "What's on Venus. Who's on Mars! Jeez! You blew it!"

Benny: "No I didn't! You got confused."

Ronny: "I didn't get confused. *You* got confused!"

Benny: "Did not! It was *you*."

And so on.

Usually by this time, their argument turned into pushing with fists flying, until other members of the group pulled them apart. "Boys, boys, settle down." Vicki, a couple of years older than Eva and often in the motherly role, calmly tried to restore order while the rest of us were limp with laughter.

Jimmy, Chuck, and Larry were pretty much interchangeable. I thought of them as a single unit—jimmychuckandlarry. Even when I called out one of their names, all three looked up. I never saw one without the other two, so I could barely tell them apart. Like a Greek Chorus, they added their own comments or laughed as one, but were kind of colorless background players in my mind.

Then there was Rob. The tall, sweet boy with bony wrists and jutting cheekbones. He never joined our discussions. He quietly watched the rest of the group with his wistful, Bassett Hound eyes, offered beer to the empty-handed, and smiled when Joey said something particularly funny. Eva told me he'd been kicked out of his house last year, when he was sixteen. He had so many brothers and sisters his parents said they couldn't afford having him around anymore. Lynn had invited him to sleep on her couch while he finished high school, worked as a bag boy at the IGA, and dreamed of making something of his life. No one dared say a cruel word about Rob or the wrath of all of the Portables would be felt.

The adorable Lynn was usually present with her fairy-like giggle and bare feet. I wondered if she began wearing shoes after Labor Day. Sort of the way you weren't supposed to wear white after the official end of summer—maybe the same rule applied to going without shoes. I tried to imitate her hippie shoeless style once, when she and I had gone cruising. After I cut my foot on a piece of glass and ended up hobbling for the next couple of days, I'd realized I couldn't pull off that image with the same 'cool' factor she could.

But, it was Kenny I wanted to know better. Since Eva told me he liked me, I'd been on the alert for him. He wasn't around quite as much as the rest of the group because he worked as a bus boy in a West Brookfield restaurant several nights a week. But, when we saw each other, we enjoyed our one-on-one conversations.

Tonight at the Common was the first time we had a chance to be alone, though. No one thought to bring munchies, so Kenny volunteered to walk to Cumby's.

"Justine, do you want to come?" he asked.

"Sure!"

The topic of this evening's intellectual debate was: *Does God exist?* Eva had already offered ideas from her Catholic upbringing; I'd played the devil's advocate by asking how we were supposed to accept what we were told simply on faith if there was no scientific evidence; Carl made some stupid comment about how his own perfection was proof God existed, while Joey had commented that, actually, Carl could be an argument against God's existence. As Kenny and I were about to walk away, Benny and Ronny joined the conversation.

Benny: "Well then, who's in Heaven?"

Ronny: "Yes."

Benny: "I mean the name."

Ronny: "Who."

Benny: "In Heaven."

Ronny: "Who?"

Benny: "The guy in Heaven."

Ronny: "God."

Benny: "Man! You were supposed to say 'Who'!"

Chuckling softly, I allowed Kenny to lead me in the direction of Cumby's. He wrapped his arm around my shoulders as I felt a little thrill go through me. That exhilarating feeling whenever I was beginning a new romance. He really was cute. He was nice too, talking about his family and what he liked to do when he wasn't working. As we walked, he told me that he doubted he'd go on to college after he graduated high school this year. He liked working at the restaurant and thought maybe he'd stick with it.

Approaching Cumby's, I spotted the police cruiser parked out front. "Should we wait until they leave?" I whispered, wishing I'd brought Visine for my eyes.

"Nah. We're fine," he said easily, steering me to the door and holding it open.

The two officers were standing at the checkout counter, chatting with the cashier. They barely glanced over at us. Hunting through the choices of salty and sweet snacks, I strained to listen to their conversation. I couldn't believe it! Standing behind them, waiting for our turn to pay, the enormity of what they were saying rushed over me.

"Evening, Officer O'Reilly. Officer Costa." Kenny nodded. As they passed us on their way to the exit, I smiled in response to Officer Costa's cordial smile.

"Justine, isn't it?" Officer O'Reilly had turned toward me as if just remembering he'd met me before. "Staying out of the cemetery at night, I hope."

"I am, sir," I said, trying to avert my bloodshot eyes.

"Good, good." He chuckled as he walked out with Officer Costa.

By the time we finished at the register, the cruiser was gone. I prayed the cops weren't headed to the Common as we turned in that direction, and couldn't wait to tell Eva what I'd heard.

Our friends were right where we left them, still talking about God. We were in time to hear Carl telling jimmychuckandlarry, "Well, if you don't believe in God, then I guess you don't believe in Jesus, either."

"Jesus was a historical figure," I interjected, stopping short of adding "you moron." "Eva! Come here! I need to talk to you."

I dragged her away from the group by the arm, almost too excited with my news to speak.

"What?"

"We're fine!" I said. "Everything's decent! They aren't looking for us!"

"What are you talking about?"

"They don't know diddly squat! They have no idea who did it."

"Justine." She heaved an impatient sigh. "You have to start at the beginning. You always come in partway through a thought and expect me to know what you're saying."

126

"The signs! The election signs! I thought you were worried about getting caught! Jeez! I don't get you!"

She grabbed me by the shoulders and pulled me so she was looking directly into my face. "Speak slowly. Start at the beginning."

"Ken-ny and I went to Cum-by's. Re-mem-ber?" I said in an exaggerated, drawn-out monotone. "The two cops were in there. They were talking to the cashier about our little adventure. The cashier asked if they knew who did it. The cops laughed and said no. They said even though some of the old folks are ticked off, they don't have the time or money to follow up. They have no leads. We're in the clear! We're fine!"

"Oh, thank you, God! All I could think about was how wicked pissed off my parents were going to be."

"I told you we wouldn't get caught! Come on." I glanced at our friends. "We'd better get over there and add something intelligent to whatever conversation they're having."

"Or," she said, "something so completely idiotic they think we're absolute geniuses."

I turned quickly toward her. I *knew* it! I *knew* she was playing the same mind games with them I was.

OUIJA BOARDS AND TIME CAPSULES

"Fly Like an Eagle" – Steve Miller Band

EVA

"SHHHH! LISTEN AGAIN!" JUSTINE HIT rewind. She turned the volume all the way up and held her finger in front of her lips. I strained my ears through the static for any other sound. Wait, wait! There it was!

She pointed toward the recorder placed between us on the dirt floor at Wausau and nodded her head excitedly at me.

"Whistling! Like that day we were exploring in the attic. It sounded as if it was coming from the far end of a tunnel. Then, a scraping noise, like a chair being moved."

"I *know* it's Uncle Harry!" she said. "This is proof he's up there! No one was home except Aunt Peggy and Uncle John, and they were down in the kitchen. After I stuck the recorder up in the attic, I went and sat in my room and read. Nobody came upstairs!"

"You don't have to convince me. Remember when we heard the whistling up there? Trust me, I'm a believer!" I stopped the recording and rewound it. "What are you going to do about it?"

"What *can* I do? It's not like I can say, 'uh, Uncle Harry, could you keep it down? I'm trying to sleep.' I'm just glad to know I'm not losing it."

Listening again, there was no mistaking it. There was a ghost in the attic!

"Well, speaking of ghosts," I said, "I have something to tell you."

"Okay...?"

"I went to Jane Williams's birthday party last night."

"You're kidding! Why would you... did she... *why?*"

"I didn't really have a choice. When Jane says you're going to her party, you're going to her party!"

"What happened?"

"It was a theme party. And, guess what theme she picked. The Occult!"

"You're kidding!" she said. "What'd you do?"

"We started out with Light as a Feather, Stiff as a Board. Did you ever play that? Jane decided she wanted to be the one to levitate. She laid down on the dining room table and we all stood around her, two fingers from each hand underneath her. There were, I don't know, maybe ten of us? Anyway, she had us chanting it over and over, 'light as a feather, stiff as a board.' Then, I swear to God on my grandparents' grave, she floated off the table!"

"No *way*! It must have been some sort of trick."

I shook my head resolutely. "If I weren't there, I might not believe it, but I'm telling you. We lifted all 200 pounds of her right up in the air! It was crazy."

"Whooooaaa!"

"Then we did the Ouija Board. You know what that is, right?" I hesitated as I remembered placing my fingertips on the heart-shaped indicator. "I never truly believed in it, but after last night, I'm not so sure."

"Why?"

"It had real answers. About boyfriends, college questions, that kind of thing."

"How about for you?"

"Well, that was wicked strange." I studied a tiny piece of dark green moss growing by the steel arm I was sitting on, absently running one fingertip over its softness. "I was asking the questions and the pointer started moving. I just didn't know what it meant."

"What did it say?"

"It kept spelling out 'Harry... bluebell... Harry... bluebell.' Over and over. What do you think it means?"

"No clue. The only Harry I know is Uncle Harry. But I don't see the connection." She drained the remainder of the blackberry brandy bottle, then stashed it in a hollow under Wausau's blade. "Did you guys do Bloody Mary?"

"No. What's Bloody Mary?"

"You stand in front of a mirror in a dark bathroom and say 'I hate Bloody Mary' three times. Some people say you'll see her ghost appear in the mirror, holding the dead, bloody baby she killed. Others say you'll get deep scratches down your back from her long, red fingernails."

"Did you ever try it?"

"My friends and I always say we're going to, then chicken out!"

"I wish I'd known about Bloody Mary last night. I could have had a lot of fun using it on Jane. Anyway, the whole night was sorta spooky."

"What about reincarnation? Did you ever decide if you believe in it?" Justine had sent me another book, *Audrey Rose*, on her favorite topic. And, many of her letters during the year contained strange occurrences she claimed happened to her—déjà vu; the feeling she knew a perfect stranger she'd just met; dreams she was certain were actually memories from previous lives. She was convinced reincarnation could happen and she had probably lived before.

I was more skeptical. "I'm not sure. A person being reborn as another person? Sounds kinda far-fetched. I was taught to believe that when someone dies, their spirit goes to Heaven or Hell."

"Then how do you explain Uncle Harry? And spirits contacting you through the Ouija board?"

"I don't know. I haven't thought about it much." I stretched my arms over my head and yawned. "What did you do last night?"

She leaned back against the rusted plow blade and pulled from her purse a long green pack of cigarettes. Using her index finger and thumb, she languidly extracted a skinny brown object.

"You're smoking cigars?" I asked.

"It's not a cigar. It's a More."

"Let me try one." I lit it, took a long draw, and forced myself not to cough on the acrid smoke. "Not bad," I croaked around my burning lungs.

"Right? Plus, they make you look really cool." The left corner of her mouth trembled. "So, about last night...."

"Last... night..." I choked.

"I went out with Kenny."

"What?" I shouted, forgetting about the fire in my throat. "How did that happen?"

She shrugged. "He called and asked. I said yes. Actually, we've hung out a few times."

"Come on! What do you mean 'hung out'? Do you like him? Are you seeing him again?"

"Yeah, I like him. He's fun. We had fun." She knew what I was really asking. Raising one eyebrow, she leaned toward me. "He's a pretty decent kisser too, if I do say so."

"What?! What's the story with you two?"

"Oh, come on, Eva! There's no 'you two'! We've gone to dinner, cruised around, met up once or twice with the Portables... hung out. That's it. End of story."

The hopeful enthusiasm seeped out of me. "You aren't seeing him again?"

"I doubt it. I leave Sunday. He's nice, but I won't be back for a long time. Besides, I've got other fish to fry back in New Jersey. A whole, great big high school full of them."

"That's too bad. I thought you'd make a good couple. Oh and, by the way, I forgot to tell you. Lynn's pissed as hell at you."

"Why? What'd I do?"

"We went over to McDonald's in Spencer to grab something to eat before heading to Jane's last night. I'd told her about what you did over there when some guys in the parking lot yelled to us."

"But why is she mad?"

"Because they were yelling, 'Hey, blondie, show us your ass!'"

"I don't see...."

"They recognized my car and thought she was you! They thought she was the one who mooned them!"

"Huh," she said with a small smile. "I guess I was wrong. I guess my ass *is* that memorable!"

"Metal box?"
"Check."
"Pack of Mores?"
"Check."
"Pack of Marlboros?"
"Check."
"Pack of EZ Widers?"
"Check."
"Roach clip?"
"Check."
"Blackberry brandy bottle?"
"Check."
"Carter/Mondale pin?"
"Check."
"Horseshoe"
"Check."

"Bell."

"Check."

"This week's *Worcester Telegram?*"

"Check."

"Letters?"

"Check. Check."

"Okay then," I declared. "I think we're ready! Let's pack everything into the box, write up our predictions, then we'll be done."

I had re-watched *2001: A Space Odyssey* on television and come up with a wicked cool plan. Since it was 1976, we put together a time capsule that, if opened in the year 2001, would be twenty-five years old. Under my supervision, we collected an array of items to represent current-day life. We gathered mementos reflecting our own interests, including letters we'd each written, sealed in separate envelopes.

"You should have brought one of your mom's doughnuts to put in the capsule!" Justine said. "That would certainly show what we like."

"Ewww! Can you imagine it in twenty-five years? It'd be rock hard, or covered in ants, or... ewww!"

"Hey! Dough-not underestimate the doughnut. Get it? 'Dough-not?' Huh? Huh? Get it?"

"Oh, yeah, I got it. It doesn't make it any less gross! Nice idea, though," I said.

"Okay, then," Justine said, picking up her pen. "What about our predictions? What will be going on in the world in 2001?"

"The guys who wrote the movie were pretty smart, so I'm guessing they have some scientific knowledge or background. First, write down that we'll have contact with extraterrestrial life—you know, aliens from another planet."

"Got it," she said, scribbling. "And, people will be living on the moon by then and have some sort of lightning speed spaceships to travel between there and Earth."

"And Mars!"

"That's good. And, we'll all have our own flying cars. Do you like that?"

"Yep," I said. "How about this? The Beatles will be reunited and there won't be any more poverty and starvation in the world. And, there'll be world peace."

"Everyone will be like the hippies—'make love, not war'!" She wrote rapidly. "And, get this. Steven Tyler from Aerosmith will be President of the United States. Wouldn't *that* be decent?!"

"Oh, and you'll be a famous actress living in California. I'll be a famous writer living in New York City."

"Okay," Justine agreed, her pen hovering above the paper. "That's fine. As long as we make a vow that even living far apart, we never lose touch or stop being friends. Promise?"

"Of course. Promise."

I had planned well and brought two shovels and a can of spray paint. Accompanied by our ever-faithful Lucky, we'd trekked into the grove of trees on the neighbor's property where it butted up against Peggy and John's to look for the perfect location. One where it would be possible for someone to find the time capsule, but not so easily that it would be discovered before the twenty-five years.

"This is the one. This tree." I pointed to one growing slightly outside of a cluster.

"Here. Give me the shovel."

In no time, we had a hole at the base of the tree, nestled between two protruding roots. I carefully lowered the box, then Justine shoveled the dirt to fill the hole. We patted it tightly and gathered a pile of stones to form a marker.

"Is that enough? What if no one knows there's something underneath the rocks?"

I held out the can of spray paint. "That's what this is for!" I made a red arrow on the trunk of the tree, pointing downward toward the base.

"Put arrows on some of the other trees—there, pointing to that one, then pointing to that one over there." Justine indicated several nearby trees. "End with the one where it's buried."

When we were done, I mused, "Wouldn't it be hysterical to see the reaction of the person who finds this?" I gathered the shovels and empty spray paint can, then patted Lucky's head to let him know we were leaving.

"I think it would be even more fun if, somehow, we remembered it was here and came back in twenty-five years and dug it up. How decent would that be? We'll be so old by then. In our forties!" Justine exclaimed.

I laughed at the thought. I couldn't picture us ever being that old!

CHAPTER 6

1977

Sweet Freedom

"American Girl" – Tom Petty

Eva

FOUR MORE STEPS. JUST FOUR... more... steps. My left thigh muscles groaned as I gripped the bannister with both hands and stretched my right leg to avoid the squeaky stair, reaching for the one below it. Crap! That one squeaked too. I waited, listening. I didn't hear anyone. Okay, two... one. Race-tiptoeing down the hallway, I grasped the back doorknob and turned it one creaking fraction at a time, then inched the door open.

"Eva?"

Damn! I turned around and slumped my way into the front sitting room. My mother had told me before I went to work that she wanted to talk to me when I got home. After a day of scouring poop and vomit, and forcing pleasantries for all of those grumpy old people, I really wanted to go see Justine. She'd arrived this morning and we hadn't even had a chance to make plans. But *noooo*. My mother and I had to talk.

Luckily it wasn't The Talk. My mother assigned that task to my older sisters who'd taken great delight in giving me the gory details of the pain and bloodiness that go with a girl losing her virginity. From the way they described it, I couldn't figure out why anyone would ever want to have sex. No, luckily I didn't have to suffer through the indignity of *that* conversation with my mother! Today, it was the what-are-you-doing-with-the-rest-of-your-life talk. As if, at eighteen, I should have it all figured out.

I threw myself onto the love seat and loudly released my breath in a long stream. She ignored my impatience. "Eva, have you even signed up for your fall classes? You can't keep putting it off."

"It's *fiiine*, Mom." I sighed again for emphasis. "I'll *get* to it. I'm only taking the basic classes all freshmen have to take."

"But you need direction, Eva. Look at your sisters. They knew what they wanted when they started college. How about teaching? Or maybe nursing? Good, solid professions."

Great. Follow in my perfect sisters' footsteps. Teaching? With a bunch of bratty kids not listening to a word I say? Nursing? After today's degradation? I don't think so.

"This isn't done, Eva," she said as I got to my feet. "You need to go over there and sign up for those courses."

As I bolted for the door, she called after me. "And you need to see about housing too!"

After picking up Justine, I recounted the conversation with her.

"A writer! Why not? You've always said that's what you wanted to be. Maybe for a show like *Saturday Night Live*. Those letters you write to me—when you get *around* to writing to me—are hilarious. Yep. It's decided. You'll be a writer." She blew out the smoke she'd been holding and nodded as she passed the joint back to me.

"Okay, Miss Decisive. That's what I'll be." No matter how crappy a mood I was in, having Justine back was like waking up after winter's hibernation. Everything was fresh and renewed, full of life. Her animated face and the way she bounced in the passenger seat proved she was just as happy to be here.

Steering around a sharp curve in the road, I slowed to a stop on the shoulder. "Hey, did you ever hear about this place?"

She gazed out the window, squinting against the late-day sun. It looked like any farm you might see as you wandered the New England countryside. A large but ordinary-looking white farmhouse with black shutters faced the narrow street, while behind it was a huge red barn with white trimmed windows. Above the triple-sized sliding doors was a white, rectangular pediment with block lettering marking its establishment: 1909, Long View Farm. It was a peaceful, secluded location, but unremarkable until you knew its purpose.

"It's a recording studio," I said. "Some of the biggest bands and musicians in the world come here to record."

"Pffff, right! Like who?"

"I'm serious! They keep it all hush-hush, but Arlo Guthrie and Stevie Wonder have been here. Alice Cooper, too. I heard Cat Stevens is coming soon."

Justine shook her head. "Why would they want to come to this little town, way out in the boonies? Don't they usually go to some big city, like…"

"…New York? That's exactly why they come here. They can practice and record in peace and quiet. They have a staff to cook and everything. Cool, right?"

"If it's so hush-hush, how did you hear about it?"

"All the locals know about it. Just not the rest of the world."

"*Excellent!* Let's go look around!"

"Justine!" I laughed. "It's private property. People can't go wandering around there."

"Chicken shit!"

"I'm not a chicken shit. Just normal! Normal people don't think they can go gallivanting on other people's property, Justine!"

"Where's your sense of adventure, Eva? It's not like it's someone's home. It's like a… like a landmark! And aren't landmarks meant for people to go and visit?"

"No. We're not doing it," I said as I began to drive away.

"Oh, you're no fun!" Her eyes remained glued to Long View, searching for evidence of its hidden world of rock 'n' roll.

"Quit bellyaching, you hoodlum. I'm plenty of fun!"

She whipped around to study me. "Fun? You're '*plenty* of fun'? How *much* fun, Eva? Hmmm? Does *Tim* think you're fun, huh? Tell me about him. Is it serious? Is he hot? Do you have *fun* together? Do you *looooove* him?"

"I don't know if I'd say it's serious. We've only been going out for three months and I really like him, but I don't know if I *looove* him!" Stopping at the intersection with New Braintree Road, I checked left, then right, then left again. "And yes, he's wicked hot."

"What's he look like? You always leave the most important details out of your letters!"

I conjured up a picture of him without even trying. Like any of the posters I had hanging on my bedroom walls, his face was stamped in my mind. "A little like Peter Frampton." Unguarded, a wistful sigh escaped before I caught myself.

Too late. Fluttering her lashes, Justine smiled coquettishly and mimicked me in falsetto. "Ahhh. My boyfriend. He's such a *dream*boat!"

"Oh, shut up, wise ass! He's smart too. He'll be studying engineering at Stanford, in California, this year. It's going to be hard for us."

"Hard? How hard, Eva?"

Punching her in the arm, I couldn't help laughing. "Shut up, Justine, you disgusting pig! It's not like that!"

"Eva, Eva, Eva. What are you waiting for? Marriage?"

What *was* I waiting for? It's not like Tim hadn't tried. Every time we were alone, either in the back of his Pontiac LeMans or out at Horse Pond, our make-out sessions got hot and heavy. I liked it when his hands made their way under my blouse, but as soon as he tried to go to third base, I pushed him away. I simply couldn't shake the images my sisters had drawn in my mind. Or, how unworthy I felt for even having those kinds of thoughts when I took Communion on Sundays, reproachful eyes staring down at me from the cross above the altar.

"Maybe. I'm just not ready." To avoid her endless interrogation, I switched to Justine's favorite topic: her fast-changing, impossible to keep up with, love life. "What's your boyfriend-of-the-moment situation?"

Kicking her feet up onto the dashboard with her attention sufficiently redirected, Justine launched into a recap of her string of liaisons. To hear her tell it, there was a never-ending supply of cute, available guys. She'd asked about Kenny in one of her letters, but he had a steady girlfriend now. I made arrangements for her to meet my friend, Matt. I thought he was attractive, but who knew what Justine would think. Her taste wasn't predictable.

"Hey! Let's hide on cars tonight. I've told my friends back home about it, but they don't get how excellent it is. And, here's the game. For every car we hide on, we have to come up with a new job for you. We've already covered teacher, nurse, and writer, so they're out."

IT WAS AN UNUSUALLY ACTIVE night on Elm Street. We hardly had time to regroup from one hiding before another car came around the curve. My list of possible professions was growing. Cop. Waitress. Movie ticket collector. Tightrope walker. Dog poop scooper. Stripper. Astronaut. Spy. Chocolate taste-tester. Catholic nun.

As the next lights pierced the darkness, appearing around the bend from behind us, we jumped into the ditch between the side of the road and the orchard. We huddled low, whispering and giggling. The sound of the engine grew louder, but didn't fade. It stopped right next to where we were lying. I could feel the cold spreading in my stomach as I peeked over the edge. What *was* this? There was no *way* we could have been spotted! This was unprecedented! What should we do? Maybe if we kept still, they'd leave.

Click. *Creeeaakk.* The car door opened and a man's voice asked, "Hello? Who's there?"

How could we have been seen? He'd go away. We had to just... keep... still.

"Are you hurt?" *Shit.* Justine wasn't going to deal with this so I'd have to. With my face on fire, I struggled to my feet and immediately froze in the headlights. The police cruiser! Not a single coherent thought was forming in my mouth. I glanced down at Justine, rigid, peering up at me with humongous eyes.

"Uh, yeah, thanks, Officer O'Reilly. I'm fine. I was just looking for my dog."

Looking for my dog? Where the hell did that come from? I heard a snort as Justine, hands over her mouth, convulsed with laughter. I stepped quickly onto the road.

"Thanks so much for your help. My dog ran off... tried to follow him... fell into the ditch. I'm fine, really."

"Do you want a ride home?" he asked.

"No thanks, sir. I'm going to get my dog... finish our walk."

"Okay, but be careful, Eva. Stay out of ditches." He offered me a kindly chuckle before tipping his cap to me. As he drove away, I pretended I was looking for my fictitious dog until the taillights were out of sight. Then, I ran back to where my so-called friend was still safely hidden by the tall grass.

"You jerk! Way to hang me out to dry!"

Scrambling to her feet, Justine was still chuckling. "Your dog? Your *dog*?! Uh, you're pretty quick on your feet, huh?"

"Well, at least I got *on* my feet. You're such a wimp!"

"I thought you were going to get arrested. He was actually pretty cool about it."

"Why would I get arrested?" I asked. "I wasn't doing anything wrong. Other than putting up with you and your shenanigans!"

She grabbed my arm. "Hey! I've got it! Quick thinking. Good under pressure. Able to lie through your teeth without batting an eye. I know what you should be. A lawyer. Right? A *lawyer!*"

UTOPIA

"Stairway to Heaven" – Led Zeppelin

JUSTINE

"**H**ERE, LEMME POUR YOU SOME more, Aunt Peggy." I set aside my collection of contemporary poetry, the one I'd read so many times the spine had broken, loosening some twenty-odd center pages I had to keep shoving back into place. Tipping the pitcher of iced tea I'd brewed earlier, flavored with sugar and fresh mint, I refilled Aunt Peggy's glass. As I handed it back to her, she smiled before setting it on the sturdy wood table next to her chair.

Leaning back in my lounge chair, the rose-scented breeze played lightly over me as I settled into my Utopia—Miller Ave. From this stretch of lawn behind the house, there was no other sign of civilization. I untied the strings of my bikini top to avoid tan lines and luxuriated in the sizzling heat of the early afternoon on my baby-oiled skin. Lucky lounged close by, occasionally dashing off to chase a rodent stirring in the grass, then returned panting, and sprawled by my side once more. The cicadas' song, like shivering maracas, lulled me to the brink of sleep.

Forcing open one sun-drowsy eye, I watched the tawny-backed sparrows, butterflies, and bumblebees. "Aunt Peggy, what's that?" I asked, sitting up and pointing to a blurry-winged critter I'd thought might be a hornet.

"It's a hummingbird, sweetheart. They've been my favorite since I was a little girl."

"I've never seen one before. It's so cute!"

"My mother used to keep a garden in the front yard. She called it the hummingbird garden. She'd plant columbine, coral-bells, bee balm, and I can't remember what else, to attract them. My brothers and sisters and I would all gather around the front window and spend hours, it seemed, watching those itsy-bitsy birds. There might be a dozen or so at any given time."

Her dreamy tone caught my attention. I watched her speak, absorbed in the far-off memories of her childhood. Her dear face where soft cheeks lined with a patchwork of heartbreak and age always accordioned with her warm smile. Her brow was deeply furrowed from decades of quiet pain, topped by dark hair, cropped to manageable shortness for her arthritic fingers. I knew every detail of that face, having treasured each moment in my life I'd had to study it.

But she was different in that instant. She was still my Aunt Peggy, only somehow less familiar. As her glazed eyes revisited her past, her face relaxed, looking almost smooth and youthful. I thought of the old pictures Eva and I had found in the attic. Many of them were of Aunt Peggy, Uncle John, my grandfather, and the rest of the Miller children posed in groups, or were candids of them around the farm. My imagination showed me a little girl of long ago, romping with her siblings—playing hide 'n' seek... exploring the trap doors and passageways in the barn, like I used to with my own brothers... lying in the front yard at night, softly lit in the brilliance of the star-filled sky... sharing secrets and making plans for when they were grown-ups. An entire life lived before I ever knew her.

"Maybe we could plant a hummingbird garden? Together?"

She looked at me for a long time, the lines and furrows returning to their places. She smiled faintly. "Maybe." She continued to examine me. "Justine, did I ever tell you that you favor my mother when she was young? I'll have to show you her photographs sometime."

I remembered the other picture Eva and I had come across that day in the attic—the one of the young couple with baby Dorothy Justine in the carriage—and how seeing my great-grandmother that young had startled me. The one I kept under my pillow back home in New Jersey. I returned her smile.

"Aunt Peggy, can I ask you something? Do you think it's true that there's a ghost in the house?"

"I can't say for sure, honey, but there sure are some strange things I can't explain."

"Like what?" I asked.

"Well, like cold spots in the house, even during the hottest part of summer. Things in one place when I'd swear I'd put them in another. Oh, but the strangest, I'd say...." Aunt Peggy took a long drink of iced tea, emptying nearly half her glass, then placed it back on the table. She unhurriedly wiped at a ring of sweat it had left on the tabletop.

I prompted her. "You'd say…?"

"The lights."

"What about the lights?"

"I used to think it was my old, forgetful brain. Thinking I'd turned off a light but finding it still on. Until the time Uncle John went down into the cellar, the part way at the very back of the house. Neither of us had been down in ages—a year, even. But I sent Uncle John down to fetch me some canning jars. The light was on all the way in the back part of the cellar!"

"Couldn't it have been left on from the last time he was there?" I asked.

"From a year earlier? The bulb would have burned out. No. It was one of those odd things that always makes me wonder."

"What about whistling?"

"Whistling?" she asked.

"Do you ever hear whistling in the attic?"

"Aye-yuh, sometimes I do."

"Do you think it's Uncle Harry?"

"Could be," she said. "He was quite the whistler."

"My mother said he fell down the stairs and died. Is that right?"

"It is. It was a peculiar accident. He'd come to visit and was staying in the attic, the way he always did. It seems he was coming down the stairs and a flash of lightning right outside the window startled him, making him lose his footing."

"Lightning?" I asked. "He fell during a lightning storm?" My mind was racing. The mysterious light Eva and I had sworn we'd turned off. The storm that day when we'd heard the whistling in the attic. Did thunder and lightning stir up his restless spirit?

"So I was told."

I fell quiet, contemplating this new information and eager to share it with Eva. Then, I had another thought. "How about Rag Doll Man?" I asked. "Have you ever heard of him?"

"Rag Doll Man?"

"Yeah. Supposedly, he escaped from a mental hospital and hides out in the woods?"

"Of course I've heard of Rag Doll Man," she said. "Not since I was a girl, though."

"What do you mean? I thought he just escaped a few years ago."

Aunt Peggy gave a hearty laugh. "Honey, that story's been around for generations. Whenever something happens no one can explain—a burglary, some kind of violence—it's blamed on Rag Doll Man."

"So he isn't real?"

"I can't answer that, Justine. It's one of those legends that, by now, no one knows if there's any truth behind it. Maybe he's real—or *was* real—maybe not. Who can say?"

"Aunt Peggy, do you know what Eva told me?"

"No, what did Eva tell you?"

I took a moment to think through phrasing it as diplomatically as possible. "She said some of the kids in town think Uncle John is Rag Doll Man."

"That's nonsense," she said.

"I know, but it still makes me mad that people talk about him like that."

"Justine, you need to not listen to gossip. You know the truth. Don't let silly comments upset you."

"I try, but it hurts when people say such ugly things about him."

She gave me the gentle smile that was a healing balm on my heart. "You'll live a much happier life, honey, if you ignore hurtful comments. We can't control what someone else says or does. Only how we let it affect us. Anything new since you got back this summer?" she asked, closing the subject. "Are your old friends still around?"

"Yeah, we've run into most of the Portables. Eva's okay. Trying to figure out the whole college thing. Oh! I do have some exciting news."

"What's that?" She smiled expectantly.

"Well, you know our friend, Vicki? Eva's neighbor?" I felt a growing sense of importance as I related the details. "She and her boyfriend Pablo are getting married. They're having an engagement party later this summer." I had romantic images dancing before my eyes and, feeling quite grown-up at sixteen, I added, "It's kinda strange when your friends start getting married, ya know?"

The smile on Aunt Peggy's face remained frozen in place, but her eyes misted over as she answered. "It's even stranger when your friends start dying."

Tramps and Dreams

"Heartbreaker" – Pat Benatar

Eva

IF SHE SPRAYED ONE MORE perfume on me, I was going to walk out of there stinking like a French whore. Already on overload with Chantilly, Chloe, Charlie, and Tabu, I didn't even know which was which.

"Justine, stop!" She was coming at me with another bottle. Love's Baby Soft. "Alright! I'll take that one. Jeez! What's with you?"

"Listen, Hot Stuff! I'm doing your gorgeous hunk of a boyfriend a big favor. No offense, but you're starting to smell a lot like Smokey. Sorry, but you know I'm right!"

After her incessant badgering, I'd finally relented and driven us to the Auburn Mall so Justine could "advise" me on a new wardrobe. I'd purchased shorts, embroidered tops, Lee jeans (I'd put my foot down when she'd held up Jordaches), tank tops, peasant blouses, and shoes. Not those platforms or the three-inch heeled Candies she insisted on wearing, but some cute clogs and a couple pairs of sandals. Then, she'd dragged me into the Frederick's of Hollywood shop. I felt like every set of eyes was on us as she shuffled through the stacks of elaborate lace and satin bras.

"Try this. And this. Oh, and this one! See the padding? It will give you a little lift. Emphasize that cleavage!" She hadn't even bothered to lower her voice as she called across the store.

I raced over. "Sshh! I can't wear that! I'll look like a…" My eyes did a sweep to make sure no one would hear me. "…a *hooker!*"

Her laugh rang through the store. "Trust me. You'll thank me after Tim gets a load of you in these!" She'd held the matching panties over her head.

I'd grabbed two sets of the lingerie in my size—one red with black lace overlay and the other a vibrant blue—then slunk over to the register and paid for them before hurrying from the store.

Maybe she was right. There was something about imagining Tim's reaction that sent a familiar jolt of anticipation into my... well... *down there*. I glanced over at Justine as we waited to buy my new, alluring scent and she gave me a triumphant grin. She acted like she was preparing me as some kind of sacrificial virgin but, honestly, I still hadn't made up my mind.

I hadn't told Justine yet, but I'd decided I was in love with Tim. He told me he loved me, too. I knew he was the one I wanted to spend the rest of my life with. And, I had no doubt he'd be my first. I just wasn't sure when. I'd always thought I would wait until marriage. I certainly didn't need Miss Manipulation dragging me down her path of debauchery before I was ready.

I was sagging under the weight of my growing number of shopping bags, but Justine still hadn't bought anything for herself. We stopped at the garden center on our way to the mall where she'd found hummingbird feeders and purchased two—one for Peggy and one to take home to New Jersey. Otherwise, her objective for this excursion seemed to be slut-ifying me.

"Want to get a drink at Orange Julius?" I stopped, realizing I was talking to myself. Backtracking, I found her in a novelty gift store, standing in front of a shelf filled with bells. "I thought I lost you! What're you doing?"

Justine didn't look up. She was studying the collection, picking one up, putting it down, picking up another. With a sharp intake of air and a squeal, she grabbed a porcelain bell from the back of the second shelf. Holding it protectively with both hands, she examined it, then rang it, listening closely to its tone. Her face alive with delight, she announced, "This is the one!"

It wasn't until she set it on the counter at the register and dug her wallet out of her purse that I got a good look at her purchase. It was lavender and the handle was sculptured into an older woman sitting in a rocking chair with a young girl snuggled into her lap. In flowery, deep purple writing on the bell itself, were the words 'Dearest Aunt.'

"WHAT ARE YOU LOOKING AT?"

Justine was standing before the Travel Wall in my bedroom. Taped to it were pictures I'd pulled from magazines like *National Geographic* and *Life* of all of the places I planned to visit: Mount Rushmore... Niagara Falls... The Grand Canyon... Yellowstone National Park. In the middle of my collage was a huge map of the United States. I had developed a colorful system using sticker dots: red dots to mark the places I'd been, which focused mainly around central Massachusetts; green dots for all of the places I wanted to see throughout the rest of Massachusetts and surrounding New England states; yellow dots stretching across the remaining East Coast and as far west as the Mississippi River; blue dots covering the Midwest; and, purple on the West Coast, even in Alaska and Hawaii. It was my goal to visit every one of the fifty states.

"These are all the places you want to go?"

"Yeah. Someday," I said.

"Let's see. I've been here, and here, and here, here, here. And here, a couple of times." She pointed to several places in California, Texas, New Orleans, and all up and down the East Coast. "You know what this looks like," she said. "Remember those concentric circles you told me about a long time ago? That you saw yourself as part of concentric circles, moving farther away from your starting point? Now I get it."

"I may not end up doing it quite in this order, though," I told her, a grin creeping onto my face. "I think I'll end up hitting one of my purple dots soon... in California!"

"When?! With Tim? Have you told your parents? Will you fly out on your school breaks? Are you gonna stay in his dorm room with him?"

"Shh!" I held a finger in front of my mouth. "We haven't made definite plans yet, but we might get an apartment."

Sighing dreamily, Justine lay back on the bed. "It'll be so romantic. A secret rendezvous. You'd better report back to me everything that happens."

"Well, not everything!" I picked up a pillow and threw it toward her.

"My map would be kind of the opposite of that," she said, dodging the pillow, then propping herself up on one elbow to regard the Travel Wall again. "I'd have a lot of red dots all over the place, but I'd still put most of my other colors right back there." She pointed in the upper right-hand quadrant. "North Brookfield."

"Are you nuts! Why? When you have the chance to see so many places?" I was incredulous. I'd have given my left arm to go to half of where she'd already been!

"What can I say? This is home to me."

"Justine, you live in Fantasy World, thinking there's something magical about this town."

"It *is* magical! Besides, living in a fantasy sure beats the hell out of reality sometimes!"

I rolled my eyes. "Anywho... are you seeing Matt any time soon?"

Shrugging, she said, "I think tomorrow. He's called a few times. He's nice, right?"

I could feel my mood souring. "Justine! You blew off Kenny after only a couple of dates. Then you flirt with him, right in front of Matt. Don't be such a bitch."

"I'm not a bitch! First, I didn't 'blow off' Kenny. I went back to New Jersey! Second," her voice rising, "maybe you've found your one and only, but I'm not settling down. I'd die of boredom. I'm *sixteen*, for Chrissakes!"

"You treat guys like they're… disposable! Like they don't have feelings!" I saw how hurt Kenny was when Justine didn't keep in touch with him after she'd left last summer. He finally began dating another girl, and Justine acted like they'd both simply moved on. She didn't seem to realize he was nuts about her.

"Oh, come on, Eva! We live five hours apart. I couldn't possibly last in a long distance relationship. Who could?"

"*I* could. And I *will*, this year, when Tim's in California."

"Yeah, well, good luck with that. I sure couldn't do it."

"Justine." I controlled my voice. "Sometimes you're so self-centered when it comes to guys. Maybe what you need is to get *your* heart broken for a change, so you'll understand these games you play aren't nice."

"I'm not playing games! Why don't we agree to disagree on this. Matt doesn't seem to mind. He knows I'm only here for the summer. If it's not a big deal to him, why are you all bent out of shape?"

We sat on opposite ends of my bed in silence, glaring at each other. She was stewing in her own self-righteousness, but I wasn't giving in. After last summer, I had to listen to Kenny moaning about how they'd "really connected" and "why did she have to live so far away." But, she never wrote to him—not *once*—after she went home. I was kicking myself, having fixed her up with Matt. He'd told me he knew she wasn't interested in anything serious, but I saw how he looked at her when they were together. It was obvious he hoped she'd have a change of heart. Sometimes I wondered if she even *had* a heart when it came to guys.

"In other news… remember I told you what happened to my cousin Lisa?" Justine broke the silence. This was her way of making up with me. By changing the subject.

"You mean when she said she was raped on her date?" I decided to go with it.

"When she *was* raped on her date! She told him 'no' but he didn't stop.

That's rape!" Her voice was rising again. She took a deep breath and let it out in a long stream before continuing. "*Any*way, I felt terrible for her, like I wished I could do something to help. So Mom came up with an excellent idea. She's gotten me an internship at a shelter for battered women in Trenton. She knows the director. My job is to play with the kids and listen if the women want to talk. I can't give advice or anything. Just listen."

"Do you get paid for it?"

"No. It's volunteer. Still, I'm excited!"

I regarded my friend. With all of her convictions and beliefs, how passionately she stood up for what she thought was right and for the people she loved, in a lot of ways, she was also self-absorbed. Maybe this job would be good for her. Let her see what it means to have *real* problems. "I'm glad your mom found it for you. Sounds perfect."

She got up and stretched, standing in front of my poster of Eric Burdon. "Who's that?"

"The lead singer from The Animals. You know, 'House...'"

"...Of the Rising Sun.' Yeah, yeah, I know. They did one of my all-time favorite songs: 'Don't Let Me Be Misunderstood.'" Looking at me pointedly, she added, "That could be my anthem."

"Because your intentions are good?" I laughed, thrilled my years of music instruction had sunk in. "Come on, I'll give you a ride home. It's late."

I pushed aside my frustration. I knew Justine and I didn't share the same views about boys, so I'd just have to remember not to fix her up with any more of my friends.

I grabbed my keys and we were back to our usual banter, smacking and jabbing each other as we headed down the stairs. At the bottom, my brother, Craig, who had just come home from a night out, affectionately tousled my hair.

"Well, heeeyyy, Justine. I haven't seen you in a while. What are you up to?"

Craig was two years older than me and I'd always been the closest to him of all my siblings. Recently, he'd begun to go bald, but instead of mourning it, he'd opted to shave his entire head. As I turned around to watch their exchange, I felt an uneasiness in my stomach.

Justine's fingertips skimmed his smooth scalp. "Wow! I like it! Looks excellent. Eva's taking me home. Good seeing you!"

Wait! What was *that*. I was certain I saw them exchange a look—a secret smile—before she came flouncing down the stairs after me.

"What was that all about?" In all the years Craig and Justine had known each other, I didn't think they'd ever exchanged more than a handful of words.

"Nothing!" She sounded genuinely surprised. "What? I was only admiring his head. Reminds me of Kojak!"

"Yuk!" I tried to modify the harshness in my voice. "Craig's a whole lot better-looking than Kojak."

"He sure is," Justine smiled.

Okay, there it was again! That *look*! I swear I saw a trace of that wanton-woman expression on her face. "Hey! Knock it off! He's too old for you! He's twenty! And you're... you're *jailbait*!"

"What are you talking about? He's your *brother*, ewww! I only said he's cute!"

She sounded indignant and acted like my suspicions were outrageous. She was trying to pretend her motives were purely harmless. I didn't trust her. It looked to me like she was trying to add another stud to the mosaic on her denim jacket.

"Get bent, Justine!" I slammed the screen door in her face as I stormed out.

Hello, Dearie

"Bridge Over Troubled Water" – Simon and Garfunkel

Justine

"**A**RE YOU SEEING EVA TODAY? I haven't seen her around much lately." Aunt Peggy crossed the living room holding her coffee mug in one hand while balancing herself with her cane in the other. I jumped up from the sofa to take the mug from her and set it on the tray table next to her oversized, stuffed recliner. She slowly lowered herself into the chair and settled against the rectangular pillow embroidered with the saying "Home is Where the Heart Is" that she used for back support.

"I guess she's been busy at her job. Lynn says she hasn't talked to her, either." I wasn't sure what to think. I knew she was kind of pissed at me because of the whole Matt situation, and about Craig too, for some reason. But it'd been almost a week and I hadn't seen her. Every time I called her house, her mother said she was at work, or sleeping, or out. Even her feeding schedule for Smokey was all different. I didn't know how early she'd been coming in the mornings, but it must have been *really* early. Aunt Peggy usually served breakfast by 7:30 and I could tell by the fresh pile of hay at the gate, Eva had already come and gone. When she'd been there for the late day feeding, she was so fast and quiet, I hadn't even noticed.

"Honey? Would you mind moving a couple of the bells around for me? I want the one you just got me up front so I can see it better." Aunt Peggy had been finding little chores for me to "help" her. She didn't ask me outright if there was something wrong, but she knew.

Despite Aunt Peggy's efforts, I still felt empty inside. I mean, it wasn't like I'd been sitting home without *any* social life. Lynn and I had gone cruising a few times. And, of course, there was Matt. Although Eva thought I was leading him on, the truth was that I did like him. He was sweet and always planned fun things for us to do. Last week, he even took me to

152

Whalom Amusement Park. I hadn't been there since I was a kid when Mom and I went every summer so I could play my favorite game—the one where you shoot the water gun into the clown's mouth until his balloon explodes. Matt had wanted to keep going on the rides, but I insisted on trying for the 'Choice' prize at the water balloon race. After I'd won the gigantic stuffed Scooby Doo, it was a little hard to fit on the roller coaster.

"Justine, Eva's across the street. Don't you want to go see her?" I got up from Uncle John's chair with an uncertainty I hadn't felt since the first time I saw her all those years ago, when I'd rescued her from the briar patch.

Glancing out the window I did a double take, then sank back into the rocking chair. The rustic scene of the girl caring for her horse was as familiar to me as the label of a Hiram Walker Blackberry Brandy bottle. So familiar, the details barely registered in my conscious mind. Except when everything in the scene was wrong. Her car was nowhere in sight. Instead, her old ten-speed was propped against the gate. No wonder I hadn't heard her coming. And, those clothes. I hadn't seen her dress in those baggy old jeans and shapeless flannel shirts since she was fourteen. Her luxurious, auburn hair, always long and free, was pulled back into a grim ponytail. Watching Eva interact with Smokey, an eerie dread settled in my gut. It reminded me of the way she used to cling to him when she was being bullied in her early high school days. Instead of purposefully swiping the brush along each side, she was stroking him in a slow, hypnotic motion. Her other hand was resting on his back, never breaking contact. Anyone else would simply see a girl and her horse. I saw my hurting friend clinging to her security blanket.

Should I go out and try to talk to her? Should I leave her alone? I rested my forehead on the heels of my hands as I rocked slowly, thinking. Was this about me? My instincts were telling me no. Problems at home? Her mother never said anything when I called. Maybe she and Tim had a fight? But I'd be the first person she'd tell. I needed to go find out.

Lifting my head, I looked out the window. She was gone.

"Now what, God damn it!" Despite my exasperation, I chuckled as I imagined Eva's reaction to my taking the Lord's name in vain. Even after all of these years, she was still nudging me toward subscribing to her Catholic morals. I always nudged right back, thoroughly content with my own set of morals, thank you very much. Meanwhile, I studied the flat tire on my bike, knowing I'd have no other choice but to walk it the mile back to Aunt Peggy and Uncle John's while lugging a heavy bag of apples.

Aunt Peggy was having a rough day because her arthritis had flared up. Nonetheless, she was determined to make the Dutch apple cake she'd promised to mark the end of my summer visit. I'd offered to go buy the apples from Brookfield Orchards, but look at me! I was stuck with a worthless bicycle and what felt like ninety pounds of apples. The late August humidity wasn't helping. My clothes stuck to my damp body and little streams of sweat wormed down my scalp and face.

I hooked the bag over the handles of the bike and began to push. *Shit! This is going to take all day!* I set out, feeling like the tortoise from Aesop's fable. *Slow and steady wins the race.* I entertained myself by reciting the story, taking pleasure in exaggerating the arrogance of the hare who thought the pokey tortoise was no match for his speed. But, like that tortoise, I knew if I kept putting one foot in front of the next, I'd eventually make it home. *Slow and steady wins the race.*

As I trudged along, my mind wandered. I'd be going home in a few days, starting the eleventh grade in a week. I was excited to see my friends and check out the guys. There was Chris, a senior, who I'd begun a flirtation with right before the end of school last year. I was interested to see if it went anywhere. Plus, I'd be starting my internship at the shelter for battered women. This could be a very good year!

I rounded the corner onto Elm Street and passed the last of the apple trees when my cumbersome bike got the best of me. I laid it on the ground, making sure not to turn over the bag of apples, and plunked down on the ground next to it. I was sopping with sweat and berating myself for not having had the foresight to buy something to drink back at the orchard. My mouth was parched, my body soaked and exhausted, and I was becoming increasingly grouchy. *Stupid bike! Stupid apples! I didn't even want that stupid Dutch apple cake anymore! Stupid hot, humid weather! Stupid gnats, buzzing all around my face and getting caught in the sweaty bug trap I'd become! Stu—*

"Hello, Dearie."

I started at the sound of the hoarse voice behind me. I leapt to my feet and spun around. Standing four feet from where I'd just been sitting, partially obscured from sight by a tree at the edge of the woods, was a lanky man, definitely taller than my 6'2" dad. The face was almost covered by the brim of a tattered hat tipped forward over his eyes. But I could see his mouth. He was smiling, showing crooked, stained teeth with gaps where a few were missing.

I ran. I left the bike and the bag of apples. I forgot about my physical discomfort. My adrenaline transformed me from that tortoise into the hare.

I ran faster still, never looking back, straining for a glimpse of the Miller Ave street marker. Shadow Hill Cemetery flew past on my left as I concentrated on where I was going. *Don't look, don't look!* I pushed my cramping legs harder as I heard a car draw up next to me until, from the corner of my eye, I recognized it. I stopped and bent over with my hands on my knees, gasping for breath.

"Justine, is there a problem?" he called through the open window, touching his fingertips to the brim of his hat.

"There was... I saw... Rag Doll Man... scared me...."

"Did you have an accident?" Officer O'Reilly asked, then thrust his thumb towards the back seat. "Is this your bike I picked up from near the orchard?"

I explained about the flat tire and the creepy guy who'd spoken to me.

"Oh, you must mean Drifter Drake."

"Who?"

"Drake's a Vietnam vet. He's harmless. When he came back from war a few years ago, his parents had both died and he had no money, no job, nothing really waiting for him. He's been living in a shack he built back in those woods ever since."

"So, he's Rag Doll Man?" I asked.

"Rag Doll Man? Is that old story still going around? No. Drifter Drake is a hermit who generally wants to be left alone."

The cop leaned across the passenger seat and opened the door. "You've had quite a scare. Let me give you a lift back to your house."

I had an attack of apprehension, but pushed it away. Eva was right. I was too quick to assume all police were suspect. This guy had never been anything but nice to me. I took a step toward the open door.

KEEPING UP APPEARANCES

"Riders on the Storm" – The Doors

EVA

J USTINE LOOKED VICTORIOUS WHEN SHE finished her tale. I hated that, but in this case, had to admit she was justified.

"Was he wearing a trench coat?" I asked, glancing at my friend as I brought the car to a stop at the red light. This was the first time we'd hung out in over a week and I was doing my best to pretend everything was fine. "I've been so busy at work," I'd told her when she asked where I'd been. "My car's still in the shop," in answer to why I was driving my mom's old Ford Pinto.

"No," she said. "Pants and this long tunic. Like those Hare Krishnas you always see hanging around airports."

"I've never been in an airport, so I wouldn't...."

"You've *never* been in an *airport*!? How is—?" Her question was cut off by the revving engine of a souped-up Camaro, complete with racing stripes, dual exhaust pipes, and spoiler that had pulled along beside us. Two guys in their late teens or early twenties grinned at us.

"I've never flown any—" I yelled back as the driver next to me pressed his foot on the accelerator, making it impossible to finish my sentence.

Justine held her finger up to me, then made a circular motion to the boy in the car next to us. He rolled down his window and leaned out, allowing the motor to idle.

"Hey, baby," he said with a smirk.

"Hey. Could you do me a favor, please?"

"Anything for you, gorgeous." He nodded, revving the engine once more.

Justine shook her head and he stopped. "Seriously. My friend and I are trying to talk, and it's impossible for me to hear her above your overcompensation!"

I had just taken a sip of my beer and it spewed all over the inside of the windshield as I burst into laughter. The guys looked baffled as they tried to understand what she meant, and I sped away when the light turned green.

"Justine! You never change, do you?"

"I spoke to them politely."

"I thought you'd have learned your lesson after that whole mooning fiasco last year."

"It wasn't a fiasco for me!"

I took a moment to appreciate my friend. Her energy and humor. Her irreverence and sharp tongue. No matter how emotionally paralyzed I was, she could always distract me. *Star-filled sky... stinging burn as he slapped my face... the ripping sound of my shirt... the rusty taste of blood... the metallic flash of moonlight on the handcuffs.* Those images poured through me until my heart was racing.

"Eva?"

I looked up. "I'm sorry. What were you saying?"

"We were talking about Drifter Drake. That he's the one people keep thinking is Rag Doll Man. But, ha! I told you! You can tell Jane Williams and all of her little idiots, not only is Uncle John not Rag Doll Man, there's no such *thing* as Rag Doll Man! So there!"

As fascinating as this revelation was, I couldn't fully enjoy it. This was the time of the summer I usually dreaded. Justine was leaving in two days and we'd be apart for nine months with only our letters to keep us connected. I spent hours, sometimes days, putting my every thought and feeling into those letters. I treated them as a combination of Dear Diary and a writer's forum, cathartically baring my soul while perfecting my comedic craft. Justine was the master of both appreciating my humor and dispensing advice, and her responses never got to me fast enough when I'd been fighting with my parents or had started dating a new boy.

Not this year. I needed her to leave. I needed space from her questions. Today, she'd tried to get me to pick up one of our favorite games—wandering through the cemetery and making up stories about the people buried there. Shadow Hill. I hated it. I never wanted to go anywhere near it again.

"How did you hear all of that stuff about Drifter Dan?" I asked, trying to remain engaged in our conversation.

"Officer O'Reilly told me about him. After Rag Do... I mean, Drifter Dan... freaked me out."

My stomach heaved. I careened to a stop in a grocery store parking lot and dove under the seat, mumbling something about having dropped my cigarette pack. *Officer O'Reilly!* Even hearing his name made me physically ill.

I managed to pull out a cigarette and light it. My voice sounded bizarrely nonchalant to my ears. "Oh, Officer O'Reilly? You ran into him too?"

"Yeah. He gave me and my bike a ride home. You're right about him. He's okay," she paused for effect, "for a cop."

"Uh, yeah," I said, unconsciously pulling my knees together tightly to guard that place, deep inside of me, still bloody and tender. Like a kaleidoscope, fragments of colors and images and words cascaded through my mind, trying to reconstruct a complete picture of what happened That Night. I was exhausted, keeping the pieces from coming together, all while pretending everything was normal.

"Hellooo!" Justine called. "You're not listening to me."

"Sorry."

"What's going on, Eva?"

"I was, uh, thinking about college. I start next week."

"Did you sign up for your classes?" she asked.

"Uh, yeah, I did. I'm only taking four this semester."

"Do you have a roommate?"

"I'm going to live home and commute. Worcester is only a forty-minute drive and it'll save me a lot of money. Plus, there's no way I could leave Smokey."

She didn't say anything for the longest time.

I peeked over and found her staring at me, scrutinizing me, waiting for me to flinch, to give her a hint at what I wasn't saying to her.

Finally, she said, "I thought you were looking forward to getting out of North Brookfield. Doing the whole 'college experience.' Wasn't that the point?"

"This works out better."

I held my breath. It didn't take a genius to know where her third degree would lead next.

"How's Tim? Have you seen much of him, with work and all?"

"Uh, Tim and I broke up. He left last week, anyway, for California. It's better like this."

"Oh, Eva!" She was unable to disguise her shock. "He was so great! What happened?"

"We weren't as compatible as I'd thought."

"You won't be going out to see him? What about when he comes home for vacation?"

"No. It's over," I told her, choking on the words. "And, I'm fine. Really."

"Okay, okay, sure," she said, then quietly added, "I'm really sorry, Eva."

THE ENGAGEMENT PARTY

"Hotel California" – The Eagles

JUSTINE

G ENERALLY, I LOVED A PARTY. Friends, booze, music, boys. What's not to love? But Vicki, Eva's neighbor and informal mother figure of the Portable Party, and her fiancé Pablo's engagement party was unlike anything I'd ever attended. From the moment Eva opened the door into their cramped apartment above The Pub, I'd been as skin-pricklingly uncomfortable as if wearing clothing two sizes too small on my premenstrual bloated body. The thundering stereo with its woofers, subwoofers, decibels, or whatever the techno-terminology was, made my eardrums feel like they were about to rupture. I don't know if it was the noise, or the oxygen-sucking blanket of smoke, or the cramped, suffocatingly humid atmosphere, but within seconds of entering, I developed a crushing migraine.

"Excuse me… pardon me… excuse me…." I squeezed my way through the wall-to-wall people. Across the room, I waved to some of the Porta-Party kids, crammed into various groups.

"Hey, Carl!" I shouted to be heard above the din. He gave me a semi-smile and a quick chin jerk. His sweaty face was bright red.

"…stine," Rob, standing by the open window, was smiling toward me.

At the hint of my name, I managed to raise my hand to wave to him, only knocking into three people in the process. Still as gangly as ever but somehow glummer each time I saw him, he averted his sorrowful eyes after I acknowledged him.

And, there was one of the jimmychuckandlarry threesome. Eva informed me it was Larry, who'd gotten a job downstairs as a bartender. I tried to ram my way toward him, but couldn't find a path through the bodies. Instead, I feigned enthusiasm as I congratulated Vicki and Pablo when they pressed past. Warm, skunk-tasting beer in hand, I made every effort to keep my nose from wrinkling at the overpowering stench of patchouli and body odor.

I gave up mopping the perspiration trickling down my neck and shouldered my way through the throng in search of the bathroom. A little cold water on my face might help my throbbing head. Passing through the kitchen, I paused to see what the big attraction was around the dinette set. On the table, there was a small pile of white powder. Several people were intently scooping smaller rations from the pile, using the edge of a razor blade. Dropping the powder on the table in front of them, they'd work at it with the blade, chopping and scraping until satisfied with the line they'd created. Leaning over with one end of a rolled dollar bill up the nose, each would snort the substance, moving the dollar-tube along the length of the line until it vanished.

Staggering down the short hallway with my vision starting to blur from pain, I knocked on a closed door. There was no answer. Turning the knob, I asked, "Is anyone in here?" A voice called, "Come on in." *Shit!* I'd walked into the bedroom, with a huge king-sized bed right in the middle of it. I couldn't even begin to guess how many naked bodies were all draped and intertwined with one another. Girls? Guys? Some of each? Several heads lifted and invited me to join them.

"Uh, yeah, umm, no thanks," I mumbled, backing out of the room as quickly as possible. I'd heard about orgies—my friends and I had even joked about them, but people actually did this? I bumped into someone in the hall and mumbled, "Excuse me."

"Well, hey, Sexy. Are you coming to join our little party?" A shirtless guy—an un-hot Jim Morrison wannabe—hovered over me, backing me against the wall. He pressed his body against mine and I could feel his hot, rank breath on my neck as he bent to kiss me.

"Get off me, scumbag!" I shoved him away and bolted to hunt down Eva. I found her engaged in conversation with Vicki and Pablo.

"Hey, Eva, I'm not feeling well. Can you drive me home? Thanks for a great time, you guys." I offered a wavering smile.

In the fresh, cool air outside, I sank to the ground to rest my pounding head in my hands as I gave Eva a rundown of what I'd seen. "Holy shit! Who does that? So much for my image of country bumpkins and hayseeds. I've never seen *any*thing like that back home."

"I don't know most of those kids. Maybe they were Pablo's friends. Do you need Excedrin? Water? Food?"

"No, I'm fine. Seriously. It was kind of freaky, though," I admitted, chuckling at the image of all those bodies writhing on the bed. "I'm already planning the story for my friends back home. Maybe I'll say I actually considered joining in. Or, better yet, that I did! Excellent! And, it was all guys and I was the only girl." I thought about other story possibilities. "I know! I'll tell them—"

"I mean the guy who attacked you in the hall! Did he hurt you? How did you get away from him?"

"Oh, that creep? He was nothing! I pushed him off me."

She continued staring at me. "Justine, I'm really sorry. You sure you're okay?"

"It's no big deal. Really, Eva. It's fine."

After I'd washed off the filth of the evening with soap and water, I climbed into bed and thought about the party. The packed, sauna-like apartment; the skin-crawling sensation from dozens of bodies pressing against me; the horrible smell; the ear-splitting noise. The vacant-eyed kids snorting coke and the mass of bodies on the bed had left me feeling empty inside. I remembered something Eva said to me a few years ago. That I had romanticized North Brookfield. She'd accused me of not seeing its gritty underbelly. I was beginning to understand what she meant.

WHAT HE DID THAT NIGHT

"Have You Ever Seen the Rain?" – Creedence Clearwater Revival

EVA

JUSTINE WAS HEADED BACK TO New Jersey. They usually left right after lunch. It would be easier with her gone. She required so much attention and, while I usually loved her high-spirited presence, it was exhausting. I barely had enough strength for myself. I'd write to her soon.

All I wanted was sleep... and escape. When my body finally did shut down, the nightmares started again and my racing heart woke me up, my body soaked in sweat.

A do-over. Wouldn't it be great if, in everyone's life, God let us have one do-over? One chance to make a different choice? I'd use it now. I wouldn't have gotten into his car That Night. Instead, I would have run.

Snuggling deeper into the sheltering comfort of my bed, soft pillows cradling me, the light from the full moon glowed through my curtains. Without turning my head, I could scan my entire refuge and its familiarity was consoling. My record collection; my books; the ashtray I made in ceramics class in tenth grade; my knickknacks collected through the years; my newest posters of Mick Jagger, which replaced the pictures and map on what used to be my Travel Wall; the long, wooden keepsake box, containing every letter Justine had ever written to me. And, the brightly decorated hatbox with the oversized rose blooms where I'd saved each ticket stub, pressed flower, card, note, photograph, and memento chronicling my life with Tim.

My parents' voices drifted up from downstairs. They were worried about me. They liked Tim. Justine liked Tim. So did Lynn. Everyone in North Brookfield liked Tim, and I bet everyone in Stanford, California would like him too. But, no one liked him more than I did. And, no one understood why we broke up. Least of all, Tim. It was better this way. He wouldn't want me anymore. After what I did That Night.

I stepped into the car, modestly gripping my mini skirt in place as I sat. "How are Peter and Jennifer?"

"Good, good. Getting big. Eight and ten."

"Oh, wow. If ever you need me to babysit again..."

"Yeah, is forty too old for a babysitter?" He chuckled, turning to look at me. The light from the dashboard cast an unearthly glow on his face and turned his blond hair green. "How old are you, Eva? You must be sixteen?"

"I'm eighteen, sir."

"Eighteen! All grown up. And, Eva, no need to be so formal, right? I've known you since you were little, after all." He reached his hand to pat the inside of my naked left thigh. I jerked my leg away and scooted as far as I could get against the door.

He's only being friendly, I'd told myself. He's a good guy. He's got two children—eight and ten. I turned to look out the passenger window into the darkness, the backdrop of my childhood speeding past. Dunn Brook, where Craig and I used to hunt frogs. The town dump where I went every Saturday morning with Dad to take the week's garbage. There was the Humphrey's house with the biggest pool around, a favorite hangout for the local kids on steamy summer days. Rural roads past Brookfield Orchards where my family went on Sundays for the bushel of apples that would last us until the following weekend. Where Justine and I stole apples a couple of years back.

"You don't mind if I do a quick drive through the cemetery, do you? To make sure everything's okay. It is my job, you know." He winked at me as he steered the car through the main gate and past the engraved limestone sign. Shadow Hill Cemetery.

He's a good guy. Everybody in town says so.

Was it too late for me to go visit Smokey in his pasture? The illuminated numbers on my clock read nearly ten o'clock. Yeah, definitely too late.

A shower. I'll take a shower. It'll be my fourth one today. That's okay. Other than being with Smokey, it's the only place where I feel something besides this numbness. The place where I can cry without being cross-examined. The place where I can try to wash away my disgrace.

He drove down the narrow main road past the discreetly hidden sensors that triggered melancholy music. In the moonless night. Surrounded by the graves of long-dead town residents. The lament of church hymns. He stopped the car in the farthest back corner, deep in the cemetery. Only woods and crumbling stone walls around us. Shivering, I crossed my arms in front of me. Pulled my poncho tighter.

"Eva," He swiveled his body and leaned toward me, pushing my bangs away from my eyes. "You've grown into quite the beauty."

"I n-n-need to go home." I shrank away from him.

"You didn't think I noticed you, did you?" His words were seductive. Intimate and practiced. He inched closer on the bench seat to stroke my hair. "I've noticed you. Have you noticed me too, hmm?" He lowered his lips to my neck.

"P-p-please. I need to go h-ho—" I pulled back. The rotten egg stench of alcohol on his breath made my stomach heave.

"I've seen you looking at me, Eva. I've seen you." He peered at me with eyes lit only by the glow from the dash. His icily unfamiliar eyes that never crinkled to match the grin on his mouth, went dark when he turned off the engine. His words sounded wrong too. Elongated and drawn out. Like a 45 record being played at 33. "I know you want this... Oh, baby, you feel so good... Oh, Eva, be nice to me."

"Please! Don't! I need to—"

He kissed my neck. My chest. Pressing the scratchy wool from my poncho into my skin. "Eva," he murmured, "...feels good...."

"Please, don't." I tried to push him away from me. I didn't want him to be mad. He's a good guy. Everybody likes him. He's got two kids—eight and ten.

He pinned me firmly with one hand. Pulled up my poncho. I struggled to pull it back down.

"Eva." His voice turned harsh. "Be nice. I know you want this."

"I don't... please... I need to go...."

He whipped out handcuffs. Slapped the freezing steel around my right wrist. Threaded the other cuff through a handle over the door. Imprisoned my left wrist. Shredded the yarn of my poncho. Tore open my blue embroidered peasant blouse. Revealed I picked the wrong day to go braless.

"No, no, no, no... please..."

"You like that?" he asked, his sour breath filling my mouth. I bucked my hips, momentarily knocking him off me. He slapped me across the face. My head snapped to one side. "Knock it off, bitch," he said in a deep, threatening growl.

I gasped for air and opened my eyes to stop the spinning. Concentrated on the star-speckled sky above me. There's the North Star. And the Little Dipper. *His mouth on my breast. Kissing me. Biting me. Bile surged into my throat. I fought it down. My knee lurched upward toward his crotch. He punched me in my left cheek. Lights flashed before my eyes and, all at once, I had that surreal feeling—out of body—like when I'd been smoking pot. I existed on a physical level, I knew I did. But, my mind was free, escaping the flesh he was brutalizing.* There's the Big Dipper. There's Cassiopeia. Is that Orion's belt?

"Mmmm, baby. You taste so good." His voice sounded as if it was coming from a great distance. He slowly licked my quivering lower lip, then my upper.

Block it out, Eva. Block it out.

Dragging myself from bed, I retrieved my discarded shoes and carried them to my closet. Opening the door, it fell forward. Mocking me. The garbage bag I'd stuffed as far as possible into the armoire spewed its contents to remind me. I yanked it closed, then pushed it, beat it, tried to bury it, in the darkest, farthest back corner. I didn't want to see it… *any* of it. Any of those clothes or the shoes or the horrible perfume Justine had picked out. Buried deep in the bottom of the bag was the outfit. The tattered peasant blouse and mini skirt. The ragged poncho my mother had lovingly made for me with her own two hands. I told her I'd lost it. Everything except the shredded, bloody panties that I'd buried in the bathroom trash. That Night.

Smokey. I was with my beloved Smokey. Brushing him as the warmth of the sun radiated off his dazzling, silver coat. The stiff, leather saddle creaked when I threw it over his back. As I tightened the straps under his belly, checking that they were holding firm, his velvety nose nuzzled my ear.

Repulsive tongue slimed down my stomach. "So pretty… sweet baby… mmmm, taste good." Skirt jammed up around my hips. Scratching of lace panties yanked down my thighs. Sound of a pants zipper. All so far away.

With my left foot in the stirrup, I threw my other leg over Smokey. Sitting high on my perch, I gently nudged his sides with my heels. We began a slow, easy trot across the field.

My virginity was ripped from me. But, I was only conscious of galloping at full tilt with my Smokey, the rhythmic pounding of his hooves drowning out my pitiful howls, our hair billowing loose and carefree behind us. We raced away, speeding on and on and on….

That Night.

I wondered how Justine's cousin, Lisa, was doing. After she was… I wish I'd asked more questions, but… I couldn't bring it up. Justine would get suspicious. I couldn't take the chance. No one could ever know what he did to me. Not even my best friend.

"This is our little secret, okay, Eva?" He grinned at me as he buckled his belt. "You wouldn't want your parents to know what you did."

He unlocked my arms and I absently massaged the red scrapes on my wrists. I didn't feel the raw skin.

"Those cuffs a little tight, baby?" he asked in a soothing tone, then added, most sincerely and graciously, "You were great. Thank you." As if I'd simply delivered a sermon at church. I was just a girl he knew from around town.

He had two kids—eight and ten. I knew his wife. They sat three pews behind my family on Sundays. Behind me, my parents, my brother Craig, and whichever other siblings happened to be in attendance any given week. And, Tim. My love. Every Sunday, Tim sat next to me, secretly holding my hand in his on the bench between us.

"Here you go, Eva," he declared chivalrously.

I was home. Somehow, I had pulled on my tattered clothing and was sitting in the cruiser with him in front of my house as if we'd merely gone for a pleasant drive. As if he'd rescued me from the side of the road and driven me straight here.

I glanced toward him, unable to meet his eyes, and the friendly expression on his face was the one I knew from church. He's a good guy. Everyone says so.

I needed to get into the shower before my parents came up, like clockwork, at 11:30. I spun the knobs to adjust the temperature, hiccupping as tears worked their way down my face. Safely in the deluge of water, I finally relaxed. I pictured the water washing away his awful words—*come on, baby, I know you want this*—his brazen hands touched me in places no one had ever touched before. I imagined the water cleansing my body of his disgusting mouth and tongue, and suppressed a wail when I tried to lather away the humiliation left behind in my battered vagina.

Finally, when not another single tear squeezed from my eyes, I shut off the water. In the morning, in about seven hours, I'd be back in here, going through this ritual once more. I needed to get out and into my room before my parents saw me like this. They'd be so ashamed if they knew what I did.

CHAPTER 7

1978

SUGAR COATED THREATS

"The End of the Innocence" – Don Henley

EVA

"Zena, who's four, was real protective of her little brother and sister. You should see the looks she gave me." Sitting with her back against Wausau's blade, Justine crossed her arms, raised one eyebrow, and pursed her lips, imitating the distrustful posture of the little girl she'd met at the women's shelter. "It took us two weeks to find them a safe house so I got to know her family pretty well. I went to see them almost every day after school. At first, Zena never looked at me. And never smiled. But the day they were leaving, she gave me this huge hug, like she didn't want to let me go." Justine added quietly, "I hope they're okay."

"Don't you keep in touch with them?"

"No. It doesn't work like that. To keep the women and children safe, it's all done secretly. It's for their protection... and ours."

I studied my friend's face and saw a serenity unlike anything I'd ever seen there before. "But, it must be so hard. Getting close to them, then never seeing them again."

"Yeah, but it's nothing compared to what they're going through. I like knowing I've done something, even in my small way."

"It doesn't sound so small. Working with the kids. Getting them to trust you. It sounds like you help them," I said. "And that you like it."

"It's fab. I hate seeing those babies, though, their eyes so... empty... and scared. They're too young to have seen so much."

"I'm glad it's worked out for you, Justine." I examined her more closely. "You seem, I don't know, more subdued? Something's different."

"Not *too* different, I hope!" She laughed. "Nope. I'm still your wild and crazy friend. That'll never change."

"Oh, I don't know. I was pretty impressed with you earlier at the package

171

store. When those guys honked and yelled at us? I half expected you to take a baseball bat to their headlights."

"I was never *that* bad!"

No, she was never *quite* that bad. But, she didn't fly off the handle the way she used to. Even with me, she was more diplomatic. Instead of making some snotty comment about dressing like a hick, she'd eyed me up and down and asked me how I was doing.

"So, tell me the truth. You really only went out with two guys this year, Justine?" I asked in disbelief. "Chris and Dennis?"

"That's right, Eva," she said. "Can you believe it? And, Chris and I were together for *six months*! That's definitely a record for me."

"Were you in love with him?"

Tilting her head to one side, she said, "Come on, Eva. You know me. I fall in love for about five minutes, then it gets boring. With Chris, it took a little longer, but it *definitely* got boring."

"How so?"

"Eh, he got all possessive and, you know, acted like he owned me." Smiling, she added, "You can imagine how well that went over with me."

"What about the other one? Dennis?"

"Nah. He was cute, but played head games. He was more immature than the kids I work with at the shelter." She shook her head and said, with a touch of self-importance, "I'm too busy for that nonsense."

I thought about the blur of boys I'd dated this past year. Nothing serious. No one particularly interesting. Nothing but lots of warm bodies, temporary shields against the demons that visited me every night. As happened a dozen times each day, my thoughts strayed to Tim, sending waves of misery all the way to my fingertips. Forcing his image from my mind, I looked up to find Justine scrutinizing me.

"So…" I began.

"Eva, when are you going to tell me what's going on with you? I hardly heard from you this year. Nothing about your family, the Portables, a boy… or why you quit school."

"Oh, you know." I studied the small patch of moss growing by Wausau's left arm. "There's no one worth mentioning. There's been a bunch of guys. No one special."

"That's not like you. You've never been the love-'em-and-leave-'em type. In fact, I seem to recall you giving me a whole lot of shit for my dating history."

"I just haven't found anyone yet."

"Have you heard from Tim?"

"*No.* We haven't spoken. I told you we're over."

Justine leaned toward me and took a long breath as I braced myself for Round Two of her cross-examination. Some things don't change. "So, why'd you leave college? What'd your parents say about it? Are you going back in September? What are you doing with your time? Working?"

"Jeez, Justine! Give me a chance already! I left college because I was burned out and needed a break. My parents were pissed off, but it wasn't working for me. Yes, I'm planning to go back in September. Yes, I've been working full-time."

Justine's face flashed a riot of thoughts as she processed what I'd told her. To her credit, she didn't continue to badger me and whatever millions of questions were racing through her mind, she kept them to herself. Mostly. "*This* September?"

With a burst of laughter, I gave her a little push. "Yes, *this* September!"

She leaned back against Wausau, crossed her arms, raised one eyebrow, and looked at me skeptically. I watched her eyes search mine. I knew her brain was working overtime, processing and analyzing every word I said, every gesture I made, putting together every piece to try to figure out the puzzle I'd become to her. If there was one person on this Earth who would persist until she understood exactly what was going on with me, it was Justine. And I couldn't risk that.

I pulled out a joint, lit it, took a long hit, and handed it to her. "Welcome home. Here's to a great summer. Quit looking at me like that. You look exactly like the little girl, Zena, you told me about!"

I COULDN'T CLEAR THE FOG out of my head. It wasn't only the joint we smoked before picking up munchies. I was also trying to keep two mental steps ahead of Justine so she wouldn't quiz me to death. Luckily, when she was stoned, her brain couldn't hold a thought for more than a second before it went whizzing off to the next.

We wandered down one aisle of the IGA and up the next, each potato chip bag and caramel candy bar setting off Justine's enthusiasm. "Ooo, my favorite! Oh, this is what I'm craving! Ahh, this looks fab!" She stood transfixed in the freezer section, trying to figure out how we could cook a frozen pizza.

"Where'd you get that?" I asked, nodding toward the open soda can in her hand.

"Don't worry," she said. "I'll pay for it." Then she leaned closer to me and whispered, "Cotton mouth!" before erupting into hysterics.

"Ladies." A masculine voice spoke from behind us.

"Oh, uh, hi, Officer O'Reilly," Justine said, snapping to attention. "I'm going to pay for it, I swear! I was thirsty and, well... I'm now... to pay for it."

"I'm sure you will," he answered. "Hello, Eva." He tipped his hat at me. I forced myself to nod in return.

"We were looking for snacks. Out driving, ya know... got hungry... needed food... drinks."

Damn it! Justine and that mouth! I, on the other hand, couldn't find a single word to push out of mine. Even though we'd smoked a short time ago, I was suddenly sober. From the corner of my eye, I glimpsed his blond crew cut and those blue eyes I'd once thought were so kindly. They were hard, even cruel. And his thin-lipped mouth twisted into a sneer.

"I know how that is, Justine." He pulled those smirky thin lips into an amiable smile.

"Didn't have lunch... got hungry... snacks...."

The cop ran his hand down Justine's arm, as if demonstrating his concern for her plight. As she reached for a box of Screaming Yellow Zonkers from the next to the bottom shelf, he watched me above her head. His smile was gone. His eyes squinted with hostility.

Justine dropped the package of glazed popcorn into the cart, oblivious to the unspoken conversation I imagined had occurred.

Him: *You'd better keep your mouth shut.*

Me: *I haven't said anything.*

Him: *And you'd better not.*

Me: *Just leave me alone.*

Him: *You wouldn't want anything to happen to your friend, would you?*

"It was nice seeing you again, Officer O'Reilly," Justine said cheerily. "We've got to go... help my aunt... take care of Eva's horse... feed the dog...."

"Glad you're back, Justine. I'm sure I'll see you around this summer." He touched her shoulder, then turned toward me. "Eva, you take care." He held my eyes until he was confident his message had been received.

My body began to tremble.

Once he was gone, I hurried us to the check out. "You know, Justine, I'm going to need to head home. I have to get my run in for today, then take a shower before dinner. My mother's expecting me."

"Ya sure? I thought we had the afternoon together."

"Yeah, I forgot we're having a family dinner tonight. We'll talk later?"

"Okay. Besides, what's this new fitness kick you're on? Training for a marathon? Or to outrun the cops?" She chuckled at her joke.

"Well, uh, you know." I didn't bother to finish. We'd paid for our food and Justine was engrossed in her Choco'Lite bar.

Break Down and Turned On

"Spirit in the Night" – Bruce Springsteen

Justine

"Justine. Can you come here, honey? I think we have a problem." I found Aunt Peggy sitting at one end of the kitchen table with her bills and bank statement laid out in front of her. "I don't know what some of these charges are and my monthly budget is off."

I pulled up a chair and sat next to her. Scrutinizing the Visa bill, I ran down the fees item by item, reading them aloud. "Lane Bryant, $76.89... IGA, $23.54... Sears, $231.50." I looked up. "Sears? Did you buy a new appliance or something?"

Shaking her head firmly, she insisted, "It must be wrong."

I studied her other credit card bill. MasterCard. Several small amounts from stores and restaurants Aunt Peggy frequented. "Wait. FTD. Flowers?" She shook her head. "Sears, again? $499.95?" Aunt Peggy was still shaking her head.

"Okay. If it was one credit card, I'd think maybe it's a mistake. But two?" Grabbing the statements, I made a couple of phone calls and within twenty minutes, I was sitting back at the table.

"Who's Maryann O'Connell?" I asked.

"She goes to our church. Why?"

"Those weird purchases were delivered to her, but paid for with your credit card. You don't think she stole your information somehow, do you?"

"Justine, she wouldn't do that. She's a nice lady, married with three children." The panic rose in her voice. "I can't afford this! I don't know what to do!"

I'd learned how tight money was for her on her modestly fixed income when I began helping her with the household budget last summer. Patting her arm, I said, "I'm gonna call Mrs. O'Connell and see what she says. It's probably a big misunderstanding. Then, we'll go from there, okay? Don't worry. I'll take care of this."

I'D CHEWED AT THE HANGNAIL on my ring finger until I'd ripped it off and made it bleed. Eva waited patiently for me to finish my story.

"Pass me a beer?" Taking a long drink, I relaxed against Wausau and stuck the bloody cuticle in my mouth. "Uncle John gets out of the hospital tomorrow. It turns out, even though Aunt Peggy's been setting out his pills for him every day, he hasn't been taking them. Neither of us realized he'd had a break until I talked to the woman in town. Then we put two and two together."

"Does Peggy still have to pay for all of the things he bought her?" Eva asked.

"No. Mrs. O'Connell sent back the refrigerator and the TV. And, thank God, she and her husband were nice about it when we explained. The other things, the flowers and the candy, Aunt Peggy has to pay for. I called Dad and he's sending me a check to help."

"John really believed he and Mrs. O'Connell were engaged?"

I shrugged one tired shoulder. "Yeah. That's the mark of schizophrenia. He can't tell fantasy from reality."

"What if it happens again?"

"I took his credit cards out of his wallet. Aunt Peggy's gonna start hiding her purse because she thinks he's been taking money from it. We'll have to watch and make sure he's actually taking the pills." I sighed, the heaviness in my chest easing for the first time since morning.

"I bet Peggy's wicked glad your parents made that deal with you, right?"

It was a great offer. My dad was paying me to help Aunt Peggy around the house —cleaning, shopping, errands, whatever. While it involved a lot more responsibility than I was used to having, it meant I got to be here for the whole summer, instead of having to find a job in New Jersey. "Yeah. And he said if it works out, I can do it every summer, if I want. Pretty awesome, huh?"

"Yes, but I can see that it will be *my* job to help get your mind off things for a while. Come on." She dragged me to my feet. "I'm taking you to a party."

THE PORTABLES WERE DODGING THE cops by meeting north of town at

Horse Pond. With the windows down in Eva's new Mustang II, the gentle summer evening breezed through the car. All I saw in the dim light on either side of the packed dirt road was dense woods to our right and water on our left.

"Will there be any cute guys? Will I know anyone? How did you hear about this place? Where *is* everyone?" I stuck my head out of the window, searching for any sign of the gathering.

"We have to go a bit farther. And, yes. I'm sure there will be guys. Cute? Who knows? We don't exactly have the same taste."

I caught the growing strains of "Blinded by the Light" by Manfred Mann as we made the final turn. "Fab!" The velvety black surface of Horse Pond reflected the moon in a sea of sparkling light.

"This is it. Looks like a huge turnout."

All of the heaviness from the long day lifted from my shoulders. I hadn't seen any of the old gang since I'd been back, and Eva'd heard several of them would be here tonight. My eyes adjusted to the smoky atmosphere, lit by headlights from several cars and the full moon.

"Uh, there's Matt. Do you want to say 'hi'?" Eva nodded toward one of the groups.

As we approached, he dropped his arm from around the shoulders of a red-haired girl. I felt a tiny twinge of regret, thinking about all of the time we'd spent together last year.

"Justine!" He hugged me as his companion shot me the death glare. "It's great to see you. Back for the summer?"

I glared back spitefully at the girlfriend, holding Matt's embrace a little longer than necessary. "You look amazing, Matt." Eva dragged me away from the crowd, moving us quickly to another group. And, who was with them? Kenny! He too had a date who eyed me with hostility. I was half-tempted to reassure her Kenny and I were simply old friends, and half-tempted to flirt outrageously with him just to piss her off.

"Skank."

I whipped around to see who'd said it. No one met my eyes. Instead, I heard sniggers and saw sidelong smirks. My heartbeat pounded in my ears. Yanking my moist shirt sleeves out of my sweaty armpits, I'd taken two rapid steps toward the blur of faces when Eva grabbed my arm and pulled me away.

"So, have you seen this lovely pile of, uh, what is this?" she asked, pointing to the ground. "Worm poop? Or, maybe they're gold nuggets? We could—"

"Eva, stop!" I was in no mood to be pacified. "What the hell's their problem? What'd I do to them?"

"Don't antagonize them. You know you were trying to piss off their girlfriends. Ignore them. Come on, let's go find the rest of the gang."

I started to insist I wasn't afraid of a bunch of insecure girls, when… *Holy Hotness, Batman!* That boy standing by the edge of the parking lot was cute. *Really* cute. All my anger, all my hurt, and every thought of Kenny, Matt, and their bimbos evaporated. That gorgeous hunk. That tall, lean, muscular body. That tight blue t-shirt. Those low-slung, slightly flared, perfectly-fitting jeans—not baggy with a droopy ass and not so tight they hugged him obscenely. Those Converse. Not the typical loafers or Sperry Top Siders of the boys back home, or the combat-style boots worn by most of the boys around here. But black, low-top Converse sneakers. I've always had a thing for a guy in Converse.

And that hair! The guys at school obeyed the dress code, keeping theirs short—fussy-looking. Even the 'rebels' had it fastidiously clipped around their ears. In North Brookfield, I'd met few guys with hair shorter than mine. But this boy had dark brown, nearly black locks, falling to his collar, all full and curly—loose, touchable curls. My fingers twitched, imagining the silky bounce as they burrowed in those curls.

How long have I been staring? When I snapped my gaping jaw shut, his grin widened, displaying beautifully straight, white teeth, as my heart, like a guitar string that'd been plucked by tender, yet commanding, fingers vibrated and enfolded me in its melody. Dear *God*, was he good-looking! I raised my eyes to his and stiffened. It wasn't that even from here I could see they were light-colored, framed by long, black lashes. It was the *way* he was staring at me. Intimately, but not in the undressing-me-with-his-eyes sort of way. More like somehow he knew me. The *real* me, carefully hidden deep inside.

In that moment, I knew him too. Not a word had been exchanged or a kiss shared, but I knew.

I gave myself a shake. Yeah, he was cute. So what? Turning toward Eva, I focused on her moving mouth and the buzz of conversation floating around me. Benny and Ronny had joined us and were babbling something so unintelligible I couldn't be bothered to decipher it. My thoughts kept straying fifteen feet away.

Stop it, Justine! You aren't one of those idiot girls who acts like a doofus over some guy. Was he still looking at me? Please *be looking at me.* With my peripheral vision, I could see he was. *What should I do? Should I go over there? Speak to him?*

"…ready? We need to get going." Eva shook my arm to get my attention.

"Huh? What'd ya say?"

"You're going to be late if we don't leave. Come on!"

"Already? Okay." I risked it and looked over at him. His eyes bore into me and, again, my heart twanged.

Shit!

Eva filled me in on the gossip as we drove away. Who everyone was. Who those bitchy girls were. How Kenny had kept looking at me all evening, hadn't I noticed? I guessed I should be more interested in what she was saying, but all I could think about was that boy. Finally, as we approached the center of town, I casually mentioned him.

"What's his story?" I asked.

"Who's story?" She looked pensive for a moment, then recognition washed across her face. "Ooooh! Danny Stevenson!?"

"Yeah," I said with practiced casualness. "I'm thinking he's someone I might like to know better."

"Danny Stevenson?! *Really*?!"

"Yes, *really*!" My words shot out a little too fast and forcefully. "What's wrong with Danny Stevenson?"

"Okay, okay. Nothing. Nothing at all. He's great. It's just…."

"Just?"

"He grew up down the street from me. I remember playing softball when we were five. He was such a spaz! And, the time he went trick-or-treating as a lamb. Oh! And when he was in sixth grade and asked every girl in his class to be his girlfriend! And, *and*… the time—"

"*Any*way," I interrupted with a haughty tone. "I thought he was cute."

She immediately began backpedaling. "Oh, yeah, yeah. He's great. He did go out with Jessica Taylor, last year's senior class prom queen. I guess he's kinda cute."

"Kinda? *Really*?! He's adorable! Where does he live? Where does he work? Does he go to college? Where does he hang out?"

"Whoa, there! He lives in the next town over. Hey! Actually, I do know where he spends a lot of his time. Remember that recording studio I showed you? Long View Farm? He's, like, good friends with the owner, or the manager or something, and hangs out there."

"Hmmm." Despite Eva's reluctance, I'd decided Danny Stevenson was definitely someone I was going to get to know.

WHAT IS LOVE?

"Because the Night" – Patti Smith Group

EVA

"I DON'T KNOW WHAT IT FEELS like to be in love. Lust, definitely, but love? Doubtful. Does it even exist? A couple of girls I went to school with were always claiming to be in love. I might be more inclined to believe them if the objects of their undying affection didn't change as often as their underwear." Justine's eyes glazed over as she became lost in her reverie. Suddenly, they refocused and landed on me. "Like Romeo and Juliet. Love at first sight? *Pffft*. You can't love someone you don't really know. The whole idea is ridiculous. They were only a couple of horny teenagers!"

"Whaaat are you talking about?! You're in love every time you turn around!"

We were hanging-out in my bedroom on the hottest afternoon in July that summer. I sat cross-legged on my vanity bench, facing Justine who lounged on the bed, dreamily studying a crack in the plaster ceiling and absently twirling a lock of hair around her finger while she recounted her reaction to Danny.

"Listen to you!" I was livid and on a mission. I leapt to my feet in the most graceful and passionate movement I ever made, and covered the length of my bedroom in one stride. Reaching to the back of my closet, I pulled out a long, wooden box, then thrust it in front of her triumphantly as if sharing my discovery of the Ark of the Covenant.

"There!"

"Whaa…?" Justine propped herself up on an elbow, seemingly annoyed I dared disturb her blissful daydream about Danny.

"Your letters! Evidence!!" I planted my face within two inches of hers, and grinning ear to ear, held the box up to her nose.

182

"Whaa...?"

"The let-ters!" I cackled in my best yet imitation of the Wicked Witch of the West. "How quiiickly we forget, my pretty!" I extended my hands and waved my fingers, and it was not difficult to imagine those fingers were long, green, and crooked as I pointed at her accusingly. "The let-ters!" Pointing my index finger straight up and then slowly aiming right between Justine's eyes, I grinned. "Let's seeee..." I cackled again, then shot a long green finger and thumb into the box and emerged with a random piece of stationery, which I theatrically waved in front of her nose. I scanned the letter briefly before finding the damning paragraph. I waved my finger at her, still in witch mode, and read:

"Dear EEEEEva,

Today in study hall, my friend, Tessssssa passed a note to me. (Cackle) It said that someone by the name of... The Tin Man... wants to go oouuuut with me... I never heard of him before, but she said he sits behind me in fourth period. When I got to claaasss, I turned and looked, and there was the most (I changed my voice to a high-pitched, breathless imitation of hers) there was the most gorgeous guy I had ever seen in my life!! His skin was the most beautiful color of aluminum, and he had the most adorable pointy hat! Like a funnel! Eva, *I think I'm in love!*"

With that, I collapsed on the bed, amused with myself to the point of hysteria, while Justine crossed her arms and tried to look angry.

"That does not sound like me!! It does not!" Her voice rose with indignation.

"That does not sound like me!" I mocked in falsetto, literally rolling on the bed from laughter. I was laughing so hard I was afraid I might choke and, for a minute, she looked hopeful that I would.

She sat on the bed, arms crossed, waiting for me to recover. "That's not me. I *don't* fall in love."

I was still giddy. "Okay, then, what is it? I could pull ten more letters out of this box, and every one of them would mention a new boyfriend. The next, new great love. Everything perfect. *Compatible.* Until... the next letter, and then it's on to someone else. That's why I was nervous to introduce you to Kenny, Justine. Or to Matt. These guys play for keeps and, to you, it's just a little..." I was searching for words, "...it's a little *square dance*! Grab the next partner, do-si-do!"

"You're ridiculous, Eva," Justine said. "After all of these years, how could you be so wrong about me?"

"Or is it that you know I'm right, Justine?"

I'm Not in Love

"Something" – The Beatles

JUSTINE

THROUGH PHONE CALLS AND WORD of mouth, the Portable Party mainly managed to keep just out of reach of the police. After the group was busted at the Common last summer, we realized there must be pressure to 'clean up' the town. So as law enforcement became more determined, we became more crafty. Tonight, the hangout was at the Dikes—a series of dirt roads carved through the woods on the outskirts of town. If you were one of those 'in the know,' you could navigate the twisting, turning maze and find the roughly one-acre clearing with a party in full swing.

Eva said Danny called her and they prearranged tonight's meeting. She studied me, eager to pounce on any indication I was interested. Consequently, I was determined not to give her the satisfaction.

"New shorts?" She eyed my frayed denim cut-offs.

"These old things?" I said, thinking about the better part of an hour I'd spent snipping off the legs of my outgrown jeans, then carefully pulling at the horizontal threads until the perfect amount of shredded fringe framed the upper part of my thighs.

We stood with Eva's high school friends at one edge of the clearing, near the parked cars. A bonfire provided just enough light to see. Resting my back against an old Chevy pick-up, I set my mouth on auto-pilot and scanned the crowded gathering. I glanced from one group to another and spotted Kenny, Matt, and some of the bitchy girls we'd seen at Horse Pond. I bent forward pretending to scratch my knee, fully aware my white eyelet halter top gapped in front, emphasizing my cleavage and barely restraining my breasts. I inwardly gloated as I watched from beneath lowered eyelids, bitch-girls smacking their drooling boyfriends.

"Right, Justine?"

I whipped my head in Eva's direction. *What had she said? She's waiting for my answer.* "Yes!" I improvised. "She's absolutely right!" This seemed to be the appropriate response as I was greeted by a collective nodding of heads.

Having done my part, I allowed myself to continue casually surveilling. At last, my eyes landed on a van parked in the shadows on the edge of the woods, opposite where I was standing. Leaning against it was the one person I'd prayed all day would show up. When our eyes met, he broke into a smile that caused my heart to leap. Without thought, I started in his direction.

Oh, shit! Eva! I turned back toward her.

"See ya later!" She waved me off.

Yesterday's letters-are-proof episode raced through my mind once again as I drew nearer to him. *You're in love every time you turn around... the most gorgeous guy I had ever seen... these guys play for keeps... I don't fall in love.*

"Hi, Justine. It's good to see you again."

My legs turned to rubber beneath me.

He grabbed me around the waist as I crumbled toward him.

What the hell was wrong with me?

"You okay there?"

I forced my eyes to meet his. They were blue. Deep blue. Gorgeous blue. Sky blue. Wait. Cobalt. No... sapphire? *Ocean* blue. Long lashes. Captivating. Endearing crinkles at the corners as he smiled at me.

"Justine?"

"Oh... yeah, yeah. I'm good, Danny. I'm... really fab." Releasing my breath, I steadied myself on feet solidly placed eight inches apart. I tried to ignore the heat in my cheeks, my damp palms. *Come on, Justine. He's only a boy like any other boy you've known.*

Eva's accusations continued to haunt me. *That's why I was nervous to introduce you to Kenny, or to Matt... the next, new great love.* Her words reverberated. I felt my hand involuntarily go to my temple as I tried to blink those words away.

"Hey...?" The crinkles around those ocean blue eyes had smoothed. I couldn't look away. Then he extended his hand and lightly grazed my shoulder.

"I, uh...."

I'm not in love. That hair. I reached up and touched it, sank my fingers into it. It was soft and full. I twirled my finger around one curl, then another.

I'm not in love.

Soft and full. Like his lips. Those lips. They curved upward into the most luscious grin I'd ever seen. Involuntarily, my tongue quickly ran over my own before I yanked my gaze back to meet his. With my fingers still laced through his thick tangle of curls, I pulled him toward me and, as my heart exploded in my chest, his lips touched mine for the first time. In that blissful moment, every single one of those sappy, hackneyed, trivial love songs I'd ridiculed over the years made perfect, brilliant sense.

"WHERE'VE YOU TWO BEEN?" ASKED Eva when we rejoined the rest of the group at the Dikes.

You two. Lyrical, magical words sang in my heart while I savored the exquisite burn on my face from his five o'clock shadow. The vibrations he left on my lips and the hint of his Pierre Cardin cologne in my clothes sent waves of electricity shooting to my groin. I was acutely aware of every fiery point where his body pressed against mine.

Did I even answer Eva? Who else was around us? All that mattered was the chilled, tingly bitterness of the beer Danny and I shared. By far the most intoxicating drink I'd ever had. His potent, blue-eyed gaze permeated my soul and I knew I'd follow him to the ends of the Earth....

Stop it! Stop it! STOP IT! Reason, or rational thought, or whatever had been instilled in me from the time I was little demanded I take a mental step backward and stop acting like a simpleton. Mom would be horrified. And, quite frankly, this wasn't me! Justine Andrews didn't behave all silly and giddy over anyone, especially some guy!

Setting a smile on my face, I forced myself to engage in the conversation around me. These girls were a whole lot nicer than the Kenny/Matt groupies from last night and the boys were pleasant and amusing enough. When I glanced up at Danny, confident I'd regained my composure, he grinned at me. My legs went weak and I grabbed his arm for support.

Shit! I may be in trouble with this one.

Eva was understanding—almost as if she expected it—when I told her Danny was taking me home. As the van bounced along the unfinished roads, he reached over and intertwined my fingers with his on top of the center console.

"When do you go back to New Jersey? Can I see you before you leave?"

"I'm here for another month. When are you free?"

"How about tomorrow?"

"I'm open all day," I said.

"I have some stuff to do in the morning, for my brother. Then I'm open."

"You have a brother?" I asked. "I have two older brothers."

"Actually, I'm the oldest of five boys."

"You're kidding!"

"Three of them are pains in my ass. Then, there's my youngest, Teddy." His tone softened. "He's special. He was born prematurely and has cerebral palsy. He never learned how to walk, can't even dress himself. But, he's smart, Justine. He really is!"

"Go on."

"Well, when he was born, Dad seemed real angry. My mom hardly ever got out of bed. Neither one of them was able to give him the care he needed. When Teddy was a baby, he'd be crying in his crib and no one went to get him. So, I started going in and picking him up. Changing him, feeding him. Doing what needed to be done. Pretty soon, I'd be out in the backyard or over at the ballpark, and I'd hear Dad screaming at me, 'Danny, your brother needs you... Danny, your brother needs to be fed... Danny, this... Danny, that.'"

My heart ached for this guy, who I envisioned as a ten year-old, shouldering more responsibility than any kid should have to.

"Jeez, Danny, I'm sorry."

"I'm used to it. After I take care of Teddy tomorrow morning, I'll pick you up."

I told him I was staying on Miller Ave, but when I gave him directions, he shot me an amused look and said, "I know where it is."

Almost noiselessly, he pulled the van in the driveway. Turning off the engine, he flicked on the inside light. "We've met before. At the ballpark on Elm Street, right? You and Eva were upset about some birds?"

"Yeah, I remembered after we left Horse Pond the other night."

He reached toward me and my palms began to sweat. Instead of kissing me, though, he ran his hand through my hair, studying me.

"What is it? Why are you looking at me like that?"

"Justine, what's your connection to this house?"

"My great-aunt and great-uncle live here. It's always been in my family. Why?"

"So you come up here a lot? Stay at this house?"

"Yeah. All my life. I've spent my summers here since I was born. Why, Danny, what's wrong?"

187

He chuckled, shook his head, then rubbed his hand across his eyes. "You wouldn't believe it if I told you."

"Try me."

"I grew up on Elm Street. Right near Eva. I've been friends with the guys who live up at the farm at the end of this street since I was a kid."

"Okaaayy...?"

"I used to ride my bike up there all the time, to go hang out with them. For years, I noticed a girl who came during the summers and stayed at this house."

"Wait! I'm not following you."

"I figured out this girl was always here in the summers so I would come up this way, almost every day, hoping to see her. She had long blonde hair and, when she was a lot younger, she wore glasses."

"Are you *serious*? That was me! I'm the only girl who spends summers here."

"I know, *now*, it was you. I just put it together. I've had a crush on you for years. How weird is that?"

"Danny," I whispered, "why didn't you ever speak to me?"

"I don't know. Shy, maybe? Awkward? You were so pretty, even back then. Besides, you'd have thought I was some kind of stalker, riding my bike back and forth, hoping to see you."

"Well, I think that's kinda the definition of a stalker, isn't it?" I laughed, reaching to kiss him. "Actually, I think it's adorable. Look at us. All these years later. Obviously, it was destiny we met."

"You were made perfectly to be loved and surely I have loved you, in the idea of you, my whole life long," he whispered, lips against mine.

I pulled back sharply. "Elizabeth Barrett Browning?! You're quoting Elizabeth Barrett Browning?? She's my all-time favorite. I love her! How in the world do you know her?"

He looked equally surprised. "How do *you* know her?"

"I love literature, especially the classics. It's my escape. I'm not much into sports, so reading's how I spend my spare time. I've gone through so many library cards back home, it's become a running joke with the librarian."

"Well, I read to Teddy all the time. It's sort of our thing. When he was little, it was Mother Goose and the Brothers Grimm. When he got older, he liked the Hardy Boys, then The Lord of the Rings books. He likes me to read him poetry right before going to sleep."

Later, I hurried to wash my face and brush my teeth, eager to climb into bed and nestle under the covers so I could imagine my cocoon was Danny's embrace. I could feel my muscles starting to relax toward sleep as I fantasized I was lying in his arms. Outside, the rain which had started as a gentle sprinkle when Danny kissed me goodnight was pounding on the roof. A flash of lightning exploded in my room simultaneously with a crack of thunder, jolting me upright in bed.

The storm was fast-moving and the noise rapidly grew more distant. Relaxing against my dream Danny, I heard something above me but floated on my cloud toward unconsciousness.

Slam!

Again, I jumped up and listened. Dresser drawers opening and closing. Or was it the rain? Tiptoeing into the hallway, I put my ear to Aunt Peggy's door. Silence. Farther down the hall, I stopped at Uncle John's door. No light shining from under his, either, and not a sound from the other side. I crept back to my room, trying to tiptoe around the creaky floorboards, and settled back into bed, but my ears were on full alert. Footsteps. Right overhead. Coming from the attic! I was certain of it. Back and forth. More drawers opening and shutting. Then, quiet. I waited and listened. Nope. Nothing more.

Curling up with the blankets over my head, I prayed Uncle Harry was finished for the night. I concentrated on the sound of the clock on the shelf above the bed *tick-tick-ticking* rhythmically, the tension slowly easing from my body. Gradually, my thoughts drifted back to Danny. Everything about him intrigued me. The way he looked. The way he felt and smelled. How sweet he was with his little brother. How incredibly well-read he was. And, the romantic notion of him having a years-long crush on me. I doubted I was going to get much sleep.

What is a Good Girl?

"Only the Good Die Young" – Billy Joel

Eva

TEN MORE MINUTES. THE NURSE said it would take ten more minutes. It'll be positive, I knew. I had all the symptoms. I was late. My boobs were sore. I was moody. I'd gained weight. Nauseous. *It must be morning sickness.* The second hand on the big clock moved so slow, I swear, it was about to start going backwards. *How can Justine look so unperturbed? I'm a basket case, but there she sits, reading her Cosmo as if she doesn't have a care in the world.*

"Evelyn? Evelyn Jones?" We both sprang to our feet and followed the nurse back into the examining room. She placed the file on the desk and left, closing the door. I looked over at Justine, but she was studying a poster on the wall showing the diagram of a woman's reproductive organs. I sank onto the examining table, the white paper crinkling beneath me and sticking to my sweaty thighs, and tried to make my hands lay still in my lap. I stared at the huge, full-color, smack-me-in-the-face picture of the uterus. With a baby growing inside. *I'm going to puke.*

"Really? You're sure. A hundred percent sure?" My heart was doing backflips while I tried to grasp what the doctor told me. *I'm safe? I'm not pregnant? I don't have to start making plans? I don't have to tell my parents!*

"Yes, Miss Jones, I'm sure. It's what we call false pregnancy. Your body became convinced you were pregnant and developed the symptoms you've been having. You should get your period any time. Then, I want you to start on birth control pills. Here's a prescription and a starter pack. Use condoms for the first month to make sure you're protected."

Outside the clinic, Justine put her arms around me while I finally allowed my pent-up anxiety to surface. I sobbed until the shoulder of her shirt was soaked. The past three weeks had been a nightmare.

Steering me toward the car, she helped me in before going around to the passenger side. Rubbing my back as my breathing slowly quieted, she repeated over and over, "It's okay. You're okay."

At last, I drew a long, steadying breath and put the car in drive, ready to leave behind the clinic and this emotional roller-coaster. That was when Justine began the inevitable third degree I'd been dreading. "Eva. Why haven't you gone on the pill already? When you first had sex?"

"I don't know. I kept planning to, but never got around to it. Obviously, I won't make that mistake again."

"Eva, I have to ask. You're such a devout Catholic, I figured you were saving yourself for marriage."

"Well," I replied defensively, "things don't always go the way we plan. After Tim left, I wondered what I was waiting for."

"Hold on. Are you saying you and Tim never slept together?"

"No. My first was someone you don't know. Then, I guess it didn't seem to matter anymore, ya know? Like once I'd done it, what's the big deal?" This may have been the first time I ever shocked Justine.

She stared at me with her mouth hanging open.

"Yeah, well, what about you, Miss Wild Thing?" I turned the tables. "When did you go on the pill?"

Her mouth slowly spread into a wide grin. "Eva! I'm still a virgin!"

"What?! You're joking! *You?*"

"Ha! Who'd have thought it? That you'd turn out to be the promiscuous one while I'd be the good girl? Guess you can't always judge a book by its cover, right?" She chortled and repeated, "Who'd have thought?"

"Wait! Go back! Go back!" Justine spun around to look over her shoulder as Salem Cross, a historic inn built in the 1700s, faded into the distance.

"What? Why? I thought you needed to go home to get your 'beauty sleep' for your big date with Danny tomorrow!" I slowly pulled the car to the shoulder, the gravel softly crunching beneath my tires. No sign of car lights, so I cranked the steering wheel and made a U-turn back toward the restaurant. There was not a single house on this deserted stretch of road outside of West Brookfield. Only the inn, long since closed for the night and alone on its hundreds of privately owned acres. Nonetheless, a wave of anxiety swept over me as apprehension churned in my stomach.

"I want to see something real quick. There, pull into the parking lot!"

"Justine! It's wicked late. The place is closed. What are you doing?"

It was our last night together and had been relatively sedate. Dinner at McDonald's in Ware, a couple of beers as we drove around talking, a few comments exchanged with guys we passed on the road. I should have realized she wouldn't be satisfied until she caused some sort of mischief.

"Over there, over there! Hurry!" She pointed to the far right corner of the lot where the dark night was even darker under a strip of giant Eastern White Pines.

"Justine! What are...?"

"Shhh! Trust me!"

"Ha! You must be..." I began, but she'd already leapt from the car. Sighing, I followed, crouching low as we crept stealthily toward the marquee by the street.

Spelled out in large changeable letters with a single light illuminating the sign was the advertisement for the inn's upcoming event:

Welcome Back Class of 1928!
50th Reunion
Dining Room Is Open Regular Hours

She giggled, looked all around, then giggled again and started pulling off each of the letters on the last line, dropping them to the ground.

"What the hell are you doing!?" I asked, muffling the dread in my voice behind the hand clasped over my mouth. "Are you crazy? We're going to get busted!"

Her hands flew as she shuffled and arranged letters on the ground, stepped back to study her work, then moved them around some more. I peered up and down the road through the darkness, certain I'd see lights approaching any second. *Come on, come on!* I silently pleaded, as I waited for the sound of a police siren. *Flashing lights... freezing steel around my right wrist... biting me... 'mmmm, baby. you taste so good....*

"Okay. Got it! Go get the car and get my camera out of my purse. Hurry! I'm almost done." She began placing the letters on the sign.

I raced to the Mustang and left the headlights off as I rolled the car as quietly as I could back toward Justine. "Give me the camera! The camera!" She flapped her hand at me.

I jumped out to give it to her and looked to see what she'd done. Oh *shit*! She'd changed the message on the sign and was happily taking pictures of it to document her creativity. Dashing back to the driver's seat, I cast one last, brief look as Justine scrambled into the passenger side.

192

Welcome Back Class of 1928
50th Reunion
Our penis Is Huge!

"I'll send you a copy as soon as I get this roll developed," Justine assured me, kicking her feet up onto the dashboard and lighting a cigarette. "I'm sure you'll want to keep *that* for posterity!"

I glanced at my friend and laughed. Hard, until my stomach cramped. I kept laughing. A truly earnest laugh. The kind that made me feel free, without a care or worry in the world. The kind that made me feel like I was a kid again. Feelings I forgot I knew how to feel since That Night.

When I dropped her back to the house, she hugged me longer and tighter than usual to say goodbye. To her credit, she didn't needle me as much this summer as in years past. She'd only made one or two 'suggestions' about my clothing, but took the hint when I refused to discuss it. She hadn't lectured when I told her I was taking another year off from school, and stopped quizzing me about the guys I was seeing. Part of it was because I'd stopped telling her about them. After the whole pregnancy scare, I knew to be a whole lot more careful, anyway.

"Be good and stay out of trouble this year. I don't want to get a letter from you saying you've been expelled from school. Or, worse. A letter from prison!"

Laughing, she replied, "Where's the fun in being good?" Looking me directly in the eye, she quietly added, "Take care of yourself. I'll write soon."

Where's the fun in being good? I thought about that as I drove toward home. Justine certainly loved to create a ruckus. She had no compunction about causing mischief. Even breaking a law or two. But, what did it mean to be good? As I pulled up to the curb in front of my house, I turned off the engine and thought about it. Being good. Was someone good if they always played by the rules? Or, did being good mean having a good heart—being a true friend? Because Justine certainly was good in that sense. At nineteen, I'd come to understand people aren't all good or all bad. It wasn't as simple as black and white.

A horn from a passing car blasted, startling me out of my reverie. Black and white. The black and white police cruiser. His eyes bore into me with such force the air was knocked out of me. As the car crept by and he continued to glare at me, his warning was clear.

Keep your mouth shut.

Eye Rolling

"I'm Not in Love" – 10cc

Justine

"**S**o, you want to be Peggy's assistant again next summer?" Mom asked once we got on the road heading home from Aunt Peggy's. "You weren't bored? Missing your friends back home?"

Bored?

Hot lazy days soaking up the sun with wafting aromas of lilacs and freshly mowed hay. Adventurous nights wrapped in protective darkness, hiding from cars on nearly deserted roads with only the peepers and our giggles breaking the stillness. Quiet times with Aunt Peggy and Uncle John, playing a board game or watching television while Lucky slept faithfully nearby. Countless clandestine gatherings with the Portable Party, swigging beer, getting stoned, laughing at the absurdities we discussed.

And, Danny. Spending every possible moment together this past month. Dinners, movies, parking in his van. Hanging out at Long View Farm, getting to know the people who run the recording studio. Yesterday, for our last date, we'd gone to Quabbin Reservoir.

"No. It was good," I assured her. "I was busy a lot of the time. I'd love to do it next year."

"Aunt Peggy says you had a pretty active social life. Anyone in particular?"

Even though Quabbin Reservoir had bored me when I was little for its lack of a swing or sliding board or other piece of playground equipment available, the other day it was paradise. The weather was perfect for our picnic lunch and we'd found a secluded alcove at the edge of the dense woods, overlooking the water. I'd tried to ignore the jitters in my stomach, attributing it to my usual dread of leaving North Brookfield. Truth was that Danny's sheltering arms wrapped around me, his lips electrifying every nerve in my skin, made the

194

thought of going home terrifying. I would have been content to stay where we were forever.

"Justine, I'm not a great pen pal. But I'll try," he'd said.

"Why can't you call me?"

Sighing, he'd pulled me closer. "I have nosy brothers, remember? And one phone. But I'll try."

"Don't worry about it," I'd answered, half-wanting to convince him I wasn't going to be waiting for his call anyway and half-wanting to hurt him for not making more of a commitment.

Briefly, he'd rested his forehead on my shoulder, then turned me until I faced him. "Justine. You know how I feel about you. I promise I'll do the best I can to stay in touch with you. Maybe I'll come see you in New Jersey?"

"Sure, if you have time. I'm busy too, though, with school, my volunteer work, and all." I'd tried to sound aloof. "Seriously, Danny. I'm fine. We're good," I said, turning to look out across the crystal clear water of the reservoir so he wouldn't see the tears welling up in my eyes.

"Don't do that. Don't put up this wall and pretend everything's fine when, obviously, it's not. Justine, look at me." He'd placed his fingers under my chin and gently turned my head until I faced him. "We'll figure things out, but not if you hide what you're feeling. Can't you drop the act and be yourself with me?"

"I am myself with you."

"No, you aren't. You're upset and hiding it; I can see that."

My heart had hurt in a way new to me. I'd never believed long distance relationships could work, but then, more than anything, I'd prayed they could. "I don't want to go home." I felt the tightness in my heart unravel. "I'm afraid we'll never get this back. I'm afraid you'll forget about me." As my truth seeped out of me, so had my pent up panic.

Pulling me tighter, he'd kissed me on my forehead, comforting me almost as a parent would a child. "I could never forget you, Justine. We'll work it out."

I'd furtively swiped at my tears. When I'd finally trusted my voice, I said, "And, I am myself with you, Danny. That's why leaving is so hard for me. I'm more myself with you than I've ever been in my life. I'm more myself with you than with my parents, who I live in constant fear of disappointing. I'm more myself with you than with my friends, who only want 'fun Justine.' Even Eva. I've always felt like I needed to act a certain way—more grown up, or something—or she'd think I was a child."

"You know that's not true."

"I know. It's my own crap I have to deal with." I'd kissed him on his cheek,

then gently on his lips. "With you, I've always been myself. I'm more myself with you than I am with me!"

"I know a lot of people. Eva's friends. We like to hang out, ya know," I told Mom vaguely.

"Like who?"

I looked over at her, but her eyes were still fastened to the highway. Her jaw was tight and her hands gripped the wheel in a stern, no nonsense way that didn't exactly invite confidence. She didn't usually ask about my private life. She knew most of my friends back home and had met Chris while we were dating, but she generally wasn't too interested.

"Well, there's Lynn, who's Eva's closest friend. Besides me, that is." I laughed. She gave a glimmer of a smile in return. "And Vicki, and her husband Pablo." Even though I hadn't seen them at all this summer. "And, you know, a bunch of other local kids. They're nice. Fun. We have fun together."

"No boys?"

"I'm buying a house, Justine. I can't live with my father anymore. My whole life has been about how much he resents me. My parents were still in high school when he got my mother pregnant. Somehow it's my fault his dreams never came true. After my mother died, he began to show me how he feels about me. He'd beat the shit out of me every time he got drunk. Which was often. I finally stopped taking it and began hitting back. Anyway, I'll be moving out the second I have enough for the down payment."

I'd looked into those bottomless blue eyes and seen the injured boy beneath. Words were unnecessary. I'd wanted to take him in my arms and protect him. I'd wanted him more than I'd ever wanted another person. Heart, body, soul. But I could barely wrap my own head around the depth of my emotions, let alone try to explain them to him. So I'd said nothing. When he'd kissed me at that moment, I could have done anything for him. And would have, if that family with two little kids hadn't interrupted us with their gasps of horror.

"Well, I did meet one guy. Danny. He's really nice. And cute," I replied, noncommittally.

"Tell me about him. What's he like?"

"He's sweet. About six foot two, dark curly hair. He does construction type work."

"Oh," she said, lips tight. "That sounds nice."

"He's good at what he does," I insisted, a hint of a plea in my voice. "Not just pounding nails, but artistic stuff too. He designs and finishes rooms, and he's starting to branch off on his own. Actually," I added with pride, "he landed a huge account last week. A developer for a new housing community. Danny's the lead contractor."

"So, he isn't in school?"

"He has his associate's degree. He's smart. And, self-educated. He reads everything." Mom didn't need to know about how his father's drinking had made it necessary for Danny, at fifteen, to find work to help put food on the table. She didn't have to know how his delinquent brothers were always needing to be bailed out of jail and it was usually Danny they called. I didn't mention Teddy and everything Danny did to care for him. I also excluded information about when Danny had no money for college, he had scraped together enough to put himself through community college while working full-time.

"How old is he?"

"Twenty."

"That's a little old for you."

"Only three years older."

"Hmmm. Well, he sounds... industrious."

I turned away to face the window before rolling my eyes. This was simply Mom being Mom. I'd heard her thoughts in every variation over the years: "If you put half the energy into your studies as you do boys, you could change the world." "Why do you feel the need to have a boy to complete your life? You're a whole person on your own." "What are his ambitions, Justine? You don't want to waste your time with someone who's going to hold you back." Always the same song about independence and self-sufficiency, just to slightly different tunes.

We rode along in silence as I turned up "I'm Not In Love" by 10cc playing on the radio.

He'd parked in the gravel driveway at Aunt Peggy and Uncle John's house. My heart had nearly burst at the uncertainty of tomorrow, and the day after, and the next nine months. We'd sat in the darkened van holding hands, but neither quite knowing what to say. I hadn't wanted to open the door to get out because it would mean it was done. Our beautiful summer together. I'd wanted to stretch out this moment for as long as possible.

"Justine," he'd finally said. "I've never met anyone like you before. This last month has been the best of my life."

Why couldn't I admit I felt the same?

He'd reached over and kissed me, then looked deeply into my eyes. A lump threatening to turn me into a blubbering fool had formed in my throat as I'd turned away.

"I've never felt like this before. I've never been able to tell anyone the things I've told you. Justine," he'd tucked a piece of stray hair behind my ear and trailed his fingers gently down my face. "I...."

Don't say it! my mind had screamed. I can't bear to hear it! Quickly, I'd planted my lips on his. When at last I pulled away, I'd told him, "I need to go in. Please write me, Danny. I'll miss you so much," and gotten out of the van.

Swallowing around the lump in my throat, the one stubbornly refusing to go away even after crying myself to sleep, I said, "He is. He's a really good guy."

When I got back to New Jersey, my first stop would be to drop my film off at Fotomat. I'd promised Eva I'd get those pictures of the Salem Cross sign to her and I wanted to see how the pictures I took of Danny at Quabbin Reservoir turned out. There were only two shots left so I used up the film on him. My friends at home would want to see this guy I'd written them about.

I didn't know what I was feeling for him—just that it would be a long, long time until next summer. As close as I felt to him, I knew how long distance relationships went. It was just as well not to get my hopes up. Besides, I knew what I was *not* feeling for him.

I was *not* in love.

CHAPTER 8

1979

CHATTING WHILE DRIVING

"Runnin' with the Devil" – *Van Halen*

JUSTINE

"**I** MET A GUY," EVA SAID on our first evening together since my return for the summer. We were catching up during our favorite recreation: aimlessly cruising to nowhere. "I think he really likes me."

My ears perked up. I wasn't sure what happened with Tim, and she'd made it clear she didn't want to discuss it. In fact, she hadn't mentioned anyone special in nearly two years. Just countless dates with random boys. I'd met several last summer, but none made a lasting impression. "That's bitchin'! What's his name? What's he like? Where did you meet him? What does he look like? Where's he from? What color is his hair?"

"Whoa! Down girl. Hold your horses!"

"Come on... *tell* me!" I switched off the radio in Eva's Mustang. "Is he a fox?"

"A fox? A *fox?!* I haven't heard that one before except in the Jimi Hendrix song. Hmmmm. He's cute, let's say. At least I think so!"

"Details! I want details!"

"Well...." Eva gazed out over the steering wheel, prolonging the suspense. "His name is Lester and he's from Ware. He left high school to start his own band called Wired, and plays the guitar. And..." Eva broke into a big grin as she revealed the pièce de résistance. "And, he has long, blond hair. Wicked long. Down to here!" Eva gleefully leveled her free hand near her lower back and glanced sideways, eagerly awaiting my squeals of approval.

"Ewwwww."

"What do you mean, 'ewwww'?" Eva was clearly deflated.

"I mean *ewww*!!!" I nearly choked on the word. "Ewwwwww! Yuck!"

"Yuck? *Whaaat?*"

"I hate really long hair on guys. You know that. Hate it!" I'd thought Tim's wasn't bad—wavy, right to his shoulders. But nearly to the ass? "It's so… so dumb. You know I can't stand any guy to have hair longer than mine." With that, I gave my own mane a defiant little flip, the underside of my fingers flicking the hair away from my neck.

"Hmmmpf. Well, I *like* long hair on guys." She looked at me indignantly. "I like long hair on guys, Miss Prissy Pants!"

In spite of my protests, Eva seemed convinced I'd find Lester irresistible. "I have a picture of him, and he looks a lot like Gregg Allman. You know, the long blond hair, blue eyes—"

"Greg who? I don't know. Lemme see."

Eva reached for her purse while steering the car, narrowly missing trees and telephone poles by the side of the road. She retrieved it and hauled it up to the console between us.

"God! Watch out!" I braced my legs against the imaginary brakes. "Did you see that?"

"See what?"

"A padiddle! A one-eyed car. You know, one headlight out?"

"Must be another one of your weird New Jersey terms." Eva exultantly produced a picture of Lester.

I couldn't find any words for a moment. I could only study the photo she'd thrust before me. I snapped on the inside light and examined every detail. Then, shoving it back in her purse, I gave my verdict. "He looks like Chewbacca!"

AN HOUR LATER, WE WERE nearly out of gas after meandering through all of the neighboring towns. As Eva pulled behind the last car in line on the side of the road, a quarter of a mile from the Sunoco station in Spencer, she asked, "So, have you heard from Danny?"

I studied the 'Question Authority' bumper sticker on the car in line ahead of us. "Turn off the car while we're not moving. It saves gas," I told her. "Why don't you guys have odd-even days here?"

"I don't know. Does it make the lines shorter in New Jersey?"

"Shorter? Well…." I doubt I'd ever noticed how long the wait was back home. My friend Laura and I had turned sitting in gas lines into an opportunity to meet guys. We distracted ourselves from the fact that we were riding around in Mom's embarrassing spaceship-shaped AMC Pacer by dressing as provocatively as possible. Last week, when we'd waited on line for nearly two hours clad in micro shorts and bikini tops, we ended up with dates for the following night. Who'd have thought the energy crisis would produce new opportunities for us to spice up our social lives?

Eva pulled her Marlboros from her purse, lit one, and held the pack toward me.

"I quit."

"*Really?* How come?"

"Hmmm. Lots of reasons. Too expensive. It ruins the smell of my Aromatics Elixir. And I don't want to taste like an ashtray." Eva smiled at my last comment. "It completely lost its appeal for me."

"Wow! I remember how shocked I was when you were a little girl, lighting up a cigarette out behind the barn. Now look at you. All grown up!" She nudged me with her elbow. "Speaking of shocking, I gave up pot."

"*Nooo!* How'd that happen? I figured you'd be getting high the rest of your life. You know, one of those gray-haired fifty-year-olds, sneaking into the bathroom, lighting incense so her kids don't smell it."

She started the car and moved it forward in line, then turned it off again. "I guess it was one night last fall. Lynn and I went to a party over at the Dikes. None of the Portable Party kids are around much anymore. There were all of these geeky, zit-faced high school freshmen hanging out, smoking pot, listening to that disco crap and, I don't know. It felt so… mainstream. Everyone is doing it. And, there they were, trying to have these profound conversations like we used to, but honestly, they just sounded like a bunch of morons."

Eva was one of the most sensible people I knew. I wondered if she thought I sounded like an imbecile when I was in the throes of one of my pot-induced revelations. The only downside I'd ever considered was how it affected my weight. Eva had taken up running, and worked her way up to ten miles a day. I wished I could claim that passion, but I was less inclined toward physical fitness. Grudgingly, my post-party munchies had driven me to the gym so I could still squeeze into my skin-tight clothes.

"Well, if you're not gonna get high," I said, "I'm certainly not doing it around you. You'd be screwing with my head and making me sound like an idiot!"

"You don't have to be stoned to sound like an idiot!"

She grinned as she passed me a piece of Hubba Bubba, popped one in her mouth, and began chewing it vigorously. I chomped on mine, working for perfect bubble-blowing texture. Gazing out the window, I decided I was ready to broach the subject I'd avoided. I assumed my offhand, just-asking-not-that-I-really-care voice. "So... Danny. Have you seen him?"

"No. I don't think I've run into him since last summer. I told you, he keeps to himself. Didn't you let him know you were here?"

"We kind of lost touch. He doesn't write letters much and he stopped calling around Christmas. Eh, I was only curious. You know me." I cracked a bubble with a loud pop. "I moved on once I got home."

"You should call him. I know you liked him. Justine, *call* him!"

I couldn't talk about how hurt I was that he hadn't tried harder to stay in touch. I thought we had a real bond. By spring, I'd given up and gone with Walter to the Senior Prom. But still, my heart beat a little faster and my temperature rose a degree or two every time I thought of the moments Danny and I shared.

As the car crept forward, I asked about her job. Eva was still working long hours at the nursing home, complaining about some of the cranky residents but mainly satisfied with her steady income. She asked about my college plans.

"I love what I do at the shelter so I've decided to study social work with a concentration in women's issues."

"How does your mom feel about that? I know she wanted you to go into law or business."

"You know what, Eva? I've stopped worrying about living her dreams. This is *my* life!"

"*Okaayy*, then! So, which college did you pick?"

My old New England family had always gone to school in Massachusetts. My grandmother was a graduate of Mount Holyoke, my aunt of Smith, and my grandfather and uncle both went to Amherst. They were all fabulous colleges and it had long been assumed I'd end up as a legacy at one of them.

"I'm going south. I found a great college in Virginia with the exact programs I want."

"Uh-oh. Bucking the system? Were your parents mad?"

"What do you think?" I asked, eyes wide in mock-horror.

"Ha! Oh *man*! I wish I could have been there when you told them. I bet they went ballistic! I guess things you do shouldn't surprise me anymore, but I swear, you still manage to find some way to shock me!"

"Yeah, I knew you'd like that." I popped my gum triumphantly. "Also,

I've already found a job at a women's shelter near the school. I'll be able to keep doing the kind of work I've been doing back home."

"But I thought you loved Massachusetts so much that you'd want to move here to go to school."

"Lemme tell you, it was a tough call," I admitted, holding my hands out like the scales of justice. "On one hand, I love Massachusetts. On the other, I hate being told what to do."

"I hope your choice is really what's best for you. Not what's the best 'screw-you' to your mother."

"Well, what about you? You're the one who was always itching to get *out* of Massachusetts. But look at you, two years later. You're still stuck. What's keeping you here, Eva?"

When we were finally on our way back to Aunt Peggy and Uncle John's, I reveled in the comfort of the familiar landmarks, most barely visible in the darkness: the reflected lights from the bungalows on Lake Lashaway; the sign for Brookfield Orchards; the outline of gnarled apple trees; the hill where Wausau overlooked the cemetery; and the watchful stones in Shadow Hill, standing at attention as we passed.

Turning right onto Miller Ave, that lifelong thrill surged inside me. I was home, straining to see the first glow of the house lights emerge past the tunnel of trees. I was still baffled by Eva's about-face in goals. Breaking up with a cute and brainy guy like Tim to take up with this Lester, the plain-looking high school dropout. As confusing was her indifference to the idea of college and leaving North Brookfield.

I didn't want to start our time together this summer badly. I was back in my favorite place with my best friend in the world and was going to enjoy it. I forced enthusiasm into my voice and said, "Tell Lester 'hi' for me and that I can't wait to meet him!" and hopped out of the car.

WHEN REALITY COMES CRASHING IN
"(Don't Fear) The Reaper" – Blue Oyster Cult

EVA

"**D**ON'T LOOK, DON'T LOOK!" JUSTINE said. "They'll know we're talking about them! Just be cool."

I couldn't help myself. I'd been trying to form a picture in my head based on Justine's descriptions, of the guys sitting behind me. Long, greasy hair, "the way you like it," was the chief characteristic she mentioned. Every time I turned to steal a peek, as if just nonchalantly looking around the bar, she barked, "No! No! Don't look! You're too obvious!"

"Okay. I'm going to go find the bathroom. I'll get a look at them when I go past."

Climbing off the barstool, I casually stretched and surveyed the three in question. Greasy? Their hair wasn't *greasy*! What was she talking about? All three of them were reasonably attractive. Yeah, their hair was long, but it was well-kept. One even had his pulled back into a neat ponytail. Justine was nuts. I wasn't really checking them out, of course, because they weren't even in the same league as Lester.

Their eyes followed me as I walked past them. By the time I returned, Justine was engaged in an animated discussion with them.

"Eva, this is Jack, and this is Bill and Kevin."

What the hell was with her voice? Nodding my head toward the guys, I grabbed my beer and listened as she continued her conversation.

"…and we met when I was out riding one of the horses. You know Eva is a jolly good equestrian. I was positively gob-smacked when I first saw her ride! She's the only person I've met in this area who can keep pace with me. Because, of course, back home in England, I'm able to ride whenever I like." She tossed her hair over her shoulder.

That's it! She was speaking with a British accent! What stunt was she pulling now?

"So, Heather. How often do you go to Long View with your father?"

"Oh, this is my second time. It's rather secluded and picturesque... a little like our farm in Scotland, with the animals and all. Peaceful."

Heather McCartney? Had she convinced these slosh-brains she was *Heather McCartney*?! She rambled on about her jet-setting lifestyle, taking tea with the Queen, dining with President Carter, partying at Studio 54. And there they sat, slack-jawed and bleary-eyed, living vicariously through the tales she was weaving. The bartender caught my eye, and we both hid our smiles.

I must admit, she never broke character. It was like watching an intricately choreographed tennis match. Questions lobbed at her, Justine ably returned with plausible and artful answers. Who knew if what she was saying was even close to accurate. Her self-confidence was enough to convince these oafs. But, when she responded "Sure! My Uncle Ringo" in answer to "Have you seen *The Godfather*?" the bartender and I couldn't help laughing out loud.

With autographed bar napkins from this celebrity grasped in their fingers, the three young men staggered toward the exit. Justine and I stared at each other, eyes wide and lips clamped shut, as we listened to their excited jabbering. Once they'd left, we collapsed into hysterics.

"Well, that was fun to watch," the bartender said as he dried the bar glasses. "Something tells me those boys will never forget this night."

"WHAT IS THAT?" JUSTINE PEERED through the windshield toward the side of the desolate road, two miles from the bar we'd just left.

Slowing my car to a crawl, I strained to see through the haze. A ghostly image with waving arms appeared beside an upended motorcycle, its front wheel bent at a peculiar angle. As my headlights illuminated the site, I realized the ghost was Jack, the pony-tailed guy we'd been talking with at the bar less than an hour ago. Behind him on the grass in the curve of the road was an overturned Dodge with the roof crushed in, smoke billowing from under the hood.

Dreamlike, I watched myself moving in silent slow motion, bringing my car to a stop, opening the door, and stepping out. Each action was disjointed and distinct. Jack was hobbling, the gaping tear in his jeans revealing a long, hideous gash. Through my fog, I was aware of Justine rushing toward him and saying something. Their mouths were opening and closing, their hands moving and pointing, then they both ran toward the smoldering vehicle. I headed to the driver's side, step by robotic step. As if a phantom hand slapped me across the face, my senses snapped into focus and my instincts kicked into full gear.

Noise and chaos. Screaming and shouting. I tried to draw a deep breath, but coughed against the smoke burning my throat and the acrid stink of gasoline. I dropped to my knees to peer into the car and found the crumpled hindquarters of the driver blocking the side window. Scrambling toward the front of the car on all fours, I found the top half of the body dangling face down, trapped partway through the shattered windshield.

"Eva, come on! *Fire!*" My stinging eyes made out Jack and Justine supporting a dazed-looking Bill between them. Justine frantically beckoned for me to follow. I then realized Kevin was moaning as he regained consciousness, and he was trapped. A million miles away, I heard the wail of sirens. There was no other option here. We had to get the injured boy out before the car exploded. I couldn't leave him alone, shrieking in terror.

"You'll be okay, Kevin. There's been an accident. Do you understand me?"

I heard a bubbling, guttural noise, followed by another howl.

"Okay. Shh. Shh. Don't try to talk. We're getting you out. We'll get your shoulders, but you need to push with your legs to come through the front."

I rapidly evaluated my patient as Bill tore off his shirt. Wrapping it around his hand, he knocked away the remaining jagged fragments of the windshield. I placed my hand under Kevin's down-turned forehead to support him, but felt the slickness of blood. "Your shirt!" I yelled to Jack. "Give me your shirt!"

Bunching it, I placed it against Kevin's face and gently lifted, supporting his head.

"Eva, *hurry!*" Justine's panic prompted me to move faster.

"Okay. Jack, get one shoulder. Bill, hold the other. When I count to three, you guys pull and Kevin, you push. Justine, get his legs. Ready? One, two, three."

In one fluid motion, we had Kevin out. We carried his upper body while Justine supported his legs. The sirens were getting closer, but urgency spurred us away from the burning car. Together, we carefully turned Kevin over, adjusted our hold on him, then continued as rapidly as possible to safety. We laid him on the ground as the ambulances and fire trucks screeched to a halt.

With the rescue vehicles lighting up the site, I removed the cloth from Kevin's face and we got our first real look at him. Where his face had been resembled ground meat. No nose, no lips—the skin sheared off. My heart dropped to my stomach and, next to me, Justine groaned before collapsing to the ground.

"YOU KNOW YOU SAVED THAT guy's life." Justine regarded me with respect the following afternoon, leaning back against Wausau. "You were amazing!"

"Nah, anyone would have done it!" I was making a pretense of modesty, but honestly, I was proud of how I'd taken charge at the accident site.

"What did they say at the hospital?"

Using my connections through the nursing home, I was able to get information about Kevin's condition. There would be multiple surgeries to reconstruct his face, including skin grafting. Luckily, he had not sustained any brain trauma.

"They said it will take awhile, but he'll pull through. Poor guy."

Last night had been exhausting. We'd gone to the emergency room and waited while Jack had his leg treated, and he and Bill were released. Once Kevin's mother arrived, we had finally left. I dropped Justine to her house and went home to get a couple of hours of sleep. Instead, I lay awake, picturing that boy's mangled face and thinking how his life had changed in one horrible second. Moments prior, he'd been young, carefree, with a clear and optimistic view of his future. He'd been hanging out with his buddies at his favorite dive, flirting with a couple of girls, then heading home. Gone. Life as he knew it. Facing a future of pain, disfigurement, regrets, and countless 'what ifs.' If there was anyone who could empathize with how radically Kevin's life had changed in a single instant, it was me.

Now, my lack of sleep had caught up with me. I struggled to my feet and stretched. As I let out a huge yawn, I scanned the cemetery but saw it was empty. "I'm tired, Justine. I'm going home. How about if we hang out tomorrow?"

Back at my house, although my heavy eyes felt gravelly and my head stuffed with cotton, I was more centered than I had been in ages. I thought about what I'd given up over the last couple of years. What he stole from me That Night, and what I'd allowed him to continue taking from me since.

I thought about the brightness in Justine's eyes the day she told me how fulfilling she found her work at the shelter. My response to the wounded boy in the car accident had given me that same sense of purpose.

Flipping through the phone book, I finally found the number I wanted. I dialed and waited. When I heard the voice on the other end, I said, "Uh, yes. I want to find out how to apply for admission into your Nursing Program. Yeah, sure, I'll hold."

LOVE

"Tonight's the Night" – Rod Stewart

JUSTINE

I T'D BEEN NINE MONTHS. *NINE months* since I'd seen him. Six since we last talked. I should have believed him when he warned he wasn't a good correspondent. I'd poured my heart into letter after letter, filling them with light-hearted humor and words of longing. They went unanswered. Phone calls trickled off after several interceptions by his obnoxious brothers and my overbearing mother. The endless, hurt-filled weeks had faded into lonely months, and I'd crammed him into that I-can't-deal-with-it place inside of me.

As the months passed and the silence lengthened, I chose to move on. I dated other boys, including the much sought-after Walter, but there was always something missing. What was missing, I realized in this moment, was that none of them were Danny. Even though I'd convinced myself he had only been a summer romance, my heart demanded I recognize the truth.

The past several months of apathy evaporated because there he stood. In the driveway, eyes glued to mine. He smiled.

"Hi, Danny." I grinned in response. He looked the same. His irresistibly touchable hair. Those magnetic blue eyes. The little indent at the base of his neck where my tongue had spent so much time exploring last summer. And, that mouth.

That mouth was still smiling, not saying a word.

As I reached for him, I kissed that mouth and it obliterated every hesitation, question, and insecurity of the past nine months.

After the accident, I needed to see him again. Every other guy I'd dated had quickly faded from mind when someone new tickled my fancy, and I'd never looked back. But not with Danny. Either I could go on denying he was different or I could stop playing games. Because life wasn't a game. The

211

image of Kevin's tattered face made this quite clear. I had to know if what I felt for Danny last summer was real and how he truly felt about me.

We spent hours catching up. I told him about my school year, how well I did in my classes, and about my college plans. I told him about the pressures back home from my family and friends. Danny was my greatest cheerleader when I told him I was intimidated by my cousin Lisa, who had graduated as valedictorian of our class. He couldn't conceal the shock in his eyes.

"You? Intimidated? Justine, I've never met anyone as smart as you. Remember when your aunt and uncle's finances were in such a mess? And you figured out what all those credit card charges were? You ended up saving their house from foreclosure."

Danny told me about his jobs, the work he was doing with the housing development, and ongoing problems with his family. Ever since his mother died, Danny had faced increasing strain, trying to balance the care of his brother with his own budding career. I could see the heartbreak in his eyes when he told me his father recently had made the decision to place Ted in a state home. For the first time, I saw past Danny's rugged exterior to the sensitive young man who not only rescued injured birds, but also genuinely adored his disabled younger brother.

We both conspicuously avoided mentioning 'us' or 'others,' but I needed to know. "Why did you stop calling, Danny? Did you meet someone else?" My stomach soured when he pulled away from me.

"Nothing serious, Justine. Just a girl I hung out with once in a while."

I drew a painful breath around the bile in my throat. My reaction was unfair, but jealousy was a vice I wasn't used to dealing with. After all, I hadn't exactly spent this past year sitting at home, dateless. Should I expect him to have committed himself to a monastery? Did she touch him the way I had? What had she done with him I hadn't? Was she prettier?

"Are you still seeing her?" I asked.

"Not since you called."

We spent the evening at Long View Farm. We had gone plenty of times last year, and I had gotten to know the folks who ran it. This was different because it was my first time when musicians were there to record. We didn't hang out with the band, only spoke briefly to them in passing, but we got to listen in as they practiced the songs for their next album. And, it was their title piece "Love Stinks" that would become the soundtrack of this day in my mind.

By the time we left, I was floating on a natural high. I was with the man of my dreams and had met my first rock stars. We'd planned to go to a late dinner, but before we were even out of the farm's parking lot, I wrapped myself around Danny, nibbled his neck, and whispered into his ear all of the naughty things I wanted to do to him. I thought about how close we'd come at Quabbin last year. Tonight, there was no young family to interrupt us.

"Forget the restaurant, Danny."

"Restaurant? What restaurant?" With me still hanging on him, he managed to steer the van to Horse Pond without crashing.

"Rubbers! Danny, do you have rubbers?"

"In the glove compartment!"

I popped open the door in front of me. *Shit!* Does he always carry all of those boxes of Trojans? Did he buy them for me? Or for *her?* Shoving the thoughts from my head, I grabbed out a foil packet.

Skidding to a stop on the unpaved lot by the water, Danny threw the gearshift into park and, in one fluid motion, sprang from his seat, grabbed my arm, and dragged me onto the bed in the back. In seconds, we were both stripped of our clothing and reveling in the feel of our moist, burning skin pressed together. He was commanding, instructing me, unabashedly enjoying what I was doing to him.

Then, Danny touched me in a way I'd only heard the kids back home make jokes about. I imagined I would be too embarrassed to have his mouth on me so intimately, but with his encouragement, I let go of my inhibitions and opened myself up to him. Every nerve sizzled and my insides shuddered with each touch of his tongue.

Danny kissed me deeply, then pulled back to hold my eyes with his. "I love you, Justine."

"I love you too, Danny." Words I'd never said to another guy. I was scared about what I knew was next. He tried to be gentle, but my hips met his with the force I craved. My flash of pain was immediately overcome by ecstasy beyond my wildest teenage dreams. Greater than anything I'd ever read about or experienced in all of my eighteen years.

Much Ado About Lester

"Magic Man" – Heart

Eva

"**H**OW CAN YOU EVEN *SAY* that?" Justine ducked her head, at least having enough sense to recognize her words were hurtful. "I'm simply telling you the truth."

The heat crept up my face as I crossed my arms and leaned back against the porcelain sink. I opened my mouth to retort just as a group of girls opened the door to the bathroom, a waft of smoke from the bar following them in. I released my breath and slammed my lips shut, unable to take my eyes off of my alleged best friend. I clenched my fists tighter as I fought back the impulse to slap the superiority off her face. She refused to look at me as we waited for the girls to finish reapplying their lip gloss before finally leaving.

"How would you feel if I told you Danny wasn't good enough for you? That you could do better? Huh? How would that make *you* feel?"

"Like shit, I'm sure, but Danny—"

"And you're being really shallow, don't you think? Is it because of his hair, Justine?"

"It's not his hair. It's…."

"Then what's your problem? He's a good guy with a lot going for him."

"Oh, come on, Eva. What do you have in common? When Danny and I—"

"Shut up about Danny Stevenson, already!" I screamed at her. "He's not God's gift, Justine. I'm sick of hearing you talk about him like he's perfect. Trust me, I've known him a lot longer than you."

Justine's eyes flashed with anger before she arranged her face in a neutral position.

"Lester's talented. He's good to me. And, he loves me."

At this, Justine rolled her eyes. "I doubt he loves anything as much as he loves getting high. Come on, Eva! That's all he talks about! His pot, the new bong he wants to buy. He's a burnout! You don't even smoke anymore, Eva!"

"Okay. So he has his one downfall. Other than that, he's a great guy."

"He doesn't listen when you talk. He's too busy looking around to see who's checking him out! Half the time, he cuts you off in mid-sentence."

"That's not true!"

"Are you kidding me? Besides being a stoner and ignoring what you say, what ambition does he have? Huh? To play in these dive bars and get paid in beer and weed? Wow! Big dreams. He didn't even finish high school and... *and* he actually thinks Ronald Reagan would be a good president!"

"Well... Carter hasn't exactly...."

"Oh, come on, Eva! Reagan's not even a good *actor*! Plus—"

"Justine, please!" My eyes filled with tears.

She sagged, resting her back against the wall. In unreadable silence, she watched me. The pulse in her neck was jumping. "Alright. I'll give him a chance, okay? But I do have one question." A hint of her trademark smile tugged at her mouth. "When the hell was the last time he showered?"

"WHAATT?" I SHOUTED TO JUSTINE over the noise of the band. Fanning at the cigarette smoke cloud between us, I leaned forward to catch her words.

"I said," she yelled back, cupping her hands on each side of her mouth, "will Lester be able to sit with us during their break?"

I nodded, distracted by the complex guitar solo of Lynyrd Skynyrd's "Free Bird" that Lester was nailing. He'd never been in better form. Even Justine's eyes were riveted to his fingers as they flew up and down the neck of the guitar and across the strings, commanding every breath and heartbeat in that jam-packed room. Each vibration and every soul-stirring stroke from his fingertips fed the thrill that started in my stomach and whirled faster with the music, leaving me panting at the final climaxing chord.

"That was *bitchin'*!" Justine gushed as he approached our table, bending to give her a kiss on the cheek.

He smiled his answer right before I yanked him close to kiss him full on the lips. Out of the corner of my eye, I saw the group of girls at the bar who had been ogling him all night, turn away in disappointment.

"Thanks." He tossed his hair over his shoulder before pulling up a chair and settling his 6'3" frame into it. Grabbing his Heineken, he downed half the bottle in one long drink. "Allen Collins is a genius. I've been working real hard to get his guitar riffs down."

"Well, it shows! That was awesome!" Justine said. I hoped she was being sincere and not putting on an act for my sake. Either way, I was happy she was being so nice to him.

A man in a black Stetson leaning against the bar and chatting with his buddies had been keeping a close eye on our table. As Lester leaned in to kiss my neck, sending electrical shocks to my loins, the cowboy ambled over, nodded towards us, and tipped his ten-gallon hat to Justine. She cocked her head to one side and half-smiled, waiting.

"Ma'am," he began with a terrible fake Southern drawl. "If I told you that you have a great body, would you hold it against me?"

Justine's eyes widened as she glanced at me. We both turned back to him and collapsed into laughter. Lester grinned and shook his head at the poor guy, shifting in his leather boots.

"I'm so sorry," Justine giggled. "I've never heard that one before. That's so, uh... cute!" She picked up her beer bottle and regarded her hopeful suitor. "No, I wouldn't hold it against you, but I have a boyfriend."

After a mumbled "nice meeting you, anyway" to Justine and a "great job, man" to Lester, Buffalo Bill swaggered back to the bar. I kicked Justine under the table and she kicked me back. Lester shhhhsh'd us both and changed the subject.

"So, hey, Justine, did you hear what my little nurse did the other night?" Lester nodded his head toward me.

"Oh, Lester, don't."

"Tell me!" Justine insisted.

"A customer passed out right here. In the bar! My gorgeous girlfriend went rushing over and did CPR until the paramedics got here. We found out later he'd had a heart attack, but is going to be okay. How 'bout that?" It was Lester's turn to look proud as he lightly brushed the hair away from my face and kissed my forehead.

"Why didn't you say anything?" Justine asked. "See? There you go again. Saving lives!"

My face was burning even though I doubted anyone could tell in the dim light.

"Wanna go?" I asked after Lester rejoined the band to start their final set.

With a quick look around, Justine said, "Yeah, sure. It looks like Hop-along Cassidy left. I don't want to embarrass him anymore."

"Come on. He's the one with the corny pick-up line. What were you supposed to do?"

As we walked to the car, she said, "I must admit, you're right about Lester and the guitar. He's really talented."

"Yeah, thanks. He really is a good guy. I know you'll like him when you get to know him better."

"Seriously, though." She gently pressed her shoulder into me. "When was the last time he took a shower?"

We drove back through town before heading out toward Miller Ave. Everything was great. Justine had let up on her criticism of Lester and was maybe even starting to see why I liked him. I had a boyfriend who was crazy about me. My job at the nursing home was still going well. I was getting back on track with my college studies. Yes. My life was finally going the way I wanted.

"What's he doing, just sitting there?" Justine startled me out of my musing. I followed her gaze out of the passenger window.

"Who?"

"Officer O'Reilly. Isn't that him?"

My heart leapt as I recognized the cruiser, indeed, idling in front of my house. I slowed as we passed and he turned toward us. He smiled and touched the brim of his hat. I sped past without acknowledging him.

"That's weird," Justine said. "Why do you think he's hanging out here?"

"Dunno."

"Eva...?"

"You don't mind if I drop you off, do you? It's been a long day. Plus, I need to get in a run before bed."

"A run? Are you *kidding* me? It's after midnight!" Justine was incredulous.

"Uh, yeah. I didn't have a chance earlier."

"Don't be ridiculous! You're not going running at this hour. What's going on, Eva?"

"It's nothing. I just remembered... that's all."

"You're not going running, and that's that." Justine was still staring at me. "Go on home and go to bed. Running. Jeez! At this hour!"

"Uh, okay. It was only a thought. You're right. It's too late." The words dribbled out of me without any strength. I could hear how feeble I sounded, but was unable to fake it at that moment. Not even for Justine.

All Good Things

"Landslide" – Fleetwood Mac

Justine

DANNY BOUGHT A CAPE COD style house last October. He'd gotten a great price on the fixer-upper and done all the repairs and upgrades himself: new plumbing and electrical, hardwood floors, and elaborate custom cabinetry in the bathrooms and kitchen. With the addition of several lucrative clients, his contracting business was rapidly becoming one of the most in-demand in central Massachusetts. This influx of money allowed him to renovate with few restrictions.

We had become nearly inseparable since reuniting in May and every moment I wasn't helping Aunt Peggy, I took my role of Danny's self-appointed interior decorator seriously. We'd hunted through yard sales and antique stores for furniture and bric-a-brac. I'd chosen linens in a rich, royal blue paisley for the king-size bed and filled wall space with pictures and paintings we selected together. He wanted my input on everything for the house he pointedly referred to as "our home." At the Brimfield Antique Show in July, we hit the jackpot.

We wandered hand-in-hand up one crowd-packed aisle and down the next. Row upon row of vendors with their rich assortment of wares displayed beneath an expanse of colorful pop-up canopies and over-sized beach umbrellas. We purchased a mahogany, roll-top secretary desk for Danny's home office. I found nearly a dozen vintage postcards picturing late 1800s and early 1900s North Brookfield, then purchased antique frames to display them. We bought a brass inlaid rosewood mantel clock to place above the newly refurbished fireplace and a pair of 1930s silver-plated lamps, perfect for the tables on either side of the bed. I insisted on the matching 19th century rocking chairs with curved armrests so we could enjoy cool summer evenings on the screened-in porch.

Ducking through the opening of a massive canvas tent, we discovered a vast exhibition of classical paintings in intricately carved, gilded frames. We were drawn to the same picture. The scene, in muted pastels, was a young man and woman in Victorian dress, him seated at the baby grand piano while she hovered adoringly nearby. The attraction between the couple was nearly palpable. The title penned at the bottom read, *When Love Is Young.*

"Danny, please, can we get this?"

"Where would it go?"

"Right when you walk in the front door," I answered. "Over that rustic sideboard on the opposite wall. It's a perfect fit."

"How much is it?" He searched for a price tag, but found none on the frame itself or the makeshift wall it was hanging on.

"Wait," I said, placing my hand on his forearm. The vendor was finishing up with another customer. "Sir!" I called out, waving my hand in his direction. "What are you asking for this painting?"

"Ah, yes, that." The quirky little man, a throwback to another era, strode toward us in a way I could only describe as jaunty. He could have been someone from the old time pictures in Aunt Peggy's attic with his bowler hat and bow-tie. Rapidly gesturing hands punctuated his rambling speech. "It's actually a hand-colored print from an original etching circa 1900. Yes, yes, circa 1900. Quite lovely."

"But how much is it?" I tried to suppress a swell of impatience.

"Such a charming Victorian couple, see? They're in their own world. No one else exists. Their own Utopia. Yes, so young and in love." The odd man sighed and fell silent, forgetting we were there.

I grinned at Danny, but he shook his head at me, trying hard to control his own smile.

"Sir?" My voice cracked on my restrained laughter.

"Ah, yes. The price. I'm asking $300 for it. It is hand-colored, after all, did I mention? Quite old; quite old, indeed."

"Hmmm, I don't know." Danny took a step toward the exit to start the bargaining process.

"Okay, okay. Let me tell you what I can do. I can see the lady, here, has her heart set on it. Yes, she does. Let's see." He tapped his index finger against his pursed lips, seeming to concentrate on the issue at hand. "Let me see." His eyes went from Danny to me to the picture. Suddenly, his finger paused in mid-tap. "Huh."

"What?" I asked.

"It's just that, well, no. It's silly. I'm being silly!" he prattled.

"Silly about...?" I began.

"It's that, well, look at the two of you! You could be the couple in the picture! There's more than a scant similarity, there is! More than a little, I'd say!"

Danny and I stared at the subjects in the picture. She was in a full-length dress, buttoned to the chin, and her hair was swept into a loose up-do. Facially, I saw nothing remotely resembling me. The man was in striped trousers with the tails of his charcoal colored jacket hanging to one side of the intricately carved high-back chair where he sat. His hair was smooth, combed to one side. Perplexed, we glanced back at the salesman.

He pointed to the Victorian pair. "*When Love Is Young*—that *is* you. You must have it! It belongs to you two! Tell you what. I'll give it to you for $250, yes I will."

Danny still looked hesitant.

"Well, okay, young man, you drive a hard bargain. I'll let you have it for $225. That's my final offer. $225! What a steal!"

With our latest treasure carefully wrapped in brown paper, we wandered back toward Danny's truck. We'd spent nearly nine hours strolling around Brimfield and it was time to go. I was distracted by the goods under nearly every tent we passed, when I suddenly realized I was alone. Doubling back, I found Danny leaning over a table crammed with antique jewelry—glittering gold necklaces with square-cut garnets, screw-back earrings with dangling amber pendants, bracelets with lapis, and bangles with emeralds.

"*Holyyy...!*" my voice trailed off as I bent to inspect a quarter-sized amethyst set in a delicately woven gold bracelet. "This stuff is amazing!" In a hushed voice, I asked Danny, "You don't think these are real, do you?"

"See the guy over there? Watching us? I'm pretty sure he's a guard," he said.

"I guess they're real, then!"

"What do you think of this one?" Danny picked up a ring from a slit in the velvet-backed display. The guard's eyes were glued to Danny's hand while the owner hurried over to assist.

"That's an Edwardian sapphire and diamond engagement ring," said the owner.

His name was Herb, I gathered, from the professionally engraved name tag pinned to the pocket of his buttoned-down shirt. But, I was barely aware of Herb or the guard. I only saw Danny—my love, my heart, and my soul. His eyes, deep blue and filled with promise, held mine as I held my breath.

What is this? Is this it?

The ring had a huge center sapphire—nearly 2 carats—surrounded by ten diamonds totaling another carat, bordered by tiny sapphires all set in polished platinum. I had never seen something so beautiful.

Ohmygod, ohmygod. I was having trouble catching my breath. *Yes!* my brain screamed.

I smiled at Danny.

Horror washed over his face.

"Oh, Justine. I'm sorry... I didn't mean to...."

"No, no, Danny! I was... it's just that... yes, the ring is gorgeous!"

"I was only trying to get an idea of what you like. Not for now, but, you know, someday."

"Of course. I knew that," I said, turning away to hide my embarrassment. "I have to finish college, after all."

Danny set the ring back in its holder and reached for my hand. "You're the one, Justine. The love of my life. You know that, don't you?" Pulling me to him, he tipped my face to his and leaned down to kiss me. "We'll find the perfect ring when the time is right."

ABOVE THE BED, IN THE center of the shelf built into the headboard, rested the bronze cast of the entwined hands of Robert and Elizabeth Barrett Browning Danny gave me as a graduation gift. Since I first discovered *Sonnets from the Portuguese* three years before, I'd been a devotee of the romantic verses and insisted on reading aloud to him whenever we were alone.

> *How do I love thee? Let me count the ways.*
> *I love thee to the depth and breadth and height*
> *My soul can reach, when feeling out of sight*

With his blue eyes intensely focused on me, I'd read stanza after stanza to him. He'd taken to calling me "Belovéd"—the term Elizabeth used for her husband—and could quote any line containing it. "Belovéd, thou hast brought me many flowers/Plucked in the garden...." There was something about hearing the sensuous words in his rich baritone voice that never failed to turn me on. When he'd whisper "Belovéd" in my ear and begin unbuttoning my blouse, it was impossible for me to concentrate on sonnets. The book would be set aside and forgotten.

Today, though, he seemed distracted. While we sat side-by-side on the love seat in the living room, he tried to pretend all was normal. With his fidgeting and staring off into space, I knew something was wrong.

"I'm seeing Eva later, so I thought we could, you know...." I jerked my head toward the bedroom, hoping to draw him out of his funk.

"You know I'm always happy to 'you know'... but do we have time? You don't need to get home?"

"No, I've got the day off. I'll stop home, but Aunt Peggy isn't expecting me. I am worried, though."

"Her health?" he asked.

"Yeah. She's getting worse. She's having more trouble getting around. We'll have to hire someone for when I leave. They can't do it, the two of them, anymore."

"What about Randy? Is he planning to move here any time soon?"

I had confided in my brother about Aunt Peggy and Uncle John's financial situation and he devised the perfect plan. He loved North Brookfield the way I did, felt the same strong attachment to the town and our family history. When he learned Aunt Peggy could no longer afford the upkeep on the house and was thinking of selling it, he stepped in with an offer. He'd buy the house, paying them a monthly stipend toward the purchase, and would assume all repair costs and utility bills. They'd negotiated the details and all involved felt it was an ideal solution.

"No. He's not ready, but he will be someday. In the meantime, my dad will pay for a full-time aide. You know, I always loved that house. It's gotta be what, over a hundred years old? I wish I'd had the money to buy it. I know it needs work—a roof, windows, and all—but I would have loved for us to live there after we get married. Do you think it would have been a good investment for us, Danny?"

"Is what a good investment?"

"The house! Haven't you heard a word I said?"

"Justine...." His eyes were turned downward.

"Danny...?"

"There's something I have to say—to tell you. It's...."

I sat on the edge of the sofa and watched him as a chill flickered in my belly.

"I...." His eyes dropped to his hands twisting in his lap. At last he uttered the words that would change everything. "I got a phone call this morning."

The cold that had started in my gut shot to my heart, then to my hands and feet, numbing them. My face, by odd contrast, burned. "A phone call? From?"

He covered his face with his hands, deliberately rubbed his closed eyes, and then lowered his hands back into his lap. He drew a long breath and exhaled in an unsteady stream. Finally, the words burst out. "The girl I told you about. The one I saw after you left last year. I swear, Justine, I was careful! I don't know how it happened. You and I... well, at the time, I didn't think we had a chance. She means nothing to me, Justine, *nothing*! It's you I love. But what can I do? What am I supposed to do?"

"What are you telling me? Is she"—I took a deep breath—"*pregnant*?"

His eyes seized mine, pleading with me to acknowledge his torment. I struggled to wrap my head around what this meant. While he and I had spent the summer falling in love and planning our future, another girl was carrying his baby!

"Is she keeping it?"

He bowed his head. "Yes."

Hysteria rose in my voice. "You're not going to m-marry her, are you?"

"I have to," he said, barely above a whisper.

I stood up. Through my haze of shock, I stared at his defeated form. He sat there, eyes on his hands in his lap. Wordlessly, I rushed toward the door. Hanging on the wall in the entrance was the painting, *When Love Is Young*. I wiped the tears from my face and a stab of envy for that naively happy couple in old-fashioned dress rushed through me.

"Belovéd."

I didn't turn around. Instead, I spat my response over my shoulder. "Don't call me that, Danny. Ever again!" I slammed out of the house and bolted to my car. Images of my shattered dreams hung before me as I drove away.

"GIMME ANOTHER," I SAID TO Larry, my old Portable Party friend who was tending bar at The Pub.

"Don't you think you've had enough, Justine?"

I tapped my glass toward him. "'nother Bud draft."

Larry shook his head, grabbed my glass, and held it under the tap. "Where's Eva tonight?"

"Workin'."

"Is she coming by later?"

"No. She's workin' a double."

"I think you'd better get a ride home, Justine," Larry said. "I don't want you driving like this."

I didn't answer. *Who gives a shit? So what if I have an accident? Would anybody care? Danny certainly wouldn't.*

A group of older men were playing pool. Every so often they'd glance in my direction. A thirty-ish couple was at the other end of the bar. They seemed oblivious to everyone else—he'd lean close to whisper something and she'd laugh and kiss him on the lips. Their eyes never left each other as he stroked her hair and she smiled affectionately in return.

Fools!

The main door opened and a familiar figure walked in.

"Lester!" I called out, wobbling but catching myself before falling off the stool.

"Heyyy! What's going on, Justine?"

"Just 'avin' a drink, tha's all. What're you doin' 'ere?"

Lester settled into the seat next to me as Larry placed a bottle of Heineken in front of him. "Killing time. Eva's working, the band's not playing tonight. I'm on my own."

We started with some getting-to-know-you chit-chat, then graduated to playful banter. I sized him up as I emptied the rest of my beer. He did have pretty eyes. His ponytail was a golden color and clean. Clearly, he'd showered. He was not my type at all, but in this light, he wasn't half bad.

I asked for another beer, but Larry cut me off.

Lester finished his second beer, then caught me glancing at the tightness of his jeans. "I've got some new weed out in my van. Wanna get outta here?"

"Sure."

LONELINESS

"All By Myself" – Eric Carmen

EVA

"**Y**OU THINK HE'S CUTE? I don't know. He's got those huge lips and he looks kinda... effeminate... maybe?" Justine was moving slowly across my room, examining each of my Mick Jagger posters. Most pictures were of him performing in concert—one with a knee-length smoking jacket, another sharing a microphone with Keith Richards and sporting a frilly shirt with multiple layers of ruffles down his sleeves. Some were casual, like the one with a solid white suit and the close-up with his full-lipped pout.

"I sure wouldn't kick him out of bed!" I answered from where I sat cross-legged on the padded bench at the end of my bed. I took a moment to admire each of the posters individually. "Actually, I think he's wicked hot. Okay, here it is," I said, smoothing the newspaper open to the article.

Justine huddled next to me to stare at the faded picture of the little girl who'd been found murdered by Five Mile River. "How long's it been?" she asked.

"Pretty close to five years, I'd say."

"Did you read the story, Eva? How'd they finally catch the guy who killed her?"

"He confessed."

"That's it?" she asked. "No leads they'd been following or clues from the crime scene?"

"This isn't some TV show, you know. Sometimes these cases never get solved. But this guy walked into the police station and turned himself in. Apparently, he couldn't live with the guilt anymore. He told the police that he'd raped her, then panicked. He didn't mean to kill her with the rock. Just knock her out."

225

"Jeez. All of these years, no one knowing the truth except that one guy. Can you imagine if he hadn't come forward? They may never have known. Or," she added, "they might have kept blaming Rag Doll Man!"

I stood up to stretch. It was a beautiful late August day and, leaning on the windowsill to gaze outside, I thought about preparations needed to get Smokey ready to move back home. *Make sure the stall is cleaned... get fresh hay... buy a new barrel of grain from Agway.* As I scanned the street up and down, my eyes fell on the black and white cruiser coming from the direction of town. Officer O'Reilly was the driver.

Justine joined me at the window.

"What did you say?" I asked.

"I wanted to know what you were looking at," she said. "Why is that cop cruiser always around here?"

"Dunno."

Silently, we watched as he drove out of sight toward Shadow Hill. I couldn't think of a single word to say. My eyes were glued in the direction where he'd vanished.

Wait! What the hell?! The cruiser was heading back this way!

Justine had returned to the bed to read the newspaper article about the little girl, but I was frozen in place. I don't think I imagined it as he slowed directly in front of my house. Then he continued on. Moments later, he went past a third time.

"Uh, I forgot to run today," I said, forcing my voice to remain steady.

Justine's head popped up. "What? You've gotta be kidding me! You're not thinking of going now, are you?"

"Well, I, uh...."

"You can go running later. This is our last day before I leave. Why don't we grab a six-pack and go cruising?"

"ARE YOU EVER GOING TO tell me what happened with you and Danny?" I asked.

"Maybe," she said.

Other than a few mumbled phrases—"broke up... another girl... all a big mistake"— she'd turned icily reticent when I tried to get any information from her. Typical—she'd always preferred to keep her misery to herself.

I tried changing the subject. "Lester and I are making plans to go away for Labor Day weekend. We're thinking about—"

"Ugghh! I don't want to hear it!"

"Sorry?"

As we approached the town limit of West Brookfield, I lifted my foot from the accelerator. For a second, a smile crossed Justine's face as she resurrected our long-standing joke. "Uh-oh. Be careful there. Don't want to go a single mile over twenty-five miles per hour!"

I chimed in with my requisite response. "You know what these local cops are like. Pulling over speeders is what they live for."

Once we'd reached the other end of town, I resumed my lead-foot habit. "I shouldn't have talked about Lester and me. That was insensitive. Right after you and Danny, you know."

"This has nothing to do with Danny. I'm just not Lester's number one fan."

"What?" I was shocked. "I thought you guys were getting along?"

"I'm sorry, Eva. I think you can do better. He's kind of a lowlife."

And that's when I finally snapped. "You know what, Justine? Fuck you!"

Her mouth dropped open. Once I'd started, though, I couldn't stop. All of my suppressed irritation with her pretension and moodiness came bursting out.

"You think you know everything! You aren't around most of the time. You don't know some of the shit I've gone through. He's been nothing but great to me. The night we met, when he was playing at the bar, some guys were harassing me, pinching my ass, and all. Lester stopped in the middle of a song, jumped off the stage, and grabbed one guy's arm before he could touch me again. He told them they'd better lay off of me or he'd beat the shit out of them!" I paused for breath.

"Yeah, but—"

"Did you know he's self-taught on the guitar? At sixteen, he put his band together. He's been working as a musician ever since. Sometimes he drinks too much, gets high, whatever. And maybe he's got girls all over him. But he's committed to *me*! He takes care of *me*! He loves *me*! I don't know what happened with Danny and some other girl, but I'll tell you this: Lester has always been faithful to me. So whatever your problem is with him, Justine Andrews, get over it! He's here to stay!"

Her lips were pressed together so the taut, white skin around them contrasted to the splotchy red of the rest of her face. We drove on in silence.

I couldn't even look at her. I blasted the radio to fill the void and drove as fast as I dared toward Miller Ave. When I pulled through the tunnel of trees and saw Smokey standing patiently by the gate, the tightness in my chest melted and tears welled up in my eyes. I ground to a stop in the driveway as sweet Lucky came to greet us.

Taking a long, deep breath then blowing it out, Justine turned toward me. It was in that moment I saw she was crying too.

Before slamming the car door shut, she said, "Maybe you don't know Lester as well as you think you do."

CHAPTER 9

1980

What a True Friend Does

"Someone Saved My Life Tonight" – Elton John

Eva

WHEN THE DOORBELL RANG, I had no intention of answering it. Although it was early evening at the end of May, I was in bed. I wanted to sleep, but wouldn't. I felt like I should read, but couldn't concentrate. I knew I should be outside; friends were doing things, going places, and I had missed one of the best parties of the year: the annual Moose Brook bonfire. But I had no desire to do anything. It'd been two weeks since....

Bbrrrrring!

That damned doorbell again. I rolled over and folded my pillow around my head. "Go awayyy!"

Brrring! Brrrrinnng!

Someone was sure persistent.

Brrrrinnng!

Where did my parents say they were going today? To my aunt's house in Vermont? Maybe there was an accident.

Brrrinnng!!!

Okay! You win. I rolled over, pushed my flattened-out, greasy hair away from my face, and padded down the stairs to the front door. *Police? Firemen? Bible salesman? This had better be important!*

I turned the lock and pulled the heavy front door open. A diminutive blonde figure stood on the other side of the screen. Were my eyes playing tricks on me?

"Well, are you gonna invite me in or are you gonna stand there with your mouth open?" Justine breezed past me as if we had just seen each other yesterday while I held the door open in stunned silence. In her typical

231

right-at-home fashion, she surveyed the chairs, decided on the green floral recliner, and plopped herself down.

"I just ate, so don't worry about offering me a drink or anything."

With my back hugging the wall, I slid around the corner and sat on the chair facing hers. Her humor was lost on me.

"Uh… okay."

"And, by the way, Eva, you look like you saw a ghost. I don't bite, you know."

"Oh. Sorry." I searched for words. "It's that, uh, I'm surprised to see you. I didn't know you were back in town. You never mentioned in your letters when you'd be back."

Justine sagged forward in her chair. All of her swagger seemed to drain from her, and her voice assumed a tone of seriousness. "I never sent any letters. After last summer, I couldn't. But when I heard about Smokey.…"

I looked away, studying a fly on the windowsill beside me. "Oh. So you heard."

"Aunt Peggy told me. I'm so sorry. I wanted to come here and tell you, in person."

I was finally able to meet Justine's gaze. "Thank you." I only wanted to go back upstairs, get back under my covers. "Thank you. I appreciate that." *The end. Now let me go.*

Instead, Justine sat taller.

Here it comes. The questions. The intensity. Oh God… a lecture. A sermon about not giving up. Here it comes. You are worthy. Oh God, spare me.

"Hey, do you know what time it is?"

I detected a glint of a sparkle appearing in her eyes, one I hadn't seen in years. "Huh?" I looked at the clock. "It's around six—"

"No. I mean do you know what *time* it is? It's summer. It's gonna be dark in a few hours."

"And?"

Justine lowered her voice to a whisper. "It's time… *to hide on cars!*"

"Mmm. No. I'm not up for that." Nice try, but I couldn't catch her enthusiasm.

"You *are* up for it, and we're going. It'll be totally rad. Go upstairs and get some real clothes on. I brought something to help us pass the time while we wait for it to get dark." Justine opened her purse to reveal a bottle.

"Blackberry brandy? Are you crazy?!"

"Yes, but that's beside the point. Are you coming or do I have to drink this all by myself?"

I found myself coming alive, reluctantly. "Well, if you drink that all by yourself, I might end up having to do CPR on you, and that'd be awkward."

Justine jumped out of her chair, bounded to mine, and pulled me to my feet. "Go!"

"THERE WEREN'T MANY CARS TONIGHT," I observed flatly.

We had ended up hanging out with our old friend Wausau, and the night was so quiet it seemed I could hear the TV from Jane Williams's house at the back of the cemetery. Justine kept up her chatter as we passed the bottle between us, giving me a running narrative of her college life, her grades, her job at the women's shelter, her expectations, her parents' expectations, and her ongoing Danny torment. It was riveting, but I found myself to be less than good company and even less of a participant, offering only an occasional "uh huh" or "really?" or "that sucks." The old magic simply wasn't happening.

"Give me another hit of that," I said, reaching for Justine's bottle. "Whoa. Did we drink that much? It's half empty."

Justine held up the bottle and examined it, contemplating. "It's half *full*. So, Eva, my friend, that would make you a pessissimist."

"A whaaaat?"

"A peshimist."

"Justine, you light-weight. You're shit-faced!"

"Oh yeah? Oh yeah? And you're *not*?"

"Nope, not at all." I stood up to prove my point, taking a step toward Justine and the bottle. Except my knees buckled and I found myself lurching headlong into a thicket.

Justine stood over me with a smirk, stifling a laugh. "That does it! We've come full circle. This is exactly what you were doing when we first met. Enjoy your trip?"

"Yes, it was lovely. Why don't you come along?" I grabbed her free hand and yanked her down next to me, reveling in the rather ungraceful way she fell. For the first time today, we laughed, and it was heartfelt.

"Wish I had a camera for that one. I thought you never made an awkward move in your entire life."

"Come on, Eva. That's not true. I make plenty of them. I'm not so perfect, you know."

"What? Stop the presses! Justine isn't perfect?!"

"No. Really, Eva. I make mistakes too. I have problems too, you know."

"Your problems always seem to be 'which guy do I go out with?'" I was drunk enough to let a little bitterness show. "Hmmm. I'm Justine," I sing-songed. "Do I go out with Mark or do I go out with Mike? Decishions, decishions. And, do I wear my peppermint pink top tonight or the teal green one?"

Justine gave me a shove. A hard one. "Not funny, Eva!"

I turned and looked at her. Were those tears? "Uh, sorry?"

"Your teasing goes too far. It's not funny. My problems are real. Didn't you hear anything I've said? Everything seems to be converging on me, all at once."

"Well, pity you, but you're not the one who lost your best friend!"

Justine looked instantly sober. "You really don't listen, do you?"

The silence was deafening. Unable to find words, I picked up the bottle and took a long guzzle.

Justine stared at me a long while. "Let's walk down to the cemetery. I want to look at something."

"Okay." We both rose to our feet unsteadily and began walking in silence.

"I feel like I need to visit some of my ancestors."

"Sure."

"It gives me pershpective," Justine slurred. "There's something reassuring about seeing them. Comforting."

I didn't have to reply. Justine knew I felt the same way. Fascination with the past and an unexplainable connection to our ancestors were of the many shared bonds we knew would never change.

The moon had risen, giving us enough light to navigate between headstones and find our way to the Miller plot. We had traveled these narrow roadways with their crumbling pavement so many times before, we could have done it blindfolded. When we reached her family headstone, Justine lowered herself Indian style onto the cool grass. I plopped down beside her.

"Remember when we used to come here as kids and just walk around telling stories, Eva?"

"Yeah."

"Sometimes I feel like I need to see these graves again. It reminds me that my life isn't so hard." Justine took a deep breath. "When I think about my great-grandmother and how she lost so many of her children, it puts it all in perspective."

"You mean in *pershpective*."

Justine gave me a sideways look and a wry smile. "Eva, it's so complicated! Everything in my life is changing, and too fast. Aunt Peggy... school... Danny. I wish I knew what to do. And I don't."

For the first time in a long while, I felt sorry for Justine. I absently twirled a piece of grass, relishing the silence to gather my thoughts. "I wish we were kids again. My biggest problem back then was avoiding Jane Williams. I was so dumb. As if anything she thought or said mattered."

Justine laughed. "Jane Williams! Remember that night we tried to scare her?! Oh, that was a good one."

"Those early summers were nothing but 'good ones.' Remember exploring the barn... and the attic! You tried to scare me, but we both ended up scared!"

We chuckled as the memories came flooding back.

Justine gazed into the distance. "They were great summers. We were scared out of our wits. Remember Rag Doll Man? Finally finding out he isn't real? That he's some old hermit—Drifter Drake—living in the woods?" She shifted her eyes to her great-grandparents' grave marker, lost in her thoughts. "You see, Eva, people live and die. They just live and die, and for what?" She sounded drunk again. "Who remembers? Who even *knows*?! That's why I like to come here. Dorothy Justine. Sweet Alice. Baby. Faith Ellen. John Carl. They were real, Eva, and they lived and died here, in this place, and up there on Miller Ave. And someday we'll be gone too."

I sat in silence, trying to absorb Justine's logic. We lived. And we died. Someday, we'd be gone too. And who would even know?

As if in answer, the clock at the Town Hall began to announce the hour. We silently reflected while the bell sounded ten times. I closed my eyes while images forced their way in. *We live... we die... who even knows... Dorothy Justine... Sweet Alice... Baby... the thirteen-year-old murdered girl at Five Mile River.*

Smokey.

"That's *it*!" I leapt to my feet so fast I nearly knocked Justine over.

"What's '*it*'?"

"The bell!" I was so excited I could barely speak. "The bell! Justine, we've got to ring the bell for Smokey!"

"Ring the bell? Are you drunk?"

"Yes, but so what? We need to do it!"

"How do you suppose we do that?" Justine was suddenly the logical one. "Do we go walking into Town Hall and say, 'hey, um, excuse me, I want to go ring the bell'?"

"No! Not the Town Hall. The old Methodist Church! I know the way in, Justine. We can get in! Craig told me how."

"You mean that old church by the Common? The one that's all boarded up?"

"That's the one."

Justine sat looking at me in stunned silence while I barely contained my enthusiasm. A role reversal from a few short hours ago. Finally, I grabbed her hand.

"Are you coming or do I have to do this all by myself?"

"HURRY UP AND LOOSEN THAT board," I whispered. "You're killing me!"

"Hold your horses. I'm getting it!"

Since she was lighter, Justine stood on my shoulders working on freeing a window at the back of the ancient church. With a groan of protest, the old rotted board gave way, and I felt her weight lift as she pulled herself through the narrow opening. I heard the click of her lighter. Pulling as hard as I could, I only managed to hoist myself to eye-level of the bottom ledge of the window. I could hear Justine picking her way through the dark room.

"Go open the door! Hurry up!"

"Jeez! Give me a minute!"

I positioned myself by the back door and flattened against the wall. *What if I'm seen? What if the cops come by? What's taking so long?* At last, the door opened. I slithered in and Justine pushed the door closed behind me. My eyes couldn't adjust to the abrupt blackness quickly enough.

"What's in here? I can't see."

"I see some pews. Old boxes. A lot of books. Missals."

"Missiles?! What is this, a cold war depository?"

"Missals, you moron! You know, hymnals."

I couldn't help but smile to myself, loving it when Justine gave it back. "Did you see the stairs to the belfry anywhere?"

"I think they should be here, in the back."

Flick. Flick.

In the arc illuminated by Justine's lighter, I could make out shadows, and then shapes. Pews. Boxes. Books. Tall stained-glass windows with only the street light across the way revealing hints of their colors.

"There they are!" Justine whispered. "The stairs!"

Justine held the lighter aloft as she carefully picked her way through decaying cardboard boxes littering the sides of the winding stairs. I inched my way even more gingerly behind her. As we climbed, the stairs creaked and groaned. I could feel my feet sinking into something soft.

"What am I stepping in?"

"Pigeon shit."

"I can't see a thing. I'm gonna trip over something and break my neck! Justine! Slow down! Lemme grab hold of the bottom of your shirt." I groped my way in blackness. Justine paused in front of me and flicked the lighter. "Dammit, Justine, why did you have to wear such a short shirt? There isn't even anything to hold onto."

"This was all your idea, remember? Excuse me for not wearing my breaking-into-a-church outfit!"

"Breaking-into-a-church outfit," I repeated under my breath, chuckling at the picture in my head of Justine in a burglar's cat suit, when she stopped short and sent us colliding.

"Just*ine*! You have *got* to warn me when—"

"There it is! The rope!"

We stared, speechless. She raised her arm above her and flicked her lighter. The heavy rope disappeared into an abyss stretching far above our heads into pitch-black. We released our collective breath.

The bell!

I stepped in front of Justine. "I have to do this." I stared at the rope, following it up into the darkness. Uncertainty overwhelmed me. *Everyone in town will hear. Will someone call the cops? I have to know!*

I shifted my gaze to a rickety ladder in front of us. "We've got to go a little farther up. We've got to go up to the tower."

"Okay. Follow me."

God, who is this girl? Anyone else would be whimpering, pleading "no way, we'll get caught!" or "no way, there are probably bats up there!" But not Justine. She never said no to anything—never backed down. To think, a few hours ago I was making fun of her, telling her that her biggest decisions were between wearing the pink or the blue top. I felt my cheeks grow hot. Here she was, climbing a rickety ladder in near total darkness for me. How could I be so wrong about someone?

"I love you, Justine."

She stopped and turned. "You say something?"

"No."

I followed her up the ladder, my knuckles white, wondering if Justine hated heights as much as I did. At last, she stepped onto a landing.

"Rad!" Justine whistled in amazement. "Eva, hurry up! You've got to see this!"

I scrambled up the last few feet and emerged onto the landing. We were in the tower! A six-sided tower. The windows were open and the full moon lit up the sky. Far below us, the village of North Brookfield slept. Somehow, from this vantage point, the town looked different. Soft and so small, like a painting. For a moment, neither of us spoke.

Justine broke my trance. "There it is!"

"There what is?"

"The police cruiser! See him? Way over there."

I followed Justine's gaze. In the distance, over the rise of the hill, the town's lone police cruiser was unmistakable. With blue lights flashing, it sped down North Main Street towards the outskirts of town.

"He's leaving! Eva, you've got to do this *now*!"

I'm doing this. God damn it, I'm doing this! For Smokey! I grabbed the rope with both trembling hands and took a deep breath. *How does this go?*

"Two times for a male!" Justine interjected as if she'd been reading my thoughts.

I pulled the rope as hard as I could. The bell was enormous and far heavier than I had imagined, but the sound it let out was lovely. A plaintive, lonely peal, and to me, the saddest sound on Earth.

I felt a lump rise in my throat, then tears began streaming. "Smokey, this is for you."

Justine bowed her head in reverence. "Can't you go any faster?"

"I could, but that's not the right way. When you toll the bell for someone, you have to wait for the reverberation to stop completely in between each time."

"Whaaat?"

"I said," shouting to her, "The right way to toll the bell is to wait for the reverberation to stop each time."

"How old was he?"

"Thirty-two! What are we on?"

"Twenty-nine!"

"Whaaat?"

"Twenty-*nine*!"

Just three more. I had been ringing the bell for at least five full minutes. As I yanked the rope, I watched the town. One by one, lights had come on in windows scattered across the awakening village. I was possessed. *Good! I hope the whole town wakes up!*

Justine bit her lip while scanning the scene.

Thirty.

"Police!" Justine screamed so loudly I had no trouble hearing despite the echoing in my ears.

"Go! Run!"

Thirty-one. *Fuck him! He's not taking* this *away from me! Just one more.*

"Run, Justine!"

"No!"

The cruiser screeched to a stop in front of the church. From our perch far above, we saw the door slam as the unmistakable brawny figure with the blond buzz cut hurried straight for the front door.

My hands were shaking. My entire body began to shiver. I shut my eyes tight. *I* will *do this! He can't stop me!* "Thirty-two!"

There! Let's go! I turned and half-scrambled, half-jumped down the ladder. Behind me, Justine didn't even bother trying to negotiate the rungs but jumped to the landing and overtook me on the stairs. We took them two at a time, at last emerging at the base of the choir loft, right as the main door swung open.

We were out the back door and didn't stop running until we reached the railroad tracks. We ducked behind the old depot and then ran some more, down the abandoned railroad tracks, all the way to the path leading to Peggy and John Miller's house.

HEARTBREAK AND FORGIVENESS
"Yesterday" – The Beatles

JUSTINE

O*HSHIT!OHSHIT!OHSHIT!* ABANDONING MY GROCERY CART in the middle of aisle three, I made a mad dash for the front door. I'd been searching for Uncle John's Chips Ahoy! when I'd caught a glimpse of Danny at the other end of the aisle, carrying a package of Pampers under his arm. I didn't think he saw me and prayed I could get out of there without a confrontation.

Stumbling across the parking lot, I foraged for the keys somewhere in my oversized purse and snagged them just as I reached my car. I steadied my hand long enough to shove the key into the lock. The footsteps were right behind me.

He grabbed me and whirled me around to face him. "Justine! Come on, Justine, talk to me!"

"Don't touch me!"

Several people in the parking lot turned to stare at us.

Danny dropped his hand. "*Please*, can we talk?"

I fell back against my car and waited. Every clenched muscle melted into shivering defeat. "Why, Danny? Why do you keep calling me? Just leave me alone."

His voice cracked. "I'm in hell, Justine! Please. You have to know I still love you." The tears welling in his eyes broke free and streamed down his face.

Watching him as he wept, he was *my* Danny again: the boy I fell in love with, who'd trusted me with his deepest secrets. I'd trusted him, too. I'd trusted him to honor and treasure the heart I'd given to him. But he'd destroyed it.

His eyes seized mine, pleading with me to acknowledge his torment.

For one moment, I forgot everything. I put my arms around his neck and pulled his mouth to mine. Those sweet lips that had confided in me the heartbreak of his lonely, miserable childhood. Those loving lips that had coaxed and teased me from innocent girl to passionate woman. Those cruel lips that had betrayed me and crushed my heart.

"Danny, no!" I pulled away. "I can't."

"Justine, please! I love you. *Only* you. I'll figure this out. I'll make it right, I swear!"

I gasped as I stumbled a step backwards.

"What are you talking about? Make *what* right? They exist, Danny! They aren't... hypothetical!" A child. He had a *child* with another woman.

He gripped my wrist. "Justine, I—"

"Go home to your family, Danny," I said, yanking my arm away. "And throw away my number. Don't call me anymore."

It wasn't until I got into my car and drove away that I wondered if the Barrett-Browning hand sculpture he'd given me was still resting in the headboard above the bed.

Their bed.

FUNNY HOW THIS TOWN, so much a part of me, could be the source of both unbearable grief and the greatest comfort. I knew where I needed to be. I drove to the gravesites of my great-grandparents, John Carl and Faith Ellen, and of the three little ones, including Dorothy Justine. I dropped to the ground by the larger headstone.

Stop with the tears, Justine! Enough already!

I'd spent the past nine months replaying our last moments together. How one phone call had destroyed all of our plans. Seeing Danny had ripped open my wounded heart, which had barely started to heal.

"Faith Ellen?" I spoke to my great-grandmother as if she had materialized in front of me. "What am I supposed to do? How'd everything get so screwed up?"

No one answered. I pulled a blade of grass from the ground and twirled it between my thumb and forefinger. A gentle breeze tousled my hair. I glanced up.

Faith Ellen? "I thought I was okay after all this time. I guess I was kidding myself. I spent this past year practically living at the school library and my job at the shelter so I wouldn't think about him. I was an idiot to come back here this summer."

It had been a mild spring with regular rainfall. The cemetery was in full color. The rolling hills had never been a more vibrant emerald. Mini-gardens of geraniums and lilies-of-the-valley flourished at gravesites scattered from one end of the cemetery to the other. For once, the beauty of my surroundings was lost on me. I was completely immersed in my pain.

And in my guilt for what had happened with Lester.

"That's the other problem, Faith Ellen. What do I tell Eva?"

I'd made Lester swear he'd never speak of what we did last summer. *Almost* did. I'd been drunk, out of my head with grief. I wasn't thinking. Especially after Lester fired up the Hawaiian Gold he'd recently scored. I'd allowed myself to pretend I was with Danny. I'd closed my eyes and felt fingers gently stroking my hair, then tracing my face. A shiver went through me as they trailed down my neck and grazed my breast. When I burrowed my hands in his hair, the straight, course strands didn't spring and curl around my fingers. And his lips felt foreign and greedy.

Simultaneously horrified and sober, I'd jerked myself away from Lester as I pictured Eva in my mind. Why was she even with this creep? How did I get myself into this predicament? He'd roughly pulled me against him and shoved his tongue in my mouth, groping my breast with his free hand.

"Take me home!" I'd yelled. "Now!" I'd pushed his 260-pound frame away from me.

"I thought you wanted this, Justine."

"No, I don't want this! Eva's my best friend!"

"Then what are you doing here?"

"I don't know. This was a huge mistake. Just take me home."

"Should I tell her?" I asked Faith Ellen's headstone. "I mean, nothing *really* happened with him. Still...."

I didn't get a reply. The flower-scented breeze caressed me again as I swept my hand across the soft grass surrounding me. A bird trilled from a nearby tree and I squinted against the sun in search of it. I was suddenly aware of the beauty of this pastoral backdrop, as if I'd only just opened my eyes. I was about to resume my self-reproach when a gentle wave of warmth swept through me like an ethereal embrace.

"You made a mistake, Justine." I heard a voice in my head. *"Forgive yourself and move on."*

THE OUTRAGEOUSNESS OF JUSTINE
"Double Vision" – Foreigner

EVA

OOOHHH, BOY. *THAT'S TROUBLE!*
My notoriously untamed friend was downright trashed. She didn't notice me standing in the doorway, watching her with her old flame, Kenny. I could hear her voice above the music on the jukebox and the din of the people chatting at the bar. She swayed on her feet as she leaned forward to shout into his ear. When he pulled back, she stumbled before catching herself.

This was the fourth time in the two weeks since she'd run into Danny at the grocery store that I'd been called to come pick her up. One time, Justine had phoned me from a bar after she'd been unable to find her keys. It turned out the waitress had confiscated them for her own safety. Twice, Larry-the-bartender here at The Pub had called to say Justine wasn't in any shape to drive. And this morning, Lynn had reported that when she and Justine went to a new bar over in Belchertown, our wayward friend vanished for over thirty minutes with some guy she'd just picked up. When she returned, her shirt was inside out.

"Fuck you, Kenny! You're not my father!"

Oh, Lord! Before she could continue with her tirade, I hurried to her side and reached for her arm, but she jerked it away. Her face relaxed when she discovered it was me.

"Eeeeevaaa! Whatcha doin' here? Aren'tcha workin'?" She threw her arms around me with such force she nearly knocked me down.

"Kenny called and asked if I wanted to come join you." Looking over Justine's head, I mouthed "thank you" to him. He gave me a rueful look and nodded.

"Ooooh, m' boy, Kenny! Isn' 'e great? Isn' 'e the best? I love 'im so much, don' I, Danny?"

"Uh, I'm Kenny."

"I *know* you're Kenny!"

The record ended, followed by the *click-click* and static at the start of the next. Justine plopped down on a bar stool as the drumbeat of the new song began. Staring unseeingly toward the music, a tear began to edge its way down her face. Kenny and I looked at each other mystified, and I shrugged my shoulders. It was "Love Stinks" by the J. Geils Band.

When the melody faded, she sat unmoving for the longest time. At last, she directed her unfocused eyes on me. "Hey, Eva! When'd ya get here? I'm sosorry... sosorry... I never meant... Lester...."

"Lester?"

Her head began to droop and, as her eyes drifted shut, I grabbed her before she slid off the stool.

"Come on, Justine. It's time to go."

By the time I got her to my house and helped her into bed, she was nearly unconscious. After she'd downed two Excedrin with black coffee and made a face at the scrambled eggs and toast I placed in front of her the next morning, I broached the subject.

"So, are we going to talk about last night?"

"What do you mean? I got drunk. You came and got me. What's to talk about?"

"Why were you there all by yourself, drinking?"

"I wasn't all by myself. Kenny was there." She inspected a triangle of toast.

"Justine, listen. You thought you'd gotten over Danny. Seeing him again brought it all back. I get it. But you can't keep on the way you've been going. You're a mess!"

"Why don't you tell me how you really feel!"

"I'm serious, Justine. As long as I've known you, you've always taken great care of yourself. It looks like you haven't brushed your hair in weeks; your make-up's always smeared. And how much weight have you lost? It's gotta be fifteen pounds!"

She turned her red, swollen eyes toward me. "Sorry if I offend you. Really, I'm fine."

"You're lucky it was only Kenny last night. Anybody else might have taken advantage of you. In your condition."

"What are you talking about? I told you, I'm fine!" She gave me a weak smile, then took a small bite of toast and chewed it deliberately.

"Justine, sometimes I don't know how to handle you."

"Sometimes I don't know how to handle myself," she said softly, flipping the toast triangle around. "Really, thanks for your concern, Eva. I'll be okay."

I couldn't help myself, though. I needed to make her understand her behavior was begging for trouble.

"Justine, *please*, going out by yourself, dressed the way you always dress, getting drunk, losing judgment. It's a good thing Kenny was there for you last night. Someone else might have done something terrible to you. *Wicked* terrible!" My voice ended in a near-scream.

She sat back in her chair. Her bloodshot eyes never left my face. She took a long drink of coffee while continuing to watch me over the brim of the mug. Studying me. I waited for her to speak, but instead of her usual barrage of questions, she remained silent. I could practically see her brain cataloguing, sorting, and dropping the last pieces of the puzzle into place.

Oh shit! Oh no! Here it comes.... My palms began to sweat.

Her mouth opened and I prepared myself. Instead, she closed it and swallowed.

Her eyes narrowed and her face reddened. Reaching across the table, she placed her hand on top of mine and asked in a tight-throated voice, "Who? Tell me who, Eva. Who did it to you?"

THE NEXT HOUR FELT LIKE a month. Justine altered between table-banging, fork-throwing outrage and clenched-jaw calm. I resisted telling her who for fifty-nine minutes.

"Am I an idiot?" she asked herself out loud. "I must be. I'm a complete moron! How could I not have known? *How!*" She slammed her palm on the table, making the dishes and silverware clink as they bounced against each other.

"I, er, uh...."

She stopped, deliberately lowered the volume of her voice, then continued. "It's so obvious now. The way you're dressing. Avoiding Lynn and me. All those random guys you dated. Lester...." She didn't even bother to mask her distaste. Then, her eyes widened. "And Tim!"

I dropped my gaze.

"God *damn* it! The bastard ruined it for you with Tim, didn't he? Who was it Eva?" She was shouting, scaring me with the ferocity of her anger. "*Who?*"

"Justine, please," I began. "I can't...." Raising my eyes, I saw her struggling to get a hold of herself.

The self-recriminations started again, followed by more table banging and yelling, then silent introspection. "Listen to me, Eva," she said, forcing a soothing tone. "First, and you have to believe this—it was not your fault. You got it? You did *nothing* wrong. Second, you aren't alone with this anymore. I'm here for you if you want to talk... or not. Third, I'm going to check around and find you someone who's trained to help rape victims."

I winced when she said that word.

She leaned forward and locked her eyes on me. "So help me, he will not get away with this. I will hunt him down and kill him, do you understand?"

It was then, at minute fifty-nine, that she finally broke me. "Give me his name."

I replied, "Tom O'Reilly."

UNDERCOVER

"One Way or Another" – Blondie

JUSTINE

M

Y CAR WAS NEW. WELL, it was new to me, but used. The old Chevy Malibu I'd bought to drive myself to college blew a gasket on my way to work one day in Lynchburg, Virginia. The local mechanic had shaken his head, saying the estimated repairs would be more than the car was worth. I'd scoured the newspaper and ended up with a cute, gold-colored Honda Accord hatchback. It was better on gas, anyway, so I never looked back. Its anonymity was coming in handy as I lurked in the shadows of the early evening, slumped in the front seat with the 35 mm camera my parents gave me for my nineteenth birthday on the passenger seat.

Tom O'Reilly. I did my best to control myself when Eva said his name. She didn't need me to go ballistic. She needed me to help her. *Tom O'Reilly?* He'd seemed so nice. Our paths had crossed countless times over the years. She'd known him her entire life. He was married with three kids. And, he was recently promoted to Police Sergeant.

Once I knew who my target was, I needed a plan. I'd decided if I actually killed him, he'd be getting off easy. I wanted to make him suffer. But how? I was nineteen years old and he was, what? Forty-something? How could I possibly get him back for what he'd done to my friend?

I decided I'd follow him so I'd know exactly what I was up against. Clearly, he wasn't the person he pretended to be around town—the public servant protecting local citizens, the faithful family man. I knew he'd hurt Eva and suspected she wasn't the only one.

I didn't tell Eva what I was up to. She'd warned me he was dangerous and about him hanging out in front of her house, the driving by, the pointed looks meant to keep her quiet. Eva didn't need to know I was hell-bent on making sure that psychopath paid for what he'd done.

I pulled the Red Sox cap I'd borrowed from Uncle John farther over my face and glanced toward the police station. I found my new role as vigilante was successfully providing me with the distraction I needed from both my own problems. Besides, who knows? Maybe the detailed notes taken during my surveillance could help convict him someday. At the very least, it gave me an outlet for my inner chaos.

July 2 – SA (Sergeant Asshole) left station at 7 PM. Learned his personal car is a blue Cutlass sedan. Drove to East Brookfield Pizza. Came out about 8:30 PM with blonde woman. Drove back roads to Brookfield Orchards. I turned off my lights to follow. He pulled his car between rows of apple trees. I didn't get a good view. Poor lighting, couldn't get too close. I left about 9 PM.

July 4 – SA left station about 7 PM. Drove his Cutlass to his house, stopping in front of Eva's house for a few minutes before continuing. Around 8:15, he and his family drove to Spencer. Fireworks. I lost them in the crowd.

July 7 – SA left station about 7 PM. He saw me! He looked right at me, sitting in my car across the street. I pretended I'd pulled off the road to look for something in my glove compartment and didn't notice him. Then, I drove home.

July 8 – I brought Aunt Peggy's car tonight. SA left station about 7:15 PM in his Cutlass. I followed at a farther distance than before. He drove to Ye Olde Tavern in West Brookfield. He left about 9:00 with a small, dark-haired woman. I followed them down by a deserted warehouse. I stayed fairly far away and turned off my headlights so he wouldn't see me. I kept snapping pictures using my telephoto lens even though I couldn't clearly see what was happening. There seemed to be a definite struggle going on in his car. It was even rocking a little bit. At one point, I thought I heard a scream. I got out of there as fast as I could. Then I felt guilty. Should I have checked to see if she was in trouble? I'll have to see what shows up when I get my film developed.

July 9 – SA went home after work, stopping in front of Eva's house first. Was driving police cruiser.

July 10 – SA went home after work, stopping in front of Eva's again before continuing on. Was driving police cruiser.

July 11 – SA left station about 7 PM in his Cutlass. Drove back to the pizza place in East Brookfield. Came out with a woman. Tried to follow them, but I got stuck at a red light. I suspected he went back to Brookfield Orchards, but I couldn't find him.

July 14 – Shit! Tonight, I didn't think I'd make it home alive!! SA left the station his usual time, around 7 PM in his Cutlass. I had Aunt Peggy's car, but did he recognize it somehow? He drove over to Ye Olde Tavern again. I waited outside for two hours until he and a woman came out. He never looked to where I was parked across the street, but must have known I was there. I followed them down one of those backroads by Wickaboag Lake. I didn't know it was a dead end! He whipped his car around and his headlights shone right on me. I struggled to turn Aunt Peggy's huge car around and ended up driving across someone's front lawn. I didn't know what to do so I drove as fast as I could, but he was right behind me. I got to the stop sign and he pulled up and started flashing his headlights. I've never been so terrified! Then, he tapped my bumper with his car. I sped off, but he stayed right on my ass. Once I got onto Route 67, I floored it. It took all I had to keep the car on that twisty-turny road. I wasn't looking in the rear view mirror so I don't know when he turned off, but by the time I got back to North Brookfield and checked in the mirror, he wasn't there.

July 18 – I've been too scared to try following SA again. Two days ago, I saw his cruiser going past my house. I thought maybe he was going to see the people at the farm at the end of the road, but it was only a couple of minutes before he drove back again. Yesterday, I saw him go by twice! Today, I decided to spy on him at work. He came out of the station about 7:30 PM and started walking directly toward me parked down the street. Somehow he knew I was out there! I started driving, but when I passed him, he looked directly at me and then put his hand on his gun holster. I don't think it was a coincidence.

I didn't tell Eva what I'd been up to. She was upset enough already. I'd have to pull back and regroup. I needed to figure out how to help Eva, not make things worse. Or put myself in danger, for that matter.

I picked up my eight packages of developed pictures from Fotomat. There were a lot of fairly clear shots and it didn't take much imagination to see the woman was not enjoying what was happening to her. She wasn't smiling in a single one of them. Instead, she looked positively terrified. I tucked them into my drawer until I could decide how to use them.

I Keep My Promises

"White Room" – Cream

Eva

"No, I'm still figuring things out," Justine said. "Don't worry. I'm gonna get that bastard!"

"I haven't seen him around lately. Maybe he's decided to leave me alone. We should let it go."

Her eyes were on me, but I couldn't read what she was thinking. After a moment, she said, "I'm glad he isn't bothering you at the moment. We aren't letting it go, though."

"It's not really your call, Justine. It's been a couple of years. What would happen anyway? The statute of limitations has probably expired."

"I don't know anything about the statute of limitations, but what he did to you will never expire. Whether it's this year, or next, or the one after, I'm going to make him pay. I promised you, and I always keep my promises."

"I don't know," I began, then stopped.

"What?"

"It's, well, I have enough on my mind."

"Such as?"

"Lester," I said. "Things have been a little rough lately."

"Did you break up with him?" Justine asked, her face brightening.

"No, I didn't break up with him! But he's back to his old ways—partying, disappearing for days on end, not telling me where he is or what he's doing."

Justine clamped her lips shut and I could see her internal struggle as she tried not to badmouth him. But I could read her mind. *Lowlife, burnout, scumbag.* I changed topics.

"I saw Danny the other day," I said.

"Rad," Justine said, averting her eyes.

"He was with his wife and baby," I continued. "His little girl is adorable. Curly black hair, just like her father. His wife is really pretty too. I heard she's the daughter of his boss over at the construction project in Oakham. I guess that's how they met. I'd never seen her before. She's tall, maybe five foot—"

"Eva, I'm glad you had a chance to see the baby, but…."

"…seven, long dark hair. Very Italian looking. Wicked nice, too."

"Seriously? You think I want to hear this?" Justine asked.

I'd been so lost in relating my story I hadn't stopped to think that it would upset her. Or was I feeling a bit vindictive because of that smug look when I told her things between Lester and me weren't so great?

She stared at me again. Assessing me silently with those blue eyes. Probably mentally watching me end my relationship with Lester and reveling in it.

"So…." I began.

"I'm going to get that cop, Eva. Somehow. I always keep my promises."

An Old Friend

"Lean On Me" – Bill Withers

Justine

"**I** swear, Larry. Two's my new limit."

"Glad to hear it, Justine." The bartender set my second Bud on the bar. Eva was working, Lynn was off with her new boyfriend, and I couldn't sit home alone after Aunt Peggy and Uncle John had gone to bed. With the endless commotion in my mind—everything Eva said about Danny and his family, my loathing of Lester, trying to figure out how I was going to pay back the cop—I needed a distraction. Usually, I could find one of my old Portable Party friends hanging around at The Pub. If no one else, Larry and I had been buddies for a lot of years.

By the time I finished my drink, I was ready to go. I didn't know anyone in the bar and the two old guys playing pool, looking at me in a lecherous way, were starting to creep me out. Eva'd be so happy with me listening to her advice. Two beers and I was done.

Saying goodnight to Larry, I wandered out and settled on a bench. The fresh air felt great. I forced thoughts of Danny from my mind and, instead, concentrated on the cop. I was starting to develop some rudimentary plans to get him back. I had the photos, but I'd be leaving soon. Could I do something from home? Send him something in the mail? I wasn't sure and was trying to heed Eva's years of advice about not acting impulsively. I wanted my revenge to be well thought out and calculated.

The town was quiet; most people had already retired for the night. Despite my heartache for Danny and my concerns about the cop, my connection to this town pulled stronger. The familiar sights—the Congregational Church, the Town Hall with its bell tower, the shops and businesses along Main Street—were old friends.

"Well, hey there, Justine. What're you up to?"

Looking up, I found Eva's brother Craig standing in front of me.

"Nothing. Hanging out. Care to join me?"

He draped his arm along the back of the bench behind me and we sat for a few moments in companionable silence. Resting my head on his shoulder, I allowed myself to settle into the moment.

At last, Craig broke the silence. "Justine, how old are you?"

"Nineteen. Why? How old are you?"

He laughed as he dropped his arm around my shoulders and hugged me against him. "Just checking. I'm twenty-three. Wanna take a walk over to the Common? See if anyone's around?"

It felt so natural to be with him as we strolled through town. I was slightly startled when he took my hand, but decided I liked the way it felt. By the time we reached the empty village green, I was more than ready when he wrapped me in his arms and kissed me. Not with the uncontrollable passion Danny and I shared, but with tenderness.

"Justine, Eva's told me what you've been through. If you ever want to talk, I'm here, you know."

Looking into his gentle eyes, I felt grateful but tormented. "I'm sorry, Craig." I choked on my tears. "I'm such a mess! I don't mean to be blubbering all over you!"

Kissing me on the head and holding me tightly, he said, "You might feel better if you tell me about it."

So, that generous, sweet guy was subjected to forty-five minutes of my ranting, sobbing, whining, and sniveling as I replayed all of my hurt and misery in having lost Danny and my inability to move past my feelings for him. Finally, after he'd patiently listened to my pitiful tale, I asked him the one question which had plagued me since the day Danny told me he'd received the phone call.

"Why did he have to marry her? He got her pregnant, but he didn't have to *marry* her!"

"Why do *you* think he married her, Justine?"

Why did he have to marry her, the slut, the bitch, the... all of the epithets I'd assigned her over the past year crowded my head. I loved him still and couldn't resolve in my heart that he was with her. He told me it had been casual. The pregnancy was an accident. But why did he *marry* her?

"I don't know. Probably her father forced him or he felt guilty."

"Come on, Justine. Think about it. I've known Danny my entire life. You know him even better. Why did he marry her?"

I sighed, wanting Craig to give me the answers instead of having to figure it out for myself. "Well, I'm sure a lot of it had to do with his own family life. His father was always telling him he was a mistake. That Danny being born ruined his life."

"I can remember hearing his father scream at him all the time, when we'd be outside playing," Craig added. "Mr. Stevenson was the town drunk and Danny's mother was so sick for all of those years, she wasn't able to help much."

"Since Danny was the oldest, he ended up pretty much raising his brothers. Up until his father put the youngest, Teddy, in the home a year or so ago, Danny practically took care of him singlehandedly. And, the other ones...."

"I know about the rest of those Stevenson boys. They're kind of a worthless bunch. Ending up in jail for one thing or another."

"He was always bailing them out." All of the stories Danny had told me about his childhood rushed to remind me of where he'd come from. "Since he was fourteen, when his mother died, he's been juggling school and work, trying to make enough extra money to keep a roof over their heads."

"Maybe he didn't want to turn out like his own father?"

I caught myself smiling wistfully at the irony. I'd lost him for the same reasons I'd fallen in love with him. Raising my eyes to Craig's, I said, "Danny married her because he's a good guy. He thought it was the right thing to do."

CRAIG AND I SPENT A lot of time together during the rest of the summer. Ours never blossomed into more than a close friendship, but we enjoyed each other's company. We went to see Zeffirelli's newest movie about forbidden romance, *Endless Love*, and I secretly searched for parallels to Danny and me in every scene. We hung out on the Common with the other locals, mainly Craig's friends. And we had many quiet dinners together. Labor Day weekend, we went to the Spencer Fair.

Going to the Fair with Craig as an adult was an entirely different experience. The yearly event had been a highlight of my childhood summers. It was a huge county fair, sponsored by 4-H and surrounding businesses, and lasted for days. There were ring-toss and fishing games for small children, and games of strength and speed for older folks; there were rides of every description; and a petting zoo. Mom would shout over the calliope cranking out carnival-style music, people laughing, and children screeching. The heavy smell of fried foods mixed with the odor of hay and animal dung. I was so small—I'd bump along like a pinball from one group to the next, pressed on all sides and walking on my tiptoes, trying to peek through the crowds. The pinnacle was the demolition derby. People brought their old junker cars and rammed them into each other while spectators cheered. The winner was the last car running.

This year, we rode the Ferris Wheel, shared some cotton candy, and Craig won me a big, stuffed panda bear at the water balloon race. I didn't mention to him that I was an old pro at the game.

When it was time for me to leave for New Jersey, Craig came to the house to see me off. Putting my arms around his neck, I gave him a long, gentle kiss. "Thank you."

Brushing my hair off of my forehead, he smiled and asked, "For what?"

"For being a real friend when I needed one." I let my fingers glide over his smooth scalp once more before getting into my car. Waving as I backed the car out of the driveway, the nostalgia I'd always felt when leaving at the end of the summer rushed through me. This time, though, as I said goodbye to North Brookfield, I knew I was finally saying goodbye to my dreams of a future with Danny.

He's Dangerous, Not Stupid

(December 8, 1980, 11:45 PM)

"Imagine" – John Lennon

Justine

"Eva? Eva? I'm sorry to call so late, but did you hear about John Lennon?"

I'd been sitting on my bed in my dorm room, studying for an exam, when the radio newscaster interrupted the music. The words "John Lennon" and "shot twice" caused my head to snap around.

What the hell? I jumped up to get a closer listen. As the reporter repeated that Lennon had been pronounced dead upon arrival at the hospital, I didn't stop to think. I ran to the phone hanging on the wall and automatically punched in Eva's number.

"Why would anyone want to shoot him?" she asked. "He was all about peace and love."

"All I keep thinking about is his music. Remember when we learned every word to 'Imagine'? And we spent that one night driving all over the place, singing it over and over?"

"And the 'Instant Karma' phase we went through, when we kept telling random people that instant karma's gonna get you.'" She chuckled at the memory. "They had no clue what we were talking about!"

"My Happy X-Mas (War Is Over) record got all scratched up from me playing it over and over every Christmas. For years! I think my parents were glad when I finally had to throw it out."

"Yeah, he was a genius. Way ahead of his time."

"This is *that* event of my life. The one I'll always remember. Where I was when I heard Lennon had been murdered. Sort of like how my parents talk about always remembering where they were when they heard Kennedy was shot."

"Me too. I can't believe he's gone." She drew a long breath, then said, "I was going to call you, anyway."

"Did something happen? Did you finally dump Lester?"

"Stop it, Justine. No, it's the cop."

"What about him?"

"He's started again. Going past my house a hundred times a day. Sometimes, I'll be driving somewhere and look in the mirror, and he'll be behind me. I thought I was being paranoid at first, but he's definitely stalking me. Then the other day...."

"What?" I pressed.

"I ran into him at Cumby's. I pretended I didn't see him at the check-out, but he was waiting for me outside. He said, 'Tell your little friend to knock it off or *you're* going to pay!' Justine, what's he talking about?"

"Oh, shit!"

"What did you do, Justine?"

"I sent a couple of letters to his house."

"Letters? Are you out of your fucking mind?" she asked. "What *kind* of letters?!"

"Like you see in the movies where they cut out letters from magazines, you know, then piece them together to make the message?"

"Justine! What'd they say?"

"Stuff, like, 'I know what you did'... that kind of thing."

"How many have you sent?"

I quickly counted them in my head. "Five, I think."

"How did he know it was you?"

"He's dangerous but not stupid, I guess."

I strained to hear something other than silence through the phone. "Are you still there? Eva?"

"This is bad, Justine. Really bad. I don't think he's bluffing."

"Shit. I didn't think it'd push him over the deep end!"

"What *did* you think? That he'd just go away quietly? You've got to stop!" Her voice was filled with panic.

"Okay, I will. I'm really sorry. I thought it'd scare him if he thought other people knew what he's been doing."

After we hung up, I sat at my desk for a long time. My mind was racing every which way. *My Econ exam was tomorrow... the cop... the new family I was working with at the shelter in town... John Lennon... had I caused Eva even more trouble?... Danny... going home for Christmas. Okay,* I stood up to get ready for bed. *Once exams are done, it's time for me to really concentrate on how to finally put a stop to that Sergeant O'Reilly. Before he puts a stop to Eva and me!*

CHAPTER 10

1981

I SHIVERED IN THE BLAZING HEAT

"Iron Man" – Black Sabbath

JUSTINE

FOR THE FIRST TIME IN my life, I didn't have the spontaneous flutter of excitement as I turned onto Miller Ave and entered the tunnel of trees. Lucky was gone—hit last winter by a car he was chasing. When I'd suggested we find a new dog for them, Aunt Peggy rejected the idea, citing her increasing disability as too much of a hindrance. Danny was out of my life. The pasture across the street was empty and overgrown. Plus, there were all the upgrades to the house my brother Randy had been making. He spent every spare minute coming to North Brookfield since having officially purchased it from Aunt Peggy and Uncle John. He'd installed new windows; knocked down the old garage and built a new one; replaced the roof; and the siding, which I had always known as white, was now a pale gray, accented with deep navy shutters. The old house looked terrific. But different.

I turned my Honda onto the gravel of the circular drive and skidded to a halt on the slippery gravel. Parked in front of the barn was a black and white police cruiser! *What... the....* I felt a paralyzing cold shoot through me and my terror made me want to turn around, go right back through that tunnel of trees, and head for the safety of New Jersey. Then I caught a glimpse of Aunt Peggy's walker near the Adirondack recliners.

I pushed the gear shift into park and turned off the ignition. Trying to quell my panic, I caught the low murmur of conversation. Aunt Peggy's dulcet tones blending with the harsh chuckle from her visitor. *Why is he...? What should I...? How long will he...?*

"Oh, there's my grand-niece now!"

Fuck me!

"Come here, Justine! I want you to meet someone."

I forced myself out of the car and plodded on trembling legs toward the back yard.

"Honey, this is Sergeant O'Reilly." Aunt Peggy sounded proud as she made her introductions.

He gripped the brim of his cap as he nodded at me. His mouth turned up in a sinister smile and his eyes bore into me. A sweaty glass of iced tea with a fresh mint sprig poking over the rim rested on the table next to him. "It's a pleasure to meet you, Justine. When I ran into your Aunt Peggy last week at the grocery, she told me you were arriving today to help for the summer. Aren't you the caring niece, coming up from New Jersey to be with your great-aunt and – uncle? I understand you and Eva Thompson are thick as thieves. I know her quite well. She and I go way back."

As each word fell from his sneering lips, I got his underlying message. *I know you know. I know where you live. I know everything about you.* Under the blaring heat of the noontime sun, I shivered. I tried to swallow... tried to draw a breath.

"Justine?"

I was jerked out of my abstraction by Aunt Peggy's concerned voice.

"Sergeant O'Reilly was asking if you ever do any babysitting... if you might be available at all this summer?"

Those dead eyes were on me. He reached out and picked up his glass of tea, took a leisurely drink, then set it back down. He never looked away from me.

I stared back. *He handcuffed my best friend! He raped her!* My fear evaporated. A familiar storm began raging in my gut. *She was only eighteen!* I took a deep breath and blew it out slowly, counting to ten in my head. Then, I cocked my chin, placed one hand on my hip, and fixed a smile on my mouth. "Well, aren't you nice to think of me? I wish... I really *wish*... I could help, but I have a very, *very* full schedule. You know how it is, Sergeant. I mean, I'm sure you have your hands full, catching bad guys, protecting the people in town, and all. Right?" I conjured up a flirtatious sounding giggle before continuing. "I *will* let you know if I find the time, though, okay?"

His eyes narrowed as he rose to his feet. "No, no, don't get up," he said to Aunt Peggy. "Thank you for the tea. I need to be moving along. You know, catching the bad guys." He laughed as his icy eyes shifted toward me. Touching the brim of his hat in Aunt Peggy's direction, he ambled toward his car. As he brushed past me, he spoke so low only I could hear. "You'd better watch your step, you little bitch."

"Have a nice day, Sergeant... O'Reilly, was it? It was a pleasure to meet you!" It wasn't until his tires spewed dirt into the air as he shot around the house that my legs gave out and I collapsed into the nearest chair.

LITTLE TROUBLEMAKER

"Dirty Deeds Done Dirt Cheap" – AC/DC

EVA

SLAPPING ON THE HEADPHONES OF my Walkman, I finished tying my sneakers, glanced at the threatening sky, and stepped off the porch. I wanted to get in a quick run before the storm arrived. I cranked up my new Journey cassette and set out up Elm Street. That's when I noticed the first piece of paper. Then another. Then seemingly countless more. Sheets of paper tucked under car windshield wipers, straining in the wind to escape. Other rogue pieces had broken free and were scurrying up the street in front of me. People holding paper in their hands; some were laughing and shaking their heads; some were wide-eyed and silent. By the time I got to the Quabaug factory, I could see the paper, like jumbo-sized confetti, had rained down all over town.

Slowing to a walk, I grabbed a leaflet tumbling past me on a draft of air. Glancing at it, I dropped onto the bench on Main Street across from Cumby's. I yanked off my headphones, draped them around my neck, and studied the sheet in my hand.

There were six photographs laid out in two rows of three. At the top, in hand printing, was the header: Tom O'Reilly, North Brookfield's Finest. While dark and grainy, each picture showed the police sergeant with an unidentifiable brunette. He was unmistakable with his golden crew cut and square jaw.

In the first picture, Tom was kissing her and the caption 'Officer Friendly' was beneath it. The second showed him pinning her against the seat back, her mouth gaping open. Underneath was printed 'Officer Affectionate.' In the third, he was shirtless and the woman's head was twisted away from him. But, he was titled 'Officer Happy.' Three more pictures, all showing the determined cop with his companion, were labeled, 'Officer Horny,' 'Officer Accommodating,' and 'Officer At-Your-Service.'

Posters—larger versions of the flyer in my hand—were slathered all over each pole and tree trunk on Main Street. Throngs of North Brookfield residents had congregated and were doing what I was. Holding onto the incriminating proof in disbelief.

"Eva! Eva! Did you hear?" Lynn shouted as she pulled her car to the curb in front of me. Leaning across the passenger seat to speak through the open window, she filled me in on the news. "O'Reilly's wife threw him out!"

"Huh?"

"I drove past their house and saw the car in the driveway all loaded up. Everyone's driving by to see. Wanna go?"

"Uh, no. I have to do something. Talk to you later." I'd spotted Justine's car parked in front of The Lunchroom. I ran across and found her sitting on a stool at the lunch counter, watching out the window. As I approached and caught her eye, she returned my wave.

"What's up?" she asked, taking a bite of her egg salad sandwich.

"What did you do, Justine?" I demanded, pulling another stool close to hers.

"What do you mean?" She continued chewing, studying the sandwich, her legs dangling like a child's.

"You know exactly what I mean, you little troublemaker!" A flash of lightning momentarily lit up the darkening sky.

"Nope. Don't know what you're talking about." But I could see a trace of a smile tugging at the corners of her mouth as she swallowed.

"Justine, I know you did the posters. And the flyers. I *know* it was you!"

"Why, Eva," she turned her wide, faux-innocent eyes toward me, "I believe you have faulty information! Why would I do such a mean, low-down, despicable, horrible thing?"

"Justine. Admit it."

"Nope. No such thing." A sharp *crack* of thunder made us both jump.

"Justine, you've been writing me letters for the past eight years. Tons of them. You don't think I recognize the handwriting? I'd know it *anywhere*! Your capital Os, with the loop at the top? Come on!"

A huge grin spread across her face as she turned back to her sandwich. Taking a bite and chewing, her eyes crinkled in mirth as she crowed, "Pretty proud of me, aren't you?"

"I can't figure out how you pulled it off. How you put up so many posters and flyered so many cars. By yourself!"

Pausing in mid-chew, she gaped at me. "You're kidding, right? After all the schemes I've watched you pull?"

"Watched *me* pull? Who are *you* kidding? *You've* always been the instigator!"

Shaking her head, she said, "You're getting senile, Eva. I remember things a bit differently!"

That drew a laugh from me. I watched outside as a strong gust sent hundreds of flyers twirling and swirling. Once they'd dispersed and settled, I remembered what Lynn had said.

"Did you hear his wife kicked him out?"

"Sick!" she said. "Next he'll be in jail."

"Justine! He hasn't done anything *illegal*. Immoral, yes, but not illegal."

Setting down her sandwich, she sipped her Tab and swallowed. "Listen. I can't say *exactly* what happened with that woman. Or other women." She lowered her voice and leaned toward me. "But what he did to you is *absolutely* illegal! You need to understand. He forced himself on you, Eva. That *is* against the law!"

"But no one knows that. Except you!"

"So, I came up with a more… *creative*… way to get him."

"What do you think he's going to do, Justine? Leave it alone? He's lost his wife, probably his kids, and his reputation—look at them." I jerked my chin toward the people on the street. "Everyone's laughing about it. You don't think he's going to forget about this, do you?"

"He wouldn't dare try anything. He's not stupid. He'll know people are watching him. He wouldn't risk it." Just then, the sky burst open and water dumped down all over the flyers strewn up and down Main Street.

"I don't know. I think you've poked the beast. Or stirred the hornets' nest. Whatever the saying is. He's not stupid, but he *is* dangerous."

"They'll arrest him," she said, her legs swinging in an unperturbed arc.

"They're *not* going to arrest him! They would have done it already."

"Well, how would he know it was us, anyway?"

"Oh, come on!" I was exasperated with my friend. "Who else would it be?"

"Well, I'm not scared." But her legs were suddenly still. "Don't mess with a Jersey girl. We're mean and we're tough." Picking up what was left of her sandwich, she took a bite. "Here. Do you want my pickle?"

For the umpteenth time in my life, I wondered who this girl was. This Justine. As I stared at her in silence, her jaw working to finish her food, she winked.

It finally occurred to me as the drumming of the rain on The Lunchroom's asphalt shingles worked to soothe my frazzled nerves. I may never totally understand what drove her, but it didn't matter. It only mattered that she loved me.

TIME TO PULL THE SHADES DOWN

"Psycho Killer" – Talking Heads

JUSTINE

"WHAT'S THIS?" EVA ASKED, TAKING the envelope I held out to her. 'Justine' was scrawled on the front.

"Open it," I said, wrapping my arms around my legs until I was curled up like a ball. Moss was spreading on the ground between Wausau's arms and I'd plunked myself down onto the cushiest patch I could find.

Slowly, she opened the back flap, then looked inside, her eyebrows scrunched together. She reached in and withdrew a stack of roughly a dozen photographs. She glanced at the first one, then the second, then quickly rifled through the entire pile.

"Justine, where did these come from?"

"They were in the mailbox. Thank God, it was me who got the mail today. Usually Uncle John gets it."

"Do you think...?"

"I don't think. I *know*! Who else would it be? He's been following me and he wants me to know it. These pictures," I pulled out the first seven or so, "are bad enough. This one, pumping gas. This one, coming out of Cumby's. This one, after church with Aunt Peggy and Uncle John. But the one at the graves in Shadow Hill? I can't believe I didn't see him there!"

"You weren't expecting him. You didn't know he was following you."

"This is the one that really pisses me off. Where was he hiding that he got a picture of me in my bedroom? He went there—to my house! What the fuck? I never took pictures of him in *his* house!"

"Justine. You know what this means, right?"

"Yeah. I need to start pulling the shades down!"

268

"That's not funny! This is serious. He's threatening you. These pictures are a threat! What are we going to do?"

"I don't know," I said, gathering the pictures together and tapping them so their edges lined up and they formed a perfect rectangle. "Obviously, we can't go to the North Brookfield police. They'd never believe us."

"The state cops?"

"What would we tell them? I can't prove these pictures are from him. I've got no proof of anything!"

"Fingerprints? Handwriting analysis?"

"Come on! He's too smart for that! You know he probably wore gloves… disguised his handwriting!"

"Okay, okay," Eva said, taking the pictures from me and stuffing them back in the envelope. "Let's be calm and think about this. How about your dad? He's a lawyer. He'd know what to do."

"He'd have a fit if he found out I'd let it go this long without saying something. The letters I mailed, the flyers and posters. No, he'd be really mad."

"I obviously can't tell my parents. That's the last thing I need."

We both sat in silence. Sunday was always the popular day to visit dead relatives and today's beautiful weather had brought people to the cemetery in droves. Still, hidden behind our metal structure and the surrounding woods on the hill, we felt alone as we debated our next move. How would we ever get lose from the grip the cop had on us?

"You know," I said at last. "There are only two ways that would finally prove what a psychopath he is. First, if the women he's raped came forward. How could they ignore it if a lot of women tell the same story?"

"I can't see that happening. No one's come forward yet. *I* certainly can't after all this time. Who'd believe me? My word against a cop's? I thought maybe after the flyers and posters, someone he's hurt might have said something. Especially the woman in the pictures. I guess not, though. I haven't heard a word."

"The other way to get him would be if he got caught in the act."

She gave a single mocking, "Ha!"

"You know what? I'm not scared of him anymore. I'm pissed off!" I squared my shoulders and pointed my index finger at her for emphasis. "He's not going to get away with this, Eva. I promised you. He has no idea who he's dealing with!"

Eva leaned toward me and shook her own finger at me. "Hey. You be careful. You're doing that thing again."

"What thing?"

"Letting your temper control you. You need to think first."

"I *am* thinking! I'm thinking it's time for that *bastard* to be behind bars!"

"Justine, you need to stay away from him." She shot me an admonishing look.

"I'm going to get him, Eva."

THE SEPARATION PARTY

"Dream On" – Aerosmith

EVA

"**A** SEPARATION PARTY?" JUSTINE ASKED WHEN I phoned her. "Engagement parties, bridal showers, bachelor parties... those I get. But throwing a party to celebrate the *end* of their marriage? I've never heard of such a thing!"

"Vicki and Pablo are still the best of friends, but they realized they aren't in love with each other. This is their way of showing their family and friends there are no hard feelings. It's all wicked grown up and civilized, don't you think?"

"I guess you could say that. What are they going to do after their divorce?"

"Vicki's keeping the apartment over The Pub; it was hers to start with. And Pablo," I placed my hand over the mouthpiece of the phone trying to muffle my laughter.

"Pablo what?"

"Pablo's going in... going into... the priesthood. He's going to become a Catholic priest!"

"Get the hell out of here!" Justine let out a gasp. "Oh shit! I guess I can't say hell around him anymore!"

"He's not like that. But it's weird, don't you think? We knew him before he found his calling. Not exactly what you'd expect of a Catholic priest, right?"

"Jesus Christ, hardly. Oh shit! I've got to watch my mouth! Listen, can you pick me up? Lynn's borrowing my car while hers is in the shop and I don't want to take Aunt Peggy's in case she needs it."

I had one of those déjà vu moments a few hours later when we walked into the sweatbox of an apartment where the separation party was in full,

271

ear-piercing swing. Many of our old Portable Party crew had shown up in support of the impending divorce.

"I'd know that laugh anywhere," Justine said as she waved in Carl's direction. "He looks good with his hair cut short. Well, shoulder-length is considered short in these parts, right?"

"He's gotten a good job as a custodian over at the school. He really got his life together. And there's Kenny!"

Justine smiled toward him as she said to me through her gritted teeth, "I haven't seen him since last summer when I made a fool of myself. Remember?"

"Oh, I remember! Rob's here, see him? Over in the corner by the window?"

"How's he been? He looks like he's still scared of his own shadow."

"No one sees much of him. He's hardly ever around. Hey, Joey!"

"Eva, it's great to see you. And, Justine! It's been years. Where've you been?" Our pint-sized buddy reached for two beers from a nearby cooler and popped the tabs on each can before handing them to us.

"Away at college, mainly," she said. "How about you?"

"I'm at my old man's dealership, selling cars, but he's training me for management," Joey said. "He says someday it'll all be mine."

"That's so sick! I'm glad things are working out for you."

Lynn had squeezed her way through to where we stood.

"Ugh," she said, bunching her hair on top of her head with one hand while fanning her neck with the other. "I've gotta get outta here. I'm dying in this heat. Thanks again, Justine, for the car. I should have mine back by tomorrow. I'll take it to the car wash and fill up the tank for you, okay?"

"You don't have to do that!" Justine said. "I'm happy I could help. Who else is here? I haven't even seen Vicki and Father Pablo yet. I can't get over that. A priest! And isn't this crazy? A separation party?"

"I know, right?" Lynn said. "Only Vicki would come up with something like this. I'm not sure who else is here. It's so crowded I never made it out of the living room. I've gotta get to work, though. I'm subbing on the late shift at the diner tonight. Gotta pay that car repair bill!"

Justine and I managed to elbow our way through the bodies, intent on finding the happily—or *agreeably*—divorcing couple. It was nearly impossible to see. The heavy layer of smoke didn't help. I gripped Justine's wrist and followed her as she carved a path through the mass of people. In the back hallway, she stopped abruptly and I rammed smack into her, causing us both to stumble forward.

"Justine! Stop doing that! One of these days you're really—"

Then I saw. Right outside of the bedroom, pressed against the wall, was Lester with his tongue down a girl's throat. They were so engrossed in each other that they didn't even know I was standing there.

LIFE FLASHED BEFORE YOUR EYES

"Don't Look Back" – Boston

JUSTINE

LESTER AND HIS FLOOZY BOTH jumped when Eva yelled, "Hey, Asshole!"

Later, disjointed fragments of the next two minutes would replay in my memory to create the patchwork impression of a vacant-eyed Lester, Eva stumbling backward as he reached for her, and the sea of curious stares as I dragged her through the front room and out of the apartment. My focus sharpened only after I'd helped my sobbing friend into the passenger seat and took control of her car.

Speeding away, I glanced occasionally in Eva's direction, but kept my raging emotions to myself. I drove aimlessly through town, past the Common, past Eva's house, and headed toward Shadow Hill Cemetery. At last, she drew a long, shuddering breath.

"I guess you were right about him. He is a lowlife."

"I'm so sorry," I said. "Really. I didn't want you to find out this way."

"What do you mean 'find out'?"

"Well, it's just, uh, I had suspicions."

"You suspected he was cheating on me?" she asked.

I couldn't decide how to answer her, so I remained silent.

"It doesn't matter." She straightened up in her seat and turned the rear view mirror toward her. Pulling a tissue from her purse, she wiped the mascara from her cheeks. "I've suspected too. This has been coming for a long time."

An unwelcome image of my fingers woven through Lester's sandy hair forced itself into my mind before I could push it back. We were approaching Wausau's hill as my guilt engulfed me. "Eva," I heard myself saying.

"Justine! Your car!"

274

All thoughts of Lester evaporated because, directly ahead of us, my little gold Honda hatchback was helplessly stuck nose down in a ditch, its hazard lights pulsing red through the darkness.

"Lynn!" I jumped out and raced toward her as she staggered onto the street. "Are you okay?"

"He kept swerving into me! He was behind me… then next to me… kept swerving into me!"

"Who? Who was swerving into you?" Eva was gripping both of Lynn's arms, speaking directly into her face.

"I couldn't see!" Lynn said. "It was dark. I don't know who was driving!"

"It was a blue Cutlass." A tall, thin man appeared on the other side of my disabled car. "Are you okay, ma'am?" he asked Lynn.

Lynn, Eva, and I gaped at the figure that had emerged from the woods. This harmless war veteran who had been blown up into mythical proportions by years of active adolescent imaginations. His gentle face regarded Lynn with concern.

"Drake, isn't it?" I asked, quickly stepping around the car toward him. "You saw what happened?"

"Yes, ma'am. The other car was all over this lady, here, like a B-52 jet-jockey all over the Viet Cong."

With one decisive assessment, I commanded, "Drake, stay here with Lynn. Eva, come with me! I know exactly whose car it was!"

THE TWO POLICE OFFICERS BEHIND the desk barely tried to disguise their smirks. When I'd first stormed into the station, Eva scurrying behind me, my thoughts were still in a jumble.

"He ran my car off the road!" I'd shouted as I crashed through the door and spotted one officer at the reception desk.

"Are you hurt, ma'am?" He'd leapt to his feet and started toward me.

"I wasn't driving!"

"But he ran *your* car off the road?" Confusion and doubt in his voice said more than his words.

"My friend was driving it!"

"Your friend?" His eyes moved to Eva.

"Not her!"

"Where is the car, ma'am? Here. Sit down so we can get all of the information we need." He gestured toward two chairs on the other side of his desk and pressed a button on the intercom as he sat down. Seconds later, he was joined by another uniformed officer who heard the tail-end of my explanation.

"…and when we were almost to Shadow Hill Cemetery, we saw my car in a ditch and our friend Lynn was there! Thank God she's okay!"

"Ma'am," said the first officer, "who did you say ran your friend off the road?"

With a quick glance at Eva, I said, "Sergeant O'Reilly."

As if in practiced unison, both cops sat back in their chairs and crossed their arms. They stared at me without saying a single word. Or hiding their smirks.

"I, er, know it was him. I swear!"

"Did you see him?"

Two sets of skeptical eyes studying me gave me pause, but I pressed on. "Not me," I said. "But there was a witness."

"Lynn?"

"She couldn't see him. But Drifter Drake did."

Eva nudged me in the ribs as I spoke.

More smirks.

"This isn't the only thing he's done! He's been stalking us for ages. Threatening us!"

"Threatening you?" asked one cop. "How?"

"Saying things to us. Telling us to keep quiet. Following us. Lurking outside our houses. He even sent me pictures he's been taking of me!"

"And… why would he possibly do this?"

I hesitated for a moment as I looked into Eva's eyes. Silently pleading with me to drop it. Not to reveal what she still considered to be her shame. I understood. It was clear our gut feeling about the cops closing ranks was coming true.

"Because…."

"Oh, Justine," Eva said in a forced, playful tone. "You have to get a handle on that crazy imagination of yours!" Leaning toward the officers, she said in a confidential tone, "She's from New Jersey, you know."

I'm not sure why "New Jersey" was sufficient explanation for my behavior, but it was. As we rose to leave, one of the cops called after us. "You'd better be careful about the things you say. That's a Sergeant on the North Brookfield police force you're talking about."

MY HEART ACHED WITH FAILURE. I was angry too. I couldn't begin to tally all of the things that made me angry about Tom O'Reilly. I forced back tears.

Eva didn't make a move for her car keys so I stepped into the driver seat. Every movement I made received my concentrated attention. Slipping the key into the ignition. Turning the key while pressing the accelerator. Checking the mirrors. Noting the occasional couple or solitary figure on the sidewalk. Putting the car in drive. Easing away from the curb and veering toward Shadow Hill.

"What?" I hadn't heard a word Eva was saying.

"I said, I knew the cops would never listen. It's time to let it go. I hate it as much as you do, Justine, but let's face it. He won. In this town, he could probably get away with murder!"

"Let's go back and get Lynn," I said. "We'll talk about it tomor—"

Thump!

"What was that?" Eva asked, turning to look out the back window.

All I could see in my rear view mirror was the dark outline of a car. Its headlights were too close to be visible.

"It's him!" My slippery hands wrapped tighter around the steering wheel as he rammed us again from behind. Our heads whipped forward, then back. "He *hit* us!"

"Don't stop!" Eva yelled as we approached my disabled car. "Go!"

I shot past, peripherally aware of the blur of Lynn and Drake's faces, white from the moon's reflected glow.

"Go right! *Right!*" Eva perched on the front edge of her seat, alternately looking ahead and behind us.

While the scenery outside whizzed past us, I memorized each tree, each branch, each leaf. I knew, years later, I would recall every detail of the numbness in my fingers, the tickling of the sweat traveling down my back as I hunched forward over the steering wheel, and the faded yellow line dividing the narrow street down the center.

"Justine, he's pulling up next to us!"

I swerved toward the middle of the road and he dropped back. He furiously wove back and forth behind us, but I blocked each of his attempts to draw beside us. Then, he rammed us from behind again, momentarily causing me to lose my hold on the wheel.

"Justine!"

"Shit! Shit! Shit!" I regained control and pushed harder on the gas. The speedometer needle hovered at 65 mph as we raced along the twisty road toward West Brookfield. Still, the other car was glued to us.

"What'll we do?" she asked.

"Dunno!"

"He'll catch us!"

"No!"

"His gun!"

"What?" I asked.

"His gun! I bet he has his gun!"

I couldn't answer her. I was barely keeping the car on the road.

"Justine! West Brookfield! *Slow down!*"

I saw the speed limit sign. My brain registered that I needed to drop to 25. I lifted my foot off the gas pedal.

Thump!

"Justine!"

In that instant, I found the answer. I put my foot back on the pedal and pushed harder. 50 mph. 55. 60. We tore down Main Street toward the only traffic light in town. Ahead, under the street lights, were two police cruisers parked on the side road. 63. 64. Right through the red light. With Sergeant O'Reilly still in fierce pursuit.

"*Justine!* Slow *down!*"

Sirens wailed and blue lights flashed. Quickly, I veered to the shoulder and slammed on the brakes. The Cutlass screamed past us with one cruiser in pursuit. Eva and I sprang from our seats and stumbled toward the policemen from the other car.

"Chased us! Gun! Tried to run us off the road!" Eva and I blubbered over each other as the two West Brookfield cops tried to quiet us. "From North Brookfield!"

"It's okay. You're okay. They've got him."

Sergeant O'Reilly was out of his car, wildly gesturing. I could hear him yelling to the cops from where we stood, fifty yards away.

What if he convinces them we were in the wrong? Would they believe him because he's a cop?

The other officer opened the passenger side door and a woman emerged, clutching her tattered blouse across her chest. Even from that distance, I could see her disheveled hair, bloodied face, and that she was hysterical.

Ten seconds later, our nemesis was in handcuffs.

Endings And Beginnings

"Turn, Turn, Turn" – The Byrds

Eva

"**I** know I fucked up. I'm so sorry, Eva." Lester turned his bloodshot eyes toward me. "I'm really trying, man, but it's hard. I'm with the band... at the bars... you know how it is."

I fixed him a cup of Maxwell House and slammed it down on the kitchen table in front of him. "Just drink the damn coffee, Lester." I picked my way past the piles of dirty clothes and trash strewn across the floor. Hurling myself out of his house, I let the screen door crash shut.

"Eva!" I heard his strangled cry as he stumbled to his feet.

"I won't do this anymore, Lester!" *What happened to him?* Shirtless, with his beer gut hanging over his low-riding jeans. Filthy, tangled hair. And he reeked.

"Please, Eva! I'll stop. Please, don't give up on me!"

"For days, Lester! I couldn't reach you for *days*! I find you passed out... *wasted!* I would have thought... after the party...."

His head fell as he dropped into a wicker chair. "I barely even remember that night. I don't even know her name!"

"And that makes it okay? You think so little of our relationship that you fool around with random girls? How many have there been, Lester? While I'm working my ass off. Or waiting for you when you say you're with the band?"

He didn't answer.

"What about your job at Howe Lumber? Have you even worked since your parents left for vacation?"

"I don't work there anymore," he whispered, studying the peeling paint on the floor of the porch.

I looked away from him. "Are you getting high again, too?"

"Eva, I don't know what to say. I'm so sorry."

A resolute calm settled over me. "I can't help you, Lester. I thought I needed you once, but no more. We're done. It's over."

He didn't speak as I walked down the steps. I called over my shoulder, "Clean this place up before your mother gets back." I heard him sob and, as much as my own heart ached, I also felt relief. Climbing into my car, I took one last glance at the house. He was sitting exactly where I left him. Watching me drive away.

THERE IT WAS. RIGHT ON the front page of today's paper. As I sat at the kitchen table, I scanned the article that included his department photo, complete with that arrogant smirk. He'd been denied bail because he was considered a flight risk. The prosecutor's office was compiling a list of charges to bring before the grand jury, including first degree assault and battery, sexual assault, and kidnapping. If convicted, he could get ten years in prison.

Justine had been true to her word. Last year, she'd found me a therapist I could trust. After speaking with the Medical Director she worked with in Virginia, Justine had handed me a piece of paper with a name and phone number. "She comes highly recommended."

My most recent visit had felt celebratory.

Dr. Cannon: How are you feeling, Eva? Knowing he's finally behind bars?

Me: Free. For the first time in years, I feel free.

Dr. Cannon: Have you thought about what you can do with your freedom?

Me: What do you mean?

Dr. Cannon: I want you to think about what you lost that night. You've told me about some of the changes you made in your life to protect yourself against what he did to you. If he's no longer a threat, what does it mean for you?

Me: Not always looking out the window to see if he's in front of my house, I guess.

Dr. Cannon: Okay, good. What else?

Me: Making better choices in my relationships with men. Dumping Lester was a good start.

Dr. Cannon: What do you mean by better choices?

Me: I guess looking for someone who's more suited to me. The same interests. Someone who doesn't have a lot of his own baggage. Someone more like Tim.

Dr. Cannon: Have you thought about reaching out to Tim?

Me: No. He stayed in California, married a girl he met in college.

Dr. Cannon: What about your parents? Do you think you're ready to tell them what happened? You really need their support.

Their voices murmured in the front parlor as I tiptoed up the back stairs to my room. They knew something was wrong, but I hadn't been able to face the shame of what he'd done to me. It had taken me nearly a year of working with the therapist to accept it wasn't my fault. It was bad luck I'd been stranded on the deserted road that night and he'd been the one to come along. It was understandable I'd gotten into the car of a police officer I'd trusted my entire life. And what I was wearing that night, no matter how short my skirt, was not an invitation.

Dr. Cannon: What else do you think you could do to start taking back the control in your life?

Me: Uh, I'm not sure. What do you mean?

Dr. Cannon: Didn't you tell me something about the way you dress? Your appearance?

Me: That's true. That's definitely changed. I guess I could start with seeing what clothes I've got. Maybe start dressing like a twenty-two-year-old woman instead of a teenage tomboy.

I tossed open my closet doors. Wow! Nothing but loose-fitting, unflattering, redundant jeans. Hanger after hanger after hanger. Opening the doors at the other end of the closet, I realized my shirt choices weren't much better. Mostly flannel—granted, in different plaid patterns, but.... And the sweatshirts. When was the last time I bought myself new clothes?

What, in my subconscious, had made me believe dressing in these baggy, nondescript clothes would make me feel secure? Maybe I thought nobody would notice me if I faded into the background? Made myself appear asexual? I've never been as audacious as Justine, but there was a time when I enjoyed looking pretty, and sexy in young, stylish clothes.

My bureau was jam-packed too. Mainly cut-off shorts and graphic t-shirts. With a similar diagnosis: drab and boring. Regarding my reflection in the mirror, I wasn't unhappy with what I saw. It was time for me to start looking as great as I was beginning to feel.

I made a mental note to ask Justine to go shopping for new clothes with me. Go with me to the hairdresser. I needed a complete overhaul. I paused as my fingers landed on one blouse I'd almost forgotten about. Holding it up, I admired the green and tan earth tone variations and the lightweight cotton fabric with the V-neck and bell sleeves. This was one of the purchases I'd made when we'd gone shopping before.

I clearly recalled the last time I wore it too. It was right after Christmas when Justine and her brother Randy came to North Brookfield to visit Peggy and John. We'd hung out at The Pub, drinking and laughing all evening. At one point, I'd caught Randy staring at my breasts. He'd tried to cover by saying how much he liked my shirt. I'd laughed it off, but tried to shrink into myself so the shirt would hang loosely on my frame instead of clinging to any of my curves.

I loved this blouse. I loved the way it looked on me. Looping it onto an empty hanger, I smiled as I put it in the closet. This one, I was keeping. The rest could go.

Something caught my eye on the high shelf above the clothing rod, pushed into the corner so it was almost completely hidden. With a jolt, recognition swept over me. The flower covered hatbox with all of the mementos from my time with Tim. I realized that while my heart still ached a bit at the thought of him, at some point over the years, it had pretty much healed. I think the time had come to let go of those memories too.

With one last glance around the room, I skipped downstairs feeling light and optimistic. I'd make that phone call to Justine. Maybe we could go shopping tomorrow. Reaching the bottom of the stairs, my mother's laugh erupted as my dad related one of his silly stories. I paused in the hallway with my hand on the phone. Glancing in the direction of my parents' voices, I took a deep breath.

"Mom. Dad. I need to talk to you."

Consequences

"Hold on Tight" – Electric Light Orchestra

Justine

"IT'S ON ME. TRUST ME. It's my pleasure." I reached into my purse and pulled out my checkbook and a pen. "How much?"

"Oh, Justine. Really. I can pay for the repairs on my own car."

"Hey. If it weren't for me, your bumper wouldn't have gotten all banged up. I'm going to pay to fix it."

"Justine...."

I held up my mug of beer and waited until Eva lifted hers. When we clinked the glasses together, I said, "Here's to finally putting that bastard where he belongs. I don't even care how much your car repairs will cost. Or mine, for that matter. It was *sooo* worth it!"

"True," she said after taking a drink and setting her beer down on the bar. The Pub was nearly empty that Tuesday afternoon. Eva had the day off and I was heading back to New Jersey in the morning, so we had chosen our old hangout for our last hurrah of the summer. "What'd the garage say about your car?"

"They replaced the headlight. The front end needs to be realigned, but it's drivable enough for me to get home tomorrow. Who cares? I'm only glad Lynn wasn't hurt."

"Hey, I talked to her yesterday. You know she's got one more year until she finishes her social work degree, right? Well, it seems she's decided to make Drifter Drake her newest project."

"Really?" I asked. "How?"

"I guess the night of the Big Chase, they got to talking. Then she invited him to her house the next day, cooked for him, let him shower and shave. Now, she's arranging for him to move into the group home over in West Brookfield. She's even helping him find a job."

"That's sick! I can't say I'm surprised, though. Typical Lynn, always helping the underdog," I said. "I didn't know she wanted to be a social worker."

"Yep. Another way you guys are alike."

Larry the bartender set fresh mugs of beer in front of us. We sipped our drinks in companionable silence. No underlying hostility about boyfriends. No secrets to guard. Most importantly, no more Tom O'Reilly. After having been haunted and hunted by him for so long, the void he left was replaced with calm.

"By the way," I said, breaking the quiet. "It's nice to see the girls again." I nodded toward her breasts on full, liberated display in her curve-embracing, cleavage-exposing halter top.

"Yeah, you like? I'm loving my new wardrobe. Thanks for helping me with it. Actually, I'm feeling wicked good about everything."

"Consequences," I said, unable to resist an opportunity to tease my friend.

"Consequences?" Her puzzled look made me laugh.

"You've always warned me about the consequences of my actions, remember? Telling me I have to be careful of what I do or who I might piss off because I'll have to deal with the consequences. Well, sometimes the consequences can be good. Like this time. We finally put a stop to that cop."

Smiling, Eva acquiesced. "Okay, I'll hand it to you. This time your actions were justified." She gently shoulder butted me. "Seriously, I gave up a long time ago, Justine, on hoping anything would ever happen to O'Reilly. I figured he's a cop. He'll just keep getting his way. You never stopped, though. You're, like, the righter of wrongs."

"That's me! Your own personal superhero!" I raised my beer mug. "I told you. I always keep my promises."

Eva lifted her glass and clinked it against mine. "To promises."

CHAPTER 11

1982

MY CHILDHOOD. IT'S ALL OVER

"Dust in the Wind" – Kansas

EVA

JUSTINE WAS DOING WHAT SHE always did. Wearing her occasion-appropriate façade. It was a little like watching an actress. You thought you knew the person, but in reality, you only saw the carefully crafted character she permitted you to see.

Today, she was the 'gracious hostess,' shaking hands and thanking the guests for coming. But her accessories hid what she chose not to show. The oversized sunglasses covered her swollen eyes and her affected smile lacked any trace of her characteristic mischief.

Few people in this town knew her well enough to see past the tidy ponytail and sophisticated black dress to understand it was all an act. But I knew Justine. Behind the poised and confident exterior she'd honed to perfection huddled a frightened, lonely girl.

Even I might have been fooled if I hadn't had the chance to speak with her in private. Right after the funeral, when her pretense faltered.

It was a lovely service. Justine and her mother had planned it together. Their combined efforts were evident in the eclectic mix of traditional with contemporary. The mourners joined voices for several of the dirges. We listened to glowing eulogies from friends and prayers recited by the minister. And we all cried openly when the cantor sang an impassioned rendition of "Amazing Grace." But Justine's thumbprint on the ceremony was clear when various family members took turns at the pulpit reading poetry verses written by Emily Dickinson and Henry Wadsworth Longfellow. The closing song was performed by Justine's cousin Lisa, with only her guitar as accompaniment. I smiled when I heard her play the opening notes of Pink Floyd's "Wish You Were Here," then foraged through my purse for a wad of tissues as she sang the poignant lyrics.

I escaped out the back door of the church and got to the house on Miller Ave to lay out the food for the reception before anyone else arrived. As others began trickling in, I kept my eyes on the door to intercept Justine before she became too involved in her duties.

"I wanted to tell you what a great job you did with putting together the service." I led her into the pantry and pulled the door shut behind us. "I know Peggy was smiling down on us during it."

Her mouth twitched, barely perceptibly, as she remained unmoving. "Thank you."

I couldn't read what she was thinking because her eyes were still hidden behind those enormous, dark shades. "I put all of the food out. The way you asked me to."

"Thank you. Where's Danny?"

"What?"

"Danny. I saw him at the church. Where is he?"

"I told him not to come back to the house, that you didn't need any more stress today."

"Stress? Why would you tell him that?"

"I thought it'd make it too hard for you. Was I wrong? You haven't talked to him in a year."

"A year. I haven't talked to him in a year."

A numbness spread through my stomach. "Justine, are you okay? Do you need to sit down?"

"I'm fine. I really wanted to see Danny, though." She opened the pantry door and looked around the kitchen as if he might have magically appeared. Wandering toward the table, she poured some Coke into a plastic cup.

"Justine, honey, listen," I said, following her. "Danny's at home with his wife and little girl. You know that, don't you?"

Her head whipped toward me, eyes still masked by those opaque sunglasses. She didn't speak or move a muscle. I waited, listening to her rapid, shallow breathing. At last, she said in a tight-throat voice, "Of course, I know that."

"Um, okay, then...." I reached over to straighten the pile of napkins, then organized the plastic utensils. "It was such a beautiful day today. The weather was perfect."

"It should have rained."

"Well... uh...." I took several plastic cups from one stack and added them to the other to even them out. "So, have you decided what you're doing for the rest of the summer? Will you be staying here with John?"

"Mom's staying. She's looking for someone to help out with Uncle John. I'm going home."

"You know this will always be your home too."

She remained frozen. Didn't turn, didn't flinch. I might have thought she hadn't heard me until I saw the single tear roll down from behind her sunglasses. "Don't you see, Eva? It's over. My childhood. My life here. Everything. It's all over."

JUSTINE

CHRIST, WHEN WILL THIS STOP? I just want to go upstairs, climb into bed, and pretend none of it is happening.

I was grateful for all the people who showed up. So many who'd been lifelong friends of Aunt Peggy, some who knew her more casually, but everyone with sweet memories and funny anecdotes. My own friends had come to support me. Eva, of course, and Lynn. Vicki, whose divorce from Pablo was finalized, came with Eva's brother Craig. Those two were an item now. Larry from The Pub. Kenny had come to the church but not to the house.

And Danny. He'd sat in the back of the church and given me a sympathetic smile as I'd retreated. Through my grief, my heart had jumped as it always had when I was with him. It was understandable, right? That for a moment, I'd allowed myself to imagine him still in my life.

Hanging from the bottom branch of the maple tree was the hummingbird feeder I gave Aunt Peggy all those years ago. She used to tell me it was a hit with the local hummingbird community and she'd spend afternoons sitting in her chair, watching through the window as they fluttered about. My heart ached as I thought about it, empty, with no one to feed the birds or admire their tiny bodies and flitting wings. Uncle John was never interested. I doubted he'd remember to make their nectar. It would just hang there without a single visitor, remnants of crusty sugar fused to the bottom. Forgotten and ghostlike. Like the people up in Shadow Hill. Like Aunt Peggy. Like all of us someday. Who would ever know?

"Justine? Are you okay?" Mom asked, interrupting my deepening gloom.

"Sure, Mom. I'm fine." I attempted a smile. *Ting-a-ling.* "Did you hear that?" I asked, startling upright.

"Hear what?"

I listened for the sound before finally shaking my head. "Nothing, I guess." Then I heard it again! A faint, distant tinkling of a bell, almost like a bell on a cat collar. I whipped my eyes up to Mom, but her face remained placid. "There! The bell. Don't you hear a bell ringing?"

She concentrated, brows pulled together. "No, Justine. I don't hear anything."

It was still jingling. I *knew* I wasn't imagining it. But no one else seemed to be paying any attention. I looked at the barrister shelves, still housing Aunt Peggy's bell collection, but the windowed doors were all shut. Of the dozen or so people remaining at the reception, no one was holding a bell or seemed to notice anything unusual. *I must be imagining it.* Staring at the assortment I had so carefully arranged under Peggy's guidance last summer, I noticed my stained glass turtle and Christmas elephant had been moved to the front. The unrelenting ache in my heart worked its way into my throat.

Swallowing hard, I glanced around, then hurried from the room. Forcing back my tears, I crashed through the outside door. Finally, the flood burst as I dropped into the nearest Adirondack chair. Sobbing, I pulled my legs up to my chest, wrapped my arms around my knees, and buried my face.

Even as I rocked myself in this comforting oasis, nothing was as it should be. Lucky no longer lounged faithfully by my side while I read. I didn't see a single sparrow and the Rose of Sharon wasn't in bloom yet. No toads or chipmunks, not even the chirp of a cricket from the stacked-stone wall. The sliding door of the barn that once groaned in rusted protest when Eva and I had barged our way through hung at a cockeyed angle with one wheel off-track. The six-paned window on the lower floor, at the base of the cow ramp, had several glass squares cracked or shattered, jagged fragments stubbornly remaining jammed in the rails. The pear tree hadn't produced fruit for a couple of years, and the sounds of construction came from a new house being built on Miller Ave at the corner of Elm.

This was the place where Eva and I shared secrets over the years—where she told me about her childhood insecurities, her adolescent dreams, and her adult fears. This is where I'd come face to face with her rapist and made the decision that, whatever it took, I'd see him brought to justice. And, this was where she'd informed me last week, when I'd rushed to Massachusetts to be with Aunt Peggy at the end, that she was going to Florida. With

Lester. He was entering a rehab center near his grandmother's house and needed Eva with him. She'd told me she felt an obligation after all of the support he'd given her during her darkest period, to help him as he struggled with his sobriety. I understood why she was going. I didn't agree with her decision, but I could see she still cared about him. I only hoped she was strong enough in her own emotional recovery to hold up under the strain of what was ahead of her.

Most importantly, this outdoor space was where I grew up with Aunt Peggy's doting heart accepting me for who I was. Through my self-centered younger years, my rebellious teens, and the highs and lows of my relationship with Danny, she listened and loved me.

Now, she was gone. I'd already paid the local stone cutter who promised he'd make my job a priority. Within the month, Aunt Peggy's name would be etched on the same headstone as her parents, up in Shadow Hill. My feeble attempt at making people know she was special and had once lived in North Brookfield. That someone remembered her. *I* remembered her.

Taking one last look around, I opened the door, but froze when I heard it. The bell at Town Hall. The slow, lamenting *bong... bong... bong*. I knew what it meant. I knew it was for Aunt Peggy. My heart couldn't take it today. I closed the door behind me, shutting out the sound.

CHAPTER 12

1983

Moving On

"Changes" – David Bowie

Justine

"**E**VA! I NEED YOUR HELP.**" Covering my eyes with one hand, I sobbed, "I can't deal with this all by myself!"

I smelled smoke the moment I entered the house an hour earlier, and found it billowing from the cast iron skillet on top of the gas flame. Through the suffocating haze, I automatically grabbed the searing handle, then slung it into the sink. With blistered fingers, I'd fumbled the windows open and yelled, "Uncle John! Uncle John! Where are you?"

The kitchen table was overflowing with his personal belongings. Clothes, toiletries, shoes, socks, underwear, books, sports magazines. There were toppling stacks of newspapers along the far wall. Grime coated every surface, the countertops were slimy, and the floor was dangerously greasy. The breeze swept the smoke from the room and spread the stench from the rotting garbage heaped by the cellar door through the house. Just then, my dear great-uncle ambled into the room.

He set a suitcase on the floor and straightened, turning toward me. I stifled a gasp. He was filthy and stank. His rumpled clothes were stained with blotches of dried food down his front. His shirt, one of the batch I'd bought him last summer, no longer strained to contain his belly. Baggy on his shrunken figure, buttoned haphazardly, one side was stuffed into his pants while the other flapped loosely over his unbuckled belt. But his face startled me most. Gray whiskers, nearly an inch long, concealed much of his usually clean-shaven skin. His shattered glasses were perched crookedly above his hollowed cheeks, and the corners of his toothless mouth were pulled into a foolish grin.

"Justin," he chortled. "Justin Case."

I fashioned a relaxed smile on my face before I spoke. "So, Uncle John, you going somewhere?"

"Aye-yuh."

When he didn't continue, I pressed, "Where ya going, Uncle John?"

"I'm getting married."

Fighting to keep my breathing even, blood hammering in my temples, I pulled paper grocery sacks from the pantry, willing my hands not to tremble.

"I read a new book, Uncle John," I said, trying to force the hysteria from my voice. "It's called *Two Thousand Pounds!* Do you know who wrote it?" I opened up the bags and set them in a row.

"Aye-yuh, nope," he said.

"It's by Juan Ton," I replied, choking back a sob. "Have you ever read *The Excitement of Trees?*" When he didn't respond, I muttered, "By I M Board."

He simply stood there, grinning.

I instructed Uncle John to sort his possessions into the bags and told him I'd be right back. In the next room, away from his vacant eyes, I fell into Peggy's chair. The numbers on the keypad kept jumping away from my convulsing finger, but after several misdials, I finally connected.

Eva answered on the third ring.

EVA

"WHEN DOES RANDY ARRIVE?"

Justine opened one bleary eye and looked at me. She'd been resting them, stretched out on the three-seater sofa in the hospital's visitor lounge. "In a couple of weeks, I guess. He's tying up some loose ends back home. He's already been mailing out résumés to places up here."

"What about your mom? What's she going to do?"

Sitting up, she stretched and put one hand on the back of her neck to massage it. "She's coming at the end of the week. She wants to be here when Uncle John gets out of the hospital."

It was incredible how much had been accomplished in the short twenty-four hours since Justine's frantic phone call. When she'd found John in the midst of his breakdown, she'd kept him calm while I'd called for the ambulance. From New Jersey, her parents orchestrated a long-term plan. Her dad had called and threatened legal action against the negligent home-aide agency. Her mom had found John a group home where the medical personnel would keep an eye on him. Randy, who was to become his legal guardian, was expediting his relocation to North Brookfield.

"What about you?" Somehow, she seemed so small to me, so frail, as she slowly pulled herself into a sitting position and wrapped her oversized cardigan tightly around her.

"I'll stay at the house for a week or two until everything settles down." She lifted her chin and gave me a self-assured nod. "I have to get Uncle John's stuff together and be here to talk to the doctors, social worker, staff." She slumped back against the sofa, the oldest twenty-two-year-old I'd ever seen.

"Eva," said my colleague, Bruce Levanduski, as he entered the lounge. Turning to Justine, he smiled. "Your uncle is doing well. He's responding the way we'd hoped and, as long as everything stays on track, I think we can release him by Friday. We need to keep him the few extra days for observation."

"Thanks, Dr. Levanduski," Justine's heavy-lidded eyes filled with tears. "Thanks, for everything."

"HERE. GIVE ME THE LAST plant." Justine held her gloved hand toward me while I pulled the remaining geranium from its pot. Her other hand held her trowel, ready to complete the task of decorating the Miller grave.

Once she'd patted the dirt back into place, she grabbed the plastic watering can from the spigot nearby, filled it, then saturated the newly planted garden around the base of the stone. When everything was finished, we both stood back to admire our handiwork. The engraver had done his job and carved Peggy's name and information right below John C and Faith E. Justine studied the etching without moving.

"I *will* remember her! And I'll tell my children and grandchildren all the stories I can think of about her. You know how Kunta Kinte's family in *Roots* kept passing his story down through the generations? If I do that with Aunt Peggy, she'll never die the second time."

"Second time?"

"A long time ago, don't you remember telling me about that saying? People die two times. The first, when their body dies. The second, when no one remembers them anymore. I won't let Aunt Peggy die the second time!"

I fell silent, contemplating the idea. I hadn't understood it as clearly when I was younger, but now I got it. A person will always be alive in some sense as long as someone remembers him or her. I waited until she indicated she was ready to go. At last, she turned to me.

"What do you want to do? I guess it's just you and me. Kind of like the old days."

"How about Wausau? We haven't done that in a long time."

"Okay. Lemme throw these things in the trunk of the car, then I'll meet you up there."

By the time she reached the old bulldozer blade, I'd dug my little surprise from my purse. Holding up the joint, I said, "Speaking of the old days… what do you think, Justine? It's been a long time since we've done this."

The old, mischievous glint lit up her eyes. "Why not?"

Passing it between us felt simultaneously familiar and strange. Like meeting an old friend you hadn't seen in a while. It didn't take long before we were drifting on our cloud of relaxation, reminiscent of our younger years.

Eva said, "All that's missing are our doughnuts. I used to always steal them for when we'd have our munchies. Remember? They were the best."

"They *were* the best," Justine sighed dreamily. "So, you never told me about Florida. What happened? How did things work out with Lester? Is he doing better? Why did you come back so soon? Is he still down there? Are you guys giving it another go?"

I wasn't up to her interrogation. I wanted to enjoy this feeling and not have to answer her questions or even think about my eight months in Florida. "It didn't work out," I said. Remembering how distractible my friend was when stoned, I changed the subject. "So, did you hear about Tom O'Reilly?"

Sitting upright, she leaned toward me, squinting through glassy, red eyes. "No! What about him?"

"Well, his divorce is finalized and he's been convicted. Not for sexual assault, though. It seems the prosecutor didn't think he could get it to stick. They got him for assault with bodily harm."

"But he's guilty as hell!" Her voice rose. "He's a damned rapist!"

"Justine! This is good news! Since two more women came forward, the judge gave him five years. He's going to the state penitentiary. Trust me, an ex-cop won't do well up there."

"Rapist!"

I tried not to chuckle at her indignation. "Lynn's uncle—you know,

298

the one who's a cop in Ware?—said O'Reilly will have a tough time finding a job when he gets out. Not too many places will hire someone with an assault conviction on their record."

Settling back against Wausau, she offered a tiny smile. "Okay. I guess that's something."

"So, hey, Justine, do you know what time it is?"

She angled her wrist, trying to catch the light from the half-moon. "Uhhh…" she peered, pulling the face of her watch closer to her eyes.

"Oh, come on! You don't need your watch. You *know* what time it is!"

She dropped her arm and flashed her Justine-grin at me. "It's time to hide on cars!"

"Hmmm." Justine sat back on her heels and stared into the barrister bookshelves.

"What's wrong?"

"There's a bell in here I've never seen before."

"Maybe you just never noticed it."

"No. I know every single one of these bells. I can't even begin to count how many times I've cleaned them and rearranged them. Aunt Peggy and I did that together since I was little. This one is new."

"Could someone have given it to her since the last time you looked?"

"I guess it's possible. I cleaned the whole case last summer, right after the funeral. I didn't see it then. Maybe someone stuck it in here afterwards?"

"That does seem weird. What else could it be?"

"Hmm, I wonder…." She studied the bell.

"Let me see it."

It was ceramic, traditionally shaped with a plain handle. It was the color of a late summer sky with flowers outlined in a deeper blue. In the midst of the flowers was a pair of praying hands.

"It's pretty distinctive," Justine said, her eyes glued to the object I was holding. "I absolutely would have remembered it."

"Odd," I agreed, reaching for a piece of newspaper. Wrapping it carefully, I gave it back to her to pack. She looked around.

"I guess that's it for the bells. Can you help me put these boxes into my car?"

"You're sure no one else wants the collection? You aren't going to start World War III in your family or something, by taking them?"

"Aunt Peggy would have wanted me to have them. I *know* that. I don't think anyone else cares."

After loading them into the car, it was time to tackle the attic. I hadn't climbed the steep stairs in years. Not since we were teenagers. My eagerness to revisit the artifacts was shot through with apprehension as we reached the top.

"Hey, Justine," I said, breaking the silence, "do you think Uncle Harry still hangs out up here?"

"I don't know, Eva. The last time I heard him was when he was slamming around in some drawers. I don't think I've heard him since." Justine pulled the string on the light bulb and turned to smile at me. "Maybe he found what he was looking for!"

"What he was looking for," I murmured, distant memories flashing through my mind. *Uncle Harry... Jane Williams's occult-themed party... Ouija board... Uncle Harry... blue bell.* "Justine!" I shouted, grabbing her arm.

She spun around to face me. "What is it?"

"Uncle Harry! Blue bell! Remember?"

She shook her head.

"At Jane Williams's party that one time. Years ago. Remember? I told you there was this message that didn't make any sense, but the Ouija board seemed to mean it for me. 'Uncle Harry... blue bell.' Remember?"

"Oh, riiiiighttt... I *do* remember. You don't think...?"

"How is it even possible?"

"I don't know. But in some abnormal—"

"Or, *para*normal."

"Or paranormal way, it kinda makes sense."

"Okay," I said with a shiver, "I'm officially freaked out! I never would have admitted it when we were kids, but this place gives me the heebie jeebies!"

Justine burst into laughter. "Come on, chicken! It's only Uncle Harry letting us know he's watching and everything's okay. Actually, somehow, it makes me feel... protected, or something."

I opened the creaky door. We both stood in the doorway regarding the contents of the room, almost exactly the same as the last time. There may have been a few additional cobwebs, a thicker layer of dust, and a denser coating of grime on the windows, but otherwise, nothing had changed. The old iron bed was still pushed against the far wall. The steamer trunk stood at the base of it, with its rounded lid partially open. The row of worn shoes still waited for someone to return. In the corner was the little school desk where children, decades ago, learned to write and do their arithmetic. And, the piles of boxes.

Crossing to the center of the room to pull the string on the naked ceiling fixture, I tripped over a shoe out of line with the rest. Kicking it with the side of my foot, it slid across the floor to where the others had remained obediently in order.

"Where do you want to start?" I asked, scanning the treasures that once captivated us.

"With the dishes. Those are mine. Mom said Aunt Peggy had finally completed the collection about a year and a half before she died. She'd called Mom to let her know. She was excited about giving them to me as a wedding gift someday."

Once we were done taking the dishes to the car, Justine surveyed the attic. Finally, she dragged a couple of the empty containers we'd brought with us toward the countless boxes. We spent the next couple of hours sorting through photographs and books and documents, and history.

"Hey," she called, studying a certificate she'd unscrolled. "Check this out."

I leaned over her shoulder and read it out loud. "This commendation is awarded to Faith Ellen Lane, in appreciation of her service, commitment, and dedication to the work and mission of the North Brookfield Chapter of the Women's Christian Temperance Union. This twenty-third day of September, Nineteen Hundred and Thirty-Six. And it's signed by Chapter President, Florence Boyne."

"What was the Women's Christian Temperance Union?"

"It was an organization started in the 1800s, at first to talk about concerns related to alcohol use. As it went on, it broadened its interests to other social reforms, especially suffrage."

"So," Justine suppressed a smile, "you're saying my great-grandmother supported teetotalism?"

"Yes. Just like you!" I looked at the date again. "Hmm, 1936? Even though women had gotten the vote by then, there was still a lot of inequality. That was during the Depression too. I'm guessing she must have felt strongly about women's rights to have gotten involved. That *does* sound like you!"

She studied the document a moment longer, then rerolled it and tucked it into one of the cartons she planned to take home.

As we were about to pull the string for the last time, Justine glanced at me, then walked to the steamer trunk. She lifted out the wedding dress with the buttons from neck to waist and puffed sleeves. She stared at it, turning it carefully. I watched her pensive face, waiting to hear her decision.

"I'm taking this with me. Randy doesn't care and Uncle John has no use for it." She turned to me for confirmation.

I nodded, reminding her of the Nancy Drew–type adventures we'd had that one summer several years ago, tracking down the history of the dress, solving the mystery of its owner. We wrapped it carefully in tissue paper and packed it.

Sighing, she said, "There's always been something about this attic. Do you know what I mean? I always feel closest to my ancestors up here."

"It's the ghosts, Justine. We both know this place is haunted. I think you're especially sensitive. You've always reacted when you come up here—feeling things, hearing things."

"It's true. I always told myself it's because they liked having me here." Her eyes swept the room as she walked toward the door.

I headed down the stairs, certain I heard her whisper, "Goodbye, Uncle Harry. Thanks for the bell."

In the driveway, after we'd packed the last of the memories into her car, Justine turned to me. No longer trying to fight back her emotions, she put her arms around me and held me closely before stepping back, smiling through her tears. "I'll talk to you soon?"

She was leaving for New Jersey in the morning. Randy would be coming within the next week. Waving to her as I backed my Mustang out of the driveway, I glanced at the abandoned pasture where my precious Smokey once lived.

"Bye!" I called out the window.

"Bye!" Justine called back, waving as I drove up Miller Ave.

"Bye!" I yelled, entering the tunnel of trees.

Faintly, not more than a whisper, I heard "Bye!" as I made a right on Elm.

I bellowed one last time, "Bye!" but heard nothing in return.

As I passed Shadow Hill Cemetery on my left, I couldn't help but wonder when I would see her again.

EPILOGUE

PRESENT DAY

Looking Back

"In My Life" – *The Beatles*

Justine

TURNING ONTO MILLER AVE FROM Elm Street, I marveled how despite some obvious changes, the town felt almost exactly the same as it did when I was a child. There was the new house on the corner, of course, which must be about thirty years old. As I came out of the tunnel of trees and saw the colonial style house rising on the left with the barn set behind, I felt the old flutter of anticipation in my stomach. There was a swing set and sliding board where the vegetable garden used to be, and Smokey's pasture was overgrown and unoccupied, but the old farm across the grassy sweep at the end of the road stood as it had for over a hundred years.

Parking at the top of the driveway, I saw my brother must have painted the barn recently because the red was vibrant and the white trim was pristine. The old Adirondack chairs in the space behind the house had been replaced by an updated version, including a love seat and a glider, all painted in muted pastel shades.

I'd only been back twice since Randy moved in. The first time, when he got married, and the other in 1996, for Uncle John's funeral. I'd made excuses—too busy with marriage, children, my career. But the truth was, I couldn't bring myself to return. Then time passed and it was no longer a priority. Randy and his family had been down a lot to visit us. While they always extended the invitation for me to stay with them, I suspect they understood why I hadn't come. After Dad passed away, followed several years later by Mom, I'd begun to feel an urge to come back to the place that would always hold my most cherished childhood memories.

Getting out of the car and grabbing my suitcase, I surveyed the area. The ghosts of my past felt like old friends all around me. As if to confirm their presence, a gentle breeze blew my hair into my face and stirred the wind chimes by the back door, making them jingle in welcome. Involuntarily, my eyes were pulled to the attic window.

"Justine! We were starting to think you got lost!" My brother's wife bustled out of the back door and hurried toward me.

I dropped my luggage and threw my arms around her. Even though they were down just six months ago for Christmas, it had been too long.

"DIG, YOU LAZY SACK. *DIG!*" Eva chuckled as she commanded me, one hand on her hip.

I wiped at the sweat dripping down my face and jammed the tip of the shovel into the ground so it stood upright on its own. "Are you kidding me? Are you *kidding* me?! *You* dig then, Miss Bossy Pants! Sheesh!"

She laughed as she grabbed the handle, rammed the blade into the ground, and jumped onto it with both feet. Lifting out the clump of dirt, we both peered into the hole. She emptied the shovel then poked it around in the crater as we listened for the sound of it hitting any sort of object. Nothing.

"Where the hell did we bury that thing? We marked it so well, remember? All those arrows on the trees, pointing us to the tree where we'd left it. Why can't we find it?" We'd been at it for over two hours. The floor of the grove, long-forgotten and unblemished when we arrived, looked as if giant moles had been vandalizing it.

Eva contemplated our predicament. Wiping her hands on her pants, she replied, "I guess we never thought about new trees growing or older ones falling down. Plus, trees get bigger and some shed their bark." She craned her neck, looking thirty plus years' worth higher on the trees, for any trace of red paint.

"I guess we out-clevered ourselves. We were so afraid someone would find our time capsule too soon that we made it impossible for *anyone* to find it, including us!"

"Oh my God! Weren't we a hoot? Can you even remember what we put in it? Or what predictions we made?"

Sighing, I searched my memory. "Not really. I'm sure we thought we were so smart, though. Hey! Maybe the reason we can't find it is because someone else already did! Maybe it's been dug up and it's not even here anymore. What do you think?"

"Maybe. But didn't we put our names in it? So if someone found it, they might have tried to contact us?"

"No, I don't think so...."

"Listen!" Eva grabbed my wrist. "Did you hear that?"

My heart leapt. "What? Hear what?"

"I'm not sure," she whispered. "Shh! There it is again! Someone's calling 'Justine... Justine!'"

"Oh, shut up, you big jerk! I'm too old to fall for your crap anymore." I gave her a push. "You used to really freak me out when we were kids, you know. With all of your ghost stories."

"Yeah, well, you had a few of your own, Justine!"

"I was mainly just getting back at you, Eva! So how is Uncle Harry, anyway?"

Shaking her head, Eva said, "Never hear him. Not once since moving in. Still, there are weird things, feelings or something. Nothing obvious. Like sometimes I'll feel a sudden chill. Or, I might be in the kitchen and get this sense that I'm not alone. It's subtle—a presence or a slight change in atmosphere, like someone is there. Sometimes I might see a chair rocking a little, or things I've put in one place are shifted or moved somewhere else. Once, when I was shelling peas, I felt a hand on my shoulder. I looked up, expecting it to be Randy, but no one was there!"

"Doesn't it make you nervous? Living there with all that going on?"

Eva pinched her eyebrows together in thought. "Not really. I've gotten used to it. In fact, it's almost comforting."

"Wow. Even though they're my relatives, I still don't know if I could live with them. I think it'd make me too jumpy. Guess it's good Randy bought the house instead of me, after all."

"So, you never told me what happened after Lester's mother called. Did you see her?" I shoved a fried clam into my mouth, reveling in my first taste of Howard's Drive-In in many years.

"Yeah. It was hard. A lot harder than I expected."

"What did she want?"

"She gave me his old guitar. She said even though Lester knew I was married and had kids, he never really got over me. She wanted me to have something to remember him by."

Poor Eva. Her relationship with Lester all those decades ago still haunted her. Even though he died in 2003, his wasted body finally succumbing to his years of addictions, he was a part of her history. If anyone could understand the complexities of a woman's past and how some feelings would always live secretly within her, it most certainly would be me.

"Did you tell Randy?"

She eyed me, knowing I straddled the narrow line between being her husband's sister and being her best friend. "No. There's no point."

"You're probably right."

"I also gave her a signed copy of my book. I figured since Lester was mentioned in a few of the stories, she might like it." While she still practiced nursing in Ware, Eva had realized her lifelong dream of becoming a published author. Her first book, a collection of funny sketches about growing up in North Brookfield, was in its second printing.

"Justine," she said, clearing her throat, "I've got something else to talk to you about."

"Yesss...?"

"It's about Danny."

I frowned at her.

Throughout the years, I'd never asked her about him. She'd mentioned him in conversations and I'd listened, but his name had not crossed my lips in decades. After graduating from college, I'd returned to New Jersey. My father's health was beginning to fail and Mom had asked me to come home. I'd begun my career at the Board of Social Services, and within weeks, I met a rising star in the local Democratic Party—the oh-so-hot and eligible attorney, Ken Bernard. Five years later, we were married with two children. Our son, Carl, was in law school, following in his father's footsteps. Our daughter, Faith Ellen, had gone into public health. My own path had led me to where I was today, as the director of a women's clinic in central New Jersey. By all appearances, I had the dream life. Handsome, successful husband, two fantastic kids, and a fulfilling career.

In that deep place inside me—the one where I tucked away those feelings best left unexamined—was a nagging, unresolved question. *What if?*

I kept my voice neutral as I said, "What about him?"

"I ran into him the other day, Justine. You know, he asks about you every time I see him."

"Mmm hmmm."

"He's divorced, Justine. He's living right over in Oakham."

Divorced? It was tempting to think about him, especially since my own marriage had struggled over the years. But I kept my voice casual as I said, "I'm not sure how that pertains to me. What happened between us was a million years ago."

"Things are better with you and Ken?"

"We're working on it."

"So, what are you going to do about Danny?"

I thought for a moment about my relationship with Ken. We'd been together for so long, it felt comfortable and dependable. But I could still picture Danny in my mind as if we'd seen each other last week. The striking boy with the dark curls and heart-robbing, blue eyes. I could see us together as we used to be, and my body conjured up a trace of the erotic reaction it always had to him. Even after all of these years, I had never forgotten.

My face was warm as I turned to my friend. "There's nothing for me *to* do, is there?"

What if?

YOU KNOW THAT EXPRESSION? "HER jaw hit the floor." Now I know what it means. My mouth literally fell open when, after trudging to the top of the wooded hill, we discovered Wausau was gone! Vanished! Without a trace. I turned to Eva, who was also gaping in shock.

We'd been so excited to visit our old hangout. During our walk down Miller Ave and climb up the hill, we'd bantered with "Remember when…" and "How about the time we…" as we'd anticipated revisiting our youth, kicking back with drinks and memories. Instead, it was as if someone had kicked us in our stomachs. Eva's eyes were filled with tears of disbelief.

"How in the world did someone get it out of here? And why?" Poking around on the ground with my shoe, I brushed aside dried leaves and twigs. "Hey! Check it out. The moss has covered the whole ground. No more dirt floor!"

"They must have cut down the trees that had grown up around it. See?" Eva pointed to a cluster of young saplings. "These new ones have filled in where it used to be."

"I wonder who did it? Maybe the town officials? Interesting how when we were here, I always thought we were the only ones who knew about it."

Eva offered the bottle of white Zinfandel. "What do you want to do? We've got the wine and the glasses," holding up her other hand to display the plastic champagne flutes from the dollar store.

"Oh, what the hell? It's still the spirit of Wausau, isn't it? I'm fine sitting on the ground, if you are."

Eva filled my glass and handed it to me, then poured her own. Where we once leaned against the old bulldozer blade, we used nearby trees to support our backs, the mossy carpet soft beneath us.

"So, catch me up on what everyone's been up to. Craig and Vicki? How are they? Their kids must be about grown."

Nodding, Eva filled me in on all of my old friends. Craig and Vicki, who would be joining us for dinner later in the week, had two kids still in college, while their oldest worked at an accounting firm in Worcester. Lynn, divorced and raising her son alone, lived in Boston. She sent her regrets that she wouldn't be able to make it while I was visiting. Larry, who would always be my favorite bartender, had been killed in a freak accident several years ago. It was during a tornado, something rarely seen around here, when an uprooted tree had landed on his car and crushed the roof, killing him instantly. He'd left behind a wife and two children. My heart caught when I learned sweet Rob, the shy boy from the Portable Party we'd all felt protective toward, died not many years ago too. Suicide. Eva said hardly anyone showed up at his funeral. Many of the other Portable Party kids—Jimmy, Chuck, Carl, Joey—scattered throughout the years and Eva had lost touch with them long ago. The comedy team of Benny and Ronny could be found hanging around some local dive most Saturday nights. Eva said they still entertained the crowd with their fumbled attempts at Who's On First. And my old flames, Kenny and Matt, were both married and living in the area.

Closing my eyes, I could see our old gang. Our profound, pot-induced exchanges always made me laugh. The acrid scent of burning weed and bitter taste of cheap beer. I could picture my leisurely days in the backyard with Aunt Peggy, with the innocent sense of constancy and security also left in the past. Walks with John while listening to his silly banter; playing with Lucky, always nervous when he went dashing off after a car. I could smell the cinnamon and ripe fruit aromas wafting in from the pantry, mixing with the crisp, grass-mown breeze. The stagnant, mothball air of the attic where the top floor of the house was an archive for my family's history. Romping with my brothers through sun-burned fields; with Eva, sneaking around town under the velvety protection of night. Smokey, chomping on a crabapple while standing in the cool, morning shade of the tree, tail briskly whooshing away the flies. Danny. I could conjure up sensory cues that were the backdrop to my entire childhood.

"You okay?"

"I was just thinking." I opened my eyes and turned to my life-long friend. "Remember how you used to tell me that photographs were a moment frozen in time? If that's true, then our memories are like a book, you know? The crazy things we did and some of the stuff we used to talk about. All of the people we used to hang out with, like the Portables. What we used to think was so important. Looking back, it's hard to believe Jane Williams mattered so much. At the time, she practically ruled your life, remember? All of those bits and pieces that we experienced make up the storyline of our history. Of our lives."

"Of our lives, *so far*," she amended.

"Okay, *so far*. Speaking of lives, how are you guys doing? You and Randy? Everything good there?"

She finished her wine. "We've never been better. Ever since the day we met, or I should say, met again, right after he moved up here."

I remembered when she'd called me about a year after Randy relocated to North Brookfield, with a taunting lilt in her voice, and said, "You'll never guess who I've been seeing."

"Who?" I'd asked, tuned into her upbeat attitude. I hadn't heard her sound so hopeful since she'd started dating Lester.

"Someone you know."

I ran the gamut of names in my mind and couldn't imagine who she'd be interested in romantically. "Come on! Just tell me! You know I suck at this whole guessing game!"

"He's really cute. And sweet. And fun to be with…" she drawled.

"Eva! Come *on*!"

"And likes the same things I do. And tells me I'm beautiful—"

Click! I hung up the phone, impatient with her shenanigans and knowing she'd call me back. Sure enough….

"Okay, okay!" she laughed. "It's Randy. We were both volunteering at the Historical Society. I told him how you and I used to love to go through the stuff in the attic, so he asked if I wanted to come help him sort stuff. Anywho, we've been spending a lot of time together." Lowering her voice as if sharing a confidence, she admitted, "I really like him, Justine."

"Eva! That's awesome! I'm so happy for you. For both of you. Wouldn't it be funny if, after all these years, we ended up as sisters-in-law?"

"We need to finish up so I can get dinner going." Eva grabbed the plastic containers which had held the flowers we planted around her parents' headstone. The Miller stone was still in full bloom so I emptied a can of water over the geraniums, picked a few dead leaves, and stepped back. The information etched on it was complete. Beneath John C and his wife Faith E were Aunt Peggy and Uncle John's names. While I was happy my brother had chosen to live his life on our old family homestead, I viewed him, Eva, and their children as the future. Standing before this grave, I saw the past. Mom had finally relented when I'd said I wanted to include a line from a poem beneath the names of my beloved great-aunt and – uncle. Engraved near the bottom of the stone was: 'How do I love thee? Let me count the ways.'

"So," Eva quietly interrupted my daydream, "how is it for you? Being back? Is it weird to see us living in the old house instead of Peggy and John?"

"I'm not sure what I expected. The house… Miller Ave… the town—it looks pretty much the way it always did. At the same time, I don't recognize any of it. Do you know what I mean?"

She hesitated for a moment, then said, "Because the people from your childhood are gone."

I nodded. "I have my family history here. That always made it feel like it was my hometown…."

"But Peggy and John are gone. And your connection with Danny. Right?"

"Yeah. You're the only person left from those days, you know. So, even though the actual town hasn't changed much, that's not what made it special. It was the people. And the way I felt when I was growing up here. It was like…" I searched for the precise description.

"…like a state of mind. Not the physical place as much as a…"

"…*a state of mind!* That's exactly it! Even though I'm glad I came to see you guys, the truth is *my* North Brookfield exists only in my mind."

We fell silent once more.

After a moment, she asked, "Remember how we used to make up stories about the people who are buried here? What do you think people will say about us?"

"Hmmm." I considered her question. "We were a whole lot of fun, maybe a little bit scandalous. At least I *hope* they'd say that about us." I gave her a shoulder check as I asked, "Assuming you croak first, what do you want me to have them inscribe on your stone?"

Laughing, she replied, "My name, of course, but instead of 'loving wife and mother', or anything like that, I only want it to say 'Justine's sister-in-law.' That's it. Because, *obviously*, that's how I should be remembered!"

Sidestepping as I reached to smack her, she continued, "Or something like, 'She raised hell on Earth... she's still raising hell!' Or, how 'bout, 'She may be gone but she's still on Facebook'? You like that?"

"Yeah. I'll keep it in mind."

"What about you? What would you want on your stone?"

"Jeez, I'm not good at this. You're the wordsmith. You make up something."

"Okay. Let's see. How about 'Youth is fleeting, Beauty fades, but a Rebellious Spirit lives forever'?"

"I like it! Yes, use that for me. Who said it?"

"I said it!" she laughed. "I just made it up. Fitting, isn't it?"

"Wait! So you're telling me I'm ugly?"

Grinning, she dragged me after her, back toward the house. "Yes, that's exactly what I'm telling you. Come on. We'll need to hurry. Craig and Vicki will be there in about an hour."

Walking past the Memorial Garden, we tripped the sensor for the carillon music and, even as we exited the main gate of Shadow Hill, the peaceful music drifted after us. Crossing Elm Street and beginning down Miller Ave, we chatted easily about her kids and mine, about old times, about our lives. As we passed through the tunnel of trees, the old house rose to our left with the red barn set behind it.

THE SMELL OF SAUTÉING ONIONS made my stomach grumble. I'd already made a huge salad and stuck the garlic bread in the oven. We were having an easy dinner tonight, and Eva was cooking the pasta. The doughnuts—the ones Eva now made with the same regularity as her mother had—were cooling. As I had passed along stories about Aunt Peggy to my children to keep those memories alive, she'd done the same with her mother's doughnut recipe. Her kids could make them as skillfully as Eva. The fourth generation of the famous doughnuts, produced while reminiscing about the matriarchs who had once baked them, all made from the heirloom recipe.

Ducking into their home office, I took a quick look at my emails from work. Nothing that couldn't wait. Pushing back my chair, I was about to log off the internet when I stopped. *I'll check in real fast, with my Facebook account, see what my friends have been up to, if anyone's commented on any of my posts, or sent me a message.*

"Justine, I think the bread's about done," Eva called to me from the kitchen.

"Can you take it out?" I scrolled through my newsfeed and nothing grabbed my attention. I moved the mouse up to the search bar, paused, then typed in 'Danny Stevenson' and hit Enter. Way too many possibilities came up and, rapidly scanning through page after page of them, I didn't see the one I wanted. Next, I tried 'Daniel Stevenson.' Same thing.

"Wait! It doesn't look all the way cooked, Justine."

"Then stick it back in the oven!" I tried 'Daniel P. Stevenson, Oakham, MA.' Bingo! Only one option and, even though I hadn't seen him in thirty years, I'd know him anywhere. The hair was much shorter, and grayer, but the smile was the same. I clicked on his name and it directed me to his page. He must have had some pretty tight filters applied, though, because I could access very little of his information. Profile pictures, photos of his kids. But what made me fall back in my chair was the cover photo. A picture of the Barrett/Browning hand sculpture he gave me as a graduation gift, next to a cover shot of *Sonnets from the Portuguese.*

I knew what this was. This entire Facebook page he'd constructed was for me, so I would know he had never forgotten. Scrutinizing the pictures, it was clear the years had been kind to him. *Ridiculously, unfairly kind! Those eyes.* Even on a screen, they seemed to reach right into my soul.

Closing my eyes, I allowed myself to do the forbidden. I permitted the mental dalliance I'd suppressed for decades. He was with me once more. I could smell the faded hint of cologne caught in the threads of his well-worn tee-shirt. A tingle spread down my body and shot to my groin as I felt his hands on me. His mouth. I tasted the slight saltiness of the indent at the base of his neck. His silky curls twirled easily around my fingers, bouncing back into place when I released them. Pressing my hand to my racing heart, I opened my eyes and stared at the computer screen.

What should I do? If I sent him a Friend Request, what was I really saying? We were never simply friends. Would this open me up to a whole lot of problems? Would I be reigniting something left smoldering over thirty years ago?

"Justine! They'll be here any minute! We need to finish getting ready."

"I'll be right there!"

Maybe I was only curious. I would have loved to know how he was after

314

all of this time. I wouldn't have to try to see him or anything. We could communicate electronically.

"Justine! Come on!"

"Okay!"

But how would Ken feel about me trying to contact an old boyfriend? And not just *any* boyfriend. He knew about Danny. I think he'd always been a little insecure about him. What about my kids? Would they understand? Did *I* even understand?

Consequences. Out of nowhere, like another ghost from my childhood, the word popped into my head. *Consequences.* How many times did Eva attempt to bridle my reckless actions? When she would try to teach me to think before doing. Reminding me there were always consequences.

"Justine!"

How many times over the years did I torture myself, reliving the consequences of Danny's decisions? Decisions that irrevocably changed our lives.

"Justine!"

"Coming!"

Consequences. Standing up, I looked at the cursor hovering over the Add Friend box. One click and it would be done. The possibility would suddenly exist. It was as simple as one click. One little click.

What if?

DINNER WAS LONG FINISHED. CRAIG and Vicki had left. My brother Randy and the kids had gone up to bed. Eva and I had taken our decaf coffees to the Adirondack chairs behind the house. With a sliver of moon and a sparkling swath of stars above us, we relaxed into the comfortable quiet of the night.

"Eva," I said, leaning toward my friend, "I'm really glad I came. Even after all of these years, there's no one in this world I can talk to the way I can with you. No one who knows me like you do."

"You aren't going to get all sappy and sentimental on me, are you?" She chuckled through the dim light.

"What can I say? You bring out my mushy side!"

"Come on. What about Ken?"

"My husband and kids certainly don't know much about my youth. And the people at work, at church, in the community? To them, I'm the wife, the mother, the businesswoman, the volunteer. My current friends know the image I've created. This *person* I want them to know. You're the only one who knows the real me."

"I get what you mean. The people in your life who've known you since you were young, knew you before you became... *you*! Before you became this respectable grown-up who I barely recognize!"

"Exactly!" I smiled at my friend, knowing no further discussion or explanation was needed. My friend who had always understood me. My friend who, like Aunt Peggy, had always loved and accepted me for who I was.

I settled back into my chair and sipped my coffee. I thought about what Aunt Peggy said to me, so long ago. *"There's a girl from town who's keeping her horse in the pasture across the street...."* She could never have imagined how that one offhanded statement would have altered the course of both our lives... Eva's and mine.

HIRAETH

(N.) A HOMESICKNESS FOR A home to which you cannot return, a home which maybe never was; the nostalgia, the yearning, the grief for the lost places of your past

PRONUNCIATION | 'hEr-rIth (HEER-eyeth) ORIG. Welsh

Eva's Mother's French Doughnut Recipe

1 egg
1/2 cup sugar
1/2 cup milk
1/2 teaspoon nutmeg
1/2 teaspoon vanilla
1/2 teaspoon salt
2 tablespoons melted lard or vegetable shortening
2 teaspoons baking powder
2 1/2 cups all-purpose flour

One-Bowl Method

Beat egg and sugar with spoon for five minutes, until sugar is dissolved. Add melted lard/vegetable shortening. Add nutmeg, vanilla, salt and beat again for three minutes. Sift flour and baking powder together. Add to egg mixture gradually, (saving out 1/4 cup) stirring and beating until dough leaves the side of the bowl to form a ball. Use remaining flour to dust pastry cloth or board. Roll out dough to one-fourth inch. Cut with medium-sized doughnut cutter with approximately 1-inch hole. The dough should make just 22 doughnuts. Fry in two or more pounds of lard/vegetable shortening heated to 350 degrees F. Remove the doughnuts as soon as they are golden brown and drain on brown paper.

About the Authors

Lifelong friends, brought together by their shared love of adventure and battling of wits.

Jocelyn Avery Dorgan lives in Robbinsville, New Jersey with her husband, three dogs, one cat, and occasionally one or both of her adult children. When she's not playing with the characters that live in her head, she dabbles in vegan cooking and works at the family business.

Sandy Fairbanks lives in Ware, Massachusetts with her husband, son, and a rotating cadre of cats. When she's not honing her comedic writing skills, she splits her time between working as a nurse and combing yard sales for her endless home improvement projects.

Acknowledgements

Writing a book has been both an exciting and frustrating journey. It is only with the support, guidance, and encouragement from countless people in our lives that has made this possible.

To Cynthia and Dorland Avery who are still vitally present in spirit.

To Elinor and Dave Lane who will always represent "home."

To all of our cohorts during the 1970s with whom we shared laughter and adventure. Our memories of those times together were helpful during this process.

To those who acted as our beta readers to catch us when the story went off track. In particular, thank you to Jeanine Consoli, Kathleen Mathews, Lori Wood Mihalik, Jacqueline Reid Wagner, Karen Roby Winterkamp, and Patricia Snyder.

A special thank you to Shelle Sumners whose feedback corrected the course of the book. Your perspective helped us refocus on the main objective of our story.

To Valerie Avery and Breanna Harding for being the Justine and Eva models during our photo shoot. You brought visual life to our characters.

To Brandon Avery, President of the North Brookfield Historical Society, for providing historical accuracy to our story.

To Debra L. Hartmann, our editor and publishing guru, who put the polish on our raw gem and guided us through the process of bringing the final book to market. She made us believe that the seven years spent writing this weren't a complete waste of time.

To Guy, the voice of reason when his wife was ready to toss the computer out the window. Without you, this would never have happened. Avery and Tara, for having faith that their mom could do this.

To the sights, sounds, and smells of summer that take us back forty years to a certain dead-end country lane, with a red barn and a white clapboard house and a pasture with an old white horse. Where a certain fourteen-year-old girl met an eleven-year-old girl, where magic was made, and the inspiration continues.

It really does take a village to write a book.